CONQUEROR

Conn Iggulden is one of the most successful authors of historical fiction writing today. His two No. 1 bestselling series, on Julius Caesar and on the Mongol Khans of Central Asia, describe the founding of the greatest empires of their day. Conn Iggulden lives in Hertfordshire with his wife and their children.

www.conniggulden.com

CONQUEROR

CONN IGGULDEN

HARPER

While some of the events and characters are based on historical incidents and figures, this novel is entirely a work of fiction.

Harper
An imprint of HarperCollins*Publishers*
77–85 Fulham Palace Road,
Hammersmith, London W6 8JB

www.harpercollins.co.uk

This paperback edition 2012
1

First published in Great Britain by
HarperCollins*Publishers* 2011

Copyright © Conn Iggulden 2011

Conn Iggulden asserts the moral right to
be identified as the author of this work

Map copyright © John Gilkes 2011

A catalogue record for this book
is available from the British Library

ISBN: 978 0 00 747599 5

Typeset in Minion by Palimpsest Book Production Limited,
Falkirk, Stirlingshire

Printed and bound in Great Britain by Clays Ltd, St Ives plc

MIX
Paper from
responsible sources
FSC™ C007454

To Clive Room

Acknowledgements

Without the sterling efforts of a number of skilful and dedicated people, these books would probably never see the light of day. In particular, I must thank Katie Espiner for editing a monster, as well as Kiera Godfrey, Tim Waller and Victoria Hobbs. Yes, it would have been easier without you lot interfering, but more importantly, it wouldn't have been as good.

Chagatai Khanate
late 13th century

Dnepr

Volga

Irysh

Black Sea

Caspian Sea

Aral Sea

Syr Darya Riv

Lake Balkhash

Tigris

Bukhara

Tashkent

Baghdad

Samarkand

Kashgar

I l k h a n a t e

Amudar'ya (Oxus)

Euphrates

Herat

Persian Gulf

Kabul

Kandahar

Delhi

Arabian Sea

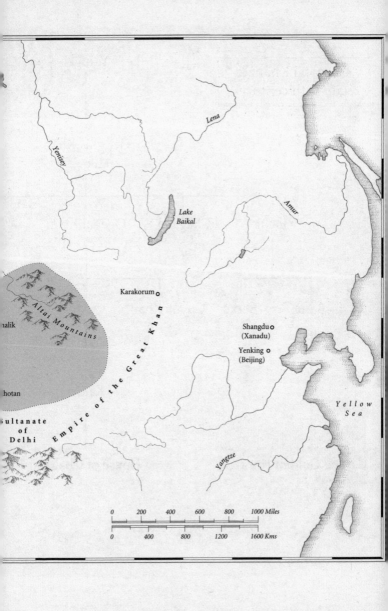

Lena

Yenisey

Lake
Baikal

Amur

Altai Mountains

nalik

Karakorum ○

Empire of the Great Khan

Shangdu ○
(Xanadu)

Yenking ○
(Beijing)

Yellow
Sea

hotan

Sultanate
of
Delhi

Yangtze

| 0 | 200 | 400 | 600 | 800 | 1000 Miles |

| 0 | 400 | 800 | 1200 | 1600 Kms |

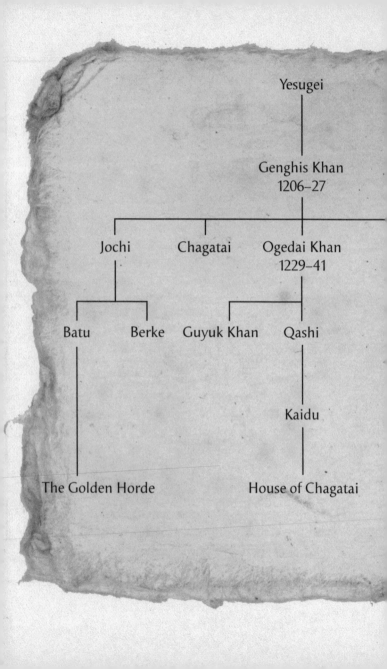

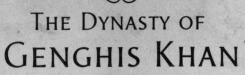

THE DYNASTY OF
GENGHIS KHAN

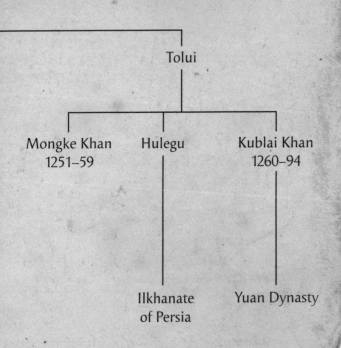

Tolui

Mongke Khan
1251–59

Hulegu

Kublai Khan
1260–94

Ilkhanate
of Persia

Yuan Dynasty

MAIN CHARACTERS

Mongke, Kublai, Hulegu and **Arik-Boke**
Four of the grandsons of Genghis Khan.

Guyuk
Son of Ogedai Khan and Torogene.

Batu
Son of Jochi, grandson of Genghis. Becomes Russian lord.

Tsubodai
The great general of Genghis and Ogedai Khan.

Torogene
Guyuk's mother, who ruled as regent on the death of Ogedai Khan.

Sorhatani
Mother to four grandsons of Genghis – Mongke, Kublai, Hulegu and Arik-Boke. Wife to Tolui, the youngest son of Genghis, who gave his life to save Ogedai Khan.

Baidur
Grandson of Genghis. Son to Chagatai, father to Alghu. Ruler of the Chagatai Khanate based around the cities Samarkand and Bukhara.

PART ONE

AD 1244

CHAPTER ONE

A storm growled over Karakorum city, the streets and avenues running in streams as the rain hammered down in the darkness. Outside the thick walls, thousands of sheep huddled together in their enclosures. The oil in their fleeces protected them from the rain, but they had not been led to pasture and hunger made them bleat and yammer to each other. At intervals, one or more of them would rear up mindlessly on its fellows, forming a hillock of kicking legs and wild eyes before falling back into the squirming mass.

The khan's palace was lit with lamps that spat and crackled on the outer walls and gates. Inside, the sound of rain was a low roar that rose and fell in intensity, pouring as solid sheets over the cloisters. Servants gazed out into the yards and gardens, lost in the mute fascination that rain can hold. They stood in groups, reeking of wet wool and silk, their duties abandoned for a time while the storm passed.

For Guyuk, the sound of the rain merely added to his irritation, much as a man humming would have interrupted his thoughts. He poured wine carefully for his guest and stayed away from the open window where the stone sill was already dark with wetness. The man who had come at his request looked nervously around at the audience room. Guyuk supposed its size would create awe in anyone more used to the low gers of the plains. He remembered his own first nights in the silent palace, oppressed by the thought that such a weight of stone and tile would surely fall and crush him. He could chuckle now at such things, but he saw his guest's eyes flicker up to the great ceiling more than once. Guyuk smiled. His father Ogedai had dreamed a great man's dreams when he made Karakorum.

As Guyuk put down the stone jug of wine and returned to his guest, the thought tightened his mouth into a thin line. His father had not had to court the princes of the nation, to bribe, beg and threaten merely to be given the title that was his by right.

'Try this, Ochir,' Guyuk said, handing his cousin one of two cups. 'It is smoother than airag.'

He was trying to be friendly to a man he barely knew. Yet Ochir was one of a hundred nephews and grandsons to the khan, men whose support Guyuk had to have. Ochir's father Kachiun had been a name, a general still revered in memory.

Ochir did him the courtesy of drinking without hesitating, emptying the cup in two large swallows and belching.

'It's like water,' Ochir said, but he held out the cup again.

Guyuk's smile became strained. One of his companions rose silently and brought the jug over, refilling both their cups. Guyuk settled down on a long couch across from Ochir, trying hard to relax and be pleasant.

'I'm sure you have an idea why I asked for you this evening, Ochir,' he said. 'You are from a good family, with influence. I was there at your father's funeral in the mountains.'

Ochir leaned forward where he sat, his interest showing.

'He would have been sorry not to see the lands you went to,' Ochir said. 'I did not . . . know him well. He had many sons. But I know he wanted to be with Tsubodai on the Great Trek west. His death was a terrible loss.'

4

'Of course! He was a man of honour,' Guyuk agreed easily. He wanted to have Ochir on his side and empty compliments hurt no one. He took a deep breath. 'It is in part because of your father that I asked you to come to me. That branch of the families follow your lead, do they not, Ochir?'

Ochir looked away, out of the window, where the rain still drummed on the sills as if it would never stop. He was dressed in a simple deel robe over a tunic and leggings. His boots were well worn and without ornament. Even his hat was unsuited to the opulence of the palace. Stained with oil from his hair, its twin could have been found on any herdsman.

With care, Ochir placed his cup on the stone floor. His face had a strength that truly reminded Guyuk of his late father.

'I do know what you want, Guyuk. I told your mother's men the same thing, when they came to me with gifts. When there is a gathering, I will cast my vote with the others. Not before. I will not be rushed or made to give my promise. I have tried to make that clear to anyone who asks me.'

'Then you will not take an oath to the khan's own son?' Guyuk said. His voice had roughened. Red wine flushed his cheeks and Ochir hesitated at the sign. Around him, Guyuk's companions stirred like dogs made nervous at a threat.

'I did not say that,' Ochir replied carefully. He felt a growing discomfort in such company and decided then to get away as soon as he could. When Guyuk did not reply, he continued to explain.

'Your mother has ruled well as regent. No one would deny she has kept the nation together, where another might have seen it fly into fragments.'

'A woman should not rule the nation of Genghis,' Guyuk replied curtly.

'Perhaps. Though she has done so, and well. The mountains have not fallen.' Ochir smiled at his own words. 'I agree there

5

must be a khan in time, but he must be one who binds the loyalties of all. There must be no struggle for power, Guyuk, such as there was between your father and his brother. The nation is too young to survive a war of princes. When there is one man clearly favoured, I will cast my vote with him.'

Guyuk almost rose from his seat, barely controlling himself. To be lectured as if he understood *nothing*, as if he had not spent two years waiting in frustration!

Ochir was watching him and he lowered his brows at what he saw. Once again, he stole a glance at the other men in the room. Four of them. He was unarmed, made so after a careful search at the outer door. Ochir was a serious young man and he did not feel at ease among Guyuk's companions. There was something in the way they looked at him, as a tiger might look on a tethered goat.

Guyuk stood up slowly, stepping over to where the wine jug rested on the floor. He raised it, feeling its weight.

'You sit in my father's city, in his home, Ochir,' he said. 'I am the first-born son of Ogedai Khan. I am grandson to the great khan, yet you withhold your oath, as if we were bargaining for a good mare.'

He held out the jug, but Ochir put his hand over the cup, shaking his head. The younger man was visibly nervous at having Guyuk stand over him, but he spoke firmly, refusing to be intimidated.

'My father served yours loyally, Guyuk. Yet there are others. Baidur in the west . . .'

'Who rules his own lands and has no claim here,' Guyuk snapped.

Ochir hesitated, then went on. 'If you had been named in your father's will, it would have been easier, my friend. Half the princes in the nation would have given their oath by now.'

'It was an old will,' Guyuk said. His voice had deepened

6

subtly and his pupils had become large, as if he saw only darkness. He breathed faster.

'Then there is Batu,' Ochir added, his voice growing strained, 'the eldest of the lines, or even Mongke, the oldest son of Tolui. There *are* others with a claim, Guyuk. You cannot expect . . .'

Guyuk raised the stone jug, his knuckles white on the heavy handle. Ochir looked up at him in sudden fear.

'I expect *loyalty!*' Guyuk shouted. He brought the jug down across Ochir's face with huge force, snapping his head sideways. Blood poured from a line of torn flesh above Ochir's eyes as he raised his hands to fend off further blows. Guyuk stepped onto the low couch, so that he straddled the man. He brought the jug down again. With the second blow, the stone sides cracked and Ochir cried out for help.

'Guyuk!' one of the companions called in horror.

They were all on their feet, but they did not dare to intervene. The two men on the couch struggled. Ochir's hand had found Guyuk's throat. His fingers were slippery with blood and Ochir could not keep his grip as the jug came down again and again, suddenly shattering so that Guyuk held an oval of the handle, jagged and rough. He was panting wildly, exhilarated. With his free hand, he wiped blood from his cheek.

Ochir's face was a red mash and only one of his eyes would open. His hands came up once again, but without strength. Guyuk batted them away easily, laughing.

'I am the khan's son,' Guyuk said. 'Say you will support me. Say it.'

Ochir could not speak. His throat was closed with blood and he choked violently, his body spasming. A gargling sound came from his broken lips.

'No?' Guyuk said. 'You will not give me even that? That small thing? Then I am finished with you, Ochir.' He shoved the jagged handle down as his companions watched, appalled.

The noise died away and Guyuk stood up, releasing his grip on the shards of stone. He looked down at himself in disgust, suddenly aware that he was covered in blood, from spatters in his hair to a great slick down his deel robe.

His eyes focused, coming back from afar. He saw the open mouths of his companions, three of them standing like fools. Only one was thoughtful, as if he had witnessed an argument rather than a killing. Guyuk's gaze was drawn to him. Gansukh was a tall young warrior with a claim to being the best archer in Guyuk's command. He spoke first, his voice and expression calm.

'My lord, he will be missed. Let me take him away from here while it is still dark. If I leave him in an alley of the city, his family will think he was attacked by some thief.'

'Better still they do not find him at all,' Guyuk said. He rubbed at spots of blood on his face, but without irritation. His anger had vanished and he felt completely at peace.

'As you say, my lord. There are new sewage pits being dug in the south quarter . . .'

Guyuk raised his hand to stop him.

'I do not need to know. Make him vanish, Gansukh, and you will have my gratitude.' He looked at the other men. 'Well? Can Gansukh manage on his own? One of you must send my servants away. When you are asked, you will say Ochir left us earlier.' He smiled through the smeared blood. 'Tell them he promised me his vote in the gathering, that he gave his solemn oath. Perhaps the fool can benefit me in death as he would not in life.'

His companions began to move and Guyuk walked away from them, heading to a bathing room he could reach without crossing a main corridor. For a year or more, he had not washed without servants, but the blood was itching his skin and he wanted to be clean. The troubles that had enraged him earlier that evening seemed to have fallen away and he walked with a light step. The water would be cold, but he was a man who had bathed in freezing rivers from a young age. It tightened the skin and invigorated him, reminding him he was alive.

Guyuk stood naked in an iron bath of Chin design, with writhing dragons around the rim. He did not hear the door open as he upended a wooden bucket and poured water over his head. The cold made him gasp and shudder, his penis shrivelling. As he opened his eyes, he jumped at seeing his mother standing in the room. He glanced at the pile of clothes he had thrown down. Already the blood on them had mingled with the water, so that the wooden floor ran with red-tinged lines.

Guyuk put the bucket down carefully. Torogene was a large woman and she seemed to fill the small room.

'If you wish to see me, mother, I will be clean and dressed in a few moments.' He saw her gaze fall to the swirl of bloody water on the floor and he looked away, picking up the bucket and refilling it from the pink water in the bath. The palace had its own drains, specially constructed in fire-hardened tile by Chin experts. When he removed the stopper, the incriminating water would vanish under the city, mingling with the night soil and filth from the kitchens until no one would ever know. A canal ran by Karakorum and Guyuk supposed the water would empty into that, or into some pit where it could soak. He didn't know or care about such details.

'What have you *done*?' Torogene said. Her face was pale as she stopped and picked up his tunic, sodden and twisted.

'What I had to,' Guyuk replied. He was still shivering and in no mood to be questioned. 'It does not concern you. I will have the clothes burnt.' Guyuk raised the bucket again, then tired of her scrutiny. He let it fall back and stepped out of the bath.

'I called for fresh clothes, mother. They should have been brought to the audience room by now. Unless you are going to stand and stare at me all day, perhaps you could fetch them.'

Torogene didn't move.

'You are my son, Guyuk. I have worked to protect you, to gather allies for you. In a night, how much of my labour have you undone? Do you think I don't know Ochir was invited here? That he has not been seen leaving? Are you a fool, Guyuk?'

'You have been spying on me, then,' Guyuk replied. He tried to stand tall and unconcerned, but the shivering grew worse.

'It is my business to know what happens in Karakorum. To know every deal and argument, every mistake, such as the one you made tonight.'

Guyuk gave up the pretence, exasperated at her lofty tone of disapproval.

'Ochir would never have supported me, mother. He is no loss to us. His disappearance may even be a gain, in time.'

'You think so?' she demanded. 'You think you have made my work easier? Did I raise a fool, then? His families, his friends, will know he came to you unarmed and that he disappeared.'

'They have no body, mother. They will assume . . .'

'They will assume the truth, Guyuk! That you are a man who cannot be trusted. That alone among the nation, your offer of guest rights cannot make a man safe. That you are a wild dog capable of killing a man who has drunk tea with you *in your own home.*'

Overcome with anger, she left the room. Guyuk barely had time to consider what she had said before she was back, thrusting dry clothes at him.

'For more than two years,' she went on, 'I have spent every

day courting those who might support you. The traditional-ists who might be approached on the grounds that you are the eldest son of the khan and you should rule the nation. I have bribed men with lands, horses, gold and slaves, Guyuk. I have threatened to reveal their secrets unless I receive their votes at a gathering. I have done all this because I honour your father and everything he built. His line *should* inherit, not Sorhatani's children or Batu or any of the other princes.'

Guyuk dressed quickly, pulling the deel robe roughly over a tunic and tying a belt around his waist.

'Do you want me to thank you?' he said. 'Your plans and schemes have not made me khan yet, mother. Perhaps if they had, I would not have acted on my own. Did you think I would wait for ever?'

'I didn't think you would kill a good man in your father's house. You have not helped me tonight, my son. I am so close. I do not know yet what damage you have done, but if this gets out . . .'

'It will not.'

'If it *does*, you will have strengthened the claims of every other man in line. They will say that you have no more right to this palace, this city, than Batu.'

Guyuk clenched his fists in frustration.

'It is *always* him. I hear his name every day. I wish he had been here tonight. I would have removed a stone in my path then.'

'He would never come to you unarmed, Guyuk. Whatever you said or did to him on the trip home has made it harder for me to bring you your inheritance.'

'I did nothing. And it is not my inheritance!' Guyuk snapped. 'How much easier would all this have been if my father had named me in his will. There is the source of it all! Instead, he left me to scrabble around with all the others, like a pack of dogs fighting over one piece of meat. If you had not assumed the regency, I would be out there in the gers, looking at my father's own city in envy. Yet still you honour him. I am the khan's first-born son, mother! Yet I must bargain and bribe to gain what is mine by right. If he was half the man you seem to think, he should have considered that before his death. He had enough time to include me in his plans.'

Torogene saw the pain in her son's face and relented, her anger vanishing. She took him into an embrace, moving to ease his distress without thought.

'He loved you, my son. But he was obsessed with his city. He lived with death on his shoulder for a long time. Struggling against it exhausted him. I do not doubt he wished to do more for you.'

Guyuk rested his head on her shoulder, thinking sharp and unpleasant thoughts. He needed his mother still. The nation had learned to revere her over the years of her regency.

'I am sorry I lost my temper tonight,' he murmured. He forced a breath like a sob and she gripped him tighter. 'I just want it all too much. I cannot bear it, mother. Every day, I see them looking at me, wondering when we will call the gathering. I see them smiling at the thought of my defeat.'

Torogene stroked his damp hair, smoothing it with her hand.

'Shh. You are not the same as them,' she said. 'You have never been an ordinary man, Guyuk. Like your father, you dream of greater things. I know it. I have sworn to make you khan and it is closer than you know. You already have Sorhatani's son, Mongke. You were so clever to take his oath in the field. His brothers will not disobey their mother. That is the heart of our position. Then in the west Baidur has received my envoys. I am confident he will declare for you in time. Do you understand now how close we are? When Baidur and Batu name their true price, we will call the nation.'

She felt him stiffen as she mentioned the name he had grown to hate. 'Be calm, Guyuk. Batu is just one man and he has not left the lands he was granted. In time, the princes who look to him will see he is content as a Russian lord, that he has no ambitions for Karakorum. Then they will come to ask you to lead them. I promise it, my son. No other man will be khan while I live. Only you.'

He pulled away and looked down into her face. She saw his eyes were red.

'How much longer, mother? I cannot wait for ever.'

'I have sent messengers to Batu's camp, once again. I have promised him you will recognise his lands and titles, for his lifetime and the generations to come.'

Guyuk's face twisted into a snarl.

'I do not recognise them! My father's will is not written in heaven! Should I leave a man like Batu to roam free on my borders? To eat rich foods and ride white mares in peace? Should I leave his Golden Horde warriors to grow fat and make children of their own while I fight wars without them? No, mother. Either he is under my hand, or I will see him destroyed.'

Torogene slapped him across the face. The blow was heavy and it rocked his head to one side. As a bloom of red grew on his cheek, he looked at her in stunned shock.

'This is why I told you not to court the princes on your own, Guyuk. I told you to trust me. Listen. And hear with your heart and head, not just your ears. Once you are khan, you will have all the power, all the armies. Your word will be law. On that day, the promises I have made for you will be dust, if you choose to ignore them. Do you understand now?' Though they were alone, her hissing voice fell so she could not be overheard. 'I would promise Batu *immortality* if I thought it would bring him to a gathering. For two years, he has sent excuses to Karakorum. He dares not refuse me outright, but he sends me

13

tales of injuries or sickness, saying he cannot travel. All the time, he watches to see what will come out of the white city. He is a clever man, Guyuk, never forget it. Sorhatani's sons do not have half his ambition.'

'You are bargaining with a snake, then, mother. Be careful he does not bite you.'

Torogene smiled. 'There is a price for all things, my son, for all men. I have merely to find his.'

'I could have advised you,' Guyuk said peevishly. 'I know Batu well. You were not there when we rode into the west.'

Torogene tutted under her breath. 'You do not need to know everything, Guyuk, only that if Batu agrees, he will come to a gathering in the summer. If he accepts the offer, we will have enough of the princes behind us to make you khan. Do you see now why you should not have acted on your own? Do you see what you put in danger? What is the life of one family head compared to this?'

'I'm sorry,' Guyuk replied, lowering his head. 'You have not kept me informed and I was angry. You should have included me in your plans. Now that I know more, I can help you.'

Torogene regarded her son, with all his weaknesses and flaws. Still, she loved him more than the city around them, more than her own life.

'Have faith in your mother,' she said. 'You will be khan. Promise me there will be no more bloodstained clothing to burn. No more mistakes.'

'I promise,' Guyuk replied, his mind already on the changes he would make when he was khan. His mother knew him too well for him to be comfortable around her. He would find her some small house far from the city to live out her last days. He smiled at the thought and she took heart from it, seeing again the young boy he had once been.

CHAPTER TWO

Batu whistled as he trotted across a green field towards the small ger in the crook of hills. As he rode, he kept his eyes moving, looking for watchers or scouts. He had not announced his visit to the homeland of the Mongol people and he could name a few who would have been very interested in his presence there. Sorhatani had inherited the birthplace of Genghis Khan from her husband years before. She had brought tumans back to the open plains, tens of thousands of families who wanted nothing more than to live as they always had, in the shadow of mountains, on the open land.

There was nothing to excite suspicion around Tsubodai's ger. The old man had retired without any of the trappings of power, rejecting all the honours Torogene had tried to press on him. Batu was pleased just to find him, though the retired orlok did not move around as much as some. He had brought no great herd that had to find new grass every few months. As Batu drew closer, he could see just a few dozen sheep and goats, untethered and untroubled as they cropped the grass. Tsubodai had chosen a good spot by a stream bed, on what looked like an ancient flood plain, made smooth and flat by the passage of millennia. The sun was shining and Batu found himself admiring the man yet again. Tsubodai had commanded the greatest army of the nation, more than a hundred thousand warriors who had fought their way to the northern hills of Italy. If the khan had not died and brought them home, Batu thought they would have made an empire from sea to sea. He grimaced at the memories, ashamed that he had enjoyed the old man's failure once. That was when Batu had thought his generation could put aside the petty politics and bickering that marred the world he knew.

Batu kept up his slow approach, knowing it would not be a good idea to surprise Tsubodai. They were not exactly friends, though his respect had only grown in the years since the Great Trek. Even so, Batu needed the advice of one who was no longer part of games of power, one whose word he could trust.

Still at a distance, Batu heard a dog barking. His heart sank as an enormous black hound came out from behind the ger and paused, raising its head. Batu yelled '*Nokhoi Khor!*' for someone to hold the beast, but there was no sign of Tsubodai or his wife. The dog sniffed the air, turning its head back and forth. It was looking at him over the field, then it growled and broke into a run, skimming through the grass. Its face flopped as it charged, so that he could see white teeth and eyes. As it approached, his hand dropped to his bow, but he did not take it up. His chances of a friendly welcome would dwindle somewhat if he shot Tsubodai's dog.

His pony skittered to one side and Batu shouted madly at the hound, trying different words of command. The enormous animal kept coming and he was forced to dig his heels in and canter around in a great circle, with the dog following him. He could see white froth on its mouth as it gnashed and howled at him, no longer silent as it saw him escaping.

Out of the corner of his eye, Batu saw a woman come out of the ger. She seemed amused at his predicament and bent double as she laughed. All he could do was ride in circles, avoiding the snapping jaws.

'Nokhoi Khor!' he called again to her and she stood up, looking at him with her head cocked to one side. After a while she shrugged and put her hand to her mouth to whistle two sharp blasts. The dog dropped to the grass at the sound, his dark eyes still focused on the horseman who had dared to enter his territory.

'Stay,' Batu said to the animal, giving it a wide berth. He had never seen a dog the size of that one and he wondered where Tsubodai had found it. It watched him all the way in and Batu was very aware of it as he dismounted slowly, with no sudden movements.

'I am looking for Orlok Tsubodai,' Batu said.

He could hear a low growl at his back and it was hard not to glance over his shoulder. A smile twitched at the woman's mouth as she regarded him.

'Perhaps he doesn't want to see you, nameless one,' she replied cheerfully.

Batu flushed. 'He knows me well. I was with him in the west. My name is Batu, son to Jochi.'

A shadow passed over her face at that name, as if she had heard it many times. She looked deeply into his eyes, searching for something.

'I wouldn't touch a weapon if I were you. The dog will rip your throat out.'

'I'm not here for revenge,' Batu said. 'I made my peace a long time ago.'

'I'm glad one of you has,' she said.

Her eyes flickered behind him and Batu turned, convinced the hound was creeping up on him. Instead, he saw Tsubodai leading a horse on foot, coming out of a straggling stand of trees not far away. Batu was surprised by the feeling of relief that swept over him. Once, he had hated the man, but then in those days he had hated many. In time, he had learned to respect him.

Batu did not examine his own feelings in too much detail, but in many ways he thought of Tsubodai as a father. It was not something he had ever said. Simply to see Tsubodai alive and apparently well was a ray of light in his current mood. Nothing seemed as hard if you had Tsubodai on your side. If that was true, of course. Batu was still not at all certain how he would be received.

Those thoughts passed quickly through his mind as Tsubodai came closer. The old man whistled to his dog and Batu watched as the savage animal rose and ran to him, suddenly puppyish in its enthusiasm, so that it wagged its entire body rather than just its stump of a tail. Tsubodai walked with one hand loosely wrapped in a rein and the other reaching out to ruffle the dog's great head. He was not smiling as he looked from Batu to his wife.

'Have you offered him tea?'

'Not yet,' his wife said. 'I thought I'd leave it up to you.'

'Good. Be on your way then, Batu. I have nothing to say to you.'

Batu waited, but as far as Tsubodai was concerned, the conversation was clearly at an end. Tsubodai walked past him, clicking his tongue to keep the dog close.

'I came a very long way to see you, orlok,' Batu said.

'I've left titles like that behind me,' Tsubodai shot over his shoulder. 'I am retired.'

'I'm not here to ask you to lead, old man, just to ask for your advice.'

Tsubodai paused in the action of ducking down through his ger door. 'Goodbye,' he said without looking up.

Batu watched in frustration as Tsubodai vanished into the gloomy interior, taking his dog with him. Batu turned helplessly to face Tsubodai's wife, still standing there with the same wry smile. Her child-bearing years were surely behind her, but she looked vaguely maternal as her gaze swept over the disappointed young man.

'I don't like to see a visitor turned away with nothing,' she said. 'Will you take salt tea?'

Batu heard a grunt of irritation from inside the ger. The walls were thin enough for Tsubodai to hear every word.

'It would be an honour,' Batu replied.

He was still there as the evening came in. Tsubodai didn't seem too troubled by his presence. The old man had contented himself with a silent glare, repairing a bow while Batu sat making polite conversation for some hours. He had learned the name of Tsubodai's wife, at least. Ariuna was a pleasant woman and once she had relaxed, she was fascinated by the news he brought. Even Tsubodai snorted when Batu talked of the lands he had been given in Ogedai's will. At a stroke of an ink brush, Ogedai had awarded him a vast fiefdom in Russia. Knowing Tsubodai was listening closely, Batu told Ariuna that part of it had once been his father's, after leaving Genghis behind him. He had felt Tsubodai's gaze on him then, knowing the old man's memories would still be sharp. Batu had not looked up and, after a time, Tsubodai went back to his pots of boiling water, horn and glue.

As the sun set, Tsubodai rose, stretching his back with a groan.

'I have to check the animals,' he said to his wife.

Batu looked at his feet, and it was not until Ariuna said 'Go after him, then!' that he stood up with a grin and went out. Women were sometimes vital when it came to men talking.

He found Tsubodai with the dog, which turned and bared its teeth at him until Tsubodai checked it with a word. Together, he and Batu tested the ties holding a small corral together, before going on to feel the womb of a goat very close to giving birth. The silence between them was comfortable, much better

19

than when he had sat in Tsubodai's home as an unwanted guest. Outside, the old man seemed to relax a little and he gestured for Batu to examine the goat. Batu nodded as he pressed his fingers around the unborn shape.

'Not long now,' was his verdict. 'She seems happy enough.'

'She is,' Tsubodai said, straightening up. 'And so am I. Life is hard, Batu, but it can at least be simple. It is simple here.'

Age had made him thinner than Batu remembered, but there was still a presence to him. No one would ever mistake Tsubodai for a herder, no matter where they found him. His eyes had seen empires rise and fall. They had seen Genghis as a young man.

Batu did not reply. After a time, Tsubodai sighed and rested his hands on the wooden bar of the corral.

'So tell me what has brought you so many miles. I warn you, I know nothing of the politics in Karakorum. I have no net of spies any longer, if that's what you're hoping.'

'It's not. I just want the advice of someone I can trust.'

As Ariuna had earlier, Tsubodai searched his eyes with his own and subsided, tension drifting out of him.

'Ask, boy. I don't know if you will like my answer.'

Batu took a deep breath.

'You know Guyuk as well as anyone.' Tsubodai said nothing, so he went on. 'Did you know the new khan has not yet been chosen?'

The old man nodded. 'I'm not in a desert. I heard that much, at least.'

'It has to be Guyuk, or Mongke, or Baidur . . . or me. We are the only four in reach, and Mongke pledged his word years ago, when he heard Ogedai had died. He will support Guyuk.'

Tsubodai scratched the side of his jaw. 'It's done, then. Throw in with Mongke and Guyuk. Baidur will follow along, once he knows you are together. Guyuk will be khan and I will be left alone.'

'Is that what you would do?' Batu asked seriously.

Tsubodai laughed, an unpleasant, bitter sound.

'Me? No. But I am not you and all my choices have already been made, good and bad.'

'Then why would you have me support him? In my place, what would you do?'

Tsubodai didn't answer immediately. He stared out over the darkening fields, his gaze roaming over the stream and the distant hills. Batu waited.

'I am not in your place,' Tsubodai said at last. 'I do not know what drives you. If you want to get the best bargain, then hold on as long as you can and judge the moment when his gifts are likely to become threats. Secure your own lands and perhaps you will survive long enough to enjoy them.'

'And what if I care nothing for the best bargain?' Batu said, offended. 'What if I think Guyuk should not lead the nation?'

'Then I cannot help you. If you stand in his way, you will be destroyed, without a doubt.' The old man seemed on the verge of saying something else, but he shut his mouth firmly.

'What is it? You speak in riddles, old man. You tell me you would not follow him, but that I will be destroyed if I don't. What sort of a choice is that?'

'A simple one,' Tsubodai said with a smile. He turned to Batu properly for the first time. 'You have not come to me for answers. You know everything you need to know. Are you troubled by those who share Guyuk's bed? Is it that? Do his companions fill you with anger, or is it envy?' Tsubodai laughed.

'He could take dead goats to his bed, for all I care,' Batu said with an expression of distaste. 'What matters is that he is a small man, a man without dreams of any kind. He has only cunning, where the nation needs intelligence. You cannot tell me he would make a good khan.'

'He would be a terrible khan,' Tsubodai replied. 'Under Guyuk, we will see the nation wither away, or broken apart. But if you will not stand against him, who will? Anyway, it is too late. You are already on your way to a gathering. You will give your oath to Guyuk and he will be khan.'

Batu blinked in surprise. His warriors waited for him in a valley more than a day's ride away. Tsubodai could not have known, unless he was lying about having no sources of information any longer. Perhaps there were a few old men who still came to share tea and news with the orlok after all.

'You know a few things, for a man who claims to be nothing more than a simple herder.'

'People talk. Like you. Always talking, as if there is nothing better to do. Did you want me to say that you are making the right choice? Perhaps you are. Now leave me in peace.'

Batu stifled his irritation.

'I came to ask you what Genghis would have done. You knew him.'

Tsubodai grinned at that, showing his teeth. Two were missing at the side of his mouth, so that his cheek was sunken there. It was easy to see the shape of his skull, the skin stretched over the bone.

'Your grandfather was a man without compromise. Do you understand what that means? There are many who say "I believe this", but would they hold true to those beliefs if their children were threatened? No. But Genghis would. If you told him you would kill his children, he would tell you to go ahead, but realise that the cost would be infinite, that he would tear down cities and nations and the price would *never* be paid. He did not lie and his enemies knew it. His word was iron. So you tell me if he would support a man like Guyuk as khan.'

'No,' Batu muttered.

'Not in a thousand years, boy. Guyuk is a follower, not a leader. There was a time when even you had him trotting around in your wake. That is not a weakness in a carpenter or a man who makes tiles for a roof. The world cannot be full of lead dogs, or the pack would pull itself apart.' He rubbed his dog behind the ears and the animal grunted and slobbered at him. 'Wouldn't it, Temujin?' he said to the hound. 'They can't all be like you, can they?' The dog settled onto its stomach with a grunt, its front legs outstretched.

'You named your dog after Genghis?' Batu asked in disbelief.

Tsubodai chuckled 'Why not? It pleased me to do so.' The old man looked up again. 'A man like Guyuk cannot change. He cannot simply decide one day that he will lead and be good at it. It is not in his nature.'

Batu rested his hands on the wooden spar. The sun had begun to set while they talked, shadows thickening and merging all around them.

'But if I resist him, I will be destroyed,' he said softly.

Tsubodai shrugged in the darkness. 'Perhaps. Nothing is certain. It did not stop your father taking his men out of the nation. There was no middle path with him. He was another in the same mould.'

Batu glanced at the old man, but he could barely see his features in the gloom.

'That did not work out too well.'

'You are too young to understand,' Tsubodai replied.

'Try,' Batu said. He could feel the old man's gaze on him.

'People are always afraid, boy. Perhaps you must live a long time just to see it. I sometimes think I've lived too long. We will all die. My wife will die. I will, you, Guyuk, everyone you have ever met. Others will walk over our graves and never know

23

we laughed or loved, or hated each other. Do you think they will care if we did? No, they will have their own blind, short lives to live.'

'I don't understand,' Batu said in frustration.

'No, because you're too young,' Tsubodai said with a shrug. Batu heard the old man sigh to himself. 'There's a good chance there are bones in this valley, men and women who once thought they were important. Do we think of them? Do we share their fears and dreams? Of course not. They are nothing to the living and we don't even know their names. I used to think I would like to be remembered, to have people say my name in a thousand years, but I won't care if they do, because I'll be dust and spirit. Maybe just dust, but I'm still hoping for spirit as well. When you're older, you will realise the only thing that matters, the *only* thing, is that you had courage and honour. Lose those things and you won't die any quicker, but you'll be less than the dirt on our boots. You'll still be dust, but you'll have wasted your short time in the light. Your father failed, yes, but he was strong and he tried to do right by his people. He didn't waste his life. That's all you can ask.' The effort of speaking seemed to have tired the old man. He cleared his throat and spat carelessly on the ground. 'You don't get long in the world. These mountains will still be here after me, or you.'

Batu was silent for a long time before he spoke again.

'I never knew him, my father. I never even met him.'

'I am sorry I ever did,' Tsubodai replied. 'That's how I understand about honour, boy. It's only when you lose it that you realise how valuable it is, but it's too late then.'

'You *are* a man of honour, if I understand anything at all.'

'I was once, perhaps, but I should have refused that order from your grandfather. To kill his own son? It was madness, but I was young and I was in awe of him. I should have ridden

24

away and never sought out Jochi in the Russian plains. You wouldn't understand. Have you killed a man?'

'You know I have!'

'Not in battle; up close, slow, where you can look into his eyes.'

Batu nodded slowly. Tsubodai grunted, barely able to see the movement.

'Were you right to do it? To take all the years he would live?'

'I thought so at the time,' Batu replied uncomfortably.

'You're still too young. I thought once that I could make my mistake a good thing. That my guilt could be the force that made me better than other men. I thought in my strong years that I would learn from it, but no matter what I did, it was always there. I could not take it back, Batu. I could not undo my sin. Do you know that word? The Christians talk of a black stain on the soul. It is fitting.'

'They also say you can remove it by confessing.'

'No, that's not true. What sort of a man would I be if I could just wipe out my errors with talking? A man has to live with his mistakes and go on. That is his punishment, perhaps.' He chuckled then, recalling an old memory. 'You know, your grand-father just forgot his bad days, as if they had never happened. I used to envy him for that. I still do, sometimes.' He saw Batu looking at him and sighed. 'Just keep your word, boy, that's all I have for you.'

Tsubodai shivered as a breeze rushed past them.

'If that's you, Genghis, I'm not interested,' he muttered, so low that Batu could barely hear the words. 'The boy can look after himself.'

The old man pulled his old deel robe closer around him. 'It's too late now to ride back to your men,' Tsubodai said a little louder. 'You have guest rights here and I'll send you on your way in the morning after breakfast. Coming?'

He didn't wait for Batu to answer. The moon was showing over the horizon and Batu watched the old man walk back to the ger. He was pleased he had come and he thought he knew what he had to do.

The yam station was a surprising building to see in the middle of nowhere. Three hundred miles north of Karakorum, it had a single purpose: to work as a link in messenger chains that stretched as far as the lands of the Chin, west into Russia and as far south as Kabul. Supplies and equipment came along the same route, on slower carts, so that it could thrive. Where there was once a single ger with a few spare mounts, there was now a building of grey stone, roofed in red tile. Gers still surrounded it, presumably for the families of the riders and the few maimed soldiers who had retired there. Batu wondered idly if one day it would become a village in the wilderness. Yam riders could not move with the seasons as their ancestors had.

He had avoided the way stations on his journey from his new lands. Just the sight of his tuman would have sent a rider galloping down the line. No one travelled faster than the yam riders over rough ground and news of his movements would have been in Karakorum days ahead of him. Even for this message, he had left his warriors in a forest of pine and birch, too far away to be discovered. He had ridden ahead with just two of his scouts until they came to a ridge where he could tether his horse and send them on without him.

Batu lay on his stomach in the sunshine, watching their progress towards the yam station. There was smoke coming from its chimney and in the distance he could see the tiny figures of horses cropping at the grass. When he saw his scouts enter the building, he turned over on his back and stared up at the blue sky.

There had been a time when he wanted to be khan. If he had been offered it in those days, he would have grasped the thorn without hesitating. Life had been simpler then, riding west with Tsubodai. The death of Ogedai had done more than halt the Great Trek into the western nations. The khan had gone out of his way to raise Batu from poverty, forcing him through promotions until he gave orders to ten thousand picked men. It should not have been a surprise that Ogedai had included him in his will, but it had been. Batu had not expected anything. When he had ridden to his new lands, he had found traces of a Mongol camp, with gers falling in on themselves and rough wooden buildings. He had searched them all, and in one he came across a rotting saddle stamped with the mark of his father's tuman. Ogedai had given him the lands his father had chosen when he ran from Genghis. Batu had held the saddle then and wept for a man he had never known. He knew something had changed in him from that point. As he looked up into the perfect blue, he searched himself for the itch of desire, of ambition, but there was nothing. He would not be khan. His only purpose was to be sure the best of them took command of the nation. He worked his hand into the earth he lay on and tore out a handful of grass and dirt. In the peace of a warm day, he crumbled it into dust and let the breeze carry it away.

Above him, a distant hawk wheeled and then hovered, perhaps interested in the man who lay supine on the grass of the plains. Batu raised a hand to it, knowing the bird could see every detail even from such a height.

The sun had moved in the sky by the time his scouts returned. Well trained, they gave no sign that they saw him as they reached the ridge, not until they were out of sight of anyone watching from the yam station. They walked their ponies past him and Batu followed, checking behind occasionally. He did not need to ask them if the message had gone. The yam stations were famous for their efficiency. A rider would already be galloping towards the next one, some twenty-five miles towards Karakorum. Torogene would hold his sealed letter in her hands in just three days.

Batu was thoughtful as he trotted across the rich green grass. He knew Guyuk would lose face when the gathering fell apart. Batu's other message would reach Baidur around the same time and if he acted on the promise of support, many things would change. Baidur would be a better khan than Guyuk, Batu was certain. For an instant, Batu felt a whisper of the old voice, telling him that *he* would also be a good khan, the first-born of Genghis' first-born. It would be fitting, as if the nation had been wrenched back on the right path after too long. He shook his head, crushing the voice in him. His father had wanted to find his own path, far from khans and herds. Speaking to Tsubodai had given Batu a sense of vast reaches of time, a glimpse of decades, even centuries, through the old man's eyes. He struggled to hold on to it.

Batu tried to think of all the possible futures, then gave it up. No man could plan for everything. He wondered if his pony rode over the bones of long-dead men and shivered slightly at the thought, despite the warmth of the sun.

CHAPTER THREE

Karakorum had not seen such a gathering for many years. As far as the eye could see, the land was covered in gers and horses, the families of the nation come to see the oath-taking for the new khan. Baidur had brought two tumans of warriors from the west, twenty thousand men who made a camp by the Orkhon river and kept their boundaries secure. The camp of Sorhatani's four sons was close by, with another thirty thousand families. The green plains were hidden by them, and gers perched high into the hills as latecomers searched for good ground.

There was no quiet to be had in such a host. Great herds of bleating sheep, goats, camels and yaks drifted around the city, moving out each morning to open land where they could graze and drink their fill. The river banks had been churned into brown mud over the previous weeks and the routines established. Already there had been fights and even murders. It was impossible to gather so many in one place and not have someone draw his sword. Still, the days passed in relative peace and they waited patiently, understanding that the world was large. Some of the nation's senior men were coming home from as far as Koryo, east of the Chin territory. Others had ridden from new settlements in Persia, drawn by the summons from Karakorum. First to last, the quiriltai would take almost three months to form. Until the day of the oath-taking, the nation was content to live on the food that flowed out of the city to feed them.

Torogene could hardly remember when she had last slept. She had stolen a few hours the day before, or perhaps the one before that. Her thoughts were slow and her body ached in all its joints. She knew she would have to sleep soon or become useless. At times, she thought only her excitement kept her going. Years of work had gone into the gathering and yet there were still a thousand things to do. Simply feeding the nation from the vast stores took an army of servants. Grain and dried meat were allocated to each prince or family leader, more than four hundred of them.

She wiped a hand across her brow, looking fondly at Guyuk as he stared out of the open window. The walls of the city were higher than they had once been, but he could see the sea of gers stretching away into the blurred distance.

'There are so *many*,' he murmured to himself.

Torogene nodded. 'We wait for just a few now. Chulgetei has yet to arrive, though I think he had the furthest to travel. Batu cannot be far off. Perhaps a dozen smaller names are still making their way here, my son. I have scouts out to urge them on.'

'There were times when I thought it was never going to happen,' he said. 'I should not have doubted you.'

Torogene smiled, affection and indulgence lighting her face.

'Well, you learned a little patience. It's a good quality for a khan.' Torogene felt a wave of dizziness and realised she had not eaten that day. She sent servants running to find something to break her fast.

'Baidur is the key,' Guyuk said. 'I am sure it was his presence that changed Batu's mind for him. Will you tell me now what you promised my dear cousins?'

Torogene thought for a moment, but then she nodded.

'When you are khan, you will have to know it all,' she said. 'I offered Baidur ten thousand bars of silver.'

Guyuk turned to her, his eyes wide. Such a sum represented the entire output of all the mines they knew about, possibly for years.

'Did you leave me with anything?' he demanded.

Torogene shrugged. 'What does it matter? The silver will continue to come out of the earth. It does no good sitting in locked rooms beneath the palace.'

'But ten thousand bars! I did not know there was so much in the world.'

'Be polite when he gives you his oath then, Guyuk,' she replied with a tired smile. 'He is a richer man than you are.'

'And Batu? If the treasure rooms are empty, what did he want to buy his precious oath?'

Torogene saw the sneer on her son's face and she frowned.

'You will have to have dignity when you meet him as well. Let him see nothing in your eyes, my son. A khan does not show small men they mean anything to him.'

She sighed as he continued to stare at her, waiting.

'We exchanged letters by yam riders. He could not refuse when I told him Baidur had pledged to give his oath to you. I did not have to offer him anything, I think. I did so only to save his pride.'

'He has too much pride, but it does not matter. I will see him broken in front of all the nation.'

Torogene raised her eyes to the ceiling, suddenly frustrated. How many times would she have to explain to her son before he began to understand?

'If you do that, you will have a subject and an enemy.' She reached out and took him by the shoulder as he began to turn away. 'You must understand this, unless you think I

31

ruled Karakorum by good luck alone. When you are khan, you must court the men of power. If you break one but leave him alive, he will hate you to the end of his days. If you steal his pride from him, he will not miss a chance to take revenge when he can.'

'Genghis cared nothing for this sort of politics,' Guyuk replied.

'Your father did. He understood far better than Genghis how to rule a nation. Genghis could only win an empire. He could never have been the safe hand it needed once it was formed. I have been that hand, Guyuk. Do not dismiss so easily what I tell you.'

Her son looked at her in surprise. Torogene had ruled the nation for more than five years, ever since the death of his father. For two of those, she had been almost on her own with Sorhatani, the army in distant lands. He had not given much thought to her struggle.

'I am listening,' he said. 'I assume you promised again that I would respect the territory Batu was given, or was it to offer him the position of orlok in the army?'

'I offered both, but he refused the second. I knew then that he would not be khan. He does not burn with ambition, my son, which is why he is no threat to us. I do not know whether it is from weakness or cowardice, but it does not matter. When you have his oath, you can send him back with costly gifts. We will not hear from him again.'

'He is the only one I fear,' Guyuk said, almost to himself. It was a moment of rare honesty and his mother gripped his shoulder.

'He is the direct line of Genghis, first-born to first-born. You are right to fear him, but no longer, do you understand? When the last of them come in, you will summon the princes and generals to your tent on the plain, Batu among them. You will take their oath and for the following week you will visit each camp and let them all kneel to you. There are half a million people who will see you then. Too many to bring into the city. That is what I have given you, my son. That is what you have earned with your patience.'

Sorhatani let herself down carefully from the saddle behind her eldest son. Mongke stretched down his arm to help her and she smiled up at him. It was good to see Karakorum again. Her home in the Altai mountains was far from the seat of power, but that did not mean she had not followed every twist and turn as Torogene and Guyuk bargained for power. When she looked at Mongke, she could wish he had not given his oath so early, but that river had run its course. Her eldest son had seen his father Tolui keep his word, even at the point of death. Mongke could not be an oath-breaker after that; it was not in him. She watched as he dismounted with dignity, seeing again the traditional Mongol warrior in everything he did. Mongke looked the part, with his wide face and heavy shoulders. He dressed in simple armour and he was already known as a man who had no patience for Chin things. There would be no rich foods in the gers that night, Sorhatani thought ruefully. Her son made a fetish of simplicity, seeing a nobility in it that she could not understand. The irony was that there were many in the nation who would have followed such a son, especially the older generals. Some of them whispered that Guyuk was not a man amongst men, that he acted the woman in his father's palace. Still more spoke with distaste of the way Guyuk continued his father's practice of surrounding himself with perfumed Chin scholars and their incomprehensible scribblings. If Mongke had lifted a hand, he could have had half the nation under his banners before Guyuk even knew he was threatened. Yet her son's word was iron and his oath had been given years before. He would not even discuss the issue with his mother any longer.

Sorhatani turned at a joyous shout and held out her arms as her other sons came riding towards her. Kublai reached her first and she laughed as he jumped down from his pony and embraced her, swinging her round. It was strange to see her boys as grown men, though Hulegu and Arik-Boke were still young warriors.

She caught a delicate scent of apples from Kublai as he put her down and stood back to let her hug his brothers. It was yet another sign of Chin influence on him and the contrast with Mongke could not have been greater. Kublai was taller and wiry of build, though his shoulders had broadened over the previous few months. He wore his hair in the Chin style, with a long queue down his back and the rest scraped tight to his scalp. It flicked back and forth as he moved, like the tail of an angry cat. He wore a simple deel robe at least, but no one looking at Kublai and Mongke would pair them as brothers.

Sorhatani stood back, pride swelling in her at the sight of the four young men, each beloved in different ways. She saw how Kublai nodded to Mongke and that her eldest barely acknowledged the gesture. Mongke did not approve of Kublai's manners, though that was probably true for all brothers close in age. In turn, Kublai resented Mongke's assumption that, as eldest, he had authority over the other three. She sighed to herself, her good mood evaporating in the sun.

'There is a ger ready for you, mother,' Mongke said, raising an arm to guide her to it.

Sorhatani grinned at him. 'Later, Mongke. I've come a long way to see this oath-taking, but I'm not tired yet. Tell me how things are in the camps.'

Mongke paused before speaking, weighing his words. As he did so, Kublai replied.

'Baidur is here, all stiffness and careful formality. The gossip is that he will give his oath to Guyuk. Most of the princes are close-mouthed about their intentions, but the feeling is that Guyuk and Torogene have done enough. When Batu and the others get here, I think we will have a new khan.'

Mongke glared at his brother for speaking first, but Kublai seemed oblivious.

'And you, Kublai,' his mother said. 'You will give your oath to him?'

Kublai pursed his mouth in distaste.

'As you have ordered, mother. Not because I feel it is right, but because I do not wish to stand alone against him. I will follow your wishes.'

'You must,' Sorhatani said shortly, all lightness gone from her tone. 'A khan will not forget those who stood with him – or against him. He has your brother. If Batu and Baidur kneel to him, I will give my own oath as well, for your father's lands. You must not be a lone voice. That would be . . . dangerous. If what you say is true, I suspect there will be no serious challenger. The nation will unite in its choice.'

'What a shame Mongke swore to follow him on the Great Trek,' Kublai said, glancing at his brother. 'That was the first stone of a landslide.' He saw Mongke was glowering at him. 'Come, brother. You can't be pleased with your man! You jumped early, as soon as you heard the old khan was dead. We all understand it. Be honest, though: is he the one you would choose, if you were free?'

'He is the khan's son,' Mongke said. He looked away stiffly, as if the matter was finished.

'A khan who did not even name his son as heir in his will,' Kublai said instantly. 'That says a great deal, don't you think?

I swear, Mongke, you are the one who brought us all here today. You gave your oath rashly, before any of us knew anything. Guyuk began this race a step ahead because of you. I hope you are satisfied. However Guyuk acts as khan, it will be your responsibility.'

Mongke struggled with his dignity, trying to decide if it was beneath him to argue the point. As always, Kublai could needle him into it.

'Perhaps if you had ever commanded in battle, little brother, you would know the importance of authority and rank. Guyuk is Ogedai's first-born son. He *is* the heir to the khanate. I do not need one of your Chin documents to tell me that.'

It was a sore point between them and Mongke could not resist the barbs. While he had fought alongside Tsubodai, Batu, Guyuk and the rest, Kublai had been learning diplomacy and languages in the city. They were very different men and Mongke scorned the skills of his brother.

'And was his father also the first-born, that important position?' Kublai responded. 'No, Mongke, he was third in line. You will give an oath for something the rest of us do not even recognise. Why, because you are first-born in this family? Do you think that makes you a father to the rest of us?'

Mongke flushed. 'If I must be, yes. You were not there when our father gave his life.'

They were facing each other by then, both growing in anger.

'And did our father tell you to lead our little family, Mongke? Did he say to you: "Take your brothers in hand, my son"? You have not mentioned this before.'

'He gave his other wives to me,' Mongke replied stiffly. 'I think it is clear . . .'

'It is *not* clear, you fool,' Kublai snapped. 'Nothing is as simple as you are.'

Mongke might have struck him then. His hand twitched

36

to the sword at his waist and Kublai tensed, his eyes bright with challenge. They had fought a thousand times as boys, but the years had changed both of them. If it came to blows yet again, there was a chance it would mean more than bruises.

'Stop it, now,' Sorhatani said. 'Would you brawl in front of the eyes of the nation? You would shame your father, your name? Stand back! Both of you.'

There was a moment of stillness, then Mongke leapt in, raising his right arm to knock Kublai down. Kublai measured his distance and kicked his brother in the groin as hard as he could. There was no armour there and Mongke collapsed without a sound, hitting the ground hard. It had been a solid hit and silence fell around them. As Sorhatani turned to him in fury, Kublai's eyes widened. Mongke grunted and began to rise. The pain must have been extraordinary, but his brother's rage was roaring through him. His legs twitched in agony as he lurched to his feet. Kublai swallowed nervously as Mongke staggered a step towards him, his hand dropping to his sword hilt.

Sorhatani stepped between them, placing her bare hands on Mongke's armoured chest. For an instant, he almost shoved her aside. His large left hand rose to her collar and gathered the cloth, but he could not fling her away from him even in his pain. Panting, Mongke glared over her head at Kublai, his eyes bloodshot and watering.

'I said stop,' Sorhatani said softly. 'Will you knock me down to get at your brother? Do you not listen to your mother any longer?'

Mongke's eyes began to clear and he looked down at her and then back at Kublai, who stood ready to be attacked. Mongke's mouth curled in disdain as he recognised the Chin fighting stance taught to the boys by the khan's old chancellor.

His hand fell from her collar as Sorhatani put her hand to his cheek, demanding his attention.

'You will *not* fight, Mongke. You are all my sons. What sort of an example will this set to Hulegu and Arik-Boke? See how they watch you now.'

Mongke's hard gaze slid over to his brothers, standing with their mouths open. He grunted again and stood back, mastering himself.

'Guyuk will be khan,' Mongke said. His voice was hoarse, but it carried. 'His father ruled well and his mother has kept the nation together. No one else can say the same. You are the fool, Kublai, at least if you think someone else should rule.'

Kublai chose not to reply. His brother was like a mad bull in his strength. He did not want to set him off again. Instead, he shrugged and walked away. As soon as he had gone, Mongke slumped, almost falling. He tried to stand straight, but the pain spread in waves from his groin into his stomach, making him want to vomit. Only the presence of his mother stopped him cupping himself like a child.

'Sometimes I despair,' Sorhatani said sadly. 'Do you think I will live for ever? There will be a time when your brothers are all you have left, Mongke. They will be the only men you can trust without reservation.'

'He acts and dresses like a Chin whore,' Mongke spat. 'How can I trust a man like that?'

'Kublai is your brother, your own blood. Your father is in him, Mongke, just as he is in you.'

'He goads me whenever he can. I am not a fool, mother, just because I do not know the twenty-seven steps of his pointless Chin rituals.'

'Of course you're not a fool! You know each other well enough to hurt deeply when you are angry, that is all. You and

38

he will eat together tonight and share a cup of airag. For your mother, you will be friends again.'

Mongke winced, but he did not reply, so she went on.

'Because it hurts me to think of my sons so angry with each other. I will think I have failed as a mother. Make it up with him, Mongke, if you care about me at all.'

'Of course I do,' he replied. He knew very well that she was manipulating him, but he gave way even so. 'All right, but you can tell him . . .'

'No threats or bluster, Mongke. If you love me, you will make peace with him. In a few days or weeks, you will have the khan you want. Kublai can only bow to that necessity. Be dignified in your victory.'

Mongke's expression eased as he thought it through. He could be magnanimous.

'He blames me for Guyuk's rise,' he muttered.

'And other men will honour you. When Guyuk is khan, no doubt he will reward you as the first to come to his banners. Think of that the next time you and Kublai bicker like a couple of boys.'

Mongke smiled, shuddering slightly as the pain in his groin settled to a sick ache.

'All right, mother. You will have your way, as always.'

'Good. Perhaps you should show me where my ger is. I find I am tired after all.'

The yam rider was heavy with dust. As he followed a servant through the corridors of the palace, he could feel the weight of it in every crack and seam of his clothes, even his skin. He stumbled slightly as they turned a corner, his strength vanishing in weariness. He had ridden hard all day and his lower back was aching. He wondered if he would be allowed to wash himself in one of the palace bathing rooms. For a few steps, he indulged himself in the fantasy of hot water and servant girls rubbing him dry, but it would remain a fantasy. The riders from the yam lines were given entry wherever they went. If they said they had a personal message for the khan himself, they would be let through to him even in the middle of a battle. Yet the rider was certain he would be washing in the river that evening, before settling down to a spartan camp and a small fire of his own making. Yam riders carried no tents or simple gers, or any weight that might slow them. He would lie on his back under the stars and pull his arms inside the wide sleeves of his deel robe. In twenty years or so, the older riders had told him his joints would be sore on wet days. Privately he thought it would not happen to him. He was young and supremely fit, his life stretching ahead of him. In the course of his travels, he had seen enough of trade among the people to know which items they craved. In just a few years, he thought he would have saved enough to buy a load on one of the trading caravans to Bukhara. There would be no sore joints for him. He would make his fortune. He shivered slightly as he walked, glancing up at the arching ceiling over his head. He did not dream of owning a palace. Perhaps a house in the city would be to his taste, with a wife to cook for him, a few children and a stable of good horses to train his sons for the yam. It was not a bad life.

The servant drew to a halt in front of shining copper doors. Two Day Guards from the old khan's regiment stood there impassively in their armour of red and black, like coloured insects.

'Yam message for the regent,' the servant announced.

One of the Guards broke his perfect stillness, turning his head to stare at the dusty young rider, still reeking of horses and old sweat. They searched him roughly, removing his tinderbox and a small knife. When they tried to take the package of papers, he jerked it away with a muttered curse. The message within was not for their eyes.

'I want the rest back when I come out,' he said.

The Guard only looked at him, tucking the items away as the servant knocked on the door and opened it, letting a flood of light out into the gloomy corridor.

Inside, there were rooms within rooms. The yam rider had been to the palace before, but never so deep within it. He noted that each outer room had its attendants, one of whom rose at his entry and took him on to the next. It was not long before he saw a stout woman surrounded by advisers and scribes busy writing her words. She looked up as he entered. He bowed deeply, leaving his latest guide behind to approach. To his surprise, he saw two men in the group that he recognised, yam riders like himself. They met his eyes and nodded briefly to him.

Another servant of some kind held out his hand for the package of papers.

'This is for the regent's own hand,' the rider said, repeating his instruction.

The servant pursed his mouth as if he tasted something bitter, but he stood back. No one impeded a yam rider.

Torogene had resumed her conversation, but she stopped at his words and accepted the bundle from him. It was a slim package, folded in leather. She undid the ties quickly and pulled out a single folded sheet. The rider watched as her eyes darted back and forth as she read. He could have left immediately, but he was curious. It was the curse of his trade that he carried interesting news, but almost never learned what it was.

To his dismay, he saw Torogene's face drain of colour. She

looked up, suddenly irritated to see the young man standing there expectantly, as if she might share the news with him.

'That is enough for today,' she said to the group. 'Leave me, all of you. Send my son to me. Wake him if you have to.' She tapped the fingers of one hand on the other and crumpled the paper he had brought to her.

CHAPTER FOUR

The moon was out, the night cloudless, so that its light fell on the vast host before Karakorum. There was already a buzz of interest in the gers; rumours flying, voices calling and whispering like a breeze. The city gates opened in the dark, a troop of riders coming out fast down the western road. They held torches, so that they moved in a pool of light through a flickering landscape, catching glimpses of staring faces and grubby gers by the thousand as they navigated their way through. Guyuk rode at the centre in ornate armour, a shining figure with a wolf's-head sword on his hip. More surprising to those who glimpsed them was the sight of Torogene riding at his side. She rode like a man, stiff-backed, with her long hair bound into a thick tail. The torch-lit eye of gold covered a mile at a canter before Torogene signalled to the Guards. They swung left off the main road, plunging across the grassy plain between the gers. To ride at night was always dangerous and flocks scattered in panic as they cantered through them. More than a few bleating animals were crushed beneath hooves or sent tumbling. Voices shouted in alarm and torches sprang up all over the hills around them, pinpoints of light as more and more of the nation rolled out of their beds with swords in hand.

Guyuk whistled sharply, gesturing to a shadowy enclave

marked with the banners of Sorhatani and her sons. Three of his Night Guards yanked their mounts around and rode in a new direction. The rest went on, following the paths through the gers of the people, which jinked and turned to prevent exactly the sort of manoeuvre they attempted. There were no straight roads on the plain of gers. Guyuk strained his eyes for the banners he wanted. He knew the layout of the gathered nation, but in the darkness it was hard to find his way.

The riders swore as they came to an open area that no one recognised, but at the same moment, one of the Guards shouted, pointing. They wheeled round and drew to a sharp halt at the ger camp of Baidur. His banners fluttered in the night wind above their heads, lit by torches. As Guyuk helped his mother to dismount, he saw how many men had gathered to see what was happening. Row upon row waited with weapons drawn. Guyuk recalled that Baidur's father Chagatai had attempted a coup in Karakorum years before, on just such a night. Of all men, Baidur would be suspicious of betrayal.

Guyuk saw the man he had once called friend, made distant by the tides of the nation and his own father's murder. Baidur stood as if he expected to be attacked, his sword drawn and raised to his shoulder. His yellow eyes were cold in the torchlight and Guyuk showed him empty palms, though he would not unbuckle the wolf's-head sword he wore, not for any man. Baidur was khan of a vast region to the west and Guyuk swallowed bitterness as he realised he had to speak first, as supplicant. It did not matter that he was the one marked to be the gur-khan, over all the lesser khanates. On that night, he was merely an heir.

'I come with empty hands, Baidur. I still remember our friendship, when we were little more than boys with swords.'

'I thought all the dealing was done,' Baidur replied, his voice

44

harsh. 'Why have you come to disturb my sleep, to set my people in disarray?'

Guyuk blinked, revising his opinion of the man he faced. He almost turned to his mother for guidance, but he knew it would have made him look weak. He had last seen Baidur riding home with his tuman, stiff with the knowledge that his father was considered a traitor. There had been a time when Baidur could have been khan in Karakorum, if the sky father had willed a change in fortune for his family. Instead, he had inherited and lived quietly in the western khanate. Guyuk hardly thought of him as a threat, but authority had changed Baidur. He spoke as a man used to seeing others leap to do his bidding, as if there could be no possible alternative. Guyuk wondered if he too had that air. In the gloom, he grimaced to himself as doubt struck him.

'I have asked that Mongke join us . . . my lord.' Guyuk bit his lip. He saw Baidur had noticed the hesitation, but they stood before Karakorum! It was almost painful to give the man his titles when Guyuk had none of his own. He sensed his mother shift her weight at his side and remembered her words. He was not yet khan. Until then, he would be humble.

Instead of answering, Baidur also reacted to the movement. He bowed deeply to Torogene.

'My apologies, my lady. I did not expect you to be part of a group riding at night. You are all welcome in my home. The tea is cold, but I will have new leaves boiled.'

Guyuk seethed to himself. The greeting to his mother merely highlighted his own lack of status. He wondered if Baidur had ignored him deliberately, or whether it was genuine respect for the most senior woman in the nation. He followed his mother to Baidur's ger and watched impatiently as she ducked her head to walk in. Baidur's soldiers were staring at him. No, not at him, but at the sword on his hip. Guyuk bristled at their attempt to intimidate him. As if he would be foolish enough to draw a blade with his own mother in the ger.

To his astonishment, one of Baidur's guards stepped close to him and bowed deeply. Guyuk's men pressed around him at the threat, but he waved them back.

'What is it?' he asked, a trace of his irritation still showing.

'My lord, I wondered if I could touch the sword you wear, just the hilt. It would be something to tell my children one day.'

Guyuk suddenly understood the fixed gaze of Baidur's warriors and he smiled patronisingly. The wolf's-head sword had been carried by his father Ogedai, and also by Genghis. He had seen other men gaze on it before with reverent awe. However, he did not want it to be pawed by common warriors. The very idea made him shudder.

'I have much to discuss with your master . . .' he began.

To his anger, the warrior reached out, gazing in a trance at the hilt as if it were one of the Christian relics. Guyuk took a step back. He imagined cutting the hand off to show the man his impertinence, but he was very aware of the staring faces around him, most of them loyal to Baidur rather than himself.

'Another time,' he snapped, ducking into Baidur's ger before the warrior could press him further.

In the ger, Baidur and Torogene were seated close together. It had been some time since Guyuk had seen the inside of one of the felt and wicker homes. He felt cramped and saw with fresh senses how small it was, how it reeked of damp wool blankets and mutton. A battered old kettle hissed in the middle of the space, tended by a servant girl who fussed with cups and made them clink together in her nervousness. There was little space for the trappings of wealth and power in a ger. It was easier to live simply rather than be tripping over some expensive Chin pot at every turn. Guyuk struggled with himself for a moment. It felt like an intrusion to sit on Baidur's other side, but if he took a place next to his mother, he would be forever subordinate in the conversation. With ill-will, he lowered himself onto the bed by her.

'It changes nothing,' Torogene was saying in a low voice. 'The entire nation has come to Karakorum – *every* man and woman of power, except for one. We have enough for an oath-taking.'

'If you go on, it is a risk,' Baidur replied. 'I know Batu well, Torogene. You dare not leave him outside the nation.'

His face was thoughtful, troubled. Guyuk watched the older man closely, but he saw no sign of delight or treachery.

They all heard the sound of approaching horses and Baidur stood. He glanced at the kettle coming to the boil.

'Stay here. Serve them salt tea, Erden.'

Baidur left them alone, though Guyuk was not so naive as to believe they could not be overheard. He kept his silence, taking a bowl of tea from the girl. She presented it in the aspect of a slave, her head down between her outstretched arms. Guyuk almost reached for it before he realised it was held out for his mother. He clenched his jaw as he waited for his own. Status, once again. Well, that would all change soon enough. He would not let Batu ruin his chance to become khan, no matter what the rest of them planned.

Baidur entered with Mongke, and Guyuk rose to his feet to greet them. Torogene stayed where she was, sipping her tea. The ger was already crowded, but Mongke's presence made it stifling. He had a huge breadth of shoulder and had somehow found the time to dress in his armour. Guyuk wondered if the man slept in it. Nothing would surprise him on such a night.

Mongke greeted Torogene first and then Guyuk, bowing deeply and properly, as an oath-sworn man to his master. The gesture would not be wasted on Baidur, and Guyuk felt his spirits lift in response. He opened his mouth to speak and to his irritation his mother began while he was still drawing breath.

'Batu will not be coming to this gathering, Mongke,' she said. 'I have had word from him.'

'What reason did he give?' Baidur said across Mongke's stunned silence.

'Does it matter? He claims a hunting wound that means he cannot travel. It changes nothing.'

'It changes everything,' Mongke said. His voice was slow and deliberate. Guyuk found himself leaning forward to catch every word. 'It means this gathering is at an end. What else can we do? Batu is not some minor family head. He is a powerful voice in the nation, though he does not use his influence. If Guyuk is made khan without him, it could lead to civil war in the future. None of us wants that. I will go back to my tumans, my families. I will tell them it will not be this year.' Mongke turned to Guyuk. 'My oath is yours, my lord, I have not forgotten. But you will need more time to bring Batu back to the fold before we go on.'

'I do not need more time!' Guyuk snapped. 'You have all promised an oath to me. Well, I call it now. Honour your word and I will deal with Batu later. One man cannot be allowed to cause chaos in the nation, no matter his bloodline or his name.'

Seeing he was on the point of ordering them to obey him, Torogene spoke quickly before he could offend either of the powerful men in the ger.

'We have all worked hard so that the oaths would be unchallenged, to make one man khan without dissent. That is no longer possible, but I have to agree with Guyuk. The nation is ready for a new khan. It has been almost five years since the death of my husband. How much new land has been taken in those years? None. The nation waits and all the time our enemies grow strong again. We have already lost too much, in influence and power. Let the oath-taking go ahead, with just one name missing from the roll. Once there is a khan, Batu can be summoned to give his oath alone, ordered by the one true authority of the nation.'

Mongke nodded slowly, but Baidur looked away, scratching a dark sweat stain at his armpit. No one else in the ger knew that he had received a private message on the yam. If he revealed that Batu had promised to support him as khan, it would mean a death sentence for his old friend, he was almost certain. Unless Baidur threw himself into the struggle. For just that night, Guyuk, Torogene and Mongke were all at his mercy, surrounded by his warriors. He could take it all, just as Batu clearly hoped he would.

Baidur clenched his fists for an instant, then let his hands fall loose. His father Chagatai would not have hesitated, he thought. The blood of Genghis ran in them all, but Baidur had seen too much of the pain and blood brought by ruthless ambition. He shook his head, coming to a decision.

'Very well. Call the oath-taking at the new moon, four days from now. The nation must have a khan and I will honour my promises.'

The tension in the cramped ger was almost painful as Guyuk turned to Mongke. The big man nodded, bowing his head.

Guyuk could not resist smiling in relief. Apart from those in the ger and Batu himself, there was no one else who might challenge him. After so many years of waiting, he was in reach of his father's titles at last. His mother's voice barely registered with him, some weak promise that Batu could be brought to the city when the nation had spoken. He wondered if they truly believed he would welcome Batu as a friend after all this. Perhaps his mother expected him to act the great lord, to show mercy to those who had tried and failed to ruin him.

The tension vanished in laughter and Baidur brought out a

skin of airag and a set of cups. Mongke clapped him on the back in congratulation and Guyuk chuckled, giddy at the sudden change in his fortunes. Batu had almost destroyed years of work, but whatever he had intended, it had failed. Guyuk raised a toast with the others, enjoying the bite of the cold spirit in his throat. There would be a reckoning with Batu. That was one oath he could swear with certainty in the silence of his thoughts.

By the first light of dawn, the nation was ready. They had spent many weeks preparing for the oath-taking, from gathering vast quantities of food and drink to mending, patching and polishing every item of clothing and armour they possessed. The warriors were arrayed in perfect squares, standing in silence as the gates of Karakorum opened. There was no sign of the rush and panic from four days before. Guyuk rode out at the head of a column, sitting his mount with dignity. He wore a deel robe of grey and dark blue, deliberately choosing simplicity over anything gaudy or foreign.

There had been so few gatherings since the first one called by Genghis that there were hardly any traditions to follow. A great pavilion had been erected in front of the city, and as the sun cleared the eastern hills, Guyuk dismounted there and passed his reins to a servant. He walked to his place and stood in front of the silk tent as the first group approached him. Unless his bladder filled to bursting, he would not enter the pavilion that day, nor would he sit, no matter how hot the sun became. The nation had to see him become khan.

Baidur and Mongke were conspicuous in that first group, as well as Sorhatani, Kublai and her other sons. The first four hundred contained the heads of all the major families, for once deprived of their retainers, servants and slaves. Most of them were dressed in colourful silks, or the plainest armour, depending on their sense of occasion. Even the banners of rank were denied to them. They would approach Guyuk in simple humility, to bend the knee and give their oaths.

Even within that group there was a hierarchy. Torogene came first, then Sorhatani. The two women had ruled the nation alone, keeping it intact through the death of Ogedai Khan. Guyuk saw only satisfaction in his mother's face as she knelt to him. He barely let her touch the ground before he raised her up and embraced her.

He was not so quick with Sorhatani. Though her oath sealed her loyalty, he had never been comfortable with the woman who controlled the homeland. In time, he thought he would grant her titles to Mongke, as his father should have done. She had survived, so she had luck, but women were too fickle, too likely to make some grievous error. Mongke would never jump without thinking, Guyuk was certain. He watched in pleasure as Mongke came next and repeated the oath he had given in a far land, the first stone falling that brought them all to that spot.

Kublai followed and Guyuk was struck by the keen intelligence in the younger man's eyes as he knelt and spoke the words of gers, horses, salt and blood. He too would need some position of authority in time. Guyuk began to revel in such decisions, able at last to think as a khan, rather than just dream.

The day wore on, a parade of faces until he could hardly distinguish between them. Thousands came to the pavilion: heads of families, rulers of lands thousands of miles apart. Some of them already showed signs of intermarriage, so that the eldest children of Chulgetei had the features of Koryo. Guyuk formed an idea of ordering them to breed true, keeping the Mongol stock pure before it was swallowed in the flood of subject races. The mere thought of exercising such power was like airag in his blood, making his heart pound. After this day, his word would be law for a million people – and millions more under their rule. The nation had grown beyond anything Genghis might once have imagined.

As evening came, Guyuk toured the great camps. There was no single moment when he became khan to universal acclamation. Instead, he rode from place to place, allowing thousands of his people to kneel and chant their oaths. He had warriors ready to strike down anyone who refused, but nothing came of his worries as the light began to fade and torches were lit. He took food and returned to the palace for a time to change clothes and relieve his bowels and aching bladder. Before dawn, he was out again, travelling to the very least of those he would rule: the tanner families and a host of workers from many nations. They cried out in awe at their only chance to see the face of the khan, straining in the dawn light for a single glimpse they would remember for ever.

As the sun rose again, Guyuk felt suffused in its light, lifted by it and made mellow. He was khan and the nation was already settling down to the days of feasting that would follow. Even the thought of Batu in his Russian fiefdom had become a distant irritant. This was Guyuk's day. The nation was his at last. He thought of the celebrations that would follow with growing excitement. The palace would be the centre of it: a new generation of youth, tall and beautiful, blowing away the ashes of the past.

CHAPTER FIVE

Torogene lowered herself onto the bench in the garden pavilion, feeling her husband's spirit all around her. The summer had lasted a long time, so that the city sweltered. For months, the rare heat had built to storms, then been released into a day or two of sweet coolness before it dried out and the process began again. The air itself was heavy at such times, thick with the promise of rain. Dogs lay panting on the street corners and each dawn found a body or two to be cleared away, or a woman weeping. Torogene already missed the powers she had known. Before Guyuk was khan, she could have sent the Day Guards to beat a confession from a dozen witnesses, or to evict a family of thieves, dumping them all on the roads outside the city. Overnight, they were no longer hers to command and she could only petition her son alongside a thousand others.

As she sat among the drifts of leaves, Torogene searched for some feeling of peace, but could not find it, even in Sorhatani's company.

'You cannot tell me you are happy to be leaving the city,' Sorhatani said.

Torogene patted the bench beside her, but her friend did not want to sit down.

'No young khan should have his mother watching every move, every mistake. The old must apparently make way for the new.' Torogene spoke the words reluctantly, echoing Guyuk's pompous speech to her just that morning. 'I have a fine palace, built for me by Ogedai. I will be comfortable in my retirement. And I *am* old. I can hardly believe how weary I feel on some days.'

'He's getting rid of you,' Sorhatani said. She picked up a slender branch from the path. It must have fallen just that morning or the Chin gardeners would already have cleared it away. It flexed in her hands like a whip. 'A son should honour what you achieved, keeping the nation together when it threatened to fly apart.'

'Even so, he is khan. I worked years for it. Should I complain now that I have my desire? What sort of a fool would I be then?'

'A mother,' Sorhatani said. 'We are all fools with our sons. We wipe them and suckle them and all we expect is for them to be grateful to the end of their days.'

She chuckled, her mood turning in an instant. Torogene smiled with her, though in truth she had been hurt by her son's commands.

'He has not threatened to send *you* away, Sorhatani,' she said.

'No, because he still lavishes his attention on Mongke. Orlok of the armies. It is more than my son even wanted. I swear we never planned for that, never.'

'I know. Guyuk took my advice once, at least. Mongke has the bloodline from Genghis and the tumans will follow him. My son trusts him completely, Sorhatani. That is important.'

Sorhatani kept her silence. It was true Mongke had risen in Guyuk's first season as khan, just as she had predicted. Kublai, though, would never lead armies under Guyuk. Something in the two men brought out the worst in each of them. Twice she had sent Kublai away on some errand before he ruined himself

54

in Guyuk's presence. They angered each other like two cats and neither she nor Kublai could explain it satisfactorily. There were times when she wished Guyuk would send her back to the homeland, away from the heat and smells and crowds of the city, away from the politics that ruined every peaceful day. Even in that, she had her suspicions. She did not think Guyuk valued her as an adviser and one memory of his father still troubled her. Years before, Ogedai had asked her to marry his son. The idea could still make her shudder. Ogedai had been too good a man to force her, but Guyuk would have no qualms of that sort. As things stood, the original homeland of Genghis would pass to Mongke on her death, or perhaps one of her other sons if she wrote a will and it was honoured. She could only hope that Guyuk was content to rule the separate khanates. Yet he did not seem to have that sort of vision. In fact, he struck her as exactly the sort of greedy fool who would try to take it all for himself. It was heart-breaking to see such a handsome young man with so many shadows inside him. Power brought out the best in some men, but Guyuk showed no sign of such growth.

It was one more thing she could not discuss with Torogene. The woman still mourned a husband and had set her son to rule the nation. It was not Sorhatani's place to lay his weaknesses in front of her. Just a week before, Guyuk had refused to see a delegation of princes from Koryo, preferring instead to go hunting with his companions. Sorhatani frowned unconsciously as she recalled the tense meeting with the Koryon men. She had tried to ease the insult of his absence with words and gifts, but she could see their anger in the silent looks between them. When Guyuk had returned days later, he had sent his chancellor, Yao Shu, to hear their requests. She could have done that herself if Guyuk allowed her any authority.

The memory brought angry colour to her cheeks. For once,

she had ignored his blustering servants, forcing her way into his presence. She had hoped she could make him see that his life could not be one long feast or endless hunting with his friends. A khan had to rule day by day, to make the decisions they could not make without him.

There had been no contrition in Guyuk when she told him. Instead, he had laughed at her, sending her away in a manner calculated to insult. That, too, she would not mention to Torogene, not just as the woman was leaving, her life's work done. Sorhatani realised she would miss her friend, but there had always been subjects she dared not raise.

If Sorhatani hadn't had Kublai, she thought she would have gone mad, surrounded by a nest of fools and lies and alliances. At least her son would listen. He drank up new information, possessing an insight that could still astonish her. Kublai seemed to know everything that went on in the city, until she suspected him of having a ring of spies as accomplished as her own. Yet even Kublai had been troubled in recent days. Guyuk was planning something and orders flowed between the palace and his tumans. His warriors were exercising on the plains each day, practising with cannon until the whole city stank of gunpowder. Sorhatani had a man willing to read the messages on the yam, but they were often sealed. He would open them if she demanded it, but it would mean his life and she would not throw him away lightly. The very fact that something was secret should have told her much, but she felt as if she wandered through fog. Kublai might have learned something, she thought, or at least be better able to guess. She resolved to speak to him that evening.

She and Torogene looked up as they heard the footsteps of Guyuk's Day Guards. Torogene rose with a sigh, looking into the distance as if she could carry the memory of the city with her. As the Guards stood impassively, she and Sorhatani embraced. Carts, horses and servants waited to take her to the distant palace on the Orkhon river. Summer itself was passing and Sorhatani did not think her friend would be allowed to return. Guyuk had not been able to hide his pleasure at the orders, for all he couched them in fine words and compliments.

'I will visit you,' Sorhatani said, struggling with emotion. She could not promise to keep Torogene informed, not with men listening who would report every word said between them. Torogene smiled, though her eyes were shining with tears. She had raised her son to be khan and her reward was exile, no matter what Guyuk called it. Lies and alliances, it was all the city seemed to breed from its arid stones. Sorhatani watched Torogene walk away with the men, a frail, stooped figure against their youth and strength. Sorhatani was suddenly afraid that one of her own protectors had been removed. For all his hunts and debauchery, Guyuk was intent on consolidating his power. She could not find peace when she thought of the future. She could not even return to the homeland, unless Guyuk gave his permission. It was as if she slept with a hungry tiger in the same room, never knowing when it might leap and tear her apart.

In the distance, she heard the crack of cannons firing and she started slightly. Mongke would be out there on the field, supervising his men as they practised the skills of war. Sorhatani sent a silent prayer for her sons to be safe under this new khan.

Guyuk strode through the empty corridors. He knew he was terrifying the palace servants with his order that they stay out of his sight. Days before, he had stumbled over one young woman too slow to get out of his way. He had snapped the command without thinking. They were too used to stately progress: the pace of older men and particularly his father. He had intended to let his new orders stand for just a few days until they had learned to jump when he appeared. Instead, he had found it gave him great amusement to see men and women scurrying away at every turn, convinced their lives were at stake if he so much as glimpsed them.

He increased his pace, grinning as servants darted into side rooms far ahead, word passing quickly that the khan was on the prowl. Without pausing, he pushed open the copper doors and entered his audience room.

Sorhatani was there, as well as Yao Shu, his father's old chancellor. A dozen others waited their turn and tried not to show that they had been in that room for half a day before the khan bothered to show himself. Guyuk ignored them all and walked across the stone floor to a gilded chair, set with stones of lapis lazuli so that it glittered in the light from the windows. At least the air was freshened by a breeze from outside. He had become accustomed to Chin habits of bathing and the stink of unwashed flesh could make him retch in close rooms.

Sorhatani studied every detail of the entrance he had made, controlling her expression carefully. She could have spoken first, but she and Yao Shu had agreed an order in the hours of waiting. Again, she felt the sting of insult, as if she had no other work than to wait on Guyuk while he played games with servants. None of that could be allowed to show. She had to remember his word was law, that he could take her lands or her life at the first sign of anger in her face. Perhaps it was better that Yao Shu should open the proceedings. The old man had perfected his court manner and it was rare that she could see the emotions beneath it.

'My lord khan,' Yao Shu began, approaching Guyuk and bowing deeply. He held a sheaf of parchments and Guyuk eyed them with distaste. 'There are a great number of things that only the khan can decide.' Guyuk looked as if he might respond, but Yao Shu went straight on before he could speak. 'The governor of eastern Koryo requests a tuman be sent to repel the sea thieves who are raiding his coast. This is the third time he has sent emissaries to Karakorum.' Yao Shu paused for breath, but Guyuk only settled himself more comfortably in the seat.

'Go on, Yao Shu, what else?' Guyuk asked pleasantly.

'We have tumans in the Chin territories, my lord. Shall I send word on the yam that they can go to his aid?'

Guyuk waved a hand. 'Very well, send two. What else?'

Yao Shu blinked to find Guyuk in this odd mood. He went on quickly, determined to take advantage while he could.

'The . . . um, Xi Xia governor claims that taxes have been set too high for his region. There has been a plague in the countryside there and he has lost perhaps half of those who work the fields. He asks for a year without taxes to rebuild.'

'No, he is my vassal.'

'My lord, if we could make a gesture, he would be a stronger ally in the future.'

'And have every small man crying at my doors as a result. I have said no, chancellor. Move on to the next.'

Yao Shu nodded, shuffling his papers quickly.

'I have more than eighty requests for marriage here, my lord.'

'Put them aside. I will read them in my chambers. Are there any of special note?'

'No, my lord,' Yao Shu replied.

'Then go on.'

Yao Shu was growing flustered, Sorhatani could see. In the past, Guyuk had been lazy, barely able to mask his impatience while his councillors talked. Making decisions at this speed was so unlike him that she could only wonder at what he was trying

59

to demonstrate to them. Distaste for Guyuk made her stomach clench. His father would not have ignored word of a plague in his lands so easily, as if the thousands of dead did not matter at all, as if it could not spread. She listened to Yao Shu talk of the need for shipbuilding and the sneering tone as Guyuk refused to spend the funds needed. Yet they had a coast in Chin lands and there were nations outside it that rode the waves with skills the Mongols could hardly imagine.

Yao Shu covered dozens of topics and received quick answers each time. Sorhatani groaned to herself at some of them, but at least it was better than the stagnation of previous days. The world would not stand still while Guyuk hunted with his pretty birds. The light changed outside and Guyuk had food and drink brought for himself, though he ignored the needs of those others present. At last, after hours, Yao Shu stepped back and she was free to speak.

As Sorhatani came forward, she saw Guyuk suppress a yawn.

'I think that is enough for the day,' he said. 'You will be first tomorrow, Sorhatani.'

'My *lord*,' she said, aghast as a ripple of discontent spread through the crowded room. There were others there that he could not afford to ignore, important men who had travelled far to see him. She steeled herself to go on. 'My lord, the day is still young. Can you at least say whether Batu has replied to his summons? Is he coming to Karakorum, lord, to take the oath?'

Guyuk paused in the act of leaving to turn back to her.

'That is not the business of my councillors, Sorhatani,' he said in a reproving tone. 'I have that in hand.' His smile was unpleasant and Sorhatani wondered for the first time if he had sent the order to Batu at all.

'Go on with your work,' Guyuk called over his shoulder as he reached the doors. 'The nation does not sleep.'

* * *

At dawn the following morning, Sorhatani was woken by her servants. She still had her suite of rooms in the palace, given to her when she aided Torogene through the crisis years that followed Ogedai's death. Guyuk had not yet had the nerve to take those from her, though she thought it would come in time as he consolidated his power. She sat up straight in bed as her chamberlain knocked at the door, his head bowed low so that he would not catch a glimpse of his mistress. No one in the nation slept naked, but Sorhatani had fallen into the Chin habit of wearing just the lightest of silk robes to bed and there had been embarrassing scenes before her servants learned her ways.

She knew something was wrong as soon as she saw the man standing there rather than one of the young women who helped her to bathe and dress each morning.

'What is it?' she said sleepily.

'Your son Kublai, mistress. He says he must speak with you. I told him to come back when you are dressed, but he would not leave.'

Sorhatani stifled a smile at the man's poorly concealed irritation. Kublai could have that effect on people. Only the presence of her personal guards could have prevented him from storming in.

She pulled on a heavier robe, tying it around her waist as she padded out into a room lit by the soft grey of dawn. Sorhatani shivered as she saw Kublai there, dressed in dark blue silk. He looked up as she entered and glanced out of the window at the rising sun.

'At last, mother!' he said, though he smiled to see her tousled and still sleepy. 'The khan is taking the tumans away from the city.'

He gestured to the window and Sorhatani followed him, staring out over the plains. Her rooms were high enough to see far and she could make out the dark masses of horsemen

61

riding in formation. She thought of the way cloud shadows slipped across the land in summer, but her mouth tightened and her thoughts cleared suddenly.

'Did Guyuk tell you he was taking them out?' Kublai asked.

His mother shook her head, though it hurt to admit she had not been taken into his confidence.

'That is . . . odd,' Kublai said, his voice soft.

Sorhatani met his eyes and, with a gesture, sent her servants away to make fresh tea. Together, they watched them leave and Kublai relaxed subtly when they were alone.

'If he is making some display of power, or even just training them, I think you would have been told,' Kublai went on. 'He knows half the city will be tumbling out of warm beds to watch them go. There is no way to move the army in secret. Guyuk knows that.'

'Tell me then, what *is* he doing?'

'The word is he will head west to test the new men, to bind them to him in the mountains with hard marches and endurance. The market traders have all heard the same thing, which makes me suspicious. It feels like a story someone has planted, a good one.'

Sorhatani held back her impatience as her son thought through all the possibilities before fixing on one. She knew him well enough to be sure of his judgement.

'Batu,' he said at last. 'It has to be him. A quick strike to remove the one man who has not taken the oath to the khan.'

Sorhatani closed her eyes for a moment. They were still alone, but there were always ears to hear and she stepped very close to her son, dropping her voice to just a breath.

'I could warn him,' she whispered.

Kublai drew back from her, searching her eyes.

'You would risk all our lives,' he said, dropping his head to hers as if he comforted his mother. Even a secret watcher could not have been sure they spoke together as he muttered into her hair, breathing its scent.

'Shall I do nothing and see your cousin killed?' she replied.

'If it is the khan's will, what choice do you have?'

'I cannot stand by and watch without giving him a chance to run. The yam riders can outpace the army.'

Kublai shook his head. 'That would be dangerous. The riders would remember carrying the message. If Batu escapes, Guyuk would hunt back down the chain until he reached you. I cannot allow you to do that, mother.'

'I can have some servant take the message to the stables in the city.'

'Who would you trust when the khan comes in fury, looking for the source? Servants can be bought or broken until they talk.' He paused for a time, his eyes far away. 'It could be done, by a rider willing to use yam horses who is yet not one of them. Nothing else would have the speed to warn Batu in time. If you are sure that is what you want to do.'

'He should have been khan, Kublai,' she said.

He gripped her arms, almost painfully. 'Mother, you must not say that, even to me. The palace is no longer a safe place.'

'Exactly, Kublai. There are spies everywhere now. Just a year ago, I did not have to watch my words in case some perfumed courtier ran to his master to whisper in his ear. The khan sent Torogene away. I will not last long now, with his eye on me. Let me thwart him in this, my son. Make it happen.'

'I will take the message,' he said. 'Then there will be no papers, no record.'

He had expected her to argue, but she understood there was no one else and nodded, stepping back from him. Her eyes were full of pride as she raised her voice to a normal level.

'Very well, Kublai. Go out to the plain and watch them go. Tell me everything when you come back this evening. I want to hear it all.' A listener would have heard nothing to alarm him, though both of them knew he would not return.

'Mongke will be with the khan,' he said. 'How I envy him.'

'He is the khan's orlok, his most loyal follower,' she replied. The warning did not have to be spoken. Mongke could never know they had moved to save Batu. The older brother could not be trusted with such a secret.

CHAPTER SIX

Guyuk knew he cut a fine figure on his horse, a white stallion from the khanate herd he had inherited. Despite the nightly feasts of wine and rich foods, his youth kept him slim, burning off his excesses. He had not brought the vast panoply of carts and materials his army required for a long campaign, keeping the myth of an exercise in the mountains as long as he could. Even so, each of his warriors had two or three spare mounts. Between them, Guyuk had supplies and comforts enough to make the trip a pleasure rather than a chore.

It was easy to imagine his grandfather riding the same lands, with scouts ahead and an army behind him. Guyuk had his own memories of the Great Trek into the west with Tsubodai and it was almost nostalgic to be with an army once again. It was true that they set off mid-morning rather than at dawn, as it took time for Guyuk's head to cease pounding and his stomach to settle. He rode with bloodshot eyes, but the exertion cleared his head and he was soon hungry again. He touched his waist as he rode, dreading the first feeling of thickness there. Surely riding two thousand miles would keep him trim and strengthen the muscles in his stomach.

Guyuk's mood grew bitter as he dragged his gaze back to the plains ahead of him. He had to be discreet, though at times he thought all his generals knew his secrets. Yet he held back from complete honesty, for all he desired it. Mongke was not far behind him in the tumans, and in that serious, unsmiling face, Guyuk saw all the others who would condemn him for his appetites. He thought again of Mongke's mother, the smiling vixen who had twisted his father to her will. Guyuk wanted her gone, but he could hardly banish the mother of such a senior man. His mind worked as he rode, sinking into fantasies in which he would whisper his needs to some trusted warrior and Sorhatani would simply vanish. There were those who would not question the khan's word, though it cost them their own lives. It was a heady power, but he was still wary of it. He guarded his tongue as best he could, until the strain became impossible.

Guyuk jerked from his reverie as he heard battle horns sound on his left. He looked up to see two tumans charging with lances, as they had already done a dozen times that morning. They rode hard for two or three miles, then allowed their mounts to graze as the others caught up. It was the public face of his manoeuvres and he could not complain that he found the crashing and shouting irritating. Whenever they stopped, thousands of warriors would set up targets and practise shots at full gallop, loosing and collecting thousands of shafts. They were impressive and at first he had thrilled to see such power under his command. It had begun to pall for him after the first week, though he idled time away imagining Batu strapped to a target.

Even the thought of that brought a flush to Guyuk's cheeks. He had built a network of spies to dwarf anything his father had ever controlled. In the city, a thousand conversations were reported along a chain of men, collected at the end of each day by his spymaster, then brought to Guyuk. Even in the tumans, men who were foolish enough to criticise their khan found themselves dragged before him to answer for their foolish words. Yet there had been no criticism of Batu. He had been Tsubodai's favourite, they said, a grandson of Genghis who had not sullied his hands with politics and deals. Guyuk seethed at the details he recalled. The common warriors had learned to guard their speech, even among friends. The information coming in had died to a trickle after the first examples had been made, but Guyuk still listened. He had ordered men bound to a post and beaten bloody. He had ordered two killed on the grounds that they spoke of insurrection and disloyalty to the khan. Guyuk had watched one man's tongue being torn out with iron pincers before he was killed. He smiled slightly at the memory. There would be no more of that sort of talk.

He was sure such events could not damage his authority. If anything, he thought the examples he made increased it. It hurt nothing for the men to know their khan would enforce his rule just as ruthlessly as Genghis ever had. The warriors went in fear of him and that was only right. They would not run from an enemy with Guyuk watching them.

He rode west with his army for a hundred miles or more, stopping for two days to practise formations and charges. On the third morning, Guyuk swung the army to the north, riding towards the Russian lands his father had so foolishly granted to an enemy. It was a tainted line, he had realised. Batu's father had been a traitor and his faults had bred true. There could never be trust between them, even if he had summoned Batu to Karakorum and taken his oath. Such a line would poison the new nation and could only be cut down and burnt to the root. He thought of his mother and Sorhatani, sisters in their manipulation of him. Neither would understand the need to remove his enemies. Leaving Batu in peace was not the act of a great khan, but of a weak one, too frightened to engage. Guyuk smiled to himself. He would make an example that would light the way forward, a demonstration to all those others who sought to test the new khan's strength. Let them all see! From the princes of Koryo to the Arabs and the nations of the west. Let them hear of Batu's death and hesitate as they considered resisting the Mongol nation. Batu's fate would be public and terrible. It would move from mouth to ear across the deserts, the mountains and green plains. Batu could be Guyuk's bonfire on the mountaintop, his message to all his vassal states. In that, Batu would serve his khan well.

From two miles away, Kublai watched the army passing, a vast, dusty column of men and horses. It was dangerous to come within sight of them, but he knew the scouting patterns as well as anyone alive and he worked around them, shadowing the khan's force as they rode. It helped that he was not the only man alive on the plains. The movement of so many warriors and horses drove goatherders and poor families from their homes, so that they could often be seen on the outskirts, moving swiftly out of the khan's path. Kublai himself was dressed in a dirty old deel, his face and hands almost black with grime. He hoped he could pass for one of them if he was discovered.

As he lay in long grass, he ran his hand down the dark muzzle and lips of his horse. It lay completely flat, its cheek touching the ground as it had been trained. Even so, the animal needed his touch to remain in such an unnatural position. The liquid brown eyes watched him and he could not prevent the tail whisking at flies and disturbing the cover. Nothing was completely safe within sight of the tumans and their scouts, but he had to know. The message he had memorised would earn death for many if it ever became known to the khan. Kublai knew he had to be certain it was even needed. If the khan marched his army away from Batu's lands, Kublai could simply slip away to Karakorum. It would never be mentioned again.

The tumans had swung north that morning. Karakorum was long behind them and Kublai had watched with growing anger, certain that he saw the khan's true purpose at last. Even then, he had waited, watching to be certain they did not turn back or stop at some lake to water the animals. He had dried milk and meat in his saddlebags and he could cover almost twice the distance they did each day if he had to. At best, the khan's army made forty miles, hardly starting before noon and riding without haste. Kublai kept his eyes on them, wanting to be wrong until he could not deny the truth any longer. When the last ranks had gone, he tapped his horse on the muzzle, making it jump up. He had rested all day, but he could not race madly through the night. If his horse broke a leg on unseen ground, he would not catch them again and Batu would never get the warning.

The following dawn found him barely sixteen miles north of the army, approaching a small village that lay by a stream in the crook of small hills. Kublai's water was running low and he made the decision to stop and buy supplies from them. The hills around were clear and he knew he would be riding hard all day.

He brought his horse in slowly, making sure the herdsmen could see he was alone. There were only four small gers, rebuilt with wood to something more permanent. He passed a reeking toilet pit and nodded to himself, seeing that the families there were poor but clean.

His presence made a herd of goats scatter before him, their nervous bleating as good as any watchdog for rousing the inhabitants. It was only moments before two men faced him with drawn bows.

'I will pay for food and fill a skin with water from your stream,' he said loudly.

The men glanced at each other and one of them nodded reluctantly. Kublai tapped a small bag of silver coins on his hip, drawing their gaze to the sword he wore there. Both men stared at the weapon and he wondered if they had ever seen a long blade before. Their greed showed in their eyes and he read the looks they gave each other with a sinking feeling. It was likely such men earned a little coin by robbing anyone foolish enough to pass by on the road and they still held the bows while his own remained on his back. He decided not to dismount, where they might rush him.

'Bring enough for a few days and I will leave you,' he said.

He reached into the purse and withdrew two silver coins. Both men lowered their bows and one came forward to take the coins while the other watched closely, still suspicious.

Kublai took his feet out of the stirrups as he sat and reached down with the coins. He had half expected it, but it was still a shock when the man grabbed at his long sleeve and tried to pull him out of the saddle. He kicked out sharply, catching the man under the jaw with his boot and sending him reeling, his mouth suddenly bloody from a bitten tongue. The other one gaped and raised his bow, but Kublai kicked his mount forward, drawing the sword and lowering the tip to the man's throat.

At that moment, Kublai heard a new voice, snapping a question. He dared to glance up from the terrified man he held at sword-point and his heart sank. Two of Guyuk's scouts had approached the small collection of houses from the other side, walking their horses in while he had been distracted.

Kublai sheathed the sword and dismounted immediately on the far side of his mount, his mind racing. He could not outrun such men. They were more used to long distances than he could ever be and they would run him down before the day was over. He cursed himself for his mistake, then put it aside, finding a perfect calm he had learned at the feet of the khan's chancellor years before. There was no profit in panic and he made quick decisions as he stood and waited for them to come closer.

The scouts were wary, but they saw only three men in a scuffle, one with blood leaking from his mouth. They trotted their mounts closer and Kublai dropped his shoulders lightly, disguising his height with a stoop as he fussed at his horse. He was as filthy as the other two, his robe as ragged as theirs. Only his sword marked him out and he hoped the scouts would not look too closely at it. The two thieves bowed deeply to the khan's scouts and he copied them, his manner awed at meeting such important men.

'Stand still,' one of the scouts said sharply.

His companion stayed back a few paces, but the first one came among them. Kublai guessed he was the senior of the two, long used to the authority of being the khan's man.

'What's this then?' the scout asked. He was older than Kublai would have expected, but whip-thin despite his age.

Kublai spoke quickly. 'Just a disagreement, lord,' he said, dipping his head. 'A discussion over some goats I was buying.'

Out of the corner of his eye he saw the injured herder gape at him. A scout might be tempted to make an example of a thief on the road, even to take them all to the khan for justice. He would have no interest in settling some local dispute. Kublai only hoped the men would keep their mouths shut and let him talk his way out of it.

'I clip the left ears of my animals, two clips, as you can see there,' Kublai went on, pointing. The scout didn't look round, too old a hand to be distracted. 'My cousins do the same, which I have told them would lead to . . . um . . . disagreements like this one, lord. The animals are mine, I'd know them anywhere.

71

You are a khan's man, lord. If you could rule on this, I'd be grateful.' He rambled on and the scout relaxed, turning to grin at his companion.

The herder with the bloody mouth tried to speak and Kublai whirled on him.

'Shut your mouth, Hakhan, this is all your doing. I know that brown one like it was my own child.'

Both herders stared in amazement at the madman who addressed them in such a way, but the scouts were already losing interest. He kept his gaze down and spoke on, playing the role with everything he had.

'My lord, if you could just stay while I gather up the ones that are mine, I will send a hundred prayers to the sky father for you. My wife is pregnant again. We don't have much and I can't afford to lose some of my best breeders now.'

'Come on,' the older scout said to his companion. He had lost interest in the three grubby men who stood and argued in the road. Kublai kept pleading with them as they turned to ride away, but relief washed over him. At last, he was alone once again with the two herders. Both stared at him as they might have at a mad dog. The one with the bloody mouth spat red onto the ground and spoke, though the effort cost him dearly.

'Who are you?' he managed.

'Just a traveller,' Kublai replied. His muscles had been tensed to attack for too long and his hands shook as he unclenched. 'In need of food and water, as I said. Now, if you still have an idea of robbing me, I will not be merciful the second time. One shout will bring them back.'

The herders looked instinctively to where the scouts had ridden away and both of them seemed to dislike that thought. There was little justice on the plains. Even the distant presence of the khan's men was enough to send terror into their hearts.

Rather than turn his back on the pair, Kublai mounted again and trotted the horse behind them as they filled his waterskin and gathered a small package of fresh-cooked lamb and stone-ground bread. It smelled delicious, but he would not break his fast until the khan's army was far behind him. Batu's land lay more than a thousand miles to the north, but it was not enough to reach him barely ahead of the khan's armies. Kublai was grim as he set out again, alert for any sign of the scouts in the distance. To run, Batu would need all the time Kublai could give him.

CHAPTER SEVEN

Over three days of hard riding, Kublai ran his horse to complete exhaustion. The animal cropped grass in its sleep, but there was never enough time for it to recover before he had to mount again. He was in pain as he climbed into the saddle on the fourth day. He did not have the calluses of the scouts and great patches of skin had rubbed away on his buttocks and lower back. Each morning was an agony until the scabs broke and settled to a numb ache that would last all day. He did not know exactly how far he had come, only that the khan's army were far behind him. Batu had kept an entire tuman of warriors and their families when he travelled to his new lands. They would have grown in number and so many could not be hidden easily. Kublai expected to find signs of them, though that was a challenge for another day.

His immediate problem was that his horse had lost weight alarmingly and was sweating and chewing yellow spit at its mouth. It was time to test the yam lines in a plan that had seemed simple back in Karakorum. From his saddlebags, Kublai drew out a set of small bells sewn into cloth. He draped them over his saddle and took his bearings once again, from the hills around him. There was no one in sight, but he had seen a yam station some twenty miles back and aligned himself to the path worn by its riders. He took stock of himself for the last time and winced at his own weariness. No yam rider rode with packs on his mount. Weight was everything. With a grimace, he wrenched the buckles open and let his supplies tumble out. His bow followed and he held his sword for a long moment before placing it on top of the small pile of leather and cloth. In hostile territory, he felt as helpless as a newborn child without it, but there was no alternative. He kept only a small leather bag he could strap to his back, exactly the sort of thing yam riders carried. He had even written an innocuous letter to a false name, ready to be shown if he were stopped and searched, though that was not likely. No one interfered with a yam rider.

On a whim, he sliced the bags into strips, then wrapped the scabbarded sword securely, making a package that he could hide. The blade was valuable and though he doubted he would ever see it again, he could not just leave it in the dust for scavengers or, worse, the khan's scouts when they came riding behind him.

Kublai drew his horse into some trees and settled down to wait for dusk. There could only be a few miles to go and he wanted to arrive at the yam station at sunset, or even night. It had been Genghis himself who set the distance between yam stations at twenty-five miles. Some of them had been in operation for so long that wide roads stretched between them and families had built homes of brick and clay. He lay back against a tree trunk with the reins looped around his fist.

He awoke to find the trees were dark around him. He had no idea how much time had passed and cursed as he stood up and reached for his saddle. His horse whinnied, stepping away, so that he had to slap its face to get it to stand still.

In moments, he was back on the road, trotting and listening for signs of life. The moon had barely risen and he was thankful the night was still with him. It was not long before he saw lights ahead and forced his mount into a gallop once more.

The bells on his saddle jingled at every step, loud in the darkness.

The yam station was a small one, built of flint and limestone in the wilderness, with little more than a few outbuildings and a cobbled yard. Torches had been lit as they heard him approach and Kublai rode in confidently, seeing two men waiting. One carried a fat waterskin and the other a platter of steaming meat scraps, still dripping water from the boil-pot inside. Another horse was already being led out of the stables, made ready as he dismounted.

'Who are you?' the man with the platter asked suddenly.

'I've come from Karakorum, with urgent messages,' Kublai snapped. 'Who are *you*?'

'Sorry,' the man replied. He still looked suspicious and Kublai saw his gaze fall on the horse he had brought in. Kublai was not the first to think of stealing a yam pony in such a way, but the quality of the mounts they brought in usually gave thieves away. Kublai saw the man nod grudgingly to himself. Even so, he spoke again as Kublai took a double handful of moist lamb shreds and chewed them.

'If you're from Karakorum, you'll know the yam master there.'

'Teriden?' Kublai said around his mouthful. 'Big Christian with a red beard? I know him well.'

It was an easy test for a young man who'd grown up in the city, though his heart thumped in his chest at the thought of being found out. Trying to hide the stiffness of his saddle sores, he mounted the fresh horse, adjusting his small pack on his shoulders as he accepted the skin and knocked back a draught of airag mixed with water. It was cheap and sour, but it warmed him and he gasped as he tossed it back. From that point on, his only sustenance would come from yam stations.

'I'll tell him you keep a good house here,' he said as he took

76

up the reins and trotted the horse to the stone gate. The yam staff were already busy unsaddling his last horse and rubbing it down. The animal steamed in the torchlight and no one bothered to reply. Kublai smiled and dug in his heels, clattering out onto the road north. It had worked and it would work again. It had to if he were to stay ahead of the khan's army. No message could move faster than those riders. Until he spoke to Batu himself, the man would be completely unaware of the threat against him.

As Kublai left, the yam servant stared thoughtfully after him. He'd never seen yellow eyes like those before. Genghis was said to have had such eyes. The man scratched a flea bite on his cheek, lost in thought. After a time, he shrugged and went back to work.

The four men had watched the trail for three days, hunting in pairs, so that there were always rabbits for the stew each night. There was a huge warren nearby and it was easy enough to set strangling snares over the holes. They had a good view of the road through the mountains and so they spent their time talking, or gambling with knucklebones, or just repairing old kit. They knew they could expect to be relieved in another two days and they were approaching the end of their time. There had been little excitement. Just one family of peddlers had passed through and the men were not interested in the cheap goods they had in their little cart, drawn by an ancient pony with one white eye. With rough laughter and a kick, they had sent them on their way.

'Someone coming,' said Parikh, the youngest of them.

The other three shuffled over to the edge of their small camp, looking down at the trail below while being careful not to show their heads. Their bows were well wrapped against damp, lying unsprung so the strings didn't stretch. Nonetheless, each man had the weapons in easy reach. They could have an arrow ready to fly in moments. They peered down, cursing the morning haze that blurred the air, seeming to come from the rocks themselves before it burned off.

Despite the mist, they could see a single man walking slowly, leading a lame horse. His head was bowed and he looked like any poor warrior, stumbling home after many nights hunting, or searching for a lost animal. Even so, the watchers had been placed on that road as the first line of defence and they were wary of anyone. The oldest, Tarrial, had seen more than his share of ambushes and battles. He alone had scars on his forearms and they looked to him for decisions. Sound carried far in the mountains, and with a silent gesture Tarrial sent Parikh off on his own along the ridge. The lad would scout for anyone else creeping up on them, as well as providing a second shot from hiding if something went wrong. The others waited until Parikh reached a place where he could see half a mile along the back trail. The young man raised a flat palm to them, visible at a distance. Clear.

Tarrial relaxed.

'Just one man. Stay here and *don't* steal my food. I'll go down to him.'

He made no attempt to hide his progress as he scrambled down the rocky scree. In fact, he made as much noise as possible, rather than make the stranger nervous. Years before, Tarrial had seen his jagun officer killed on patrol in Samarkand. The officer had kept to the shadows while thieves robbed a store. As one of them passed him, he had stepped out and laid a heavy hand on his shoulder, hoping to scare the thief half to death. His ploy had worked, but the man jammed a dagger into his ribs in panicked reflex. Tarrial smiled fondly at the memory of the officer's face.

By the time he reached the trail, the stranger was close enough for Tarrial to make out his features. He was tall, unusually so. The stranger looked exhausted, his feet barely lifting with each stride. The pony was as dust-covered as he was and favoured its right foreleg.

Kublai sensed Tarrial's gaze and jerked his head up. His hand dropped to his hip, but there was no sword there and, with a grimace, he raised his free hand to show he was unarmed.

'Yam rider?' Tarrial called.

'Yes,' Kublai replied. He was furious with himself for walking so blindly into the hills. He had lost track of the days, even of the horses he'd exchanged at yam stations along the way. Now, everything he had achieved could be undone by a few thieves. Not for the first time, he regretted leaving his weapons behind.

'Who is the message for?' Tarrial asked. There was something about the man that had his instincts twitching, though he couldn't say what it was. Through all the grime that layered him, pale yellow eyes glared at Tarrial and more than once the rider's hand dropped to his hip, as if he was used to carrying a sword. Odd, for a simple yam rider who always went unarmed.

'No one stops the yam,' Kublai said sternly. 'The message isn't for you, whoever you are.'

Tarrial grinned. The man couldn't be much older than Parikh, but he spoke like one used to authority. Again, that was a strange thing for a yam rider. He couldn't resist prodding a little further, just to get a reaction.

'Seems to me a spy would say the same thing, though,' Tarrial said.

Kublai raised his eyes to the sky for a moment. 'A spy on a yam horse, with a leather bag? With nothing at all of value on him, I might add.'

'Oh, we're not thieves, lad. We're soldiers. There's a difference. Not always, I admit, but usually.'

To his surprise, Kublai straightened subtly, his gaze sharpening.

'Who is your minghaan officer?' he said curtly.

'He's about a hundred miles away, lad, so I don't think I'll be bothering him with you, not today.'

'His *name*,' Kublai snapped. There were only ten minghaans to every tuman. He knew the name of almost every man who held that rank in the nation.

Tarrial bristled at the tone, even as he wondered at it. Alone, unarmed, hundreds of miles from anywhere and the man still had an air about him that made Tarrial reconsider his first words.

'You're not like the yam riders I've seen before,' he said warily.

'I don't have time for this,' Kublai replied, losing patience. 'Tell me his name, or get out of my way.' Before Tarrial could reply, he tugged on his reins and began walking again, taking a path straight at the warrior.

Tarrial hesitated. He was tempted to knock the rider on his backside. No one would blame him, but some instinct for survival stayed his fists. Everything had been wrong about the meeting from the first words.

'His name is Khuyildar,' he said. If the rider tried to barge past him, Tarrial was confident he could put him down. Instead, the man stopped and closed his eyes for a moment, nodding.

'Then the message is for his master, Batu of the Borjigin. For his ears alone and urgent. You had better take me to him.'

'You only had to say, lad,' Tarrial replied, still frowning.

'Now.'

CHAPTER EIGHT

There wasn't much conversation as Tarrial and Parikh led Kublai through the mountains. They had left only one man behind to watch the road, while the last of the four rode back to inform their officer. Kublai's lame horse rested with the other mounts, while he had been given the smallest of the scouts' ponies, an irritable animal that tried to bite whenever it saw a finger.

Parikh shared his waterskin with the strange yam rider, but neither Kublai nor Tarrial seemed to be in a mood to talk and his first efforts were ignored. With Tarrial in the lead, they followed a wide path that wound its way upwards into the hills. Kublai could see mountains in the distance, but he had only the vaguest idea where he was, even with the maps he had in his head. The air was clean and cold and he could see for miles as they walked or trotted their mounts.

'I've already lost a day with that lame horse,' Kublai said after a time. 'We need to go faster.'

'Why's that, then?' Tarrial asked immediately. He glowered at the mysterious rider who ordered men about as if they were his personal servants. Tarrial could hardly believe the way Parikh almost came to attention every time the stranger looked at him. No yam rider was that used to authority. Tarrial knew he had to be some sort of officer, perhaps on his own business and using the yam lines without permission. He thought Kublai wasn't going to reply – until he did, grudgingly.

'There is an army behind me. A week, maybe ten days, and they'll be here. Your lord will want every moment of warning I can give him.'

Parikh gaped and Tarrial lost his frown, suddenly worried.

'How big an army?' he said.

In answer, Kublai dug his heels into the flanks of his horse, kicking it on.

'Find out when I give my message to your lord,' he called over his shoulder.

Tarrial and Parikh looked at each other for a moment, then both men broke into a canter to reach and overtake him.

As Kublai rode, he tried to assess the defensive qualities of the land around him. It looked as if Batu had made himself a camp in the valleys of the range of hills, unless the scouts were lying to him about distances. He thought back to the accounts he had read in the library of Karakorum. Under Genghis, the tumans had once destroyed an Assassin fortress, taking it down, stone by stone. No stronghold Batu could have built would stand for longer than that one. Kublai brought the worst possible news, that Batu had to move his people away. With the khan's army coming, Batu had to run and keep running, with only a small chance he would not be caught and slaughtered.

At a better pace, the scouts led him over a series of ridges and the valleys beyond. Most of them were thick with trees. There were small animal paths and they followed those, but the forests would slow Guyuk's army and force them into single file. They would expect ambushes and traps and lose days as a result. Kublai shook his head as he trotted his mount through the gloom, the canopy of branches blocking the sun. He lost track of time and distance, but the sun was setting as they reached an inner ring of scout camps and Tarrial halted to refill his waterskin, empty his bladder and change horses. Kublai dismounted to do the same, his bones creaking. He could feel the hostile stares of Batu's warriors as they nodded to Tarrial and Parikh. Perhaps a dozen or so men lived in that damp place, rotated on constant watch. Kublai doubted anyone could approach Batu without him hearing of it, but it would not help him.

Wearily, Kublai mounted his new pony and followed Tarrial and Parikh, leaving the inner scout camp behind. Darkness came quickly after that and he was completely lost. If Tarrial hadn't been leading, Kublai knew he'd never have been able to find his way through. The forest seemed endless and he became suspicious that Tarrial was deliberately leading him in a twisting path, so he could not find his way back, or lead anyone else in.

They rode all night, until Kublai was dozing as his horse walked, his head nodding in time to its steps. He had never been so tired. The last paths had vanished and Kublai began to wonder if Tarrial was as lost as he was. They could not see the stars to guide them and it seemed a walking dream as their horses clambered over unseen obstacles and pushed their way through bushes with sharp commands from the three men to drive them on. Branches and thorns scratched them as they forced their way in deeper.

Dawn came slowly, the grey light returning the forest to reality. Kublai was drenched in sour sweat and he could hardly raise his head. His back ached terribly and he straightened and slumped at intervals, trying to ease the stabs of pain. Tarrial watched him with barely hidden scorn, but then the scout had not ridden hard for a month before that, burning through his reserves and eating little until the bones of his skull showed. Kublai had reached a point where he resented Batu bitterly, without reason. He knew the man would never appreciate what he had gone through to bring him the news ahead of Guyuk's army and his temper grew with the light. At times, it was all that sustained him.

As the sun rose, Kublai had a sense that the trees were thinning from the impossible tangle of the night before. Already that was becoming a strange memory, in incoherent flashes. He raised his face to the sun when it grew warmer, opening his bloodshot eyes to see they had passed out of the trees at last.

A gentle valley lay beyond the forest. Kublai strained his eyes into the distance and saw the wall of trees begin again. It was not a natural meadow, but the work of years and thousands of men, clearing land where Batu's families could settle in peace. Around them, the forest stretched for many miles in all directions. For the first time, Kublai wondered how Guyuk would find such a place. Among the oaks and beeches, Kublai had not even smelled the smoke of their fires.

Their arrival had not gone unmarked. No sooner had the three men walked their mounts out of the trees than there were shouts and cries, echoing far. From among the clustered homes and gers, warriors gathered and rode towards them. Kublai shook the weariness away, knowing he had to remain alert for the meeting to come. He took his waterskin and squeezed a jet of warm water onto his face, rubbing hard at the bristles on his lip and chin. He could only imagine how bedraggled and dirty he looked. His disguise as a poor yam rider had become the reality.

The warriors cantered in on fresh mounts, looking disgustingly alert. Kublai massaged his eye sockets as they approached, easing a headache. He knew he would need food soon, or he'd be likely to pass out some time that afternoon.

As the jagun officer opened his mouth, Kublai raised his hand.

'My name is Kublai of the Borjigin, cousin to Batu and prince of the nation.' He was aware of Tarrial and Parikh jerking round in their saddles. He had not told them his name.

'Take me to your master immediately. He will want to hear what I have to say.'

The officer shut his mouth with a click of teeth, trying to reconcile the idea of a prince with the filthy beggar he saw before him. The yellow eyes glared through the dirt and the officer recalled the descriptions of Genghis he had heard. He nodded.

'Come with me,' he said, wheeling his mount.

'And food,' Kublai muttered, too late. 'I would like food and perhaps a little airag or wine.'

The warriors didn't answer and he rode after them. Tarrial and Parikh watched him go with wide eyes. They felt responsible for the man and they were reluctant to leave and go back to their lonely post in the hills.

After a time, Tarrial sighed irritably. 'Might be an idea to stay here and find out what's happening. We should wet our throats before reporting in, at least.'

As Kublai entered the encampment proper, he saw there were wide dirt roads running past the homes. Some of them were gers in the style he knew, but many more had been built of wood, perhaps even from the great trunks they had cut to make the clearing in the first place. There were thousands of them. Batu's original ten thousand families had raised children in the years in the wilderness. He had expected a lonely camp, but what he saw was a fledgling nation. Lumber was plentiful and the buildings were tall and strong. He looked with interest at the ones with two storeys and wondered how the occupants would escape in a fire. Stone was rare there and the whole camp smelled of pine and oak. He realised his weary thoughts had been drifting as the officer halted before a large home somewhere near the centre of the camp. With shattering relief, Kublai saw Batu standing in front of the oak door, leaning against a wooden post with his arms crossed lightly over his chest. Two big dogs poked their heads out to see the stranger and one of them growled before Batu reached down and fondled his ears.

'You were barely a boy when I last saw you, Kublai,' Batu said, his eyes crinkling with a smile. 'You are welcome in my home. I grant you guest rights here.'

Kublai almost fell as he dismounted, his legs buckling. Strong arms held him up and he mumbled thanks to some stranger.

'Bring him in before he drops,' he heard Batu say.

Batu's home was larger than it looked from the outside, perhaps because there were very few partitions. Most of it was an open space, with a wooden ladder leading to a sleeping platform at one end, almost like a hayloft above their heads. The floor was cluttered with couches, tables and chairs, all haphazard. Kublai entered in front of two of the warriors, pausing on the threshold to let the dogs smell his hand. They seemed to accept his presence, though one of them watched him as closely as the two men at his back. He stood patiently while they searched him for weapons, knowing they would find nothing. As he waited, he saw the heads of children peeping down at him from the second level. He smiled up at them and they vanished.

'You look exhausted,' Batu said, when the warriors were satisfied.

He wore a long knife on his hip and Kublai noted how he had been ready to draw the blade at the first sign of a struggle. Batu had never been a fool and there was a legend in the nation that Genghis had once killed a man with a sharp scale of armour, when everyone thought him disarmed. There wasn't much threat in a deel robe that stank of old urine and sweat.

'It's not important,' Kublai said. 'I have brought a message from Karakorum. From my mother to you.' It was a relief to be able to say the words he had hidden for so long. 'May I sit?' he said.

Batu flushed slightly. 'Of course. Over here.'

He gave orders for tea and food and one of the warriors went running to fetch them. The other was a small, wiry man with Chin features and a blind white eye. He took a place at the door and Kublai saw how the man winked his dead eye at the children above them before he stared ahead.

'Thank you,' Kublai said. 'It has been a long trip. I only wish the news was better. My mother told me to warn you that Guyuk is coming. He has taken the army away from the city. I followed them for some days until I was sure they were coming north. I've stayed ahead of them, but they can't be more than a week behind me, if that. I'm sorry.'

'How many tumans does he have?' Batu said.

'Ten, with two or three spare mounts to a man.'

'Catapults? Cannon?'

'No. They rode like raiders on a grand scale. All the supplies were on the spare horses, at least those I saw. Cousin, my mother has risked a great deal in sending me. If it became known . . .'

'It won't come from me, you have my oath,' Batu replied. His eyes were distant, as he thought through what he had been told. Under the silent pressure of Kublai's gaze, he came back and focused.

'Thank you, Kublai. I will not forget it. I can wish for more than a week to prepare, but it will have to be enough.'

Kublai blinked. 'He has a hundred thousand warriors. You're not thinking of fighting?'

Batu smiled. 'I don't think I should discuss that with you, cousin. Rest here for a few days, eat and grow strong, before you ride back to the city. If I live, I will show my gratitude – give my regards to your mother.'

'My brother Mongke is with the khan,' Kublai went on. 'He is the orlok of Guyuk's armies and you know he is no fool. See sense, Batu! I brought you the warning so you could run.'

Batu looked at him, seeing the terrible weariness in the way Kublai slumped at the table.

'If I discuss this with you, I cannot let you go, do you understand? If Guyuk's scouts capture you, you already have too much information.'

'They would not dare torture me,' Kublai said.

Batu only shook his head.

'If Guyuk ordered it? You think too highly of yourself, my friend. I would imagine that your mother survives because Mongke has supported Guyuk so loyally. And there is only room for one on that particular tail.'

Kublai made his decision, in part because he could hardly imagine getting on a horse ever again, the way he felt at that moment.

'I will stay until it is safe to go. Now tell me you are not thinking of attacking the khan's army – the army that took Yenking, broke the Assassin fortress and humbled the Afghan tribes! What do you have, twelve thousand warriors at most, some of them still untried boys? It would be a massacre.'

The food and tea arrived and Kublai fell to with a will, his hunger banishing all other concerns. Batu sipped at a cup, watching him closely. Kublai was known for his intelligence. Even Genghis had remarked on the prodigy and told his brothers to look to Kublai for solutions. Batu could not ignore Kublai's opinion when it was so completely against him.

'If I run, I run for ever,' he said. 'I was there in Hungary, Kublai, five *thousand* miles from home. There aren't many alive who understand as well as I do that the khan cannot be outrun. Guyuk would chase me to the end of the world and think nothing of it.'

'Then have your people scatter in a hundred directions. Have them ride deep into the Russian steppes as herders. Tell them to bury their armour and their swords, that they might at least survive. You cannot stand, Batu.'

'The forest is vast . . .' Batu began.

Kublai had revived with the draught of salt tea and he thumped his fist on the table as he interrupted.

'The forest will only slow them down, not stop them. Genghis climbed mountains around the Chin wall with men just like these. You say you know the army. Think, then. It is time to run. I have bought you a few days, enough to stay ahead of them. Even that is not . . . Well, it is all you have.'

'And I am grateful, Kublai. I have said it. But if I run, how many of the people in this valley will still be alive a year from now? A few thousand? A few hundred even? Their lives are dedicated to me. These lands are mine, given by Ogedai Khan. No one has the right to take them from me.'

'Why didn't you come to Karakorum? If you had bent the knee then, if you had given your oath, there wouldn't be an army on the way here.'

Batu sighed and rubbed his face. For a moment, he looked almost as weary as Kublai.

'I just wanted to be left alone. I didn't want my warriors taken for some pointless war under Guyuk. I supported Baidur, Chagatai's son, but in the end he chose not to fight for the khanate. I can't say I blame him. I didn't expect the gathering to go ahead without me, but there it is. Call it vanity, perhaps, or just a mistake. It could have gone another way.'

'But after that? When Guyuk was made khan you could still have come.'

Batu's face grew cold. 'To save my people, I would have done even that. I would have knelt in front of that perfumed toad and sworn my honour away.'

'But you did not,' Kublai said, disturbed by the extent of the man's simmering anger.

'He did not ask me, Kublai. You are the first person from Karakorum I have seen since Guyuk was made khan. For a time, I even thought you had come to call me to oath. I was ready for that.' He waved an arm to encompass the whole camp around them, as well as the dogs and children, the families. 'This is all I want. The old khan chose well when he granted me these lands. Did you know that?'

Kublai shook his head silently.

'When I came here,' Batu continued, 'I found a few rotting gers and homes of wood, deep in the forest. I was amazed. What were those things of the nation doing so far from home? Then I found a broken saddle, still marked with my father's symbol. These are the lands Jochi settled when he ran from Genghis, Kublai. The lands chosen by the first-born of the great khan. My father's spirit is here, and though Guyuk may never understand it, this is my home. If he just stayed away, I would *never* be a threat to him.'

'But he comes. He will burn this camp to the ground,' Kublai said softly.

'That is why I must face him.' Batu nodded to himself. 'Perhaps he will accept a personal challenge, between two grandsons of Genghis. I think he might enjoy the drama of such a thing.'

'He would have you cut down with arrows before you could

speak,' Kublai said. 'I do not enjoy saying these things, Batu. But you have to know the man would never risk his own life. Put aside these mad plans. You speak in desperation, I understand! But you have no choices . . .'

Kublai broke off, a thought occurring to him as he spoke. Batu saw his attention fix on some inner place and reached out suddenly to take him by the arm.

'What is it? What came into your mind just then?'

'No, it is nothing,' Kublai said, shaking off the grip.

'Let me judge,' Batu said.

Kublai rose suddenly, making one of the dogs growl at him.

'No. I will not be rushed into it. Give me time to think it through.'

He began to pace the room. The idea that had come to him was monstrous. He knew he was too used to solving problems in the safe confines of the city, without having to consider the consequences. If he spoke it aloud, the world would change. He guarded his mouth, refusing to say another word until he was ready.

Batu watched him pace, hardly daring to hope. As a young boy, Kublai had been the favourite student of the khan's chancellor. When he spoke, even great men paused and listened. Batu waited in silence, only frowning at one of his sons when the boy crept under the table and curled himself around his leg. The little boy looked up with trusting eyes, convinced his father was the strongest and bravest man in the world. Batu could only wish it were true.

Finding it hard to think with Batu's hopes and needs pressing on him, Kublai walked outside without a word. The warrior with the white eye came out after him and stood close by, watching. Kublai ignored the stare and went into the road, standing in the centre and letting the people bustle around him. The camp was laid out like a town, with winding roads running through it in all directions. He smiled to himself as he realised none of them ran straight, where an enemy could use them to charge. As with a camp of gers, the tracks twisted and doubled back on themselves to confuse an attacker. There was an energy about the place, from raised voices calling their wares to sounds of construction. As Kublai stood there, he saw two men carrying a log of wood to some unknown destination, shuffling along with a weight almost too much for them. Young children ran around him, grubby urchins still blissfully unaware of the adult world.

If he did nothing, Batu would either attack and be destroyed, or run and be hunted down. Had he truly come so many hundreds of miles only to watch the annihilation of Batu's families? Yet Kublai had given his oath to the khan. He had sworn to serve him with gers, horses, salt and blood. His word was iron and he was caught between his oath and his need.

Suddenly furious, he kicked a stone in the road and sent it skipping. One of the children yelped in surprise, glaring at him as he rubbed a spot on his leg. Kublai didn't even see the boy. He had already skirted his oath in warning Batu, but he could live with that. What he contemplated was far worse.

When he turned back at last, he saw Batu standing with the white-eyed warrior in the doorway, the dogs lying at their feet. Kublai nodded.

'Very well, Batu. I have something more to say.'

CHAPTER NINE

Guyuk loved the long summer evenings, where the world hung for an age, suspended in grey light. The air was clear and warm and he felt at peace as he watched the sun begin to ease towards the west, turning the sky a thousand shades of red, orange and purple. He stood at the small door of a ger, looking out at the encampment of his tumans. It was always the same, as they made a town, a city rise in the wilderness. Everything they needed was carried on the backs of the spare horses. He could smell meat and spices on the air and he breathed deeply, feeling strong. The light would last a long time yet and the hunger was strong in him. He tried to sneer at his own caution. He was khan; the laws of Genghis would not bind him.

Guyuk jumped onto the pony's back, enjoying his own energy and youth. His face was flushed. Two of his minghaan officers were nearby, doing their best to look in any direction but his. He gestured to his waiting servant and Anar came forward with his hunting eagle, the bird and the man quiet with tension. Guyuk raised his right forearm, where he wore a long leather sheath from his fingers to above his elbow. He accepted the weight of the bird and tied the jesses. Unlike his falcons, the eagle had always fought the hood. She was bare-headed, her eyes sharp with excitement. For a moment, the bird flapped furiously, revealing the white under-feathers of her wings as they spread and beat. Guyuk looked away from the furious wind until she began to settle, trembling. He stroked her head, wary of the great curved beak that could rip the throat out of a wolf.

When the bird was calm, Guyuk gave a low whistle and one of the minghaan officers approached with his head down. It was as if the man wished to see nothing, to know nothing of what went on. Guyuk smiled at his caution, understanding it. The man's life was in his hands at a single glance or poorly chosen word.

'I will hunt to the east this evening,' Guyuk said. 'You have brought the scouts in?' His heart was hammering and his voice sounded choked to him, but the minghaan merely nodded in response, saying nothing. Seven times in a month of riding, Guyuk had done the same thing, swept up in passions he never felt with his young wife in Karakorum.

'If I am needed, send men directly east.'

The minghaan bowed without raising his eyes. Guyuk approved of his discretion. Without another word, the khan nodded to Anar and the two men began trotting their mounts out of the camp. Guyuk held the eagle lightly, the bird looking forward.

Whenever they passed warriors, he saw bowed heads. Guyuk rode with his head high, passing out into the long grasslands. Spare mounts grazed there by the tens of thousands, a herd so vast it covered the land like a shadow and grazed the long plains grass down to nothing each night. There were warriors there too, spending the night on watch with the animals. One or two of them saw him from a distance and trotted closer until they saw it was the khan. At that point they became blind and deaf, turning away as if they had seen nothing.

The evening light was beginning to fade in soft shades by the time Guyuk passed the herds. With every mile, he felt some of his burden lift and sat taller in the saddle. He saw the shadows lengthen before him and as his mood cleared, he was tempted to chase them, like a boy. It was good to be able to put aside the seriousness of his life, just for a time. That too was something he missed when he returned to the camps. When he came back, he could always feel responsibilities closing in on him like a heavy cloak. The days would be filled with tactical discussions, reports and punishments. Guyuk sighed to himself at the thought. He lived for the golden moments away from it all, where he could be his own man, at least for a time.

Some half a dozen miles to the east of the camp, he and Anar found a stream trickling through the plains, running almost dry in its course. There were a few trees by the banks and Guyuk chose a spot where the shadows were gathering, enjoying the utter peace and isolation. Such things were precious to a khan. Guyuk was always surrounded by men and women, from the first moments of waking, to the last torch-lit meetings before he went to bed. Just to stand and listen to the stream and the breeze was a simple joy.

He untied the jesses that snared the eagle's legs and waited until the bird was ready before he raised his arm and threw her into the air. She rose quickly on powerful wings, circling hundreds of feet above him. It was too late in the day to hunt and he thought she would not go far from him. Guyuk untied his lure and spun out the cord, watching her with pride. Her dark feathers were tinged with red and she was of a bloodline as fine as his own, descended from a bird caught by Genghis himself as a boy.

He began to whirl the lure around him, the cord invisible as he swung the weight in faster and faster circles. Above his head, he saw her wheel and drop, vanishing for a moment behind a hill. He smiled, knowing the bird's tactics. Even then, she surprised him, coming from his side rather than where he was staring. He had time to see a blur that braked with outstretched wings as she plunged into the lure and bore it to the ground with a shriek. He cried out, complimenting the bird as she held it down. He fed her a scrap of fresh meat from his leather-bound hand and she gulped it hungrily as he retied the jesses and raised her up. If there had been more light, he might have ridden with her to take a fox or hare, but the evening was closing in. He left her tied to his saddle horn, silent and watchful.

While he exercised the bird, Anar had laid thick horse blankets on the soft turf. The young man was nervous, as he had learned to be. Guyuk removed his stiff leather glove and stood for a time, watching him. When the khan showed his teeth, it was the slow smile of a predator.

The expression was wiped from his face at the sound of distant hooves and faintly jingling bells. Guyuk looked up, furious that anyone dared to approach. Even a yam rider should have been told not to interrupt him that evening. With clenched fists, he stood self-consciously, awaiting the newcomer. Whatever it was about, he would send the man back to camp to wait for the morning. For a heartbeat, he wondered if some fool had enjoyed the thought of the khan being disturbed. It was the sort of simple malice that appealed to the common men and he vowed to get the name from the yam rider. He would enjoy administering punishment for the jest.

He did not recognise Batu at first in the darkening twilight. Guyuk had not seen him since they had returned from the Great Trek into the west, and the rider approached with his head down, barely trotting. When Batu raised his head, Guyuk's eyes widened. In that instant, he knew he was more alone than he had been for years. His precious army was out of reach, too far to call. He saw Batu smile grimly and dismount. Anar called some question, but Guyuk did not hear as he raced to his own

96

horse and drew his sword from where it lay strapped to the saddle. His eagle was fussing, disturbed by the stranger. On impulse, Guyuk tugged loose the cord that held her legs before he walked clear, giving himself space.

'There is no need to rush, my lord,' Batu called. He waited until he saw Guyuk was not going to try and ride away, then dismounted. 'This has been a long time coming. A few moments more won't hurt.'

With dismay, Guyuk saw Batu wore a sword belted to his hip. As he stared, Batu drew the blade and examined its edge.

Guyuk held the wolf's-head sword he had inherited, a blade of blued steel with a carved hilt. It had been in his family for generations, khan to khan. He took strength from the feel of it in his hand as he threw the scabbard aside into the grass.

Batu approached slowly, perfectly balanced and every pace sure on the ground. The light was poor and darkness was coming swiftly, but Guyuk could see his eyes gleam. He snarled, throwing off his fear. He was younger than Batu and he had been trained by masters of the sword. He rolled his shoulders lightly, feeling the first light perspiration break on his brow as his heart rate increased. He was no lamb to be cut down without a fight. Batu seemed to sense his confidence and paused, his eyes flickering to Anar. Guyuk's companion stood in shock a dozen paces away, his mouth open like a thirsty bird. Guyuk realised with a pang that he too would be killed if Batu succeeded in his madness. He set his jaw and raised his blade.

'You would attack the khan of the nation? Your own cousin?'

'Not my khan,' Batu said, taking another step. 'You've had no oath from me.'

'I was coming to you to accept that oath, Batu,' Guyuk said.

Batu paused again and Guyuk was pleased to see he had worried him. Any small advantage would matter. For unar-moured men, both of them knew a fight might last only a few heartbeats. Perhaps two masters could hold each other off for a time, but for normal warriors, the lengths of razor steel they held were too deadly. A single gash could bite to the bone or remove a limb.

Batu stalked past Guyuk's pony and Guyuk barked a command.

'Strike!'

Batu lurched away from the animal, expecting it to kick out. They had both seen the warhorses of the Christian cavalry, trained to be weapons in battle. Guyuk's pony did nothing and instead the eagle on its back launched with a huge spread of wings. Guyuk leapt forward at the same time, roaring at the top of his lungs.

In fear, Batu struck out at the bird, his sword coming down and across the eagle before its claws could reach him. The wings hid the wound from Guyuk's sight, but it screeched and fell almost at Guyuk's feet. He lunged for Batu's chest and knew a moment of exultation as he saw Batu's blade was too low to block.

Batu sidestepped, pulling his sword free from the crippled bird. It had landed on its back, its talons still raking the air and its head straining to reach him. For an instant, his arm was away from his body, outstretched. Guyuk had put everything into the lunge and could barely recover his balance, but he jerked his blade up and caught Batu along the ribs with the edge as he pulled back for another blow. The light deel opened in a gash and blood showed beneath it. Batu cursed and kept moving out of range, away from the bird and its master.

Guyuk smiled, though inwardly he was raging at the damage done to his eagle. He dared not glance down at it, but its cries were already weakening.

'Did you think this would be easy?' he taunted Batu. 'I am

the khan of the nation, cousin. I carry the spirit and the sword of Genghis. He will not let me fall to some dog-meat traitor.'

Without taking his eyes from Batu, Guyuk called over his shoulder: 'Anar! Take your horse and ride back to camp. Bring my bondsmen. I will finish this scavenger while I wait.'

If he had hoped to provoke Batu into an attack, he got his wish. As Anar moved to his white mare, Batu surged forward, his sword alive in his hand. Guyuk brought his own blade across to block and grunted as he felt the man's strength behind the blow. His confidence was jolted and he stepped back a pace before holding his ground. A memory flashed from his earliest lessons, that once you have started to retreat, it is hard to stop.

Batu's blade was too quick to see and only his childhood training saved Guyuk as he parried twice more from instinct alone. The blades rang together and he felt a sharp sting on his forearm. To his disgust, he was already breathing hard, while Batu worked with his mouth closed, chopping blows at him without a pause. Guyuk stopped another attack that would have opened him like a goat, but his lungs were aching and Batu seemed tireless, growing faster and faster. Guyuk felt another sting on his leg as the tip of Batu's blade caught him and opened a deep cut into the muscle. He took another step backwards and almost fell as the leg buckled. He could not turn to look for Anar and he could hear nothing beyond his own breathing and the clash of swords. He hoped his servant had run. Guyuk had begun to think he could not win against this man who used a sword with all the casual strength of a woodsman cutting trees. He continued to defend desperately, feeling warm blood course down his leg as he looked for just one chance.

He didn't see Anar come from the side in a rush. Guyuk's response across a lunge had put his blade right over, leaving him vulnerable. At that moment, Anar crashed into Batu and sent them both rolling on the grass. Guyuk could hear his own heartbeat thump, as if the world had grown still.

Anar was unarmed, but he tried to hold Batu as the man sprang to his feet, giving Guyuk his chance. Batu punched his sword twice into Anar's side, two hard blows that drew the air and life out of him. Even then, Anar's hands gripped Batu's deel robe, dragging him off balance. Guyuk stepped forward in a wild rage. His first blow was spoiled as Batu jerked Anar around as a shield, then let him drop. Guyuk lunged for his heart, but he moved too slowly. Batu's sword ripped into him before he could land the blow. He was aware of every sliding inch of metal as it passed into his chest between his ribs. Guyuk turned with it, his rage allowing him strength to try and trap the blade. He gasped as it tore him inside, but Batu could not pull it free. They hung almost in an embrace, too close for Guyuk to bring his own sword to bear. Instead, he hammered his hilt into Batu's face, breaking his nose and smashing his lips. Guyuk could feel his strength vanishing like water pouring out of him and his blows grew weak until he was barely able to raise his hands.

His sword fell from his fingers and he sat suddenly, his legs useless. Batu's sword came with him, still deep in his chest. Anar was lying on the ground, choking and gasping bloody air. Their eyes met and Guyuk looked away, caring nothing for the fate of a servant.

Darkness swelled across his vision. He felt Batu tugging at the sword hilt as a distant pressure, almost without pain. When it came free at last, Guyuk felt his bowels and bladder release. It was not a quick end and he hung on, panting mindlessly for a time before his lungs emptied.

Batu stood, looking down through swelling eyes at his dead cousin. The man's companion lasted a long time and Batu said nothing as he waited for the choking sounds to stop, the desperate eyes to grow still. When they were both gone, he sank to one knee, placing his sword on the ground at his side and raising a hand to his face to feel the damage. Blood flowed in a sticky stream from his nose and he spat on the grass as it dribbled into his throat. His gaze fell to Guyuk's sword, with the hilt in the shape of a wolf's snarling jaws. He shook his head at his own greed and looked around for the scabbard in the grass. Moving stiffly, he cleaned the blade before re-sheathing it and placing it on Guyuk's chest. The khan's robe was already heavy by then, sopping wet with cooling blood. The sword was Batu's to take, but he could not.

'My enemy the khan is dead,' Batu muttered to himself, looking on Guyuk's still face. With Kublai's information, he had known Guyuk would leave his guards and the safety of his camp. He had waited for three precious days, risking discovery by the scouts while he lay and watched. Doubts had assailed him the whole time, worse than thirst. What if Kublai had been wrong? What if he was throwing away the days he needed to take his people to safety? Batu had been close to despair when he saw Guyuk ride out at last.

Batu stood, still looking down. The summer darkness had come, though he was sure they had fought for just a short time. He glanced at the dead eagle and felt a pang of regret, knowing the bird's bloodline came from Genghis himself. He stretched his back and stood taller, breathing clean air and beginning to feel the aches and wounds he had taken. They were not serious and he felt strong. He could feel life in his veins and he breathed deeply, enjoying the sensation. He did not regret his decision to face the khan with a sword. He had a bow and he could have taken both men before they even knew they were under attack. Instead, he had killed them with honour. Batu suddenly laughed aloud, taking joy in being alive after the fight. He did not know how the nation would fare without Guyuk. It did not matter to Batu. His *own* people would survive. Still chuckling, Batu wiped his sword on a clean part of the servant's tunic and sheathed it before walking back to his horse.

The warriors stood around the body of their khan, stunned and silent as Mongke rode in. Crows called in the trees around them as the sun rose. The lower branches seemed to be full of the black birds and more than one hopped on the ground, flaring its wings and eyeing the dead flesh. As Mongke dismounted, one of the warriors kicked out at a crow in irritation, though it took flight before he could connect.

Guyuk lay where he had fallen, his father's sword placed on his chest. Mongke strode through his men and loomed over the khan's body, his emotions hidden behind the cold face every warrior had to learn. He stood there for a long time and no one dared speak.

'Thieves would have taken the sword,' he said at last. His deep voice grated with anger and he reached down and picked up the blade, pulling out a length of the steel and seeing it had been cleaned. His gaze searched the bodies, settling on the smears that marked the tunic of the khan's servant.

'You saw no one?' Mongke said suddenly, whirling on the closest scout. The man trembled as he replied.

'No one, lord,' he said, shaking his head. 'When the khan did not return I went out to look for him . . . then I came to find you.'

Mongke's eyes burned into him and the scout looked away, terrified.

'It was your task to scout the land to the east,' Mongke said softly.

'My lord, the khan gave orders to bring the scouts in,' the man said without daring to look up. He was sweating visibly, a trail like a tear working its way down his cheek. He flinched as Mongke drew the wolf's-head sword, but he did not back away and simply stood with his head down.

Mongke's face was calm as he moved. He brought the sword edge down on the man's neck with all his strength, cutting the head free. The body fell forward, suddenly limp as Mongke turned back to the bodies. He wished Kublai were there. For all his distaste for his brother's Chin clothes and manners, Mongke knew Kublai would have offered good counsel. He felt lost. Killing the scout had not even begun to quench the rage and frustration he felt. The khan was dead. As orlok of the army, the responsibility could only be Mongke's. He stayed silent for a long time, then took a deep, slow breath. His father Tolui had given his life to save Ogedai Khan. Mongke had been with him at the end. Better than any other, he understood the honour and the requirements of his position. He could not do less than his father.

'I have failed to protect my oath-bound lord,' he muttered. 'My life is forfeit.'

One of his generals had come close while he stood over the body of the khan. Ilugei was an old campaigner, a veteran of Tsubodai's Great Trek into the west. He had known Mongke for many years and he shook his head immediately at the words.

'Your death would not bring him back,' he said.

Mongke turned to him, anger flushing his skin. 'The responsibility is mine,' he snapped.

Ilugeiei bowed his head rather than meet those eyes. He saw the sword shift in Mongke's hand and straightened, stepping closer with no sign of fear.

'Will you take my head as well? My lord, you must put aside your anger. Choosing death is not possible for you, not today. The army has only you to lead them. We are far from home, my lord. If you fall, who will lead us? Where will we go?

Onwards? To challenge a grandson of Genghis? Home? You must lead us, orlok. The khan is dead, the nation is without a leader. It lies undefended, with wild dogs all around. Will there be chaos, civil war?'

Grudgingly, Mongke forced himself to think beyond the still bodies in the glade. Guyuk had not lived long enough to produce an heir. There was a wife back in Karakorum, he knew. Mongke vaguely recalled meeting the young woman, but he could not bring her name to mind. It no longer mattered, he realised. He thought of his mother, Sorhatani, and it was as if he heard her voice in his ear. Neither Batu nor Baidur had the support of the army. As orlok, Mongke was perfectly placed to take over the nation. His heart beat faster in his chest at the thought and his face flushed as if those around could hear him. He had not dreamed of it, but the reality had been thrust upon him by the bodies lying sprawled at his feet. He looked down at Guyuk's face, so slack and pale with his blood run out of him.

'I have been loyal,' Mongke whispered to the corpse. He thought of Guyuk's wild parties in the city and how they had sickened him. Knowing the man's tastes, Mongke had never been truly comfortable with Guyuk, but all that was behind. He struggled with a vision of the future, trying to picture it. Once more, he wished Kublai were there, instead of a thousand miles away in Karakorum. Kublai would know what to do, what to say to the men.

'I will think on it,' Mongke said to Ilugei. 'Have the khan's body wrapped and made ready for travel.' He looked at the wretched body of Guyuk's servant, noting the slick of dry blood that had poured out of his mouth. Inspiration struck him and he spoke again.

'The khan died bravely, fighting off his murderer. Let the men know.'

'Shall I leave the body of the killer?' Ilugei said, his eyes gleaming. No one loved a lie like a Mongol warrior. It might even have been true, though he wondered how Guyuk's sword could have been cleaned and laid down so carefully by a dying man.

Mongke thought for a time, before shaking his head.

'No. Have him quartered and the pieces thrown into one of the night pits. Let the flies and the sun feast.'

Ilugei bowed solemnly at the order. He thought he had seen the light of ambition kindle in Mongke's eyes. He was certain the man would not turn down the right to be khan, no matter how it had come about. Ilugei had despised Guyuk and it was with relief that he thought of Mongke leading the nation. He had no time for the insidious Chin influences that had become so much a part of the nation's culture. Mongke would rule as Genghis had, a traditional Mongol khan. Ilugei struggled not to smile, though his heart rejoiced.

'Your will, my lord,' he said, his voice steady.

CHAPTER TEN

It took a month to bring the army home to Karakorum, almost half the time it had taken to ride out. Freed of Guyuk's command, Mongke had the men up before dawn each morning, moving on at a hard pace and begrudging every stop to snatch food or sleep.

When they sighted the pale city walls, the mood amongst the men was hard to define. They carried the body of the khan and there were many who felt the shame of failing in their duties to Guyuk. Yet Mongke rode tall, already certain in his authority. Guyuk had not been a popular khan. Many of the warriors took their manner from Mongke and did not hang their heads.

The news had gone before them, by way of the yam riders. As a result, Sorhatani had been given time to prepare the city for days of mourning. Braziers filled with chips of cedar and black aloes wood had been set alight that dawn, with the approach of the army. A grey smoke rose into the air across Karakorum, wreathing the city in mist and rich scents. For once, the stink of blocked sewers was masked.

With Day Guards in their best armour, Sorhatani waited by the city gate, looking out over the road to her son's army coming home. Kublai had barely made it back before his brother and then only by resuming his guise as a yam rider. Sorhatani felt

106

her age as she stood in the breeze, staring at the dust raised by tens of thousands of horses and men. One of the Guards cleared his throat and then began a spasm of coughing that he could not control. Sorhatani glanced at him, her eyes warning him to be silent. Mongke was still some way off and she took a step towards the warrior, placing her hand on his forehead. It was burning and she frowned. The red-faced warrior was unable to reply to her questions. As she spoke, he raised a hand help-lessly and in irritation she waved him out of line.

Sorhatani felt an itch begin in her own throat and swallowed hard to control it before she embarrassed herself. Two of her servants were in bed with the same fever, but she could not think of that now, with Mongke coming home.

Her thoughts strayed to her husband, dead so many years before. He had given his life for Ogedai Khan and he would never have dared to dream that one of his own sons would rise. Yet who else could be khan now that Guyuk was dead? Batu owed everything to her, not just his life. Kublai was certain he would not be an obstacle to her family. She sent a silent prayer to her husband's spirit, thanking him for the original sacrifice that had made it all possible.

The army came to a halt and settled in around the city, unburdening the horses and letting them run free to crop grass that had grown lush in their absence. It would not be long before the plains of Karakorum were bare dirt again, Sorhatani thought. She watched as Mongke came riding in with his ming-haan officers, wondering if she could ever tell him the part she had played in Guyuk's death. It had not worked out as she and Kublai had planned. All she had intended was for Batu to be saved. Yet she could feel no regret for the loss of the khan. She had already seen some of his favourites reduced to trembling horror as they heard their protector had gone. It had been hard for her not to enjoy their distress, having so long endured their petty dominance. She had dismissed the guards Guyuk had set to watch her. She had no real authority to do so, but they had been able to feel the wind changing as well. They had left her apartments at undignified speed.

Mongke rode up and dismounted, embracing her with awkward formality. She noted he wore the wolf's-head sword on his left hip, a potent symbol. She gave no sign she had seen it. Mongke was not yet khan and he had to tread a difficult path in the days ahead, until Guyuk was buried or burnt.

'I wish I could have come back with better news, mother.' The words still had to be said. 'The khan has been killed by his servant, murdered while he was out hunting.'

'It is a dark day for the nation,' Sorhatani replied formally, bowing her head. Her chest tightened as a cough threatened and she swallowed spit in quick gulps. 'There will have to be another quiriltai, another gathering of the princes. I will send out the yam riders to have them come to the city next spring. The nation must have a khan, *my son.*'

Mongke looked sharply at her. Perhaps only he could have heard the subtle emphasis of the last words, but her eyes gleamed. He nodded just a fraction in answer. Among the generals, it was already accepted that Mongke would be khan. He had only to declare himself. He took a deep breath, looking around him at the honour guard Sorhatani had assembled. When he spoke, it was with quiet certainty.

'Not to the city, mother, not to this place of cold stone. I am the khan elect, grandson to Genghis Khan. The decision is mine. I will summon the nation to the plain of Avraga, where Genghis first gathered the nation.'

Unbidden, tears of pride came to Sorhatani's eyes. She bowed her head, mute.

'The nation has drifted far from the principles of my

108

grandfather,' Mongke said, raising his voice to carry to his officers and the Guards. 'I will drag it back to the right path.'

He looked through the open gate to the city beyond, where tens of thousands worked to administer the empire, from the lowliest taxes to the incomes and palaces of kings. His face showed his disdain, and for the first time since she had heard of Guyuk's death, Sorhatani felt a whisper of concern. She had thought Mongke would need her guidance as he took control of the city. Instead, he seemed to look through Karakorum to some inner vision, as if he did not see it at all.

When he spoke again, it was to confirm her fears.

'You should retire to your rooms, mother. At least for a few days. I have brought a burning branch back to Karakorum. I will see this filthy city made clean before I am khan.'

Sorhatani fell back a step as he remounted and rode through the gate towards the palace. His men were all armed and she saw their grim faces in a new light as they followed their lord into Karakorum. She began to cough in the dust of their passing, until there were fresh tears in her eyes.

By the afternoon, the scented braziers had burnt low and the city was beginning the formal period of mourning for Guyuk Khan. His body lay in the cool basement of the palace, ready to be cleaned and dressed for his cremation pyre.

Mongke strode into the audience room through polished copper doors. The senior staff in Karakorum had gathered at his order and they knelt as he entered, touching their heads to the wooden floor. Guyuk had been comfortable with such things, but it was a mistake.

'Get up,' Mongke snapped as he passed them. 'Bow if you

must, but I will not suffer this Chin grovelling in my presence.'

He seated himself on Guyuk's ornate throne with an expression of disgust. They rose hesitantly and Mongke frowned as he looked closely at them. There was not a true Mongol in the room, the legacy of Guyuk's few years as khan as well as his father before him. What good had it done to conquer a nation if the khanate was taken over from within? Blood came first, though that simple truth had been lost to men like Guyuk and Ogedai. The men in the room ran the empire, set taxes and made themselves rich, while their conquerors still lived in simple poverty. Mongke showed his teeth at the thought, frightening them all further. His gaze fell on Yao Shu, the khan's chancellor. Mongke studied him for a time, remembering old lessons with the Chin monk. From Yao Shu he had learned Buddhism, Arabic and Mandarin. Though Mongke disdained much of what he had been taught, he still admired the old man and Yao Shu probably was indispensable. Mongke rose from the throne and walked along their lines, marking senior men with a brief hand on their shoulders.

'Stand by the throne,' he told them, moving on as they scurried to obey. In the end, he chose six, then stopped at Yao Shu. The chancellor still stood straight, though he was by far the oldest man in the room. He had known Genghis in his youth and Mongke could honour him for that at least.

'You may have these as your staff, chancellor. The rest will come from the nation, from those of Mongol blood only. Train them to take over from you. I will not have my city run by foreigners.'

Yao Shu looked ashen, but he could only bow in response.

Mongke smiled. He was wearing full armour, a signal to them that the days of silk were at an end. The nation had been raised in war, then run by Chin courtiers. It would not do. Mongke walked to one of his guards and murmured an order into his ear. The man departed at a run and the scribes and courtiers waited nervously as Mongke stood before them, still smiling slightly as he gazed out of the open window to the city beyond.

When the warrior returned, he carried a slender staff with a strip of leather at the end. Mongke took it and rolled his shoulders.

'You have grown fat on a city that does not need you,' he told the men, swishing the air with the whip. 'No longer. Get out of my house.'

For an instant, the assembled men stood in shock at his words. It was all the hesitation he needed.

'And you have grown *slow* under Guyuk and Ogedai. When a man, *any* man, of the nation gives you an order, you move!'

He brought the whip across the face of the nearest scribe, making sure that he struck with the wooden pole. The man fell backwards with a yelp and Mongke began laying about him in great sweeps. Cries of panic went up as they struggled to get away from him. Mongke grinned as he struck and struck again, sometimes drawing blood. They streamed out of the room and he pursued them in a frenzy, whipping their legs and faces, whatever he could reach.

He drove them down the cloisters and out into the marshalling yard of the palace, where the silver tree stood shining in the sun. Some of them fell and Mongke laughingly kicked them to their feet so that they stumbled on with aching ribs. He was a warrior among sheep and he used the whip to snap them back into a group as he might have herded lambs. They stumbled ahead until the city gate loomed, with Guards looking down in amusement from the towers on either side. Mongke did not pause in his efforts, though he was running with sweat.

He kicked and shoved and tore at them until the last man was outside the walls. Only then did he pause, panting, with the shadow of the gate falling across him.

'You have had enough from the nation,' he called to them. 'It is time to work for your food like honest men, or starve. Enter my city again and I will take your heads.'

A great wail of distress and anger went up from the group and for a moment Mongke even thought they might rush him. Many had wives and children still in the city, but he cared nothing for that. The lust to punish was strong in him and he almost wished they would dare to attack, so he could draw his sword. He did not fear scholars and scribes. They were Chin men and, for all their fury and cleverness, they could do nothing.

When the group had subsided into impotent muttering, Mongke looked up at the Guards above his head.

'Close the gate,' he ordered. 'Note their faces. If you see a single one again inside the walls, you have my permission to put an arrow in them.'

He laughed then at the spite and horror he saw in the crowd of battered and bruised courtiers. Not one had the courage to challenge his orders. He waited as the gates were pushed closed, the line of sight to the plains shrinking to a crack and then nothing. Outside, they wailed and wept as Mongke nodded to the Day Guards and threw down the bloody whip at last, walking back alone to the palace. As he went, he saw thousands of Chin faces peering out from houses at the man who would be khan in spring. He grimaced, reminded once again that the city had fallen far from its origins. Well, he was no Guyuk to be baulked for years in his ambition. The nation was his.

The smell of aloes wood had faded since the morning. The city reeked again, reminding Mongke of a healing tent after a battle. He thought sourly of festering wounds he had seen, fat and shiny with pus. It took courage and a steady hand to drain such a wound: a gash and a sharp pain to let the healing begin. He smiled as he walked. He would be that hand.

The entire city was in uproar by the time darkness came. On Mongke's orders, warriors had entered Karakorum in force, groups of ten or twenty walking every street and examining the possessions of thousands of families. At the first hint of resistance, they dragged owners into the street and beat them publicly, leaving them on the cobbles until their relatives dared to come out and take them back. Some lay where they had been thrown all night.

Even sickbeds were searched for hidden gold or silver, with the occupants tossed out with their sheets and made to stand in the cold until the warriors were satisfied. There were many of those, coughing listlessly and still feverish as they stood with blank eyes. Chin families suffered more than other groups, though the Moslem jewellers lost all their stock in a single night, from raw materials to finished items ready for sale. In theory, all things would be accounted, but the reality was that anything of value disappeared into the deels the warriors wore over their armour.

Dawn brought no respite and only revealed the destruction. There was at least one sprawled body in every street and the weeping of women and children could be heard across Karakorum.

The palace was the centre of it, beginning with a search of the sumptuous rooms that had belonged to the khan's staff and favourites. Wives were either claimed by Mongke's officers or put outside the walls to join their husbands. The trappings of status were ripped down, from tapestries to Buddhist statuary. There at least, Mongke's eye could be felt and what treasures they found were dutifully collected and piled in the storerooms below. More were burnt in great fires on the streets.

As evening came on his second day back in the city, Mongke summoned his two most trusted generals to the audience room in the palace. Ilugei and Noyan were Mongols in his mould, strong men who had grown up with a bow in their hands. Neither man affected any sign of Chin culture and already those who had done so were shaving their heads and ridding themselves of the artefacts of that nation. The orlok's will had been made clear enough when he whipped the Chin scribes from the city.

Simply meeting his officers without Chin scribes to record was a break with Guyuk's court. Mongke knew Yao Shu was outside, but he would let the old man wait until the real business was concluded. He was not filled with excitement at the need to meet Guyuk's debts. The sky father alone knew how the khan had managed to borrow so much against a treasury that stood empty. Already there had been nervous delegations of merchants coming to the palace to collect gold for their paper. Mongke grimaced at the thought. With the wealth he had wrenched out of the foreigners in Karakorum, he could meet most of Guyuk's paper promises, though it would leave him without funds for months. His honour demanded he do so, as well as the practical consideration that he needed the merchants' goodwill and their trade. It seemed the role of a khan involved more than winning battles.

Mongke was not yet sure if he had acted correctly in removing the palace staff from their soft positions. Part of him suspected Yao Shu brought every small problem to him as a way of criticising what he had done. Even so, the memory of whipping them from the city was immensely satisfying. He had

114

needed to show he was no Guyuk, that the city would be run on Mongol lines.

'You have sent men to Torogene?' Mongke asked Noyan.

The general stood proudly before him in a traditional deel, his skin greasy with fresh mutton fat. He wore no armour, though Mongke had allowed him to keep his sword for the meeting. He would not fear his own men, as Guyuk and Ogedai had.

'I have, my lord. They will report directly to me when it is done.'

'And Guyuk's wife, Oghul Khaimish?' Mongke said, his eyes passing on to Ilugei.

He tightened his mouth before replying. 'That is not . . . settled yet, my lord. I had men go to her rooms, but they were barred and I thought you would want it handled quietly. She will have to come out tomorrow.'

Mongke grew very still and Ilugei began to sweat under the yellow gaze. At last the orlok nodded.

'How you carry out my orders is your concern, Ilugei. Bring me the news when you have it.'

'Yes, my lord,' Ilugei said, breathing out in relief. As Mongke looked away, Ilugei spoke again. 'She is . . . popular in the city, my lord. The news of her pregnancy is everywhere. There could be unrest.'

Mongke glared at the sweating man.

'Then take her by night. Make her vanish, Ilugei. You have your orders.'

'Yes, lord.' Ilugei chewed his lip as he thought. 'She is never without her two companions, lord. I have heard rumours that the old one knows herbs and ancient rites. I wonder if she has infected Oghul Khaimish with her spells and words?'

'I have heard nothing . . .' Mongke broke off. 'Yes, Ilugei. That will serve. Find out the truth of it.' To be accused of witchcraft carried a terrible penalty. There would be no one willing to stand up for Oghul Khaimish once that was suspected.

Mongke found himself weary as he dismissed his officers and let Yao Shu in. The days were long for one who would be khan, but he had found his purpose. The wound would be cut and it would bleed itself clean. In just a few months, he would rule a Mongol empire without the corruption of the Chin at its heart. It was a fine dream and his eyes were bright with satisfaction as Yao Shu bowed before him.

CHAPTER ELEVEN

In her husband's summer palace, Torogene sat in a silent hall, lit by a single, gently hissing lamp. She was dressed neatly in a white deel and new shoes of stitched white linen. Her grey hair was tied back tightly, so that not even a wisp escaped the twin clasps. She wore no jewels, as she had given them all away. At such a time, it was hard to look back on her life, but she could not focus on the present. Though her eyes were still swollen with weeping for Guyuk, she had found something resembling calm. Her servants were all gone. When the first one had reported soldiers coming along the road from Karakorum, she had felt her heart skip in her chest. There had been twelve servants, some of whom had been with her for decades. With tears, she had given them whatever silver and gold she could find and sent them away. They would only have been killed when the soldiers arrived, she was sure of that. News of Mongke's death lists had already reached her, with a few details of the executions in the city. Mongke was clearing away anyone who had supported Guyuk as khan and she was not surprised he had sent soldiers to her, only weary.

When the last of her servants had gone, Torogene had found herself a quiet place in the summer palace to watch the sun set. She was too old to run, even if she thought she could have lost her pursuers. It was strange to see death as finally inevitable, but she found she could put aside all her fear and anger in the face of it. The grief for her beloved son was still fresh, perhaps too great to allow any sorrow for herself. She was worn down, as one who has survived a storm and lay sprawled on rocks, too dazed to do more than breathe and stare.

In the darkness outside, she heard voices as Mongke's men rode in and dismounted. She could hear every whisper of sound, from the crunch of their feet on the stones, to the jingle of their harness and armour. Torogene raised her head, thinking back over better years. Her husband Ogedai had been a fine man, a fine khan, struck down too early by a vengeful fate. If he had lived . . . She sighed. If he had lived, she would not be alone and waiting for death in a palace that had once been a happy home. She thought suddenly of the roses Ogedai had given her. They would run wild in the gardens without someone to tend them. Her mind flitted from one thing to another, always listening for the steps coming closer.

She did not know if Ogedai would have been proud of Guyuk in the end. Her son had not been a great man. With all her future stripped away, she saw the past more clearly and there were many regrets, many paths she wished she had not taken. It was a foolish thing to look back and wish things had been different, but she could not help it.

When she heard a boot scrape at the outer door of the hall, her thoughts tore into rags and she looked up, suddenly afraid. Her hands twisted together in her lap as the warriors slid into the room, one after the other. They walked lightly, ready with weapons in case they were attacked. She could almost laugh at their caution. Slowly, she stood, feeling her knees and back protest.

The officer came to her, looking into her eyes with a puzzled expression.

'You are alone, mistress?' he asked.

For a moment, her eyes shone.

'I am not alone. Do you not see them? My husband, Ogedai Khan, stands on my right hand. My son, Guyuk Khan, stands on my left. Do you not see those men watching what you do?'

The officer paled slightly, his eyes sliding right and left as if he could see the spirits watching over her. He grimaced, aware that his companions would be listening and every word reported to Mongke.

'I have my orders, mistress,' he said, almost apologetically.

Torogene raised her head further, standing as straight as she could.

'I am brought down by dogs,' she muttered, contempt banishing her fear. Her voice was strong as she spoke again. 'There is a price for all things, soldier.' She looked up, as if she could see through the stone roof above their heads. 'Mongke Khan *will* fall. His eyes will fill with blood and he will not know rest or sleep or peace. He will live in pain and sickness and at the end . . .'

The officer drew his sword and brought it across her throat in one swift movement. She fell with a groan, suddenly limp as blood poured out of her and spattered on his boots. The watching men said nothing as they waited for her to die. When it was finished, they left quietly, unnerved in the silence. They did not look at each other as they mounted their horses and rode away.

As he faced Mongke, General Ilugei found himself strangely troubled, an unusual emotion for him. He knew it was a sound tactic for a new leader to sweep away all those who had supported his predecessor. Beyond that, it was the merest common sense to remove anyone with a blood tie to the previous regime. There would be no rebellions in the future, as forgotten children grew to manhood and learned to hate. The lessons of Genghis' own life had been learned by his descendants.

Ilugei had taken particular pleasure in putting his own enemies on the lists he prepared for Mongke, a level of power he had never enjoyed before. He simply spoke a name to a scribe and within a day the khan's loyal guards tracked them down and carried out the execution. There was no appeal against the lists.

Yet what Ilugei had seen that morning had unnerved him, ruining his usual composure. He had known still-born children before. His own wives had given birth to four of them over the years. Perhaps because of that, the sight of the tiny flopping body had sickened him. He suspected Mongke would think it a weakness in him, so he kept his voice calm, sounding utterly indifferent as he reported.

'I think Guyuk's wife may have lost her mind, my lord,' he said to Mongke. 'She talked and wept like a child herself. All the time she cradled the dead infant as if it was still alive.'

Mongke bit his lower lip in thought, irritated that such a simple thing should become so complicated. The heir had been the threat. Without one, he might have sent Oghul Khaimish back to her family. He was khan in all but name, he reminded himself. Yet his new authority stretched only so far. Silently, he cursed Ilugei's man for going into such detail of her crimes. A public accusation of witchcraft could not be ignored. He clenched his fist, thinking of a thousand other things he had to do that day. Forty-three of Guyuk's closest followers had been executed in just a few days, their blood still wet on the training ground of the city. More would follow in the days to come as he lanced the boil in Karakorum.

'Let it stand,' he said at last. 'Add her name to the list and let there be an ending.'

Ilugei bowed his head, hiding his own obscure disappointment.

'Your will, my lord.'

CHAPTER TWELVE

Oghul Khaimish stood on the banks of the Orkhon river, watching the dark waters flowing. Her hands were bound behind her, grown fat and numb in the bonds. Two men stood at her sides to prevent her throwing herself in before it was time. In the dawn cold, she shivered slightly, trying to control the terror that threatened to steal away her dignity.

Mongke was there, standing with some of his favourites. She saw him smile at something one of his officers said. Gone were the days when they would have made a bright and lively scene. To a man, his warriors and senior men were dressed in simple deels, without decoration beyond a little stitching. Most wore the traditional Mongol hairstyles, with a shaven scalp and topknot. Their faces shone with fresh mutton fat. Only Yao Shu and his few remaining Chin scribes were unarmed. The rest wore long swords that reached almost to their ankles, heavy cavalry blades designed for cutting down. Karakorum had its own foundry, where armourers sweated all day at their fires. It was no secret that Mongke was preparing for war once he had butchered the last of Guyuk's supporters and friends.

Her *husband's* supporters and friends. Oghul could not feel anything on that day, as if she had grown a protective sheath over her heart. She had lost too much in too short a time and she still reeled from all that had happened. She could not bear to look at her old servant Bayarmaa, trussed with a dozen others as they waited in sullen silence for Mongke to order their deaths.

The orlok seemed in no hurry. He was a solid figure at the centre of them, almost half as wide again as the largest warrior in his retinue. Despite his bulk, he moved easily, a man secure in his strength and still young enough to enjoy it. Oghul stood and dreamed of him being struck dead in front of them all, but it was just a fantasy. Mongke was oblivious to the misery in the huddled rank of prisoners. Even as she watched, he accepted a cup of airag from a servant, laughing with his friends. Somehow, that burned worse than anything, that he should care so little for their fate even as they stood on their last day. Oghul saw one of the bound men had lost control of his bladder, so that a thin stream of urine darkened his leggings and pooled at his feet. He did not seem to notice, his eyes already blank. She looked away, trying to find her own courage. All that man had to fear was a knife. For her, it would be slow.

It was no blessing that Mongke had agreed the wife of a khan was one of royal blood. She looked at the dark canal Ogedai had built and shivered again. She could feel the urge to empty her own bladder, though she had been careful not to drink that morning. Her face and hands felt cold as the blood was leached away and her heartbeat increased. Even so, she was sweating and the cloth at her armpits was already wet. She focused on the small changes in her body as she waited, trying desperately to distract herself.

Mongke finished his airag and tossed the cup back to the servant. He nodded to one of his officers and the man bellowed a command to come to order. All the men there straightened, even some of the prisoners, standing as tall as they could in their bonds. Oghul shook her head at the poor fools. Did they expect to impress their tormentors and gain mercy? There was none to be had.

Yao Shu was present and Oghul thought she could see the signs of great strain on the old man. She had heard the chancellor had been absent for the first executions, claiming illness. With a delicate feel for cruelty, Mongke had sensed his discomfort. Now Yao Shu played a part in all the deaths. Oghul listened to the list of names, watching sadly as each prisoner lifted his head slightly as he heard his own.

After the endless wait, the procedure suddenly started to go quickly. The prisoners were kicked to their knees and a very young warrior stepped from Mongke's group, drawing a long sword. Oghul knew he would have earned the duty as a reward for some service to Mongke. Many of the warriors desired the task if they had not yet been blooded in battle. Oghul recalled that Genghis had killed tens of thousands in one foreign city for no other purpose than to train his men in the reality of killing.

She did not listen to Yao Shu's shaking voice as he called out the charges, reading from the page in front of him. The executioner braced himself over the first kneeling figure, determined to make a good show in front of Mongke.

Oghul looked over the river as the killing began, ignoring the shouts of approval and laughter from among Mongke's group. Bayarmaa was fourth in line and Oghul had to force herself to look as the old woman's turn came. Her crime had only been by association with Oghul Khaimish, named as the one who corrupted the khan's wife to dark magic.

Bayarmaa had not bowed her head or stretched her neck and the swordsman spoke harshly to her. She ignored him, looking over to where Oghul stood. They shared a glance and Bayarmaa smiled before she was killed in two hacking blows.

Oghul looked back again to the dark waters until it was over. When the last of them was dead, she turned to see the young warrior examining his blade with a stricken expression. No doubt it had chipped on bone. Mongke came forward and clapped him on the back, pressing a fresh cup of airag into his hands while Oghul watched in sullen hatred. When Mongke looked over at her, she felt her heart constrict in panic and her numb hands twisted in the rope.

Yao Shu spoke her name. This time there was definitely a quaver in his voice and even Mongke frowned at him. Genghis had decreed that royal blood would never be shed by his people, but the alternative filled Oghul with terror.

'Oghul Khaimish, who has brought infamy to the name of the khan with witchcraft and foul practices, even unto . . . the killing of her own child.'

Oghul's hands curled into fists at the last, reaching into the coldness within to keep her on her feet.

When Yao Shu had finished reading the charges, he asked if anyone would step forward and speak in her defence. The smell of blood was strong on the air and no one moved. Mongke nodded to the warriors standing with her.

Oghul stood shaking as she was lifted off her feet and laid on a thick mat of felt. She sensed muscles twitching in her legs, beyond her control. Her body wanted to run and could not. Yao Shu suddenly began to chant a prayer for her, his voice breaking. Mongke glared at him, but the old man spoke on.

The warriors rolled her over in the felt, so that the musty material pressed against her face and filled her lungs with dust. Panic swelled in her and she cried out, her gasping breath muffled in the cloth. She felt the tugging movement as they bound the roll of felt in reins of leather, yanking the buckles tight. She would not cry for help with Mongke listening, but she could not hold back a moan of fear, dragged from her like an animal in a trap. The stillness seemed to go on for ever. She could hear her heart thud in her chest and ears, a drum pulsing. Suddenly she was moving, turning over slowly as they rolled her towards the canal.

Freezing water flooded in and she struggled wildly then,

seeing silver bubbles erupt all around her. The roll of felt sank quickly. She held her breath as long as she could.

Sorhatani lay with just a sheet over her, though the night was cold. Kublai knelt at her side and when he took her hand he almost recoiled at the heat from it. The fever had burnt its path through Karakorum and there were fewer new cases reported each day. Every summer it was the same. A few dozen or a few hundred would succumb to some pestilence. Very often it was those who had survived the last one, still weak and thin.

Kublai felt tears prick his eyes as his mother coughed, the sound building until she was choking, her back arched and her muscles standing out in narrow lines. He waited until she could draw a shuddering breath. She looked embarrassed that he had seen her so racked and she smiled weakly at him, her eyes glassy with fever.

'Go on,' she said.

'Yao Shu has locked himself in his rooms. I've never seen him so distraught. It was not a good death.'

'No such thing,' Sorhatani said, wheezing. 'It is never kind, Kublai. All we can do is ignore it until the time comes.' The effort of speaking was enormous and he tried to stop her, but she waved his objections aside. 'People do that so well, Kublai. They live knowing they will die, but no matter how many times they say the words, they don't truly believe it. They think somehow that they will be the one death passes by, that they will live and live and never grow old.' She coughed again and Kublai winced at the sound, waiting patiently until she could breathe once more.

'Even now, I expect to . . . live, Kublai. I am a foolish old woman.'

'Not foolish, or old,' he said softly. 'And I need you still.

What would I do without you to talk to?' He saw her smile again, but her skin wrinkled like old cloth.

'I don't plan . . . on joining your father tonight. I'd like to tell Mongke what I think of his death lists.'

Kublai's expression grew sour.

'From what I've heard, he has impressed the princes and generals. They are the sort of men who admire butchery. They are saying he is a new Genghis, mother.'

'Perhaps . . . he is,' she said, choking. Kublai passed a cup of apple juice into her hands and she sipped it with her eyes closed.

'He could have banished Oghul Khaimish and her old servant,' Kublai said. He had studied the life of his grandfather Genghis and he suspected his mother was right, but that did not remove the bitter taste. His brother had achieved a reputation for ruthlessness with fewer than a hundred deaths. It had certainly not hurt him with the nation. They looked to him as one who would bring a new era of conquest and expansion. For all his misgivings and personal dislike, Kublai felt they were probably right.

'He will be khan, Kublai. You must not question what he does. He is no Guyuk – remember that. Mongke is strong.'

'And stupid,' he muttered.

His mother laughed and the coughing fit that followed was the worst he had seen. It went on and on and when she dabbed at her mouth with the sheet, he saw a spot of blood on the cloth. He could not drag his eyes away from it.

When the coughing fit passed, she shook her head, her voice barely a whisper.

'He is no fool, Kublai. He understands far better than you realise. The khan's vast armies cannot return to being herdsmen, not any more. He is riding the tiger now, my son. He dare not climb down.'

Kublai frowned, irritated that his mother seemed to be supporting Mongke in everything. He had wanted to share his anger with her, not have her excuse his brother's acts. Before he spoke again, understanding came to him. Sorhatani had been his friend as well as his mother, but she would never see clearly with her sons. It was a blind spot in her. With sadness, he knew all he could achieve would be to hurt her. He closed his mouth on all the arguments he might have made and remained silent.

'I will think on it,' he said. 'Now get well, mother. You will want to be there, to see Mongke made khan.'

She nodded weakly at his words and he dried the sweat from her face before he left her.

Guyuk's body was burnt in a funeral pyre outside Karakorum and the days of mourning came to a climax. Even in the cool basements of the palace, the body had begun to rot and the pyre was thick with the smell of perfumed oils. Mongke watched as the edifice collapsed on itself in a gust of flame. Half the nation was drunk, of course, needing little excuse as they held a vigil to see the khan's spirit into the next world. In their thousands they came drunkenly to the great fire, spattering drops of airag from their fingers or blowing them from their mouths. More than one ventured too close and fell back with shrieks as their clothing caught and had to be thumped out. In the darkness, moths and biting insects crackled in the flames, drawn from the city and the gers by the light. They died in their millions, black specks that wove trails over the pyre and fell into the flames. Mongke thought of the young women, servants and warriors who had been buried with Genghis. He smiled at the thought that Guyuk had only flies to attend him in death.

When the great pyre was reduced to a glowing heap, still

higher than a man, Mongke sent for his brothers. Kublai, Hulegu and Arik-Boke fell into step beside him at his order and the small group walked back through the quiet city, leaving the nation to continue their revels. Children would be born as a result of the night. Men and women would be killed in drunken brawls, but that was the way of things: life and death intertwined for ever. It was fitting.

The city seemed empty as they walked together. Almost unconsciously, Mongke and Kublai led the group, opposites in physique and outlook. At their backs, Hulegu had the same broad forehead and heavy frame as Mongke, while Arik-Boke was the shortest, with eyes that flickered from man to man as he walked. An old scar disfigured the youngest brother, a thick line across Arik-Boke's face that varied in colour from dark pink to the yellow of callus. An accident years before had left him with no bridge to his nose, so he could be heard breathing through his mouth as they walked. Any stranger would have known they were brothers, but there was more tension than friendship in that small group. They kept their silence, waiting to see what Mongke planned for them.

Kublai felt the strain more than the others. Only he had refused to give up his Chin style, from the cut of his hair to the fine silk weave of his robes. It was a small rebellion, but as yet, Mongke had chosen not to force the issue.

There were Night Guards at the palace, holding their own silent vigil as they stood to attention under the light of lamps. At Mongke's approach, they held themselves like statues. Mongke did not seem to notice, so deep was he in thought. He swept across the outer yard and Arik-Boke had to trot to keep up with the others as they passed through the cloisters and on to the main audience room.

More of the khan's Guards waited there, by doors of polished copper. No sign of green appeared on the shining sheets and there was a smell of floor wax and polish strong in the air. Mongke may not yet have been khan, but his orders were law in the city and he worked them all hard.

Kublai watched in hidden irritation as Mongke entered and crossed the chamber, pulling off the cloth from a jug of wine and pouring himself a cup that he knocked back in quick swallows. There was nowhere to sit. The room was almost bare, except for a long table covered with carelessly strewn scrolls and maps, some of them bound in bright-coloured thread. The glittering throne of Guyuk and Ogedai had disappeared, no doubt to languish in some storeroom for the next century.

'Drink if you wish,' Mongke said.

Hulegu and Arik-Boke moved to the table with him, leaving only Kublai standing alone and waiting to be told why they were there.

The answer was not long in coming.

'I will be khan in the spring,' Mongke said. He spoke without triumph, stating it as a simple fact. 'I am orlok of the army and a grandson of Genghis. Baidur won't challenge me and Batu has written to say I have his support.'

He paused as Kublai shifted slightly on his feet. The two most senior princes of the nation had been given vast lands in Ogedai's will. They would not challenge his brother. For all Mongke's plodding reasoning, he had risen above them all. He took his position for granted, but in truth he was the only man the tumans would accept.

'So you will be khan, brother,' Kublai said, accepting Mongke's assessment. 'Our father would be proud to see one of his sons rise so far.'

Mongke stared at him, searching for mockery. He found none and grunted, satisfied at his own dominance.

'Even so, I will not leave you behind,' Mongke told his brothers. Kublai noted how he addressed himself to Hulegu and Arik-Boke, but he nodded anyway as Mongke went on. 'You will rise with me, as our father would have wanted. Tonight we will discuss the future of our family.'

Kublai doubted there would be much discussion. Mongke was confident in his new authority, dispensing wisdom as a father to his children, rather than as a brother. He clapped Hulegu on the shoulder and Kublai thought how alike they were. Though Mongke was slightly wider in the shoulder, Hulegu had the same cold eyes.

'I will not wait for spring to begin the campaigns,' Mongke said. 'The world has waited too long for a weak khan to perish. Our enemies have grown strong without a hand on their throats, a knife at the neck of those they love. It is time to remind them who their masters are.'

Hulegu made some noise of appreciation as he drained another cup of the red wine and smacked his lips. Mongke looked on him with satisfaction, seeing the same qualities that Kublai did.

'Hulegu, I have written orders for you to take command of Baidur's army of the west, with three more tumans from Karakorum. I have made you orlok of a hundred thousand and given you three of my best men, Baiju, Ilugei and Kitbuqa.'

To Kublai's embarrassment, Hulegu actually knelt and bowed his head.

'Thank you, brother,' he said, rising again. 'It is a great honour.'

'You will raze the ground south and west, using Samarkand as your base city. Baidur will not oppose my orders. Complete the work our grandfather began, Hulegu. Go further than he ever did. It is my aim that you will carve a new khanate for yourself, filled with riches.'

Mongke handed Hulegu a scroll and watched as his brother unrolled a map of the region, copied with great care and marked with the curved lines and dots of some long-dead Persian hand.

Kublai stared at it in fascination, drawing closer despite himself. The library in Karakorum had many wonders he had not yet seen.

Hulegu spread the map on the table, holding it with wine cups at the edges. His eyes gleamed as he stared across the lands represented there. Mongke patted him on the back as he leaned in, pointing with his free hand.

'The greatest city is there, brother, on the banks of the Tigris river. Genghis himself never reached so far. It is the centre of the faith they call Islam. You speak enough of the tongue, Hulegu. If you succeed, it will be the heart of your new khanate.'

'It will be done, brother,' Hulegu said, overwhelmed.

Mongke saw his pleasure and smiled, refilling a cup to hand to him.

'The line of Tolui has come to rule,' he said, glancing at Kublai. 'We will not let it pass from us, not now. The path begun by Genghis will be cut further by our family. It must be fate, brothers. Our father gave his life for a khan, our mother held the city and the homeland together when it could all have been destroyed.' His eyes shone with a vision of the future. '*Everything* that has gone before was to prepare our line for this moment, here. Four brothers in a room, with the world a sweet virgin waiting for us.'

Kublai watched silently as Hulegu and Arik-Boke grinned, swept up in Mongke's grand words. He could not be comfortable standing apart from them, and on impulse he filled the spare cup with wine and drank it. His younger brothers moved aside for him to reach the jug, though Mongke frowned slightly. As Kublai sipped, he saw with a sinking feeling how Arik-Boke was practically quivering to be told his destiny, his scar a dark pink, almost red.

Mongke chose that moment to grip the arm of their youngest brother.

'Arik, I have spoken to our mother and she has agreed this with me.'

Kublai looked up sharply at that. He did not think Sorhatani had been well enough to discuss anything.

Mongke went on, oblivious to Kublai's suspicions.

'She and I have agreed that you will inherit the homeland khanate, all but Karakorum itself, which will remain the khan's property. I don't want this pestilent place, but I'm told it has become a symbol for the people. The rest is yours, to rule in my name.'

Arik-Boke almost spilled his wine as he too knelt and dipped his head in fealty. As he came to his feet, Mongke gripped him round the back of the head and shook him affectionately.

'Those lands were our father's, Arik, and belonged to Genghis before that. Look after them. Make them green and thick with herds.'

'I will, brother, I swear it,' Arik-Boke replied. In just a few words, he had been granted unimaginable wealth. Herds and horses numbering in the millions awaited him, as well as great status in the nation. Mongke had made him a man of power in a breath.

'I will speak more to both of you tomorrow,' Mongke went on. 'Come back at dawn and I will share everything I have planned.'

He turned to Kublai and the younger brothers grew still, understanding the tension that was always present between the two men. Mongke looked every inch the Mongol warrior in his prime. Kublai stood taller, his Chin robe in sharp contrast.

'Leave us now, Hulegu, Arik,' Mongke said softly. 'I would have a word in private with our brother.'

Neither of the younger men looked at Kublai as they left. Both walked with a spring, thrust suddenly into their greatest ambitions. Kublai could almost envy their confidence and how easily it had been given to them.

When they were alone, Mongke carefully refilled the cups and handed one to Kublai.

'And what am I to do with you, brother?'

'You seem to have planned everything. Why don't you tell me?'

'You have barely left the city in your lifetime, Kublai. While I rode with Tsubodai in the west, you were here, playing with books and quills. When I was taking Kiev, you were learning to dress like a Chin woman and bathe twice a day.' Mongke leaned closer to his brother and sniffed the air, frowning at the delicate scent around Kublai. 'Perhaps a post in the city library would be suitable for a man of your . . . tastes.'

Kublai stiffened, aware that Mongke was deliberately taunting him. Nonetheless he felt his cheeks flush at the insults.

'There is no shame in scholarship,' he said through gritted teeth. 'If you are to be khan, perhaps I *would* be happiest here in the city.'

Mongke sipped his wine thoughtfully, though Kublai suspected he had already come to a decision, long before the meeting. His brother had no great intelligence, but he was thorough and patient. Those qualities could serve a man almost as well.

'Yet I promised our father that I would look after the family, Kublai. I doubt he intended me to leave you with dusty scrolls and ink-stained fingers.' Kublai refused to look down at his hands, though it was true enough. 'He wanted warriors for sons, Kublai, not Chin scribes.'

Despite himself, Kublai was stung into a reply.

'When we were young, brother, Genghis himself told his men to come to me when they had a problem. He told them I could see through the thickest patch of thorns. Are you asking me what I want from you?'

Mongke smiled slowly.

'No, Kublai. I am telling you what *I* want. Hulegu will tear down the strongholds of Islam, Arik-Boke will keep the home-land safe. I have a hundred other irons in the fire, brother, as far away as Koryo. Every day, I am presented with the envoys and ambassadors of a dozen small nations. I am the khan elect, the heart of the nation. But you have another path to tread, the work Ogedai and Genghis left unfinished.'

Kublai's mind leapt to the conclusion and he swallowed uncomfortably.

'The Sung,' Kublai muttered.

'The Sung, Kublai. Dozens of cities, millions of peasants. It will be your life's work. In my name, you will bring an end to what Genghis began.'

'And how would you have me accomplish this grand dream of yours?' Kublai asked quietly, masking his nervousness with a deep gulp of wine.

'Genghis started the conquest of the Chin with the region of Xi Xia. My advisers have found another gate into the Sung. I would have you take an army along the south-western border, Kublai, into the Yunnan region. There is only a single city there, though they can call on an army to equal mine. Still, I think it will not be too great a task, even for an unblooded man.' He smiled to take the sting out of his condescension. 'I would have you become the grandson Genghis wanted, Kublai, a Mongol conqueror. I find I have the means and the will to change your life. Swear an oath to me today and I will give you the authority to lead tumans. I will make you the terror of the Sung court, a name they dare not speak aloud.'

Kublai drained his cup and shuddered, feeling gooseflesh rise along his arms. He had to voice his first suspicion, or have it nag at him ever after.

'Are you expecting me to be killed, brother, by sending me against such an enemy? Is that your plan?'

'Still looking for games and plots?' Mongke replied with a laugh. 'I think Yao Shu had you too long in his care, brother. Sometimes things are simple, as they should be. I would lose valuable cannons and my best general with you. Would I send

Uriang-Khadai to his death? Put your mind at ease, brother. In a few months, I will become khan. Have you any idea what that means to me? I remember *Genghis*. To stand in his place is . . . worth more than I can explain. I don't need to play games or construct complicated schemes. The Sung have already raided into Chin territory, on more than one front. Unless I answer them soon with force, they will slowly take back what Genghis conquered. That is my only plan, brother. My only aim.'

Kublai saw simple truth in Mongke's stare and he nodded. In a revelation, he realised his brother was trying to fit the role he had won for himself. A khan needed a breadth of vision, to be able to rise above the petty squabbles of family and nation. Mongke was struggling to do just that. It was impressive, and with an effort Kublai shrugged off his doubts.

'What oath would you have?' he said at last. Mongke was watching him closely, his own emotions well hidden.

'Swear to me that you will put aside your Chin ways, that on campaign you will dress and act and look like a Mongol warrior, that you will train with sword and bow every morning until you are exhausted. Swear that you will not read a scholar's book for the whole time you are on campaign, not *one*, and I will give you an army today. I will give you Uriang-Khadai, but the command will be your own.' For a moment, a sneer touched his lips. 'If that is all too much, then you may return to the libraries here and wait out the years to come, always wondering what you could have been, what you could have done with your life.'

Kublai's thoughts whirled. Mongke was trying to be a khan. It seemed he thought a similar change could be wrought in his brother. It was almost endearing to see the big brute so earnest. Kublai thought of Yao Shu and the peaceful years he had spent in Karakorum. He had loved the silences of study, the glories of insight. Yet part of him had always dreamed of leading men in war. His grandfather's blood ran in him as much as it did in Mongke.

'You promised Hulegu a khanate, if he could take Baghdad,' Kublai said after what felt like an age.

Mongke laughed aloud, the sound echoing. He had begun to worry that his scholar brother would refuse him. He felt almost drunk on his own foresight as he reached for the pile of maps and documents.

His finger rested on the vast lands of northern China and he stabbed it down.

'There are two areas here, brother. Nan-ching and Ching-chao. They are mine to give. Choose either one, with my blessing. You will have your stake in Chin lands, your own estates. If you agree to this, you will be able to visit them. Before I promise you more, let me see you can win battles for me.' His smile remained as he saw Kublai examine the maps minutely, fascinated. 'Are we agreed then?'

'Give me Yao Shu as my adviser and we are,' Kublai said, letting the words spill out before he could think his choices to death. There were times when a decision had to be made quickly and part of him was filled with the same excitement he had seen in his younger brothers.

'You have him,' Mongke said immediately. 'By the sky father, you can have all the Chin scholars left in Karakorum if you say yes to this! I will see my family rise, Kublai. The world will know our names, I swear it.'

Kublai had been looking closely at the maps. Nan-ching ran close to the Yellow river and he recalled that the plain was prone to flooding. The area was populous and Mongke would surely expect him to choose it. Ching-chao was further to the north of Yenking, on the boundary of the Mongol homeland. It had hardly any towns marked. He wished Yao Shu were there to give his opinion.

'With your permission, I will take Ching-chao,' he said at last.

'The small one? It is not enough. I will give you . . .' Mongke traced a line on the map as he peered at it, 'Huai-meng as well. Estates so vast they are almost a khanate, brother. More will come if you are successful. You cannot say I have not been generous.'

'You have given me more than I expected,' Kublai said honestly. 'Very well, brother. You have my oath. I will try to be the man you want.' He held out his hand and Mongke gripped it in pride and satisfaction. Both of them were surprised at the strength of the other.

In the spring, the nation gathered on the plain of Avraga, deep in the ancestral homeland. The oldest men and women could still remember when Genghis had bound the tribes there, replacing their individual banners with just one staff of horse-tails, bleached white. The plain was vast and almost flat, so that it was possible to see for miles in any direction. A single stream ran through one part of it and Mongke made a point of drinking the water, where Genghis would have stood so many years before.

Batu had left his Russian estates to come with his honour guards, the image of his father, Jochi. He had been visibly distressed to find Sorhatani so wasted and thin, racked with a coughing illness that grew worse each day. Fevers came and went in her and there were times when Kublai believed she only hung on to life to see Mongke made khan.

From the west came Baidur, the son of Chagatai. His wealth was obvious in the gold he wore and the fine horses of a thousand guards. As khan of the homeland, Arik-Boke had arranged it all, so that they arrived over two months. One by one, the princes and generals rode in and made camp, until even that open plain was black with people and animals. Christian monks came from as far as Rome and France, and the princes of Koryo had travelled many thousands of miles to attend the man who would rule them. Until the last were in, the gathering traded and exchanged goods and horses, brokering deals that would make some rich and others poor for a generation. Airag and wine flowed freely and animals were slaughtered by the tens of thousands to feast them all.

When it was time, Mongke rode out among the host and they knelt to him and gave their oath. No one challenged him. He was the grandson of Genghis Khan and he had proven his bloodline, his right to lead. The bitter years under Guyuk were put firmly behind them. Kublai knelt with the others, thinking of the army he must take into Sung lands. He wondered if Mongke truly understood the challenge he had set. Kublai had spent most of his life in the city. He had honed his mind with the greatest philosophies of Lao Tzu, Confucius and the Buddha, but all that was behind. As Mongke became khan on a roar of acclamation, Kublai shivered, telling himself it was anticipation and not fear.

PART TWO

'Fire is the test of gold; adversity of strong men.'
– Seneca

CHAPTER THIRTEEN

Suleiman was old, but mountains and deserts had hardened his flesh, so that sinews and narrow muscles could be seen shifting against each other under his skin. In his sixtieth year, his will remained strong, simmered down to diamond hardness by the life he had led. When he spoke, his voice was gently reproving.

'That is not what I asked, Hasan, now is it? I asked if you *knew* who had stolen food from the kitchens, not if you had done it yourself.'

Visibly trembling, Hasan mumbled an unintelligible answer. He knelt on the stone floor before Suleiman's great chair. His master was dressed in heavy robes against the pre-dawn chill, while Hasan wore only a grubby linen shift. In the shadow of mount Haudegan, the room saw the sun only in the afternoons. Until then, it could have been used to keep meat from spoiling.

'Come closer, Hasan,' Suleiman said, chuckling.

He waited until the man shuffled on his knees to the foot of the chair and then Suleiman snapped out his arm, back-handing him across the face. Hasan tumbled, pulling in his legs and hiding his head in his hands. Blood dripped from his nose and he looked in terrified silence at the shining drops. As Suleiman watched, the young man reached out with a finger and smeared a red line on the stones. His eyes filled with tears and Suleiman laughed aloud.

'A few stolen cakes, Hasan. Were they worth it?'

Hasan froze, unsure whether the question held a trap for him or not. He nodded slowly and Suleiman tutted to himself.

'I wish all men lied as badly as you do, Hasan. The world would be less interesting, but so many problems would simply vanish. Is there anything in that head of yours that understands you are not to steal from me? That I always find out and punish you? Yet still you do it. Fetch me my stick, Hasan.'

The young man looked at his master in abject misery. He shook his head, but he had learned it would only be worse if he refused. With Suleiman watching in amusement, he stumbled to his feet to cross the frozen room, feeling his bruised body protest. There were few days when he was not beaten. He did not understand why his master hurt him. He wished he had resisted the honeycakes, but the smell had driven him almost to madness. Over the years, Suleiman had broken too many of his teeth for him to eat without pain and the honeycakes were soft, dissolving on his tongue with something like ecstasy.

Suleiman patted the young man's hand as Hasan gave him the stick. It was a walking cane with a weighted tip and a dagger blade hidden in the handle, suitable in all ways for the one who led the clan of Ismaili Assassins in Alamut. He saw Hasan was weeping and he put a thin arm around his shoulder as he stood.

'Hush, lad. Is it the stick you fear?' His tone was gentle.

Hasan nodded miserably.

'I understand. You don't want to be hit. But if I don't, you will steal again, won't you?'

Hasan didn't understand and he looked blankly at the old man with his cruel, black eyes and scrawny face. Hasan was both younger and wider than Suleiman, his shoulders made powerful by endless labour in the gardens. He might even have stood taller if he straightened his back. Even so, he flinched when the old man kissed his cheek.

'Better that you accept your punishment like a good boy. Can you do that for me? Can you be brave?'

Hasan dipped his head, tears spilling from his eyes.

'That's it. Dogs, boys and women, Hasan. They must all be beaten, or they are spoiled.' Suleiman brought the stick round with a sudden snap, cracking it against Hasan's skull. The young man yelped and fell back as Suleiman stepped closer, raining blows on him. In desperation, Hasan covered his face and Suleiman immediately hit him in the chest with his bony fist, at the point just above the stomach and below the breastbone. Hasan folded to the floor with a low groan, straining to suck in a breath.

Suleiman watched him affectionately, surprised to find he was panting slightly. Old age was a curse. He might have continued chastising the simpleton if his son had not chosen that moment to clatter up the stairs to the room. Rukn-al-Din barely glanced at Hasan as he strode in.

'They have sent a response, father.'

Suleiman's mood went sour at the words and he stood in thought, rubbing a spot of blood from the stick with his thumb.

'And what do they say, my son? Will you keep me waiting?'

Rukn flushed. 'They sent our man back unharmed, but the message is to abandon our fortresses.'

Suleiman gestured for Hasan to rise and handed the stick to him to be put away. It was odd, but he preferred the simpleton's company to his own son at times, like a favourite hound. Perhaps it was that Hasan could never be a disappointment, as Suleiman expected so little from him.

'Nothing else?' Suleiman said. 'No negotiation, no counter-offer? Has this khan's brother, this Hulegu, given me *nothing* for the pains I have taken?'

'No father, I am sorry.'

Suleiman did not curse or show any reaction. He regarded such displays as ultimately futile, or worse, an advantage to his enemies. Even when he grew warm from beating Hasan, he was still able to talk calmly and kindly. As he thought, he detected the distant clinking of porcelain cups coming up the winding stair to his tower. He smiled in anticipation.

'It is almost time for my morning tea, Rukn. Will you join me?'

'Of course, father,' Rukn replied. He had not heard the woman approaching and his eyes swivelled to her in surprise as she entered with a heavy tray. At times, his father's talents seemed to approach the mystical. Certainly he knew everything that occurred in the fortress, from the smallest whisper to the skills and training of each of the men.

Hasan turned quickly as he heard her step. Kameela meant 'most perfect' in Arabic and she was as beautiful as her name suggested, with black hair and smooth olive skin. Her hips swayed as she walked and Hasan could not take his eyes from them.

Suleiman chuckled at the sight of Hasan so entranced. It had been a whim two years before to give her to Hasan as his wife. Suleiman had enjoyed the confusion and terror in the fool as he understood the gift. Hasan had not been with a woman before and it had amused Suleiman greatly. If he had one area of expertise, it was in finding the weak points of other men. Hasan could be made to do anything for fear Kameela would be hurt. At times, Suleiman could treat his pain almost as artistry, with the fool as his canvas. He recorded much of what passed between them, for the edification and instruction of future masters of the order. There were few such detailed records in existence and it pleased him to add to the world's knowledge.

Kameela served tea to him without once looking at her husband. Suleiman watched her self-control in delight. A dog could be taught only simple tricks, but people were wonderfully subtle and complex. He knew she dared not acknowledge Hasan in his presence. Suleiman had thrashed him bloody at her feet on a number of occasions, for just a word or a smile. He had known the fool would fall in love with the beautiful young woman, but the miracle had been that she seemed to return his affection. Suleiman cradled his tea in his skinny hands, watching over the rim as he inhaled the delicate scent. If only he could make the Mongol generals dance as easily as his servants.

As Kameela bowed, Suleiman reached out and ran a finger slowly along her jawline.

'You are very beautiful,' he said.

'You honour me, my lord,' she said, her head still bowed.

'Yes,' he replied. Suleiman showed his yellow teeth as he drained his tea. 'Take Hasan with you, my flower. I must talk to my son.'

Kameela bowed at the dismissal and Suleiman watched as Hasan shambled after her, his hands shaking. He was tempted to call them back, indeed had intended to do so, but Rukn-al-Din began speaking again before he could. His son's eyes were irritated.

'The Shirat fortress could be taken down, as some proof of our resolve. The place is unsafe as it is, full of lizards and cracked stones. If we made a show of destroying Shirat, it would buy us another year at least. Perhaps by then, the Mongol armies will have moved on.'

Suleiman regarded his son, wishing once more that he had managed to sire a man of intelligence. For years he had hoped to produce an heir in his own image, but those hopes and dreams had long been ashes.

'You do not placate a tiger by feeding it your own flesh,' he snapped. Hasan and Kameela had made their escape and he was angry with Rukn for interrupting his pleasures. 'If such an abomination is to be my legacy, he will have to drag it out of us. We must find what this general wants and pray he is not like his grandfather Genghis. I think not. Men like that are rare.'

'I don't understand,' Rukn said.

'No, because you are a man of weakness, combined with appetites, which is why you have a belly and must visit my doctors to burn the warts off your manhood.'

Suleiman paused for a beat, waiting to see if his son would dare respond to the insults. Rukn-al-Din stayed silent and Suleiman made a sound of derision before he went on.

'When Genghis came to my father's home, he desired only destruction. The khan cared nothing for wealth and looked to himself for power and titles. Be thankful the world has not seen too many of such men, my son! For the rest, there is always something. You have offered this Hulegu peace and been refused. Offer him gold now and see what he says.'

'How much should I take to him?' Rukn said.

His father sighed.

'Not a single coin. If you return to him with carts of jewels, he will wonder how much we have kept back. He will struggle all the harder to see our fortresses brought down. Even Genghis took tribute from cities, because those around him enjoyed the glitter of fine metals and rubies. Offer . . . exactly half of every-thing in the treasury here, so that we may double the offer when he refuses.'

'You would have me give him everything?' Rukn asked in amazement.

His father slapped him viciously across the face, making him fall back in pain and shock. Suleiman's voice was utterly calm as he continued to speak.

'What comfort will it be to have gold in our pouches if Alamut and Shirat are gone? In all the world no one dares threaten us but these. The Mongols must not come here, my son. No fortress can stand for ever, not even Alamut. I would offer him the clothes from my back if I thought for a single instant that he would leave us in peace. Perhaps he can be bought with gold. We will find out.'

'And then? If he refuses, what then?' Rukn said. His cheek was flaming from the blow.

'If he refuses gold, we will make rubble of Shirat, once a jewel of our possessions. Did you know I was born there, my son? Yet I will give it up if it saves the rest.' He shook his head in weary cynicism. 'If the Mongol prince demands still more, I will have no choice but to send our best men to poison his food and wine, to strike down his officers and to murder him as he sleeps. I have tried to avoid such a course, my son. I do not want to enrage this destroyer of towns, this slaughterer of women and children.'

Suleiman clenched his fists for a moment. His father had sent men against the great khan and they had failed. The result was a whirlwind of destruction that had left cities ruined and a swathe of death across the region. There were deserts where Genghis had passed, to that day.

'If he gives us no other choice, I will take his life. The man who threatens our very existence is no greater than the goat herds tending my flocks. They can all die.'

Hulegu watched the corpses swinging gently in the breeze. Mongke would be proud of him, he was certain. He had shown no mercy as he drove south and west of Samarkand. The word would go out that there was a new khan and that he should be feared. Hulegu understood his task and he relished earning his older brother's approval. Only nine young men remained from the town after Hulegu's warriors slaughtered every other living thing. The river was running red as bodies in the water were drained by the tugging current. Hulegu was pleased at the sight, imagining that the colour would be carried for a hundred miles, bringing fear to all those who saw it. There would be no gates closed to him as he marched, not again.

He had burnt three small cities and a dozen towns as he moved west, killing few, but leaving the inhabitants destitute and hungry, with every loaf and jar of oil or salt taken for his men. He did not know the name of the walled town which had tried to resist, barring their gates with iron and retreating into the cellars while their soldiers held the walls.

It had fallen in just a day. Though he did not have the numbers of cannon that Mongke had given Kublai, there were still enough. In a line of eighty, the polished rock balls smashed open the gates with two blows, but he had not paused to assault the town. Instead, he had ordered the guns to keep firing, cracking the stones to rubble and sending defenders flying in sprays of blood. The tumans had watched indifferently, waiting for his orders.

Only the thought that he should not waste his dwindling store of black powder made Hulegu call the halt. He enjoyed the thunder he could bring with just a wave of his hand. It was intoxicating to say 'Fall' and have a city wall hammered to pieces before his eyes. He sent his men in that evening, loping on foot as they rushed to be first to loot the town.

Young women were raped, then tied together in weeping groups, ready for the gambling and bargains that would follow. Children and the elderly were killed as they were found. As with the battered men of the town, they were of no value. Gold and silver items were stripped from each house and piled in the central square to be weighed and assessed. Hulegu had his own forges with him. His habit was to melt the precious metals, skimming off the impurities and alloys as they rose out of the denser gold. Persian chemists directed the work, sending ancient items to feed the flames. They were allowed to keep a tithe of all they collected, one part in a thousand to split between them. Already they were wealthy men and Hulegu had been forced to cut hundreds of trees and wait as the new timber was made into carts to carry the wealth.

Many of the defenders had fallen as the walls collapsed, coughing and choking on dust. Some tried to surrender, and for those Hulegu had only contempt. He stared with pleasure at the swinging bodies. He did not hang them by the neck, to die quickly. A few were hung by the feet, but most were held by ropes under their armpits and gashed across their stomachs to bleed to death. They lasted a long time and their cries could be heard across the hills.

When the town was burning, Hulegu signalled to General Ilugei to cut the bonds holding his prisoners. They were all men who had fought with courage and been battered to the ground. From a town of ten thousand, it was a pitifully small number, but he could at least have the glimmerings of respect for those few. He watched in stern silence as they stood and rubbed their wrists. Two of the nine were sobbing, while the rest stared at him in mute horror and impotent rage. He felt it like good wine in his mouth, making him strong.

He did not speak the local tongue, so he had his words repeated by one of the chemists, a turban-wearing Moslem named Abu-Karim.

'I will give you horses,' Hulegu said. 'You will go ahead of my warriors, my carts and guns. Ride west and south and tell them I am coming. Tell each man you meet that he must open his doors to me, that he must give me his wives and daughters to be mine and his wealth, which will also be mine. He may keep his life. Tell them that if a city, or a town, or a single home bars its doors to me, I will visit destruction on them all, until the earth itself cries out in pain.'

He turned away then, not bothering to wait until the translator was finished. Baghdad was to the south-west and the caliph there had sent more blustering threats and lies. To the north, Hulegu felt the pull of the Assassin strongholds. He grunted in irritation at being caught between the two desires.

CHAPTER FOURTEEN

Kublai could see a multitude around him, from those digging toilet pits, to warriors leading horses and women tending cooking fires for their husbands and sons. He had never known the life of a moving tribe, but something in him found peace in it. Looking into the distance, he wondered again at the veritable nation he had brought south. There must have been half a million souls in the column that rode down the border of Sung lands. He was not even sure of the true number.

He stretched his back with a soft groan as his wife and son prepared his ger for him. Not that little Zhenjin was much use, he noticed. Mongke's orders had not extended to his family and the ten-year-old still wore a Chin silk tunic and leggings, down to a pair of soft sheepskin boots. His topknot of black hair flicked back and forth with every movement. Kublai tried not to laugh as he saw the boy sneak a handful of steaming meat scraps from the pile that Chabi was working into pouches. She had only looked away for a moment, but the boy had quick hands. Zhenjin had stuffed his cheeks before she turned back. It was bad luck that his mother chose that moment to ask a question, or perhaps not. Chabi adored and spoiled her first-born, but that did not mean her instincts were blunt. As Zhenjin struggled to reply around a mouthful of hot meat, she poked him in the stomach and he sprayed bits of food, giggling.

Kublai smiled. He could still be surprised at the strength of his emotions when he looked over his family. It wasn't just that the boy delighted him, but a moment with his family could bring sudden understanding of his own parents. His father had given his life to save a khan, and Kublai finally appreciated the scale of that sacrifice. The man had acted for the nation, knowing he would never see his sons or his wife again. In a strange way, it left a debt to be paid by all of them, as well as a sense that however they lived their lives, they could not equal their father's final act. Kublai sensed Mongke struggled with the same burden. His older brother was trying to fit an ideal, but he would never know peace looking for the approval of the dead.

At least Mongke had not stinted in men or supplies. With Uriang-Khadai as orlok and Bayar as his senior general, Kublai travelled with two hundred iron cannon and thousands more carts filled with gunpowder and equipment under heavy tarpaulins. He had a staff of ninety-four men and women to handle the moving nation. As he stood there in his reverie, he could see some of them close by. When he had eaten, they would come to him with the details, plaints and problems of so many. He sighed at the thought, but the tasks were not beyond him, not yet. He crashed into slumber each night, yet still rose before dawn and practised with the sword and bow. When the armour had begun to feel light on him, Kublai could even imagine thanking Mongke for the changes he had wrought. The khan knew more about being a warrior than his brother. Unfortunately, it was all he knew.

Kublai felt an itch in his armpit and worked his thumb under the iron scales to scratch the sores there, grunting at the small pleasure. Life was good. He had seen his Chin estates, and in his mind's eye, green shoots were rising quickly from the black earth. Just sinking a few painted poles into the soft ground had marked a grand new venture in his life. Yao Shu had arranged the lease of thousands of plots, with the rent to be paid from the first crops. If the Chin farmers prospered, two-fifths would be Kublai's and the money would go to making a city in the north.

It was a dream worth having, something beyond the mass of warriors and horses that filled his sight to the horizons. Though it was little more than a vast square marked out on grassland, his men had already begun calling it Shang-du, the 'Upper Capital'. Those who did not speak the Chin languages called it Xanadu. He whispered the word aloud.

With a sigh, Chabi wiped a hand across her brow and told Zhenjin to carry the platter inside for the stove. Kublai's mouth filled with saliva. He was always hungry these days. His wife stood and stretched her own back. He looked over at her and their eyes met, united in their weariness. His mind lost the visions of palaces as his stomach rumbled.

'Did you get me a skin of wine?' he said.

'Of course,' she replied, 'though I hope you will not leave it empty again and complain tomorrow about how your head is bursting. There will be no sympathy from me.'

'I never complain!' he said, wounded. 'I am like a stone for keeping silent.'

'Was that some other man stumbling around the ger this morning, then? Cursing and demanding to know who had stolen his hat? I thought it was you. In fact, I hope it was you, because he was very active last night, whoever he was.'

'You were dreaming, woman.'

She grinned at him and flicked her long hair back from her face, working quickly with her hands to tie it. He stared deliberately at her breasts as they moved under the cloth and she snorted.

'There is a fresh bucket of water at the door for you to wash, old goat. Don't stay out here dreaming, so the food gets cold. I know you will complain anyway, but I will ignore you.'

She went inside and Kublai could hear her berating Zhenjin for stealing some of the pouches. Kublai chuckled to himself. When he had set out from Karakorum, he had not known how long it would take to reach the Sung lands. It was almost two years since Mongke had become khan and Kublai had spent a year of that simply travelling, moving his great host south, day after day. His tumans were with their families and there was no sense of impatience in their ranks. They did not need to stop to live. For them, the journey was as much their lives as reaching the destination. In the evenings, they played with their children, sang, gambled, made love, tended the animals or a thousand other small things that they could do anywhere. For a man who had lived most of his life in Karakorum, it was a strange thing to see.

Kublai had kept his oath to Mongke and not opened a single scroll or book since leaving the city. At first, it had been a terrible hardship and he had slept badly, dreaming of old texts. On the borders of Sung lands there were many signs of that ancient culture. They had already passed through hundreds of small towns and villages and Kublai had not been able to resist snapping up written works when he found them. His growing collection travelled with him like an itch at the back of his mind.

It had been Yao Shu who offered to read them to him in the evenings. Though Kublai was uncomfortable at skirting his oath, he could not deny it was a comfort. His son Zhenjin seemed to enjoy the droning voice and sat up late when he should have been asleep, listening to every word. Kublai's mind had suffered like a desert in time of drought and the ideas poured in, reviving him.

His body too had toughened in the months of travel. Saddle

sores were just a painful memory. Like the experienced warriors, he had developed a sheath of dark yellow callus on his lower spine, about the width of a man's hand across. He reached behind him to scratch it, frowning at the sweat-slick that stayed on his skin no matter how often he bathed. Mongke could not object to his being clean, at least. Though he wore the scaled armour, Kublai suffered less with rashes and skin rot than his men. In the humid summer, a scent of bad meat overlaid even the odour of wet wool and horses. Kublai still missed the cool Chin robes he had grown to love.

The orlok of his tumans had a ger in sight of Kublai's, with three women and a host of servants tending his every need. Kublai squinted to see Uriang-Khadai standing over one of them, giving some instruction about the best way to stitch a saddle. The orlok's back was arrow-straight, as always. Kublai snorted to himself. He had already decided Uriang-Khadai was Mongke's man, the khan's eyes on their expedition. The orlok was an experienced officer of the sort who would certainly impress his brother. He had even scarred his cheeks to prevent a beard growing. The keloid ridges proclaimed that he put duty above self, though Kublai saw it as a sort of twisted vanity.

As Kublai watched, Uriang-Khadai felt the scrutiny and turned sharply to face him. Caught staring, Kublai raised his hand as if in greeting, but the orlok pretended he had not seen and turned away to his own ger, his own little world within the camp. Kublai suspected the man saw him as a mere scholar, given authority by his brother for no great merit. When they met each day, he could see Uriang-Khadai's subtle amusement as Kublai laid out his strategies. There was little liking between them, but it did not truly matter, as long as he continued to obey. Kublai yawned again. He could smell his meal on the breeze and his mouth ached for wine to take the edge off his thoughts. It was the only way to ease his mind, to stop it tearing every idea to pieces and then making new things with the scraps. With a last look around him, he realised he could relax. Some of the tension left his shoulders and back as he ducked into the ger and was immediately ambushed by Zhenjin, who had waited patiently for him.

The tumans were never quite alone as they drifted south. With such a vast and slow assemblage, they could not possibly surprise the Sung nation. There were always scouts watching from the nearest hills. Word had gone ahead. The most recent villages were all abandoned, some of them with odd markings of blood in the road. Kublai wondered if the inhabitants had been slaughtered rather than left to give aid to an enemy. He could believe it. Though he loved the culture, he had no illusions about their brutality or the sort of armies his men would face. The Sung outnumbered him by hundreds to one. They had walled cities, cannon and flame weapons, good steel, crossbows and excellent discipline. As he trotted his horse, he listed their strengths and weaknesses as he had a thousand times before. Their strengths were intimidating, impossible. The only weaknesses he had been able to think of were that they had few cavalry and that they chose their officers for nobility of birth, or with written examinations in their cities. Compared with men like Uriang-Khadai and Bayar, Kublai hoped the Sung generals would also be considered effete scholars. He could *beat* scholars.

Out of the corner of his eye, he saw one of his scouts ride up to Uriang-Khadai and report. Kublai kept facing forward, though he felt his heart beat faster in anticipation. Four days before, the Mongol column had crossed the Sung border and begun to move east. Whatever the Sung armies had been doing for the months of his approach, they would have to respond.

He had been expecting contact. He had done everything he could with their formations and battle plans, but all of that would change when he met the enemy at last. Kublai smiled as a memory of one book flashed into his mind. He did not have to read it again to know every line. He had memorised the work by Sun Tzu many years before. The irony of a book on the art of war being written by a Chin general was not lost on him. The Sung would know it just as well.

Uriang-Khadai rode slowly over to him, deliberately unhurried, though thousands of interested eyes watched the orlok's progress. He reached Kublai and dipped his head formally.

'The enemy are in the field, my lord,' he said, his voice as clipped and dry as if he discussed the rations. 'They have taken up a position on the other side of a river, some twenty miles further east and south. My scouts report two hundred thousand infantry and some ten thousand horsemen.'

His voice was deliberately unimpressed, but Kublai felt sweat break out in his armpits, stinging the scabs there. The numbers were terrifying. He did not think Genghis had ever faced so many, except perhaps at the Badger's Mouth, far to the north.

'If I may, my lord?' Uriang-Khadai said into the silence.

Kublai nodded for him to go ahead, suppressing his irritation at the man's pompous tone.

'They could have attacked after we crossed the river, but with it still between us, I suggest we ride on. We can force them away from whatever traps and trenches they have dug. The Yunnan city of Ta-li is only another hundred miles south. If we continue towards it, they will have no choice but to follow.'

Uriang-Khadai waited patiently while Kublai thought. The orlok had not minded Kublai's endless interference in the supplies and formations. Such things were to be expected from a new man. The battles, however, were the orlok's responsibility. Mongke himself had made that clear before they left.

'Look after him,' the khan had said. 'Don't let my younger brother get himself killed while he's in a dream.' The two old campaigners had shared a smile of understanding and then Uriang-Khadai had ridden out. Now the time was upon him and he was prepared to guide Kublai through his first taste of warfare.

While he waited, Uriang-Khadai rubbed the ridge-lines of his cheeks. There were a few stubborn bristles that had somehow survived the years of scarring. He was never sure whether he should cut himself again or just yank the things out when they grew long enough. As Kublai pondered, Uriang-Khadai curled one long hair around his finger and jerked it free.

'We must cross the Chin-sha Chiang river,' Kublai said suddenly. He had pictured maps in his imagination, his recall almost perfect. Uriang-Khadai blinked in surprise and Kublai nodded, making his decision.

'That is the name of the river you mentioned, orlok. It lies between us and the city I have been told to take. We must cross it at some point. They know the ground, which is why they have gathered on that side. They are content to defend it wherever we choose to cross. If we find a fording point, they will slaughter us in the waters, reducing us to the narrow ranks we can put in.'

Uriang-Khadai shook his head, struggling to find the right words to persuade a sheltered academic who had barely left Karakorum in his life.

'My lord, they already have every advantage. We cannot also give them the choice of land, or we risk annihilation. Let me lure them along the banks for thirty miles. I will have the scouts out looking for places to cross. There will be more than one. We can have archers cover those crossing and then we can come up behind them.'

Kublai could feel the silent pressure from Uriang-Khadai, waiting for him to give way. The man was too obvious and it irritated him.

'As you say, orlok, they have chosen their ground carefully. They will expect us to rush across the river like the wild tribesmen they think we are and then die in our thousands.' He thought suddenly of a way to get enough men across quickly and he smiled.

'No. We will take them on here, orlok. We will surprise them.'

Uriang-Khadai stammered for an instant.

'My lord, I must advise against your decision. I . . .'

'Send General Bayar to me, Uriang-Khadai. Return to the tumans.'

The orlok bowed his head instantly, all sign of his anger vanishing like a snuffed candle.

'Your will, my lord.'

He rode away even more stiff-backed than he had come. Kublai stared sourly after him. It was not long before Bayar was in the orlok's place, looking worried. He was relatively young for his authority, a man in his early thirties. Unlike Uriang-Khadai, he had a smooth face, except for a wisp of black hair at his chin. There was a strong odour of rot around him. Kublai had long grown used to it as he accepted the man's greeting. He was in no mood to ease Bayar's misgivings.

'I have a task for you, general. I order you to carry it out without complaint or argument, do you understand?'

'Yes, my lord,' Bayar replied.

'When I was a boy, I read about warriors with Genghis crossing a river using a sheepskin raft. Have you heard of such a thing?'

Bayar shook his head, flushing slightly.

'I do not have the reading, my lord.'

'Never mind. I recall the idea. You will need to slaughter

161

some six hundred sheep for what I have in mind. Take care to cut them high on the neck, so that the skin is undamaged as it is peeled back. The wool must be shaved away, I believe. This work is delicate, Bayar, so give it to careful men and women in your command.'

Bayar looked blankly at him and Kublai sighed.

'There is no harm in knowing a little history, general. We should not have to relearn every skill each generation. Not when the hard work has already been done. The idea is to sew up the holes in the skins, leaving just one near the neck. Strong men can blow into the skin, using tar or tree sap to seal the gaps. Do you understand? Have vats of both substances put to boil. I do not know which will work best. When they are tight with air, the skins will float, general. Bind them together in a frame of light poles and we will have rafts capable of carrying many men at a time.' He paused to run calculations in his head, one thing Kublai could always do quickly.

'With three rafts, say eighteen hundred sheepskins, we should be able to carry . . . twelve hundred warriors across the river at a time. In half a day, we could put some twenty thousand men on the opposite side. I will assume another half day to swim horses across, using the rafts to guide them. Yes, with ropes around their necks to help them swim against the current. A day in all, if there are no mishaps. How long will you need to put the rafts together?'

Bayar's eyes widened as he saw the prince had lost his internal gaze and was once again focused on him.

'Two days, my lord,' he said with false confidence. He needed to impress the man who commanded him and Uriang-Khadai had already lost face. Bayar did not want to join him in incurring the displeasure of the khan's own brother.

Kublai inclined his head as he thought.

'Very well. This is your only task until it is complete. I will hold you to two days, general. Now, give the order to halt the column. Get scouts back into the area where the enemy wait. I want to know every detail of the river: the current, the banks, the terrain. Nothing is too trivial to bring to me. Have them report after the evening meal.'

'Yes, my lord.'

Bayar swallowed nervously as he was dismissed. He had never heard of sheepskins being used in such a way. He was going to need help and he guessed that Uriang-Khadai was not the man to ask. As the horns sounded the halt and the tumans began to dismount and tend their horses, Bayar saw the cart that carried Kublai's chief adviser, Yao Shu. The old Chin monk would know of such strange things as floating rafts, Bayar was almost certain.

As the sun came up the following day, Bayar had lost himself in the challenge of the task. The first bulbous hides had been prepared by the previous evening and carried by horse to the nearby river. With great ceremony the bobbing things had been placed on the waters, with volunteers to ride them over. Both men had sunk before they reached halfway and had to be dragged out by ropes attached to their waists. It seemed impossible, but according to Yao Shu it had certainly been done on a smaller scale. They tried rubbing oil into the skins as soon as the wool had been shaved off, then blowing and sealing them quickly, before leaving them to dry. As Bayar returned to the banks, he sent a silent prayer to the earth mother. He had gambled on the oil working and so had thousands of families preparing them. If the latest batch failed as well, he would not make the limit he had set himself. Standing in the morning gloom, Bayar looked across at Yao Shu, taking confidence from his calm. They stood together as two warriors tied ropes to themselves and lay across the floating skins, pushing off from the bank. Neither man could swim and they looked deeply uncomfortable as they paddled across the dark water.

At halfway, the current was strong and those holding the ropes on the bank found themselves shuffling downstream with the floating warriors. Even so, they splashed on and Bayar let out a whoop as he saw one of them stand and raise his arm from the opposite shallows, before clambering back on for the return trip. That went much faster, with the ropes pulled by many willing hands.

Bayar clapped Yao Shu on the back, feeling the bones beneath his colourful robe.

'That will do,' the general said, trying to conceal his relief. Uriang-Khadai was not there. The orlok had decided not to notice the sudden and massive labour that had overtaken the camp. While families worked the skins, oiling and sewing for all they were worth, the orlok had his men practising their archery and the cannon teams sweating to improve their speed with the guns. Bayar didn't care. He found the work fascinating and on the evening of the second day he strode up to the ger erected for Kublai, hardly able to restrain his grin as he was allowed to enter.

'It's done, my lord,' he said proudly.

To his relief, Kublai smiled, responding to the man's evident satisfaction.

'I never doubted it would be, general.'

CHAPTER FIFTEEN

Hulegu was hot and thirsty as he rode north. The bulk of his army had gone on without him, ready to lay a siege around Baghdad. The centre of Islam was a powerful city on the Tigris river and he knew it would not fall quickly. The decision had been difficult, but he had thought his detour to the stronghold of Alamut would be a quick strike, no more onerous than crushing the head of a snake under his heel before going on with the real work. Instead, he suffered through hundreds of miles of the most hostile country he had ever seen. The sun fed a simmering anger that seemed to have been with him for weeks. He shaded his eyes as he stared up into the mountains, seeing snow on the peak of the one known as Solomon's Seat. Somewhere in those remote crags was the most powerful fortress of the Ismaili Assassins.

The last towns and villages were long behind. His warriors rode across a burning plain, over a surface of loose rocks and scree that made many of the horses go lame. There was no grazing in such a place and Hulegu had lost time securing grain and water for the men and animals. Three tumans had originally come north with him, but he had sent one back to Baghdad and another to act as a relay for water when he saw the desolation of the terrain. He had no wish to see his best mounts die of thirst. Yet Hulegu was not deterred by the difficulties. If anything, they reassured him. No worthy goal should come easily, he told himself. Suffering created value.

In another age, Genghis had vowed to annihilate the Assassin cult. The great khan may even have thought he had done so, but they had survived like weeds in the rocks. As Hulegu looked over the single tuman, he sat straighter in the saddle, his pride obvious to them all. He had grown up with stories of Genghis. To meet one of the old enemies in the field was more than satisfying. He would give orders for their precious fortresses to be taken down and left in the valleys as fire-blackened blocks of stone. Only snakes and lizards would creep where the Assassins had walked, he vowed to himself. Mongke would not begrudge him the time he lost, Hulegu was sure. Baghdad would not fall in the next season. He had time to finish the personal matter between his family and the Moslems who inhabited Alamut.

Three guides led the tuman across the plain, recruited at knife-point from the last town they had passed. Hulegu had scouts and spies across the country feeding him information, but none of them had been able to give him the exact location of the fortress. Even the letters he had exchanged with the Assassins had gone to prominent merchants in cities, passed on by their own riders. His best information gave him only the range of mountains and nothing more. Even that had cost him a fortune in silver and a day spent torturing a man given up by his friends. It did not matter. Hulegu had always known he would have to come to the area to hunt them down. He questioned the guides constantly, but they only argued with each other in Arabic and shrugged, pointing always into the mountains. He had not seen another living soul for a long time when his scouts came riding in, their horses lathered in soapy sweat.

Hulegu frowned when he saw them making for him across

the face of the ranks. From a distance, he could see the urgency in the way they sat their horses and he forced himself to keep the cold face as a matter of habit.

'My lord, there are men ahead,' the first scout said. He touched his right hand to his forehead, lips and heart in a gesture of respect. 'Twelve miles, or a little more. I saw only eight horses and a silk awning, so I went closer, while my companion stayed out of range, ready to ride back to you.'

'You spoke to them?' Hulegu asked. Sweat was trickling down his back under his armour and his mood improved at the thought that he must be close if there were strangers gathered in the foothills to wait for him. The scout nodded.

'The leader said he was Rukn-al-Din, lord. He claimed to have authority to speak for the Ismailis. He told me to say he has prepared a cool tent and drinks for you, my lord.'

Hulegu thought, wrinkling his brow. He had no particular desire to sit down with men who dealt in death. He could certainly not eat or drink with them. Equally, he could not let his warriors see he was afraid of so few.

'Tell him I will come,' he said. The scout cantered off across the lines to get a fresh horse and Hulegu summoned General Ilugei, nodding to the man as he approached.

'They have made a meeting place, general. I want to surround it, so that they understand the consequences of treachery. I will walk in, but if I do not walk out, I want you to visit destruction on them. If I fall, Ilugei, you are to leave a mark in their histories to show their error. Do you understand? Not for me, but for those who come after me.'

Ilugei bowed his head.

'Your will, my lord, but they do not know your face. Let me go in your place to see what they intend. If they plan to kill, let me be the one who draws them out.'

Hulegu thought about it for a moment, but then shook his

head. He felt a worm of fear in his stomach and it made anger rise in him like the heat of the day. He could not stop his fear, but he could face it down.

'Not this time, Ilugei. They rely on the fear they create. It is part of their power, perhaps even the heart of it. With just a few deaths each year, they create a terror in all men. I will not give them that, not from me.'

Rukn-al-Din sat in light robes and sipped at a drink cooled with ice. If the Mongol general did not show himself soon, the precious stock brought down from the peaks would all have melted. He glanced at the dripping white block sitting in a wooden bucket and gestured to have a few more shavings added to his drink. At least he could enjoy the luxury while he waited.

Around his small group, the Mongols were still riding, a wall of moving men and horses. For half a day, they had amused themselves with yells and mock screams while Rukn's men ignored them completely. It took time to move ten thousand warriors into position and Rukn wondered if he would see the khan's brother before sunset. There were no hidden forces for the Mongols to find, though he did not doubt they wasted their energies searching the hills all around him. For the thousandth time, he went over the offers he could make in his father's name. It was not a long list. Gold and eventually a fortress, offered in such a way that it seemed to be drawn out of him. Rukn frowned, wishing his father were there to conduct the negotiation. The old man could sell his own shadow at noon, but Rukn knew there was a chance he would not survive the meeting. The Mongols were unpredictable, like angry children with swords. They could treat him with honour and courtesy, or simply cut his throat and move on with utter indifference. Despite the afternoon breeze and the cool drink,

Rukn found he was perspiring after all. He did not know what to do if his offers were refused. No one had expected the Mongols to appear in the area, when good sources said they were heading to Baghdad, hundreds of miles away. Even the natural barrier of the dry plain seemed hardly to have slowed them and Rukn realised he was afraid. Before sunset, he could be just another body waiting to be reclaimed by the dust.

At first, he did not realise Hulegu had come. Rukn-al-Din was used to the grandeur of caliphs and expected at least some sort of retinue, some fanfare. Instead, one dusty warrior among many dismounted. Rukn watched him idly, noting the extraordinary breadth of the man's shoulders as he stopped to talk to two or three others around him. The Mongols loved to wrestle, one of the few civilised things about them. Rukn-al-Din was wondering if he could interest the khan's brother in a challenge from one of his own when he saw the man striding towards the tent. He rose, putting down his drink.

'Salaam Alaikum. You are most welcome. I assume you are Prince Hulegu, brother to Mongke Khan. I am Rukn-al-Din, son to Suleiman-al-Din.'

His interpreter translated the Arabic into the general's coarse tongue, making Hulegu glance at him. Rukn chose that moment to bow deeply. His father had ordered it, though Rukn resented even the idea. The warrior stared coldly at him and Rukn watched as his eyes flickered around the inside of the tent, taking in every detail. Hulegu had yet to enter the shaded awning. He stood on the threshold glaring in, while his ten thousand continued to make an appalling racket all around them. Dust drifted in wisps through the air, visible in the light of the setting sun. Rukn struggled to remain calm.

'You must be thirsty, my lord,' Rukn went on, hoping he was not overdoing the titles and honours. 'Please sit in the shade. My men have brought ice to keep us cool.'

Hulegu grunted. He did not trust the weak-faced man standing before him, even to the point of revealing his understanding of the language. He thought of Ilugei's offer to go to the meeting in his place and wondered if the stranger was who he claimed to be. Under the pressure of Rukn's open-palm gesture, Hulegu unbent enough to enter. He frowned at the sight of a chair with its back to Rukn's servants and snapped an order to his own men. One of the Mongol officers sauntered into the tent behind him, radiating danger with every movement. Rukn remained still as the chair was dragged across the carpeted floor against the silk wall. At last, Hulegu sat, waving away his own man and the servant with a tray of tall glasses.

'I told you to destroy your fortresses,' Hulegu said. He placed his hands on his knees, sitting straight and ready to leap up. 'Has that been done?'

Rukn cleared his throat and sipped his drink as the interpreter spoke. He was not used to business being discussed so quickly and it unnerved him. He had hoped to begin a negotiation that would last all night and perhaps most of the next day, but under that cruel stare, he found himself babbling part of his promises in one rush, his father's warnings melting away like the ice in his drink.

'I have been told, lord, that we will begin the work on Shirat castle next spring. By the end of next year, it will be gone and you may tell your khan that we have obeyed you.'

He paused for translation, but at the end, Hulegu did not speak. Rukn struggled to find words to go on. His father had told him to make the Mongols understand it took months to bring down thousands of tons of cut stone. If they accepted the offer, the work would be delayed over and over again. There would be great energy and effort, but the castle would take years to demolish. Perhaps by then, the distant khan would have broken his neck, or Hulegu's great army would have moved on to other targets for their bile.

'Shirat is high in the mountains, lord. It is no easy task to bring down something that has stood for millennia. Yet we understand that you will want to report success to the khan, your brother. We have prepared gifts for him, gold and jewels to fill a city.' For the first time, he saw a spark of interest in Hulegu's eyes and was partly reassured.

'Show me,' Hulegu said, his words translated in a single sound from the interpreter.

'My lord, they are not here. You and I answer to more powerful men. I am merely an emissary for my father, as you speak for your khan. Yet I have been told to offer you four thousand finger bars of gold as well as dinar coins to fill two chests.' Even saying the words made fresh sweat break out for Rukn-al-Din. The amounts were vast, enough to found a small city. The Mongol merely stared at him as the interpreter droned on.

'You do accept tribute from your allies?' Rukn said, pressing him. Hulegu waited patiently for the translation to finish.

'No. We accept tribute from those who serve us,' Hulegu replied. 'You have spoken, Rukn-al-Din. You have said what you have been told to say. Now listen to me.' He paused while the interpreter caught up, watching Rukn closely all the time. 'My concern is the centre of Islam, the city of Baghdad. I will take that place, do you understand?'

Rukn nodded uncomfortably as he heard the words.

'In comparison to that, your father and your sect mean little to me. For the honour of my grandfather, I would have been content to see them made into ashes, but you have offered me gold and friendship. Very well, I will accept twice the sum in gold and the destruction of two of your fortresses. I will accept an oath of allegiance to me and to my family.' He let the translator

171

reach the end, so that he could watch Rukn-al-Din's reaction. 'But I will not give you my word. As you say, we both have those to whom we must answer. When I return to my brother, he will ask if I spoke to this Suleiman. Nothing else will do, do you understand? There can be peace between our families, but only when I have spoken to Suleiman. Take me to Alamut, that I may meet with him.'

Rukn struggled not to show his delight. He had been afraid the Mongol would refuse everything he offered, perhaps even to the point of killing him in his tent. In his pleasure, a tendril of suspicion entered. The Mongol leader might see an advantage in getting his army close to the ancient stronghold. Rukn did not know if the man's guides could even find it on their own. He thought of the impregnable fortress, with its single path across the sheer rock face. Let them come and stare up at it. Their catapults and cannon would not reach such a height. They could roar and bluster for a hundred years at the foot of the peak and never get in.

'I will do as you say, my lord. I will send word ahead of us and you will be welcomed as a friend and ally.' His eyes grew cunning and he shook his head ruefully. 'As for the gold, I do not think there is that much in all the world. If you will accept the first part as a gift, I'm certain the rest could be brought to you each year in tribute.'

Hulegu smiled for the first time. He did not think the young man had realised yet that his life was in Hulegu's hands.

Suleiman breathed deeply, enjoying the scent of sheep droppings in the high, clear air. The tiny meadow on the far side of Alamut was a miracle of rare device, a testament to the skill and foresight of his ancestors. Small trees gave shade to the herd and Suleiman often came there when he needed to think in peace. The meadow was barely two acres in all, enough to support only a dozen sheep and six goats. They were fat and glossy in the sunshine, their constant bleating a balm to his soul. Some of them came close at the sight of him, standing without fear as they hoped for food. He smiled, showing them empty hands. At heart, he had always thought of himself as a shepherd, to men as well as animals.

He strolled across the thick turf until he reached the sheer rock on one side and ran his fingers along it. There was a small hut there, with bags of feed for the winter and grey blocks of salt for the animals to lick. He checked the bags carefully, wary of the mould that could be poisonous to his precious flock. For a time he lost himself carrying the sacks into the light and checking the contents. In such a place, it was difficult to believe he faced the utter annihilation of his clan.

It was hard to bargain with those who seemed to desire only his destruction. Suleiman hoped his son would come back with something, but he doubted it. The Mongol leader would insist on seeing Alamut and once he had found his way through the labyrinth of valleys and paths, he would lay his siege and begin to starve them out. Suleiman looked ruefully over his small field. The animals would not support his people for long. Rarely were there more than sixty or seventy men in the stronghold of Alamut, perhaps as many again in servants. It had always been a small community, unable to survive without the payments in gold from their work. He could not resist the Mongols with force, any more than his father had managed against Genghis. Suleiman grimaced to himself as he realised he had no choices left. Three of his men were out in the world, with payments expected. Silently, he listed the merchants they had been told to kill. He would not hear from them again until their work was done. Eighteen others were at the peak of fitness in

Alamut, trained in the methods of silent murder. It was tempting to send them all out, but the reality was that they would only get in each other's way. Their training had never prepared them for any kind of mass assault. Everything they had been taught was focused on an unseen approach and a single blow, either from the hand or a weapon. In his younger days, Suleiman had dispatched a wealthy merchant simply by drugging his wine, then holding his mouth and nose shut while he slept. There had been no mark on the body and it was still considered a near-perfect example of the craft. He sighed in memory of happier times. The Mongols had no respect for tradition and, it seemed, no fear of the retribution they might face. His Assassins would have to be sent against the khan himself, perhaps while Alamut endured the siege to come. Suleiman did not doubt the khan's anger if his own brother fell, no matter how they made it look. The old man calculated journey times in his head, trying to work out the best arrangement to take them both. He still hoped they could be bribed or fooled, but his role as shepherd to his flock meant he had to plan for all possibilities.

Lost in his thoughts, Suleiman did not see Hasan step out from the shadow of the little hut. Suleiman was looking out across the meadow, shading his eyes against the setting sun. The younger man suddenly darted forward and swung a flat stone against the side of his head. It struck with a crack and Suleiman cried out in surprise and pain. He staggered sideways, dropping almost into a crouch as his vision blurred. He thought a stone must have fallen from the cliffs above and he was dazedly feeling his face for blood when Hasan struck again, knocking him down.

Suleiman could taste the blood running into his throat from his broken mouth. He looked up in dazed astonishment, unable to understand what was happening. When he recognised Hasan standing there, his gaze dropped to the red-smeared stone the young man still held.

'Why, my son? Why would you do this? Have I not been a father to you?' he said, half-choking. He saw Hasan was in the grip of surging emotions, panting like a dog left in the sun. He looked appalled at what he had done, and as the world stopped spinning, Suleiman raised a hand to him.

'Help me to my feet, Hasan,' he said gently.

The young man came forward and for a moment Suleiman thought he would do as he was told. At the last instant, Hasan raised the stone again and brought it down in a great blow on Suleiman's forehead, breaking the dome of his skull. He knew nothing more and did not hear the fool run weeping back into the fortress.

Hulegu had to admit he was impressed by Alamut. The fortress was built of a different stone to the mountains all around them. He could hardly imagine the labour involved in transporting every block up to the original cleft in the rocks, widening that place with hammers and chisels, then building stone upon stone until it seemed to have grown from the landscape.

He raised his head to take it in, then craned further and further back. At the best elevation, his cannons would merely graze the surface, sending their deadly missiles skipping up the walls without force. He had nothing else that could even reach the stronghold from the valley floor and his eyes picked out a single track running up the face. There would be no assault on the gates. He doubted more than two men could stand before them without someone pitching to his death thousands of feet below.

It had taken many days to reach the fortress and Hulegu knew he would have been hard-pressed to find it without

Rukn-al-Din. His ten thousand warriors could presumably have covered every valley and dead end in the range, but it would have taken months. His three guides seemed as awed as the Mongols, and Hulegu suspected only terror had made them promise a way in.

There had been one slight disagreement with Rukn-al-Din since their first meeting. The younger man had pressed for just an honour guard to accompany Hulegu on the last stretch. Hulegu smiled again at the thought. To bargain, a man needed some advantage and Rukn had none. Hulegu had merely described the many ways a man could be tortured for the information he needed and Rukn had fallen silent. He no longer rode proudly, chattering to the men around him. He and his companions had realised they were little more than prisoners, for all the fine promises that had been made.

Yet Alamut itself dented Hulegu's confidence for the first time. With his southern army descending on Baghdad, he did not want to lay a siege that might take two years or longer to end. As he reached the foot of the path, he could see there were men wending their way down to him, presumably carrying messages from Rukn's father. Hulegu eyed the steep steps with irritation and, on impulse, sent one of his men riding up. He had some vague hope that the small Mongol ponies could keep their footing. They had known mountains in the homeland and they were nimble animals.

Hulegu watched with interest as the lone rider walked his mount up to the first bend, hundreds of feet above their heads. He heard his officers whisper bets to each other and then one of them cursed and Hulegu shaded his eyes to look up.

The horse and rider struck the ground just moments later, the crash echoing from the hills all around. Neither survived the fall and Hulegu cursed under his breath as Ilugei cheerfully collected silver coins from the other officers.

The men coming down had paused, peering over the edge and gesturing to each other before going on. When they finally made it to the flat ground, both were stained in sweat and dust. They made hurried bows to the Mongol officers, their eyes seeking out Rukn-al-Din. Hulegu dismounted and walked over to them as they bowed to him.

'Master, your father is dead,' he heard one of them say. Rukn gave a great cry of pain and sorrow and Hulegu chuckled.

'It seems I have the new master of Alamut to take me up the path, Rukn-al-Din. My men will lead the way. Stay close to me. I do not want you falling to your death in this time of grief.'

Rukn-al-Din gaped at him, dull-eyed in despair. His shoulders slumped at Hulegu's words and he walked almost in a daze, following the first of the men who would make their way up the path to the fortress high above.

CHAPTER SIXTEEN

The sun set in streaks of gold and red as Kublai halted his great host on the banks of the river. He had scouted the area and drawn them all to a halt in sight of the ford on his maps. Across the wide stretch of dark water, the Sung commander waited expectantly. The man knew Kublai would have to cross the river at some point, perhaps even that night. In the evening gloom, Kublai grinned at the sight of Sung columns manoeuvring subtly closer to the ford, ready for whatever assault he planned. The two vast armies stared at each other across a rushing barrier. Kublai could imagine the confusion in their command tents as the Mongol tumans failed to attack. He doubted they were getting much sleep.

Before the last light had gone, Kublai's gun teams finished their preparations, marking sites and placing shuttered lamps on poles. In the night, before the moon rose, the cannons were heaved forward to the marked positions, pushed in silence by dozens of straining volunteers. At the same time, the main force moved further back, away from the river. Kublai had seen no sign of similar work going on in the Sung camp, but he did not want to be surprised by some enterprising officer with the same idea. For once, his warriors would spend the night in the saddle or on the grass by their horses. The families were a mile further away from the river, well clear of danger. Kublai wondered what Chabi was doing at that moment. She had known tonight would be dangerous for him, but she'd shown no fear at all, as if there wasn't a man alive who could trouble her husband. He knew her well enough to sense the performance in it, but even so he found it oddly reassuring. The thought of telling his wife and son he had failed was a better motivation than anything Mongke could do to him.

The moon rose slowly and Kublai stood and watched it, rubbing his damp palms down his armour and wishing he wore a lighter robe. Even the nights were warm so far to the south and he was never comfortable. His cannons were covered by loose branches to confuse their shapes and he did not think the enemy would be able to see what he had done. On its own, it would be only a gesture at best, a brief taste of fear in the night before they pulled back and restored order. A young commander might have made the decision, intending to kill a few and make the enemy run about for a while. Kublai chuckled to himself. He hoped for more. Timing was going to be important and he strained his eyes in the darkness, looking for a sign. He had not spoken to Uriang-Khadai for some days, beyond the most basic courtesies. The man clearly resented the authority Kublai had exercised over him, suddenly a reality rather than an empty formality. Kublai sensed Uriang-Khadai was holding himself in check, waiting for some error to be made. The battle to come was important in many ways and the stakes worried him. Not only did he have to break the Sung army against him, but he also had to show his own generals that he was fit to lead. Kublai felt a headache begin behind his eyes and considered visiting a shaman for willow-bark powder or myrtle leaves. No, he dared not be out of position when the time came.

Bayar watched the moon rise and began a slow trot. By his best reckoning, he was less than ten miles north of the Sung army, on the other side of the river. In the end, he and Kublai had agreed to lose two more days to ferry enough men across on the sheepskin rafts. Three tumans had made the crossing, with their horses and weapons taking most of the time. The rafts worked and Bayar sensed the anticipation in the ranks. With just a little luck, the Sung would have no idea they had even left Kublai's army. Bayar stepped up the pace, judging the speed he needed to cover the ground and still keep the horses fresh. Ten miles was not far for the Mongolian ponies. They could cover it before the moon reached its zenith and at the end he could still order a gallop and be answered.

The ground was firm away from the river and there were few obstacles, though no horsemen liked riding at night, regardless of the conditions. There would be falls and casualties, yet Bayar had his orders and he was cheerful. No one loved a surprise attack more than his people. The very idea filled him with glee. It did not hurt that Uriang-Khadai was still on Kublai's side of the river. The orlok had been scornful of the great rafts and Bayar was pleased to be away from his baleful gaze for once. He sensed a camaraderie with Kublai that he had not expected. The khan's brother was out of his depth in many ways, facing one of the most powerful enemies in the nation's history. Bayar smiled as he rode. He did not intend to let him down.

*   *   *

In the distance, Kublai saw a bright spark sear a trail across the sky. From so far away, it was little more than a needle of light that vanished almost as soon as it appeared. He had feared he would miss the sign and tried to relax his cramped muscles, held tight for too long. Bayar was there, with a Chin firework he had lit and thrown into the air from the saddle. As Kublai turned to give his orders, another spark appeared, in case the first one had been missed. High-pitched voices began to roar confused orders on the other side of the river.

'Begin firing on my signal,' Kublai shouted. He dismounted to attend to his own device, a long tube of black powder resting in an iron cradle. He brought a shuttered lamp close and lit the taper from it, standing back as it fizzed and sputtered before rising into the air in a great whoosh of light.

The cannon teams had been waiting patiently for their moment and as they saw the signal the great iron weapons began to sound, cracking thunder across the river. The flashes lit up both banks for the briefest of moments, leaving ghosts on the vision of all those who stared into the blackness. They could not see where the balls landed, but distant screams made the gun teams laugh as they sponged down the barrels and reloaded, jamming in bags of black powder and fitting the hollow reeds to the touch-holes. The mouths of the cannon erupted in belches of flame, but the balls themselves were invisible as they soared across the water. Kublai noted the best rates of fire and wondered how it could be improved. There was just too long a gap between each shot, but he had the best part of a hundred heavy cannon lined up on the banks, all he could bring to bear on the Sung positions. The barrage would surely be devastating. He could imagine the flashes of light and cracks from the Sung perspective, followed by the whistle of stone balls ripping through the camp. Many of the shot balls disintegrated at the moment of firing, reducing their range, but sending razor shards along the firing path.

On any other night, the Sung soldiers would have pulled back quickly. Kublai wished he could listen for Bayar's tumans, but the noise was too great as the shots rippled on and on. He waited as long as he dared, then sent a second rocket up into the night sky. The thunder died as the teams saw it, though a last few cracks sounded as they got off one final shot. After the noise, the night was suddenly silent and the darkness was absolute. Kublai strained to hear. Far away, there was a new noise, growing steadily. He laughed aloud as he recognised the sound of Mongol drummer boys, beating their own thunder in the darkness across the river.

Bayar had never known a battle at night. He had seen the signal rocket and then watched in amazement as the river bank was lit in flashes of gold, a rolling wave of destruction. He had once seen a dry lightning storm, with the thick air lit at intervals by flashes. This was like that, but each crack of light and sound revealed chaos in the Sung camp. He had to trust that Kublai would stop the barrage before Bayar's warriors were among them. The spikes of light gave him the arrow range and he began to empty his quiver of thirty arrows, whipping them out and onto the string almost without thought. He could not aim with only the flashes to guide him, but he had a wide charging line of thousands of men and the arrows poured out of them. He lost count of the shafts he had shot and it was only when his grasping fingers closed on nothing that he cursed and hooked the bow to his saddle. Bayar drew his sword and the action was copied all along the line.

The Sung had heard them coming, but dead men lay every-where among their packed ranks. Kublai had been far more successful than he had known. The Sung soldiers had clustered on the river banks, pressing close to repel the night river-crossing they thought would come. Into that mass of waiting men, the cannonballs had torn red paths. Thousands had been killed. The forming lines dissolved in sheer panic as men ran from the terrible unseen death that was still cutting through their camp. They ran to get out of range, some of them dropping their shields and swords and pelting away.

Out of the darkness, the arrows of Bayar's tumans came slicing and tearing into them. The Sung soldiers were caught between jaws and they pushed and spun in a great crush as they tried to find a clear path out of the destruction. Bayar's first lines hit a rabble of soldiers, cutting into them at full speed. Horses and men crashed together and Bayar's own mount went down as it struck a knot of soldiers, smashing them apart. He fell hard and rolled over someone who yelled in his ear. The cannon-fire ceased at that moment and in the darkness Bayar found himself wrestling with a man he could not see. He had lost his sword, but his fists were armoured to the knuckles and he pounded the dark figure over and over until it was still.

The Sung army was in complete disarray. Bayar swore as someone else knocked into him, but the man picked himself up and ran on. They had no idea of the size of the force spearing into them from the dark night and the Sung officers had lost control. The tumans stayed together in their ranks, walking their horses onward together and killing anything in their way.

In the moonlight, Bayar saw a pony and rider loom in front of him. He shouted before the raised sword could come down.

'Give me your horse! And if you cut me, I'll have your ears.'

The warrior dismounted immediately, handing over the reins. Another rank was already upon them and once again Bayar had to shout to be recognised. He realised he could not leave the warrior to be cut down by his own men, so had him jump up behind. The pony snorted at the extra weight and Bayar calmed it with a rub of the ears before he trotted to the rank ahead. They spread across the Sung camp and Bayar saw that a few of the men had snatched lamps from sentry poles and used them to set fire to the tents and carts. The light of the flames began to restore his sense of the battlefield and what he saw amazed and delighted him. The Sung army was running and he rode over a carpet of the dead, thousands upon thousands of them. The ranks ahead were still killing and it was more to blood those behind than to save their sword arms that he bellowed orders to rotate the front ranks.

His orders were answered instantly by signal horns. The first five ranks halted and the next moved up, Bayar among them. He passed panting men, spattered in the blood of their enemies. They sat bowed over their saddle horns, resting their aching sword arms on the high pommel. Many of them called out to the ranks passing them, asking where they had been while the real work was being done. Their spirits were high and Bayar chuckled as he went through. The flame-light was increasing as more and more tents were set on fire. Ahead, he could see a mass of men, pressing desperately to get away from the dark line of horses. Bayar saw a pony without a rider and stopped briefly to let his unknown companion take the mount. There was a body nearby and he was delighted to find a quiver with half a dozen shafts. Jumping down briefly, he flipped the body over and took a long knife from the ground, though he could not find a sword. His rank had gone on without him and he trotted to keep up as the killing began again.

Kublai waited in an agony of suspense. He could hear the sounds of battle out there in the dark, the crash and scream of men and animals being killed. He had no way of knowing how Bayar was doing and wished for light as he had never wished for anything before. He wondered if the rockets could be fired together to light up a battlefield, but he had only a small store. The idea was tempting, however. It was one more thing to remember for the future.

'That's long enough,' he said, almost to himself. He took another rocket from a roll of oilcloth and placed it in its cradle, pointing to the sky. As it lifted, it made a high whistling sound, similar to the shaped arrowhead the Mongols sometimes used. The tumans on his side of the river were ready for the signal and they began to ride to the ford. If the Sung still held their side, the tumans would be crossing without proper cover. His archers would send a hail across the banks, but in the darkness it would be impossible to aim. Kublai drew his sword, preferring to have its comforting weight in his hand.

His horse hit the waters of the fording place in the midst of thousands of others, all trying to make the crossing at a canter. Kublai felt his horse lurch into a hole and quickly sheathed his sword again rather than lose it. He needed both hands and he felt his cheeks grow hot with embarrassment as he flailed about.

His horse was snorting and whinnying as it clambered up the far bank and plunged on with the rest. Kublai could not have controlled the animal if he'd wanted to and he found himself racing headlong towards the sounds of battle. All the plans he had made dissolved in confusion as he lost track of the position of the tumans, or even which way he was going. In the glow of burning tents, he could see a great mass of men. He only hoped he was not about to charge Bayar's tumans. There was no point listening for Mongol voices or even the drummer boys. The noise of horses around him drowned all that out and he had somehow managed to get water in his ear during the crossing, so that he was deaf on one side.

185

Two hundred yards ahead of him, the first ranks off the river ford met the Sung soldiers streaming away from Bayar's tumans. The Mongol warriors had not strung their bows for the crossing and they barely had time to draw swords before the forces crashed together. Kublai could not halt or turn aside. Held in the press of moving horses, he was moved inexorably forward. He tapped the side of his head to clear his ear and smelled blood strongly on the air. He was beginning to realise that, for all the benefits of a surprise night attack, the danger was complete chaos on both sides. He heard yelling voices ahead and the unmistakable sound of Mongol warriors cheering in triumph. Kublai tried to gauge how much of the night was left by the position of the moon and wondered vaguely where Uriang-Khadai had gone. He hadn't seen his orlok since the first round of cannon-fire. The cheering intensified and he headed towards it, helped by the light of burning tents, the fire beginning to spread right across the river plain.

Kublai drew to a halt in the light of three burning carts piled against each other. With a rush of relief, he saw Bayar there, shouting commands and bringing some sense of order. When he saw Kublai, Bayar grinned and rode over to him.

'Half of them have surrendered, at least,' Bayar said. He stank of blood and fire, but he was jubilant. Kublai forced the cold face, remembering suddenly that he was meant to be a figure of distant and terrifying authority. Bayar didn't seem to notice.

'We've broken the back of their best regiments,' Bayar went on, 'and those that haven't run have thrown down their weapons. Until the sun comes up, I won't know the details, but I don't think they'll counter-attack tonight. You have the victory, my lord.'

Kublai sheathed his sword, still unblooded. He endured a sense of unreality as he stared around at the piles of dead men. It had worked, but his mind filled with a dozen things they could have done differently.

'I want you to look into using signal rockets to light a battlefield,' he said.

Bayar looked at him strangely. He saw a young man sitting with his hands relaxed on the pommel, his leggings soaked. As Kublai stared around him with interest, Bayar nodded.

'Very well, my lord. I'll start testing them tomorrow. I should finish herding the prisoners. We're having to use their own clothes torn into strips to bind them.'

'Yes, yes of course,' Kublai replied. He looked to the east, but there was no sign of dawn.

A thought struck him and he smiled in anticipation as he spoke again.

'Send Orlok Uriang-Khadai to me. I would like to hear his assessment of the victory.'

Bayar smothered his own smile as he dipped his head.

'Your will, my lord. I'll send him to you as soon as I find him.'

The sun rose on a scene of complete devastation. In his imagination, Kublai could only compare it to the description he had read of the battle of Badger's Mouth in northern Chin lands. Flies had gathered in their millions and there were too many dead soldiers to consider burying or even burning them. They could only be left behind for the sun to rot and dry.

For a time, dawn had brought some excitement as the remaining Sung regiments were hunted down and the Mongol families crossed the river with slow care. Tumans rode out with fresh quivers and overhauled the scattered enemy before the sun was fully up. Thousands more were forcibly returned to the river, stripped of weapons and armour, to be bound with the rest. Mongol women and children walked among them, come to see the fearsome men their husbands, brothers and fathers had defeated.

Yao Shu had remained behind in the main camp during the battle. He crossed the ford with the families when there was enough light to ride without falling in. By noon, he was at Kublai's ger, set up at his order on the battle side. Chabi was already there, her eyes full of concern for her exhausted husband. She fussed around him, laying out fresh clothes and making enough food to feed whoever might come to speak with Kublai. Yao Shu nodded to her as he accepted a bowl of some stew and ate quickly rather than give offence. She watched until he had finished it all. Yao Shu sat on a low bed with scrolls of vellum waiting to be read to the khan and he could do nothing, say nothing, until he was given permission. Even after a battle, the rules of ger courtesy held firm.

Zhenjin entered at a run, skidding slightly as he came to a halt, his eyes large. Yao Shu smiled at the boy.

'There are so many prisoners!' Zhenjin said. 'How did you beat them, father? I saw flashes and thunder all night. I didn't sleep at all.'

'He did sleep,' Chabi murmured. 'He snores like his father.'

Zhenjin turned a look of scorn on his mother.

'I was too excited to sleep. I saw a man with his head cut off! How did we beat so many?'

'Planning,' Kublai replied. 'Better plans and better men, Zhenjin. Ask Uriang-Khadai how we did it. He will tell you.'

The little boy looked up at his father in awe, but he shook his head.

'He doesn't like me to speak to him. He says I ask too many questions.'

'You do,' Chabi said. 'Take a bowl and find somewhere else to eat it. Your father needs to speak to many of his men.'

'I want to listen,' the boy almost wailed. 'I'll be quiet, I promise.'

Chabi smacked his head and pressed a bowl into his hand. Zhenjin left with a furious glare that she ignored completely.

Kublai sat down and accepted his own bowl, finishing it quickly. When he was ready, Yao Shu read him the tallies of dead and maimed as well as the loot they had taken, his voice droning on in the thick air. After a time, Kublai waved him to a stop. His eyes felt gritty and swollen and his voice was hoarse.

'Enough. I'm not taking it in. Come back in the evening, when I've rested.'

Yao Shu rose and bowed. He had trained Kublai from boyhood and he was uncertain how to show his pride in him. They had destroyed an army twice as large, on foreign ground. The news was already heading back to Karakorum with the fastest scouts. They would race to the yam lines in Chin territory and then the letters would move even faster, reaching Karakorum in just a few weeks. Yao Shu paused at the door to the ger.

'Orlok Uriang-Khadai is waiting for your word on the prisoners, my lord. We have . . .' He consulted a scroll thick with tally marks, holding it at the full extension of his arm so he could read it. 'Forty-two thousand, seven hundred, many of them wounded.'

Kublai winced at the figure and rubbed his eyes.

'Feed them with their own supplies. I'll decide what to do with them . . .' He broke off as Zhenjin re-entered the ger. The boy's face was incredibly pale and he was panting.

'What is it?' Chabi asked. Zhenjin only looked at her.

'Well, boy? What is it?' Kublai said. He reached out and rubbed his son's hair. The action seemed to break his trance and Zhenjin spoke as if gulping words between ragged breaths.

'They're killing the prisoners,' Zhenjin said. He looked ill and his eyes strayed to the bucket by the door as if he might need it.

Kublai cursed. He had given no such order. Without another word, he pushed past his son and went outside. General Bayar was there, striding towards the ger. He looked relieved to see Kublai. At a gesture, servants brought horses and both men mounted quickly, trotting away through the camp.

Yao Shu eyed his own horse with misgiving. He had never been much of a rider, but Kublai and Bayar were already gone. Zhenjin came out of the ger and pelted off after them without looking back. Sighing, the old man called a young warrior across to help him mount.

Kublai began to pass ranks of bound prisoners long before he saw Uriang-Khadai. In lines that vanished into the distance, forty thousand men knelt on the ground with their heads down, waiting. Some of them talked in low tones or looked up as he passed, but for the most part, they were dull-eyed, their misery and defeat clear in their faces.

Kublai cursed under his breath as he saw the orlok gesturing to a group of young warriors. There were dozens of headless bodies in neat rows already and as Kublai rode closer, he saw the swords swing and more men fall to the ground. He could hear a low moan of terror from those closest to them and the sound filled him with rage. He checked himself as Uriang-Khadai looked up. He could not humiliate his orlok in front of the men, no matter how much he wanted to.

'I have not given an order for the prisoners to be slaughtered,' he said. Kublai remained in the saddle deliberately, so that he could look down at the man.

'I did not want to trouble you with every detail, my lord,' Uriang-Khadai said. He looked faintly puzzled, as if he could not understand why the khan's brother should interrupt him in his duties. Kublai felt his anger rise and strangled it again.

'Forty thousand men is not a detail, orlok. They have surrendered to me and their lives are now mine to protect.'

Uriang-Khadai clasped his hands behind his back, his mouth tightening.

'My lord, there are too many. You surely can't allow them all to walk away? We will be facing them again . . .'

'I have told you my decision, orlok. Have them fed and have their wounded looked at. Then release them. After that, I will see you in my ger. That is all.'

Uriang-Khadai stood in silence while he digested the news. After a moment too long, he bowed his head, just ahead of Kublai relieving him of his authority in a rage.

'Your will, my lord,' the orlok said. 'I apologise if I have given offence.'

Kublai ignored him. Yao Shu and Bayar had both arrived and he glanced at Yao Shu before speaking again. In fluent Mandarin, then broken Cantonese, Kublai addressed the prisoners within earshot.

'You will be allowed to live and return home. Pass the word. Take news of this battle with you and tell whoever will listen that you were treated with mercy. You are subjects of the great khan and under my protection.'

Yao Shu nodded to him in satisfaction as Kublai turned his horse and dug in his heels. He could feel Uriang-Khadai's glare on his back for a long way, but it did not matter. He had plans for the Sung cities, plans that could not begin with a slaughter of unarmed men.

On his way back to the ger, he saw his son running along, head down and puffing. Kublai reined in and reached down. Zhenjin took the arm and his father swept him up into the saddle behind him. They rode on together and after a time Kublai felt his son shift uncomfortably. Zhenjin had seen horrors that day. Kublai reached behind him and patted the boy's leg.

'Did you stop them killing the men?' Zhenjin asked in a small voice.

'Yes. Yes, I stopped them,' Kublai replied. He felt the weight increase against his back as his son relaxed.

Alamut was a place of quiet and calm. In his life, Hulegu had found little to love in cities, but there was something about the spartan fortress that appealed to him. He was surprised to feel a pang of regret at the idea that he must destroy it. He stood on the highest wall in the sunlight and looked down across a landscape of mountains, stretching many miles into the distance. He even wondered briefly if he could leave a hundred families to keep the place for the khan, but it was just a fantasy. He had seen the tiny meadow behind the main buildings. The animals there could not support more than a few. The fortress was so completely isolated that he could not imagine trade ever taking place, or anything in the way of contact with the world. Alamut guarded no pass, held no strategic worth. It had been the perfect spot for the Assassins, but it was not suited to anything else.

As he walked on, Hulegu stepped over the body of a young woman, careful not to tread in the pool of sticky blood around her head. He looked down and frowned. She had been beautiful and he assumed the archer who had put a shaft into her throat had done so from a distance. It was a waste.

It had taken a day to get two hundred men into the fortress, each warrior trudging up the narrow path in single file, then holding the door for the next. Rukn-al-Din could do nothing and he had not had the courage to throw himself off the cliff. Not that they would have let him, but it would have been a fine thing to attempt. They had spread into Alamut's rooms and corridors with calm deliberation and the Ismaili Assassins had only stood and watched, still looking to Rukn-al-Din for authority. When the killing began, they scattered, trying to protect their families. Hulegu smiled at the memory. His warriors had scoured the castle, room by room, floor by floor, stabbing and shooting anything that moved. For a time, a group of the Assassins had blockaded themselves into a room, but the door fell to axes and they were overwhelmed. Others had fought. Hulegu looked over the battlements into a courtyard far below, seeing the bodies of his men laid out. Thirty-six of them had been killed, a higher toll than he might have expected. Most of those had died from poisoned blades, when they would otherwise have survived with a gash. By dawn, only Rukn-al-Din was still alive, sitting in the courtyard in dull despair.

It was time to finish it, Hulegu realised. He would have to leave men behind, but to destroy rather than to live. It would take months for them to break down the fortress, and he could not wait while Baghdad resisted his army. It had been a risk, even a luxury, to seek out the Assassins, but he could not regret it. For a short time, he had walked in the steps of Genghis.

It took an age to descend the stone stairs running inside the walls. Hulegu finally came out into the bright sunshine, blinking after the gloom. Rukn-al-Din was sitting with his knees drawn up into his arms, his eyes red. As Hulegu came out he looked up and swallowed nervously, certain he was about to die.

'Stand up,' Hulegu said to him.

One of his warriors kicked the man hard and Rukn clambered to his feet, swaying slightly from exhaustion. He had lost everything.

'I will be leaving men here to destroy the fortress, stone by stone,' Hulegu said. 'I cannot stay longer. In fact, I should not have taken so much time to come here. When I return this way, I hope there will be a chance to visit the other fortresses your father controlled.' He smiled, enjoying the utter defeat of an enemy in his power. 'Who knows? Only rats live on in Alamut and we will burn them out when it falls.'

'You have what you wanted,' Rukn said hoarsely. 'You could let me go.'

'We do not shed the blood of royalty,' Hulegu replied. 'It was a rule of my grandfather and I honour it.' He saw a gleam of hope come into Rukn's eyes. The death of his father had broken the young man. He had said nothing while the Mongols tore through Alamut, hoping that they would spare him. He raised his head.

'I am to live?' he said.

Hulegu laughed. 'Did I not say I honour the great khan? No blade will cut you, no arrow will enter your flesh.' Hulegu turned to the warriors around Rukn-al-Din. 'Hold him down.'

The young man cried out as they laid hands on him, but there were too many and he could not resist. They took his arms and legs and stretched them out, so that he lay helpless. He looked up and saw only bright malice in the Mongol general.

Hulegu kicked Rukn in the ribs as hard as he could. He heard them crack over Rukn's scream. Twice more he kicked out, feeling the ribs give way.

'You should have cut your own throat,' Hulegu told him as Rukn-al-Din panted in agony. 'How can I respect a man who wouldn't even do that for his people?' He nodded to a warrior and the man began to stamp on the broken chest. Hulegu watched for a time, then walked away, satisfied.

CHAPTER SEVENTEEN

Yao Shu was filled with strange emotions as he rocked back and forth on the cart taking him into Sung lands. As a young monk, he had known Genghis even before he had become the first khan of the Mongol nation. Yao Shu had put aside the natural course of his life to observe that extraordinary man as he united the tribes and attacked the Chin empire. Even in those days of youth, Yao Shu had hoped to influence the khan, to bring a sense of civilisation to his court.

Somehow, as the years passed, Yao Shu had lost sight of his first ambitions. It was strange how a man could forget himself in the thousand tasks of a day. There was always some new problem to solve, some work that had to be done. Yao Shu had seen his life slip through his fingers, so that he looked up from the details less and less often with each passing year. There had been a time when he could have written his ambitions and desires on a single parchment. He was still not sure whether he had lost the ability to think so clearly, or whether he had just been naive.

Still, he had kept hope alive. When Genghis had died, Yao Shu had worked with Ogedai Khan, then Torogene as regent. He had remained in Karakorum as chancellor during Guyuk's short and bitter reign. Ogedai had shown promise, he thought, looking back. The third son of Genghis had been a man of great vision, until his heart failed and allowed a weak son to rule the nation. Yao Shu sighed to himself as he stared out at the massed ranks riding all around him. He had grown old in the service of khans.

Mongke's rise had been a terrible blow. If ever there had been a man in the mould of Genghis, Mongke was the one. Genghis had been ruthless, but then he had been surrounded by enemies bent on his destruction. He had been formed in conflict and spent his entire life at war. Yao Shu smiled ruefully at the memories of the old bastard. The philosophies of Genghis Khan would have shocked his Buddhist teachers, almost to the point of unconsciousness. They had never met anyone like that cheerful destroyer of cities. In Genghis, all things had come together. He had kept his fledgling nation safe by slaughtering their enemies, but enjoyed himself enormously while doing so. Yao Shu remembered how Genghis had addressed a council of Chin lords on the subject of ransom. He had told them solemnly that a captured Mohammedan could buy his freedom for forty gold coins, but the price of a Chin lord was a single donkey.

Yao Shu chuckled to himself. Mongke had not inherited that sense of joy. It had drawn men to Genghis as they sensed a vibrant life in him that Yao Shu had never seen anywhere else. Certainly not in the grandson. In Mongke's earnest efforts to be a worthy khan, he showed no true understanding. Thinking back through the generations, Yao Shu worried that he had wasted his life, drawn like a moth to a lamp, throwing his years of strength away for nothing.

The lamp had been extinguished when Genghis died. Yao Shu had thought many times since then that he should have gone home at that moment, the dream over. He would have counselled a stranger to do just that. Instead, he had waited to see what would happen, taking tasks upon himself until Ogedai trusted him with everything.

Yao Shu stared out at the massed ranks of horsemen in all directions. He had made the decision at last to leave the court. No, Mongke had made it for him when he whipped Chin scholars out of Karakorum and showed it was no longer a place where civilised men would be welcome. It had been almost a relief to begin his preparations for the long trip home. Yao Shu owned very little and had given most of his wealth away to the poor in Karakorum. He did not need much and he knew there were monasteries which would take him in as a long lost son. The thought of regaling Buddhist monks with stories of his adventures was appealing. He could even read from the Secret History to them and give them a glimpse of a very different world. He doubted they would believe half of what he had seen.

Back in Karakorum, Yao Shu had been looking sadly at his collection of books when a messenger had arrived with news of Kublai's destination. The old man had smiled then at the vagaries of fate. It had solved his problem of how to travel safely for thousands of miles east. He would go with Kublai to Chin lands and then one night he would get up from a fire and walk away from all his memories. He was not bound by oath to any living man, and there was a kind of balance in having the Mongols take him home, as they had once brought him out of the lands of his birth.

It had not happened. Over the months of conversation and travel, he had become fascinated again by Kublai, his interest sparked by the other man as he toured new estates in Chin lands and talked. Oh, how the man talked! Yao Shu had always known Kublai was intelligent, but his ideas and limitless curiosity had fired Yao Shu's imagination. Thousands of new farms had been surveyed and marked out in just a few months. Kublai would be a landlord who took only a reasonable share and let his people prosper. Yao Shu hardly dared to believe he had finally found a descendant of Genghis who might love Chin culture as much as he did. On a spring evening, Yao Shu had reached a point where he knew an old monastery was barely thirty miles off the road and yet he had sat on his cart all night and not taken a single step towards it. One more year would not make too much of a difference to his life, he had told himself.

Now he was on the road to Ta-li, a Sung city, and once more, there was hope in his heart. He had seen Kublai spare forty thousand prisoners, and Yao Shu doubted the younger man even understood what an extraordinary event it had been. The orlok, Uriang-Khadai, still sulked in his ger, unable to understand why he had been shamed in front of his men. Yao Shu shook his head in wonder at the thought, desperate not be disappointed once again. Genghis had destroyed cities to send a message to anyone who might resist him. Yao Shu had despaired of finding anyone in his line who did not model themselves on the great khan.

Now he could not leave. He had to see what Kublai would do at the city. For the first time in decades, Yao Shu felt a sense of purpose and excitement. Kublai was a different animal from his brothers Hulegu and Mongke. There was still hope for him.

The region of Yunnan was one of the least populous in Sung lands. Just one city connected the distant territory with the rest of that far-flung nation, supported by a few thousand farms and barely a dozen villages and small towns. There had been no growth there in living memory, perhaps for centuries, and the benefits of peace were obvious. Kublai's army passed through millions of acres of rich ground, given over to rice paddies or dry crops and a rare breed of long-horned cow that was said to produce the best beef for a thousand miles.

Ta-li city was girded around by high walls and gates, though a suburb of merchant houses gripped the inner city like moss on a stone. That part of Sung territory was a world away from the lands Genghis had conquered. No one there had ever seen a Mongol warrior, or any armed force beyond the soldiers of their own emperor.

Kublai stared across a scene of stillness and tranquillity, his vast army out of place. He could see the smoke of a thousand chimneys over the city, but the farmers had all left their crops and gone to its protection. The fields and outer suburbs lay abandoned, stretching as far as he could see.

The ground was dry and they were close enough to the city for those within to be watching in terrified silence. Kublai spoke an order to Bayar at his side and stayed where he was while it was relayed down the line of authority. The Mongol host dismounted and began to make camp.

Kublai watched his ger being assembled, beginning with the sections of wooden lattice bound together. Everything was done for him by a group of warriors, routine making them quick. They raised a central column and slotted slender roof poles into it, taking lengths of moist sinew from pouches to tie them all off. Finally, thick mats of felt were layered and bound, the small door fitted and a cooking stove carried inside. In just a short time, it was one of thousands appearing on the land, waterproof and warm. Chabi and Zhenjin came trotting up on the same pony, the boy's arms clasped around his mother. Kublai held his arms wide and Chabi guided the mount close enough for Zhenjin to leap at his father.

Kublai grunted and staggered backwards as he took the boy's weight.

'You are getting too big for this,' he said, holding him for a beat before lowering his son to the ground. Zhenjin already showed signs of his father's height and his eyes were the same light gold that marked him as the bloodline of Genghis. Zhenjin stretched up to stand as tall as he could, making his father laugh.

'I have your bow, Zhenjin. Bring it out of the ger and I'll help you practise.'

Zhenji gave a whoop and disappeared through the door. Kublai let the smile remain. He felt the responsibility of being a father acutely. In time, Zhenjin would be his own man. Yet at that moment he was still a child, long-legged and gangly, with two teeth growing through in the front. Kublai was glad he had brought his family on the campaign. Uriang-Khadai's wife and children were safe in Karakorum, but Kublai had not wanted to leave Zhenjin to Mongke's care for so many years. He would have come home to a stranger.

Kublai nodded to the warriors as they bowed and hurried off to complete their own dwellings before dark. As Chabi dismounted and kissed him on the neck, his personal servants went inside with the first armfuls of cooking implements and a large metal pot for tea. Zhenjin could be heard asking them where his quiver was. Kublai ignored the voices, choosing to spend the last moments of daylight staring at the city he must take. His first.

Chabi slipped her arm around his waist. 'I am pregnant,' she said.

Kublai turned and held her at arm's length. His heart leapt and he embraced her. Zhenjin's older brother had died in infancy and another had been stillborn. It broke his heart to see once more the mingled hope and fear in her eyes.

'This one will be strong,' he said. 'It will be born on campaign! Another boy? I'll get the shaman to cast the bones. If it is a boy, I have been thinking of names.'

'Not yet,' Chabi said, her eyes rimmed with tears. 'Let it be born first and then we will name it. I do not want to bury another child.'

200

'You won't, woman. That was in Karakorum, where the father was a mere scholar. Now the father is a fearsome general, commanding fire and iron. I will always remember you told me before my first city. I could name him Ta-li, though it sounds like a girl's . . .'

Chabi put a hand over his mouth.

'Hush, husband. No names. Just pray that it lives and I will talk names with you as long as you want.'

He embraced her again and they stood together with the camp all around them. Chabi sensed Kublai's thoughts settle on the city he must take for the khan.

'You will do well,' she murmured, resting her head on his shoulder.

Kublai nodded, but did not reply. He wondered if Genghis had ever felt the same sense of trepidation. Ta-li's walls looked solid, impregnable.

They were entering the ger when Yao Shu approached. The old man raised a hand in greeting and Kublai copied the gesture. He had known Yao Shu for almost all his life and the monk was always a welcome presence.

'Will you want me to read to you tonight, my lord?' he asked.

'Not tonight . . . unless of course you have found something worth hearing.' Kublai could not resist checking. Yao Shu had a talent for unearthing interesting texts, covering all subjects from animal husbandry to soap-making.

The old man shrugged.

'I have some minor writings on the running of servants in a noble house. They can wait for tomorrow, if you are tired. I . . . had hoped to talk to you about other matters, my lord.'

Kublai had ridden all day. Though Chabi's news had lit his blood, the excitement was already fading. He was dropping with weariness, but Yao Shu was not one to bother him with unnecessary details.

'Come in and eat with us then. I grant you guest rights, old friend.'

They ducked low to pass through the doorway and Kublai took a seat on a bed placed by the curving wall, his armour creaking. He could smell mutton and spices being seared on a wide pan and his mouth watered at the prospect. He kept silent until Chabi had handed over shallow bowls of salt tea. Zhenjin had found his bow and quiver and was waiting with them laid across his knee, fidgeting with impatience. Kublai ignored the stare as he sipped, feeling the hot liquid refresh him.

Yao Shu accepted his own bowl. He was uncomfortable speaking before Kublai's wife and son. Yet he had to know. At Yao Shu's age, Kublai was his last student. There would be no others.

'Why did you spare those men?' he asked at last.

Kublai lowered his cup, looking strangely at him. Chabi looked up from tending the food and Zhenjin stopped fidgeting, the bow forgotten.

'An odd question from a Buddhist. You think I should have killed them? Uriang-Khadai certainly did.'

'Genghis would have argued their deaths would act as a warning to anyone else who might stand against you. He was a man who understood the power of fear.'

Kublai chuckled, but it was a mirthless sound.

'You forget that Mongke and I travelled with him when we were barely old enough to stay on a horse. I saw the white tent raised before cities.' He grimaced, glancing at Zhenjin. 'I saw the red and the black tents and what followed after.'

'But you spared an army, when they might take arms again.'

Kublai shrugged, but the old man's gaze did not waver. Under the silent pressure, he spoke again.

'I am not my grandfather, old man. I do not want to have to fight for each step across this land. The Chin had little loyalty for their leaders. I hope to find the same thing here.' He paused, unwilling to reveal too much of his hopes. When Yao Shu did not speak, he went on, his voice low.

'When they face my tumans, they will know surrender is not the end for them. That will help me to win. If they throw down their weapons, I will set them free. In time, they will come to know my word can be trusted.'

'And the cities?' Yao Shu said suddenly. 'The people there are hostages to their leaders. They cannot surrender to you, even if they wanted to.'

'Then they will be destroyed,' Kublai replied calmly. 'I can only do so much.'

'You would kill thousands for the idiocy of just a few men,' Yao Shu said. There was sadness in his voice and Kublai stared at him.

'What choice do I have? They close their gates against me and my brother watches.'

Yao Shu leaned forward, his eyes gleaming.

'Then show Mongke there is another way. Send envoys into Ta-li. Promise to spare the people. Your concern is with the Sung armies, not merchants and farmers.'

Kublai chuckled. 'Merchants and farmers will never trust a grandson of Genghis. I carry his shadow over me, Yao Shu. Would you open your gates to a Mongol army? I don't think I would.'

'Perhaps they will not. But the *next* ones will. Just as your freed soldiers will carry the news of your mercy across Sung lands.' Yao Shu paused to let Kublai think it through before going on. 'In their own histories, there was a Sung general named Cao Bin, who took the city of Nanjing without the loss of a single life. The next city he came to opened their gates to him, safe in the knowledge that there would be no slaughter. You have a powerful army, Kublai, but the best force is one you do not have to use.'

Kublai sipped his tea, thinking. The idea appealed to some part of him. Part of him yearned to impress Mongke. Would he be comfortable with the sort of slaughter Mongke expected? He shuddered slightly. He would not. He realised the idea of it had been lying across his shoulders, weighing him down like the armour he was forced to wear. Just the chance of another way was like a light in a dark room. He drained his cup and set it aside.

'What happened to this Cao Bin in the end?'

Yao Shu shrugged. 'I believe he was betrayed, poisoned by his own men, but that does not lessen what he did. You are not your grandfather, Kublai. Genghis cared nothing for the Chin culture, while you can see its value.'

Kublai thought of the torture devices he had found in abandoned military posts, of the bloodstained streets and the rotting bodies of criminals. He thought of the mass suicide on the walls of Yenking, as sixty thousand girls threw themselves to their deaths rather than see the city fall to Genghis. Yet the world was a harsh place, wherever you went. The Chin were no worse than the portly Christian monks who kept their hearty appetites while heretics were disembowelled in front of them. With Yao Shu's eyes on him, he thought of the printed works he had seen, the vast collections of letters carved in boxwood and set by mind-numbing labour just to spread the ideas of Chin cities. He thought of their food, their fireworks, paper money, the compass he kept on him that somehow always pointed in the same direction. They were an ingenious people and he loved them dearly.

'He took a city without a single death?' he asked softly.

Yao Shu smiled and nodded.

'I can do that, old man. I can try that, at least. I will send envoys to Ta-li and we will see.'

The following morning, Kublai had his army surround the

walled city. They approached Ta-li from four directions in massive columns, joining up just outside the range of cannon. Those within the walls would see there was no escape for them, and if they did not know already, they would realise the emperor's army would not, or could not, come to their aid. Kublai intended them to see his power before he sent men in to negotiate. Yao Shu wanted to join the small group that would enter the city, but Kublai forbade it.

'Next time, old man, I promise you. The people of Ta-li may not have heard of Cao Bin.'

The room of administration in Ta-li was a bare place, with no comforts. The walls were white-painted plaster and the floor was of rare zitan hardwood, its surface carved right across the width of the room, so that visitors would walk on a tracery of delicate shapes and patterns as they approached the prefect of the city.

Meng Guang stared up at a small window in the rafters as he waited. He could see a drift of rain high above, almost a mist from grey skies that reflected the mood of the city so perfectly. He wore the regalia of his office, thick cloth heavy with gold stitching over a silk tunic. He took comfort from the weight of it, knowing that the ornate hat and cloak were older than he was and had been worn by better men, or at least luckier men. Once more he glanced around the open room, letting its peace soak into him. The silence was another cloak in a sense, the exact opposite of the Mongols with their childish anger and constant noise. He heard them coming from a long way off, tramping through the corridors of the government buildings with no thought for the dignity or age of their surroundings. Meng Guang gritted his teeth in silence. His awareness was so heightened that he sensed his guards straining to see the intruders, bristling like fierce hounds. He could show none of the same feelings, he counselled himself. The emperor's army had betrayed them, leaving his city at the mercy of rude and aggressive foreigners. He had readied himself for death, but then the Mongol general had sent a dozen men on foot to the city walls.

Instead of cannon shot, Meng Guang had received a polite request for an audience. He did not yet know if it was mockery, some Mongol delight in his humiliation. Ta-li could not resist the army that surrounded it in black columns. The prefect was not a man given to fooling himself with false hopes. If the Mongols waited a year, he knew there were armies that could defend Yunnan province, but the distances were great and the smooth flow of days had come to a sudden, jarring stop around his city. It was hard even to express the outrage he felt. He had been prefect for thirty-seven years and in that time his city had worked and slept in peace. Before the Mongols, Meng Guang had been content. His name would not be remembered in history, and the subtlety of that achievement was his favourite boast to his daughters. Now, he suspected he would have a place in the archives, unless future rulers set their scribes to removing his name from the official record.

As the Mongol envoys entered the room, Meng Guang repressed a wince at the thought of their boots damaging the delicate zitan wood. It gleamed in the morning light, dark red and lustrous from centuries of beeswax and labour. To his astonishment, the Mongols brought a stench with them that overcame the scent of polish. His eyes widened as the strength of it assailed his nostrils and it was all he could do to show no sign that he had noticed. The miasma of rotting meat and damp wool was like a physical force in the room. He wondered if they were even aware of it, if they knew the distress their very presence was causing him.

Of the dozen men, ten had the reddish skin and wide bulk he associated with the Mongols, while two of them had more civilised faces, slightly coarsened by mixed blood. He assumed they were from the northern Chin, the weaklings who had lost their lands to Genghis. Both men bowed their heads briefly, watched in blank interest by their Mongol companions. Meng Guang closed his eyes for a moment, steeling himself to endure the insults he would suffer. He did not mind losing his life. A man could choose to throw that away like a tin cup and the gesture would find favour in heaven. His dignity was another matter.

'Lord prefect,' one of the Chin began, 'the name of this humble messenger is Lee Ung. I bring you the words of Kublai Borjigin, grandson to Genghis Khan, brother to Mongke Khan. My master has sent us to discuss the surrender of Ta-li to his army. Before witnesses, he has made oath that not one man, woman or child will be harmed if Ta-li accepts him as its lord and master. I am told to say that the khan claims this city and these lands as his own. He has no interest in seeing the rivers run red. He seeks peace and offers you the chance to save the lives of those who look to you for leadership.'

The blood drained slowly from Meng Guang's face as Lee Ung spoke his poisonous insolence. The prefect's guards mirrored his reaction, gripping their sword hilts and straining forward without moving a step. The small Mongol group was not armed and he longed to set his men among them, cutting out their arrogance in swift blows. He saw how the Mongols looked around them, muttering to each other in their barbarous language. Meng Guang felt soiled by their presence and he had to force himself to stillness while he thought. The little Chin traitor was watching him for a response and Meng Guang thought he saw amusement in his eyes. It was too much.

'What is a city?' Meng Guang said suddenly with a shrug.

'We are not foolish Chin *peasants*, without honour or a place on the wheel of fate. We live at the emperor's pleasure. We die at his command. Everything you see is his. I cannot surrender what is not mine.'

Lee Ung stood very still and the others listened while his companion translated the words. They shook their heads and more than one growled something unintelligible. Meng Guang stood slowly and at his glance his guards drew their long swords. The Mongols watched the display with supreme indifference.

'I will take your words to my master, lord prefect,' Lee Ung said. 'He will be . . . disappointed that you refuse his mercy.'

Meng Guang felt rage suffuse him, bringing the flush of blood back to his pale cheeks. The Chin traitor spoke of impossibilities, concepts that had no place in the quiet order of his province. For a moment, Meng Guang could not even express his disdain. It did not matter if there were a *million* men waiting outside the city. They did not exist, or have any bearing on the fate he chose. If the emperor rescued Ta-li, Meng Guang knew he would be grateful. Yet if the emperor chose to let the city be destroyed, that was its fate. Meng Guang would not raise a hand to save himself. He thought of his wives and daughters and knew they too would prefer death to the dishonour this fool thought he might contemplate. It was no choice at all.

'Take them and bind them,' he said at last.

The two Chin translators did not have time to repeat his words and Lee Ung only stared glassily, his mouth opening like a carp. Meng Guang's guards were moving before he had stopped speaking.

As they came under attack, the Mongols went from bored stillness to mayhem in a heartbeat, punching and kicking in wild flurries of blows, using their boots, elbows, anything. It was more evidence of their uncouth ways and Meng Guang despised them all the more for it. He saw one of his guards stagger backwards as he was punched in the nose and had to look away rather than shame the man further. Meng Guang focused on the high window, with its smoke of moisture coming off the rain. More guards rushed in and he ignored the muffled grunts and shouts until the envoys were silent.

When Meng Guang lowered his upturned head, he saw that three of the group lay unconscious and the rest were panting and straining against their bonds, their teeth bared like the animals they were. He did not smile. He thought of the libraries and archives of Ta-li they threatened and felt only contempt. They would never understand the choices of a civilised man could not include craven surrender, no matter what the consequences. The manner of his death was always and finally a man's own choice, if he could truly see it.

'Take them to the public square,' he said. 'When I have refreshed myself, I will attend their flogging and executions.'

The smell of them had intensified as they sweated until it filled the room. Meng Guang had to struggle not to retch as he breathed more and more shallowly. He would certainly need to change his clothes before he finished this filthy business. He would order his present garments burnt while he bathed.

CHAPTER EIGHTEEN

The prisoners were bound by their wrists to iron posts in the great square in Ta-li, set into the ground long before to hold condemned criminals. By the time Meng Guang arrived, the sun was high and hot over the city and a huge crowd had gathered, filling the square in all directions. A troop of his guards had to clear the way with wooden staffs for Meng Guang to oversee the punishment, then bring up a comfortable chair for the prefect to rest his old bones. More men erected an awning to keep the sun from his head and he sipped a cool drink as he settled himself. No emotion showed on his face.

When he was finally ready, Meng Guang gestured to the men who stood by the posts, each bearing a heavy flail. The cords were of greased leather, each as thick as a child's finger, so that they fell on flesh with a dull smack as painful as a blow from a club. He hoped the Mongols would cry out and shame themselves. They were talking to each other, calling out encouragement, Meng Guang assumed. He noticed too that the Chin translators were speaking to the crowd. The little one, Lee Ung, was jerking in his bonds as he ranted at them. Meng Guang shook his head. The traitor would never understand Sung peasants. To them, nobles lived on another plane of existence, so high above them as to be incomprehensible. The prefect watched his docile people staring at the prisoners, their faces blank. One of them even reached down to pick up a stone and threw it hard, making Lee Ung flinch. Meng Guang allowed himself a small smile at that, hidden by his raised cup.

The first strokes began, a regular thumping rhythm. As he had expected, the Chin men wailed and struggled against the bonds, arching their backs and yanking at the iron posts as if they thought they could pull them out. The Mongols endured like mindless bullocks and Meng Guang frowned. He sent one of his guards with an order to work them harder and relaxed back in his chair as the sound and speed intensified. Still they stood there, talking and calling to each other. To his surprise, Meng Guang saw one of them laugh at a comment. He shook his head slightly, but he was a patient man. There were other whips, with teeth of sharp metal sewn into the leather. He would make them sing out with those.

Lee Ung had served Kublai for barely a year. He had signed on with the khan's brother when the tumans came through northern Chin lands, marking out thousands of farms over a vast area. He had known there were risks in any enterprise, but the pay was good and came regularly and he had always had a gift for languages. He had not expected to be grabbed and tortured by the old fool in charge of Ta-li city.

The pain was unbearable, simply that. He reached the point again and again where he could not stand it any longer, but still it went on. He was bound to the post and there was nowhere to go, no way to make it stop. He wept and pleaded with each stroke, ignoring the Mongols who turned their heads from him in embarrassment. Some of them called for him to stand up, but his legs had no strength and he sagged against the pole, held only by the cords on his wrists. He longed to faint or go insane, anything that would take him away, but his body refused and he stayed alert. If anything, his senses became more acute and the pain worsened until he could not believe anything could hurt more.

He heard the prefect snap an order and across the square the flogging ceased. Lee Ung struggled up again, forcing his knees to lock. He looked around and spat blood from where he had bitten his tongue. The square was part of an ancient marketplace near the city walls. He could see the huge gate that hid Kublai's army from sight. Lee Ung groaned at the thought that his rescuers were so close, yet blind. He could not die. He was too young and he had not even taken a wife.

He saw the bloody whips being cleansed in buckets, then passed on to other men to oil and wrap in protective cloth. In growing fear, he saw different rolls brought out and laid on the ground. Lee Ung strained, standing on his toes to see what they contained as the soldiers pulled back heavy canvas. The crowd murmured in anticipation and Lee Ung roared at them again, his voice hoarse.

'Hundreds of cannon lie outside these walls, ready to bring them down in rubble!' he shouted. 'A huge army faces you and yet a noble prince has promised to spare every life in Ta-li! He offers you mercy and dignity, but you take his men and break them with whips. How will he react now, when he does not see us return? What will he do then? As our blood is spilt, so yours will follow, every man, every woman, every child in the city. Remember then that you chose it. That you could have opened your gates and lived!'

He saw his tormentor unfold a long whip and broke off in despair as he saw the glint of metal in the strips. Lee Ung had seen a man scourged to death once before, a rapist caught by the authorities in his home city. His mouth went dry at the memories. His bladder would release, his body would become a twitching, spastic thing under that lash. There was no dignity in the death that awaited. In sick horror, he watched the man swirl the whip in circles, freeing the straps. Somewhere distant, Lee Ung heard a low whistling sound. It grew louder and half the crowd jerked out of their reverie as something heavy struck the great gate to the square, the sound echoing across their heads.

'He comes!' Lee Ung screeched at them. 'The destroyer is here. Throw down your masters and live, or the streets will be red by sunset.'

Another thump sounded and then two more as Kublai's gunners found their range. One ball flew overhead, missing the wall entirely and vanishing to smash a roof right across the square. The crowd flinched after the blur had passed.

'He comes!' Lee Ung shouted again, delirious with relief. He heard someone snap an order, but he was still craning his neck to look at the shivering gate when the guard reached him and cut his throat in one swift motion. The Mongols at the posts shouted in rage as his blood spattered the dry ground. They began to heave at the posts, working them back and forth, throwing their full weight against whatever held them. Meng Guang spoke again and more of his soldiers drew blades as the city gate came down with a crash.

In the roll of dust that spread out from the walls, the crowd could see a line of Mongol horsemen, black against the sunlight. They began to stream away, fear filling them as the riders entered the city in perfect ranks.

Meng Guang stood slowly as the square emptied, his face unnaturally pale. He swayed as he came to his feet, his world falling down around him. He had told himself the army outside Ta-li did not exist, that nothing the enemy could do would influence him. Yet they had entered, forcing him to see them. Meng Guang stood rooted in a shock so profound that his mind was completely blank. He was vaguely aware of his guards leaving the bloody whipping posts to protect him, their swords held high. He shook his head in slow denial, as if he could refuse entry to Ta-li even then.

With long silk banners fluttering on his left and right, the enemy rode up in shining armour that glittered in the sun. Meng Guang gaped at Kublai as he halted close to the group of armed men, disdaining their threat. Kublai knew those around him could lace the air with shafts at the first sign of aggression, but Meng Guang's guards did not. The slow approach unnerved them all, as if he was invulnerable, so far above them in status that they could not possibly threaten him. Under his glare, many of the soldiers looked down, as if the sun itself burned their eyes.

Kublai saw a withered old man in clean robes standing uncertainly before him with empty eyes. The crowds had fled and the square was utterly silent.

In the stillness, one of the bound Mongols managed to wrench his iron post from the stones beneath it. He roared in triumph, taking hold of it like a weapon and advancing on Meng Guang with clear intent. Kublai raised his hand and the man stopped instantly, his chest rising and falling with strong emotion.

'I said I would spare Ta-li,' Kublai said in perfect Mandarin. 'Why did you not listen to me?'

Meng Guang stared into the distance, his mind settling into a cold lump that could not respond. He had lived long and been prefect of the city for decades. It had been a good life. He heard the voice of the enemy as reeds whispering in the darkness, but he did not respond. They could not make him acknowledge them. He prepared himself for death, taking a deep breath and releasing it slowly, so that his racing heart slowed to a steady beat.

Kublai frowned at the lack of reaction. He saw fear in the

prefect's soldiers and rage in the faces of his own men, but the prefect stood and looked out over the city as if he were the only man there. A breeze blew and Kublai shook his head to break the spell. He had seen the body of Lee Ung hanging from its wrists and he made his decision.

'I am a noble house.' Kublai said. 'My lands in the north were once bound to the Sung territories under one emperor. It will be so again. I claim this city as my own, as my *right*. My protection, my shadow, stands over you all from this moment. Surrender to me and I will show mercy, as a father to his children.'

Meng Guang said nothing, though he raised his eyes at last and met those of Kublai. Almost like a shiver, he shook his head.

'Very well,' Kublai said. 'I see I will have to disappoint a friend. Take this one and hang his body from the walls. The rest will live.'

He watched closely as the Mongol with the iron pole shouldered through the guards and pushed Meng Guang through to the front. The old man went without a protest and his guards did nothing. They did not dare look at each other, understanding at last that their lives hung on a single word from this strange prince who spoke in the language of authority.

'My word is iron,' Kublai said to the guards, as Meng Guang was led away. 'Your people will come to know this, in time.'

Hulegu was panting slightly as he drew to a halt and passed his hunting eagle to its handler. The bird screeched and flapped, but the man knew her well and calmed the bird with a hand on her neck.

General Kitbuqa carried a white-flecked kestrel on his right arm, but he had only two pigeons on his belt and his expression was sour. Hulegu grinned at him as he dismounted and handed over a small deer, its head lolling brokenly. His cook was Persian, a local man who claimed to have once served the caliph himself. When he had been captured on the way back to the city from some distant market, Hulegu had taken him into his staff. It pleased him to eat meals the caliph should have been enjoying, though he made sure to have them tasted first. The dark-skinned man bobbed his head as he took the flopping animal, his gaze bright on the eagle as she fussed. His people loved to hunt the air. Hawks and kestrels were treasures, but the massive eagles were almost unknown in that region. The dark gold bird that settled on the handler's wrist was worth a fortune.

Hulegu looked to Baghdad, just two miles to the north. His armies surrounded the ancient walled city, even to the point of blocking the Tigris with pontoons they had constructed in his absence. In all directions, he could see the dark smears of his tumans, waiting patiently. The caliph had refused to destroy the walls as an expression of his good faith. Hulegu still had the letter somewhere in his packs. The words were clear enough, but it was still a mystery to him. The man had written of the followers of Mohammed, certain that they would rise up to defend the centre of their faith. Hulegu wondered where they all were as his army settled in around the city. In a previous generation, the caliph might have been right, but Genghis had slaughtered his way across the region, not once but twice. It amused Hulegu to think of the survivors crawling out of rubble, only to encounter Genghis on his way back to the Xi Xia territory on his last campaign. Baghdad did not have the support it had enjoyed in previous centuries, but the caliph seemed almost unaware of his isolation.

Hulegu accepted a drink of orange juice, chilled in the river overnight. He knocked it back and tossed the cup to a servant without looking to see if the man caught it. The people of Baghdad did not share their master's confidence in God. Every night, they let themselves down by ropes, risking broken bones by scrambling down the rough walls. Hulegu had no idea how many people there were inside, but each dawn found another hundred or so being herded up by his men. It had become almost a game to them. He let his men practise their archery on the groups, giving the men and boys to be slaughtered while the women and girls were handed out to those who had pleased their officers. The caliph had not surrendered. Until he did, their lives were forfeit.

Hulegu heard the sizzle as his cook put fresh-cut venison steaks into a pan of hot fat. The smell was laced with garlic and his mouth watered in anticipation. The man was a marvel. Kitbuqa's pitiful pigeons would not add much meat to the general's noon meal, he thought, but then that was the difference between eagles and hawks. His eagle could send even a wolf tumbling. She and Hulegu were the same, he thought complacently. Predators did not need mercy. He could envy the bird its perfect single-minded ruthlessness. It had no doubts or fears, nothing to trouble a mind dedicated only to the kill.

Once more, he looked to Baghdad and his mouth tightened to a thin line. His cannons barely chipped the stones. The city's defensive walls had been designed with sloping surfaces that sent the balls skipping away with little damage. When the black powder was gone, he would be left with torsion catapults and heavy trebuchets. In time, they would still break the walls, but not with the same roaring terror, not with the same feeling of godlike power. Baghdad was known to have no boulders for miles around it, but his men had planned for that, collecting them in carts as they came south. Eventually, they would run out and he would have to send his tumans to collect more.

Hulegu grimaced to himself, weary of the same thoughts

217

spinning in his head as each slow day passed. He could assault the walls at any time, but they were still strong. Stubborn defenders could take as many as four or five of his men for each one they lost. That was the purpose of castles and walled cities, after all. They would pour naphtha oil and drop rocks on those trying to climb. It would be a bloody business and he did not want to see thousands of his men killed over one city, no matter how much wealth was reputed to lie inside its walls. It would always be better to smash the walls down, or for starvation to bring the caliph to his senses.

'If you make me wait much longer,' Hulegu muttered, staring at the distant city, 'it will go hard with you.'

General Kitbuqa looked up as he spoke and Hulegu realised the man was still hoping for an invitation to share the noon meal. He smiled, recalling the eagle's stoop. There was too much meat for one man, but he did not offer to share it. Hawks and eagles did not fly together, he reminded himself. They were very different breeds.

Caliph al-Mustasim was a worried man. His ancestors had secured a small empire around Baghdad that had lasted five centuries, with the city as the jewel. It had even survived the ravages of Genghis as he swept through the area decades before. Al-Mustasim liked to believe Allah had made the Mongol khan blind to the city, so that he rode past it without stopping. Perhaps it was even true. Al-Mustasim was not only of the royal Abbasid line, but also the leader of the Moslem faith in the world, his city a light for them all. Surely there were armies on their way to relieve Baghdad? He clasped his hands and felt the sweat on them as his fingers slid together and apart, over and over. The caliph was large of body, his flesh made soft by years of luxury. He felt the clammy perspiration in his armpits and clicked his fingers to have slave girls approach and wipe him with cloths. He did not break off his fearful thoughts as they tended to him, raising his arms and wiping at the smooth brown expanse that was revealed beneath his silks and layers. They had been chosen for their beauty, but he had no eyes for them that day. He barely noticed as one of them fed him sticky sweets from a bowl, pressing them into his mouth as if they fattened a prize bull.

As he lay there, a cluster of laughing children ran into the room and he looked fondly at them. They brought noise and life, enough to pierce the despair that weighed him down.

'The qamara!' his son demanded, looking up at him beseechingly. The other children waited in hope to see the marvel and al-Mustasim's face softened.

'Very well, just for a little while before you return to your studies,' he said.

He waved his arm and they scattered before it, whooping in excitement. The device had been built to the specifications of the great Moslem scientist, Ibn al-Haitham. 'Qamara' was merely the word for 'dark room', but the name had stuck. Only a few servants went with him as he walked along a corridor to the room where it had been constructed. The children ran ahead in their excitement, telling those who had not already seen it everything they could remember.

It was a room in itself, a large structure of black cloth that was as dark as night inside. Al-Mustasim gazed on the black cube fondly, as proud as if he had invented it himself.

'Which one of you will be first?' he asked.

They leapt and shouted their names and he picked one of his daughters, a little girl named Suri. She stood shivering with delight as he placed her in the right spot. As the curtain fell, plunging them all into darkness, the children shouted nervously. His servants brought a flame and soon little Suri was lit brightly by shuttered lamps. She preened in the attention and he chuckled to see her.

'The rest of you go through that partition now. Close your eyes and do not open them until I say.'

They obeyed him, feeling their way through the layer of black cloth by touch.

'Are you all ready?' he asked.

The light from the lamps on Suri would pass through a tiny hole in the cloth. He did not fully understand how light could carry her inverted image, but there she would be, inside the room with them in light and shadow. It was a marvel and he smiled as he told them to open their eyes.

He heard them gasp in wonder calling to each other to see.

Before al-Mustasim could organise another to take Suri's place, he heard the voice of his vizier Ahriman speaking to the servants outside. Al-Mustasim frowned, the moment of simple joy spoiled. The man would not leave him in peace. Al-Mustasim sighed as Ahriman cleared his throat outside the qamara, summoning his attention.

'I am sorry to disturb you, caliph. I have news you must hear.'

Al-Mustasim left the children to their games, already growing raucous in the dark tent. He blinked as he came back into the sunlit rooms and took a moment to send a couple of his servants inside to make sure the boys did not break anything.

'Well? Has anything changed since yesterday, or the day before? Are we still surrounded by infidels, by armies?'

'We are, caliph. At dawn, they sent another flight of arrows over the walls.'

He held one in his hand with the scroll still tight around it. He had already unwrapped another and held it out to be read. Al-Mustasim waved it away as if its touch would corrupt him.

'Another demand to surrender, I am certain. How many of

these have I seen now? He threatens and promises, offers peace and then annihilation. It changes nothing, Ahriman.'

'In this message he says he will accept tribute, caliph. We cannot continue to ignore him. This Hulegu is already famous for his greed. In every town that he destroys, his men are there, asking: "Where is the gold? Where are the jewels?" He does not care that Baghdad is a sacred city, only that it has treasure rooms filled with metals.'

'You would have me give the wealth of my line to him?'

'Or see the city burn? Yes, caliph, I would. He will not leave. He has the scent of blood in his nostrils and the people are afraid. There are rumours everywhere that the Arabs are already dealing with him, telling him about the secret ways into the city.'

'There *are* no secret ways,' al-Mustasim snapped. His voice was high and sounded petulant, even to his own ears. 'I would know if there were.'

'Nonetheless, it is what they discuss in the markets. They expect Mongol warriors to come creeping into Baghdad every night we delay. This man wants only gold, they say. Why does the caliph not give the wealth of the world to him, that we may live?'

'I am waiting, Ahriman. Have I no allies? No friends? Where are they now?'

The vizier shook his head. 'They remember Genghis, caliph. They will not come to save Baghdad.'

'I *cannot* surrender. I am the light of Islam! The libraries alone . . . My life is not worth a single text. The Mongols will destroy them all if they set foot in my city.'

He felt anger grow at the frown on Ahriman's face and stepped further away from the qamara so that the children would not hear their discussion. It was infuriating. Ahriman was meant to support his caliph, to plan and defeat his enemies.

Yet the vizier could suggest nothing but throwing gold at the wolves.

Ahriman watched his master in frustration. They had known each other for a long time and he understood the man's fears. They were justified, but it was not a choice between survival and destruction. It was a choice between surrendering and keeping some dignity, or risking the wrath of the most destructive race Ahriman had ever known. There were too many examples in their history to ignore.

'The Shah of Khwarezm resisted them to the end,' Ahriman said softly. 'He was a man among men, a warrior. Where is he now? His cities are black stones, his people are broken: slaves or the dead. You told me always to speak the truth to you. Will you hear it now when I tell you to open the gates and save as many as you can? Each day we make him wait in the heat, his anger grows.'

'Someone will come to relieve the city. We will show them then,' Al-Mustasim said plaintively. He did not even believe it himself and Ahriman merely snorted in derision.

Al-Mustasim rose from his couch and walked to the window. He could smell the scented soaps in the market, blocks by the thousand made in workshops in the western quarter. It was a city of towers, of science and wonders, and yet it was threatened by lengths of sharp iron and black powder, by men who would not even understand the things they saw as they smashed them apart. Beyond the walls, he could see the Mongol armies, shifting like black insects. Al-Mustasim could barely speak for grief and tears filled his eyes. He thought of the children, so blissfully unaware of the threat all around them. Despair pressed him down.

'I will wait another month. If no one comes to aid my home, I will go out to my enemies.' His throat was thick, choking him as he spoke. 'I will go out to them and negotiate our surrender.'

CHAPTER NINETEEN

Hulegu watched the gates creak open, pushed by teams of men under the lash. He was sweating already, aware of the sun on his skin even as it grew in intensity. Naturally dark, he had never known sunburn before the endless weeks of siege around Baghdad. Now the first kiss of warmth each day felt like a branding iron held to his flesh. His own sweat stung him, dribbling over his eyebrows and lashes to irritate his eyes and make him blink. He had done his best to keep the tumans fit and alert, but the sheer boredom of a siege was like one of the rashes that spread slowly across the flesh of otherwise healthy men. He scratched his groin at the thought, feeling the cysts there. It was dangerous to allow his shaman to cut them, as infection often followed, but in the privacy of his own ger, Hulegu squeezed the worst of them each night, reducing the hard lumps each time until pain made him stop. The oily white substance remained on his fingers. He could smell its pungency even as he stood there and waited for the caliph.

At least it would soon be over. There had been two attempts to escape his grip around the city, both of them along the river. The first had been in small boats constructed inside the iron river gates. They had been destroyed with naphtha oil, the helpless men in them drenched as clay jugs were thrown from the banks, then set alight with flaming arrows. Hulegu did not know who had died that day. There had been no way to identify the bodies afterwards, even if he had been interested.

The second attempt had been more subtle, just six men with their bodies blackened in soot and oil. They had reached the pontoons his men had built across the Tigris, anchored to heavy trunks jammed into the soft riverbed. The sharp eyes of one of his scouts had seen them sliding through the water and his warriors had unlimbered their bows, taking care with each shot as they laughed and called targets to each other. It may have been the last blow to the caliph's hopes; Hulegu did not know. He had received word that al-Mustasim would meet him outside the city the following day.

Hulegu frowned as he watched a long retinue stride out of the city. He had demanded surrender once again, but the caliph had not even answered, preferring to wait for the meeting between them. Hulegu counted as the small column lengthened. Two hundred, three, perhaps four. At last it came to an end and the gates closed behind them, leaving the caliph's soldiers to march their master into Hulegu's presence.

Hulegu had not been idle the night before. He had no awning large enough to hold the caliph's retinue, but he had cleared a spot on the stony ground and covered it in thick carpets taken from towns along their route. The edges of the spot were lined with plump cushions and Hulegu had added rough wooden benches, almost like one of the Christian churches he had seen in Russia. There was no altar, only a simple table and two chairs for the leaders to sit. Hulegu's generals would stand, ready to draw their swords at the first sign of treachery.

Hulegu knew the caliph's men would have reported his arrangements, viewed from the city walls. The small column made their way to it unerringly, giving Hulegu the chance to smile at the perfect steps of the marching men. He had not limited the numbers of soldiers the caliph could bring. Ten tumans surrounded the city and he made sure the caliph's route was lined with his own horsemen, heavily armed and scowling. The message would be clear enough.

The man himself was carried in a chariot drawn by two large geldings. Hulegu blinked when he saw the size of the caliph who ruled the city and called himself the light of Islam. No warrior, then, not that one. The hands that held the leading edge of his chariot were swollen and the eyes that searched for Hulegu were almost hidden in bloated flesh. Hulegu said nothing as the caliph was helped down by his servants. General Kitbuqa was there at hand to guide him to his place, while Hulegu thought through what he wanted from the meeting. He chewed the inside of his cheek as the caliph's men took their seats. The whole thing was a farce, a mask to allow the man some shred of dignity when he deserved none. Even so, Hulegu had not refused the offer, or even quibbled over details. The important thing was that the man would bargain. Only the caliph could do so and Hulegu wondered yet again what vast wealth lay within the city known as the navel of the world. He had heard stories of Baghdad for a thousand miles, tales of ancient jade armour and ivory spears, holy relics and statues of solid gold, taller than three men. He hungered to see such things. He had turned gold into bars and rough coins, but he yearned to find pieces that would impress his brothers, both Mongke and Kublai. He was even tempted to keep the libraries, so that Kublai would know he had them. A man could never have enough wealth, but he could at least have more than his brothers.

As the caliph lowered his bulk to his chair, Hulegu clenched and unclenched his hands, grasping unconsciously at what was owed to him. He took his seat and stared coldly into the watery eyes of al-Mustasim. Hulegu could feel the sun stinging the back of his neck and considered calling for an awning until he saw the full glare was in the caliph's face. Despite his Persian blood, the fat man was not comfortable in the heat. Hulegu nodded to him.

'What do you intend to offer me, caliph, for your city and your life?' he said.

Kublai rode east through thick forest that seemed endless. He knew he did not have to fear an attack. His scouts were out in all directions for thirty miles, yet the trees were thick and made an unnatural darkness that had his horse rearing at shadows. He had been told of a natural clearing ahead, but the sun was setting and he could not yet see the vast boulder or the lake his scouts had described.

General Bayar rode just ahead, a master horseman who made light work of the thick foliage. Kublai lacked the man's easy touch, but he stayed in sight, his personal guards all around him. At least the forest was empty. He and his men had found one abandoned village deep in thick cover and miles from the nearest road. Whoever had made the wretched houses had vanished long ago.

The ground had been rising gently for half a day and Kublai reached a high ridge as the sun touched the horizon, looking down into a steep valley with a perfect black bowl of water at its foot. His horse whickered gratefully at the sight, as scratched and thirsty as its rider. Kublai let Bayar lead the way, happy to follow the path he chose. Together they guided the horses down the slope, seeing lamps ahead like a host of fireflies.

Bayar did not look as weary as Kublai felt. He was not much younger, though the man was still fitter than Kublai's life among books in Karakorum had made him. No matter how he worked his body, it never seemed to have the easy endurance of warriors and senior men. Half his tumans had gone before him and many would already be asleep in the close confines of gers, or sleeping out under the stars if there was no place to set up.

Kublai sighed at the thought. He could hardly remember the last time he had slept through the night. He dreamed and woke in fits and starts, his mind whirring away as if it had an independent existence. Chabi would soothe him with a cool hand on his brow, but she fell asleep again quickly, leaving him still awake and thinking. He had been forced to keep a leather book of blank pages close to him, so he could write down the ideas that presented themselves just at the moment he was finally drifting off. In time, he would copy his journal onto better paper, a record of his time among the Sung. It would be worthy of the shelves in Karakorum if it continued as it had begun.

After the city of Ta-li had fallen to him, three others had followed within the month. He had sent scouts far ahead of him, carrying news of his mercy. He made a point of choosing men from the Chin who had joined his tumans over the years. They understood what he wanted and of course they approved, so he did not doubt they spoke well of the Mongol leader who was as much a Chin lord as anyone could be.

There had been a moment in those first months when he was able to dream of sweeping right across the Sung lands, of armies and cities surrendering without a blow being struck, until he stood before the emperor himself. That had lasted just long enough for Uriang-Khadai to approach. Kublai frowned at the memory, certain the older general had enjoyed being the bearer of bad news.

'The men are not paid,' Uriang-Khadai had lectured him. 'You have said they are not allowed to loot and they are becoming angry. I have not seen this level of unrest before, lord. Perhaps you did not realise they would resent the mercy and kindness you have shown to our enemies.' Kublai remembered how the orlok's eyes glittered with suppressed anger as he went on. 'I believe they will become difficult to manage if you continue this policy. They do not understand it. All the men know is that you have taken away their baubles and rewards.'

As he guided his horse down through thick brush, Kublai blew air out slowly. Good decisions were never made in anger. Yao Shu had taught him the truth of that years before. Uriang-Khadai might have enjoyed telling him something so obvious, but the problem was a real one. The tumans gave their lives and strength without question for the khan, or whoever commanded them in his name. In return, they were allowed to take wealth and slaves wherever they found them. Kublai could imagine their greed at the thought of all the fat Sung towns, untouched by war and rich on centuries of trade. Yet he had refused to burn them and barely a dozen city officials had died, just those who refused to surrender. In the last city, the people had brought their prefect out and thrown him down in the dust before Kublai's men. They had understood the choice he offered – to live and prosper rather than resist and be destroyed.

Kublai dismounted stiffly, nodding to Bayar as the general took the horses away. The night was peaceful, with an owl hooting in warning somewhere nearby, no doubt disturbed by the passage of so many men through its hunting ground. He reached down and scooped up a handful of cold water, rubbing it over his face and neck with a groan of appreciation. He had a solution to the problem. He paid many of the men who accompanied the tumans and he had silver and gold coins by the hundred thousand. He could pay the warriors as well, at least for a time. Kublai grimaced, taking more of the water to slick back his hair. It would empty the shrinking war chest Mongke had given him in just a few months. He would then have no money for bribes and no source of new income. Yao Shu had assured him the farmers on his northern lands would have a crop in the ground, but he could not decide the future on unknown quantities. Armies had to be fed and supplied. Adding silver to that was logical enough, if he could only find enough silver.

Standing there, staring across the water, Kublai grew still, then raised his eyes to heaven and laughed aloud. He was in a land where the soldiers were paid like any other tradesman. He had to find the mines where the ore was dug out. He was tired and hungry, but for the first time that day, he didn't feel it. A year before, he might have seen it as an impossible task, but since then he had seen Sung cities open their gates and surrender to a Chin lord. By the time Mongke's silver ran out, he would have taxes coming in from his new lands, even if he failed to find the emperor's supplies. He could make the cities finance their own conquest!

He didn't hear Yao Shu come up behind him. Despite his age, the old man could still move silently. Kublai gave a start when he spoke, then smiled.

'I am glad to see you cheerful,' Yao Shu said. 'I would be happier if Bayar had not picked a spot to camp with so many mosquitoes.'

Still caught up in the idea, Kublai explained his thoughts. He spoke at high speed in Mandarin, unaware that his perfect fluency made the old man proud. Yao Shu nodded as he finished.

'It is a good plan, I think. A silver mine takes many workers. It should not be too hard to find someone who has heard of one, or even worked in one. Better still if we can interrupt the pay for Sung soldiers. As well as finding the coins already made, they would suffer as we benefited and perhaps lose a little faith in the men who pay them.'

'I will set scouts to the task tomorrow,' Kublai promised, yawning. 'Until then, I have enough to pay our men in good Chin coin. Will you work out the amounts for me?'

'Of course. I will have to find the price of a cheap whore in a small town as my base. I think a man should have to save for a day or two to afford such a luxury. At the very least it will teach them discipline.' Yao Shu smiled. 'It is a good plan, Kublai.'

They smiled at each other, aware that Yao Shu only used his personal name when there was no one else to overhear.

'Go to your wife now,' Yao Shu said. 'Eat, make babies or rest. You must stay healthy.' His stern tone brought back Kublai's memories of old schoolrooms. 'Somewhere far from here, the emperor of the Sung is raging as the reports come in. He has lost an army and four cities. He will not wait for you to come to him. Perhaps he hoped your men would exhaust themselves in the trek across his lands, but instead he will hear that you thrive and grow strong, that you eat well and yet are still hungry.'

Kublai grinned at the image.

'I am too tired to worry about him tonight,' he said, yawning hugely, so that he could feel his jaw crack. 'I think for once I might sleep.'

Yao Shu looked sceptical. He rarely slept for more than four hours at a time and regarded any more as appalling slothfulness.

'Keep your book close by. I enjoy reading the things you write.'

Kublai's mouth opened in protest. 'It is a private journal, old man. Did Chabi let you look at it? Is there no respect?'

'I serve you better when I know your mind, my lord. And I find your observations on Orlok Uriang-Khadai most interesting.'

Kublai snorted at the old monk's placid expression.

'You see too much, old friend. Get some rest yourself. Have you considered the Mandarin word for "bank"? It means "silver movement". We will find where they get it from.'

Hulegu enjoyed the sense of power over the caliph of Baghdad. The older man's pretensions were torn away during the hours of the morning. Hulegu watched patiently as al-Mustasim spoke to advisers and checked endless tally sheets of fine vellum, making offers and counter-offers, most of which Hulegu simply ignored until the man understood the reality. As the morning wore on, Hulegu had his cannon and catapult teams run through their drills nearby, making the scribes nervous. The caliph stared in distaste at the moving ranks of warriors, at the gers that clustered for miles in all directions. The vast army held his city in a tight grip and he had no force to break the siege, no hope to give him peace. No one was coming to relieve Baghdad. The knowledge showed in his face and the way he sat, his shoulders slumped into the rolls of flesh.

It was intoxicating for Hulegu to have a proud leader reduced to hopelessness, to watch as the caliph slowly realised that everything he valued was in the hands of men who cared nothing for his people or his culture. Hulegu waved away the latest offer. He knew the people of the region loved to bargain, but it was no more than the twitching of a corpse. Everything they could possibly offer was in Baghdad and the city would open its gates to the Mongols. The treasure rooms and temples would be his to plunder. Still he waited for al-Mustasim to give up all hope.

They paused at noon for the caliph's party to roll out prayer mats and bow their heads, chanting together. Hulegu used the time to stroll across to his senior generals, making sure they were still alert. There could be no surprises, he was certain. If another army moved closer than sixty miles, he would know far faster than hope could rise in the caliph. The man who ruled Baghdad would be killed if such news came, Hulegu had decided. Al-Mustasim was more than a lord to his people, with his spiritual status. He could be a symbol, or even a martyr. Hulegu smiled at the thought. The Moslems and Christians put great stock in their martyrs.

Hearing their droning chant, Hulegu shook his head in amusement. For him the sky father was always above his head, the earth mother at his feet. If they watched at all, they did not interfere with a man's life. It was true the spirits of the land could be malevolent. Hulegu could not forget his own father's fate, chosen to replace the life demanded from Ogedai Khan. In the sunshine, he shuddered at the thought of millions of spirits watching him in this place.

He raised his head, refusing to be afraid. They had not troubled Genghis and he had done more than his share of destruction, torn more than most from the sunlit world. If the angry spirits had not dared to touch Genghis, they could have no terrors for his grandson.

The moment he had been waiting for came deep into the afternoon, when even Hulegu had allowed his servants to drape his sunburnt neck in a damp cloth. The caliph's fine robes were stained in great dark patches and he looked exhausted, though he had only sat and sweated through the long day.

'I have offered you the riches of Croesus,' Caliph al-Mustasim said. 'More than any one man has ever seen. You asked me to value my people, my city, and I have done so. Yet you refuse again? What more would you have from me? Why am I even here, if you will take nothing in exchange?'

His eyes were weak and Hulegu took his seat once more, laying his sword across his thighs and settling himself.

'I will not be made to look a fool, caliph. I will not take a few cartloads of pretty things and have men say I never knew what else lay within the ancient city. No, you will not laugh when we are gone.'

The caliph looked at him in sheer confusion.

'You have seen the lists, the official records of the treasury!'

'Lists your scribes could well have written in the weeks before you came out armed with them. I will choose the tribute from Baghdad. You will not grant it to me.'

'What . . .' The caliph paused and shook his head. Once more he looked at the army around him, stretching into the distance so that they became a shimmering blur. He did not doubt they could destroy the city if he gave them the opportunity. His heart beat painfully in his chest and he could smell his own sweat strongly.

'I am trying to negotiate a peaceful end to the siege. Tell me what you want and I will begin again.'

Hulegu nodded as if the man had made a good point. He scratched his chin, feeling the bristles growing there.

'Have your people disarm. Have them throw every sword, every knife, every axe out of the city, so that my men can collect them. You and I will walk together into Baghdad then, with just an honour guard to keep the mob at bay. When that is done, we will talk again.'

Wearily, the caliph heaved himself to his feet. His legs had gone numb and he staggered a step before catching himself.

'You ask me to leave my people defenceless.'

'They are *already* defenceless,' Hulegu said, with a wave of his hand. He put his boots up on the table and sat back in his chair. 'Look around you once more, caliph, and tell me it is not so. I am trying to find a way to a peaceful solution. When my men have searched your palaces, I will know there is no trickery. Don't worry, I will leave you a little gold, enough to buy some new robes at least.'

The men around him chuckled and the caliph stared in impotent fury.

'I have your word there will be no violence?'

Hulegu shrugged.

'Unless you force my hand. I have told you the terms, caliph.'

'Then I will return to the city,' al-Mustasim said.

Hulegu thought for a moment.

'You are my guest. Send a man back with the order. You will stay in a ger tonight, to learn our ways. We have Moslems in the camp. Perhaps they will appreciate your guidance.'

They locked gazes and the caliph looked away first. He felt completely without choices, a fish on a line that Hulegu was happy to pull in at his own pace. He could only grasp at the slightest chance to turn the Mongol from Baghdad without blood in the streets. He nodded.

'I would be honoured,' he said softly.

CHAPTER TWENTY

It was no simple task to disarm the city of Baghdad. It started well enough, with a populace who could see the vast Mongol army around their walls. The caliph's heralds read his orders from every street corner and it was not long before the first weapons were being dragged out onto the street for collection. It was common for families to have a sword or spear in their home, relics of an old war, or just to protect the house. Many of them did not want to give up a weapon their father or grandfather had used. It was no easier to make butchers, carpenters and builders give up their precious tools. By the end of the first morning, the mood of the city had become resentful and some weapons were even taken back in before they could be collected. Before sunset, the caliph's city guards had to face down angry mobs and at one point were almost engulfed in them. Across the city, three thousand guards faced the simmering anger of the citizens, always vastly outnumbered. Groups of the caliph's men went street by street, trying to bring massive force to bear on a single point and then moving on. As a result, the collection slowed even further. It was not a promising start and the troubles grew as night fell.

The guards had to keep their own weapons to enforce the caliph's rule, but the sight of them inflamed already dangerous passions. Every father and son feared armed men when they had given up their own weapons. The guards were pelted with roof tiles and rotting vegetables as they checked each street, thrown from above or by darting little boys yelling curses at them.

As the hot days passed, shouting crowds dogged their steps. The guards grew tight-lipped with fury as they continued their work and tried to ignore the sight of people running out of each street with swords and knives as they entered.

On the fourth day, one of the caliph's men was hit by something foul that slithered wetly down the back of his head. He had been under intense pressure for a long time: called a traitor and a coward, jeered and spat at. He swung round in a rage with his sword drawn and saw a group of teenage boys laughing at him. They scattered, but in his rage he caught one and felled him with a blow. The guard panted as he turned the body over. He had killed the youngest of them, a thin boy who lay with a great red gash across his neck, ugly and wide, so that bone showed. The guard looked up into the faces of the burly men he had paid to carry the blades. One of them dropped his armful with a crash and walked away. Behind him, others pressed forward, calling for still more to come and see what had been done. The anger was growing and the guard knew about rough street justice. His fear showed on his face and he began to back away. He managed to retreat only a few paces before he was tripped and brought down. The crowd fell on him in a rush of fear and rage, tearing with their nails, smashing their fists and shoes into his flesh.

At the end of the street a dozen guards came running. As if at a signal, the crowd suddenly scattered in all directions, running away mindlessly. They left another body with the dead boy, so battered and torn as to be barely human.

The following dawn there were riots across Baghdad. Trapped as he was in the Mongol camp, the caliph lost patience when he was told. It was true that his guards were outnumbered in the teeming city, but he had eight major guard houses built in good stone and three thousand men. He sent new orders, giving his personal permission to kill any malcontents or rioters. He made sure the order was read on every street corner. The guards heard the news with relish and sharpened their swords. One of their own had fallen to the mob and it would not happen again. They moved in groups of two hundred and scoured areas, with hundreds more employed to take the weapons to the walls and drop them over. If anyone protested, the guards used heavy sticks to knock him senseless and threw in a few kicks for good measure. If a blade was drawn in anger against them, they killed quickly and left the bodies where they could be seen. There was no shame or fear in them to spark the revenge heat of a crowd. Instead, the guards stared the citizens down while they went about their work.

The mobs shrank in the face of sanctioned aggression, fading back into the shadows of normal life. They whispered the name of the fallen boy to themselves like a talisman against evil, but the collections went on even so.

After eleven days, Hulegu was at the end of his patience when the message came that the disarming was complete and he could enter and inspect the city. The sheer weight of weapons had been impressive, forcing Hulegu to use a full tuman to cart them away. Most were buried to rust, with just a few choice pieces finding new owners among the Mongol officers. Baghdad waited before him, truly defenceless for the first time in its history. He savoured the thought as he mounted his horse and waited for a minghaan of a thousand to form up around him. At the head, the caliph took his place in his chariot, his clothes filthy and his skin covered in flea bites. Hulegu laughed when he saw the man, then gave the order to go in.

There would still be an element of danger in entering the

city, Hulegu was certain. Just a few hidden bows used from roofs as he passed could set off another riot. He wore full armour as well as his helmet, the weight and solidity making him feel invulnerable as he dug in his heels and rode through the gates at last. His tumans were ready to assault the city and he left men to hold the gates open at each point of entry. He hoped he had thought of everything and he was cheerful as he trotted his mount down a main road, empty and echoing.

In just a short time, the outer walls were long behind. The city was predominantly built from a brown baked brick. It reminded Hulegu of the smaller city of Samarra to the north. His tumans had fought a pitched battle there in his absence before looting it. By the time he had come south from the Assassin fortress, Samarra had been sacked, with blood running in the gutters and parts reduced to rubble. That was one reason the caliph's city would not be relieved. Hulegu's officers had been thorough.

Baghdad was many times the size of Samarra and the brown buildings were interspersed with highly decorated mosques. Bright blue tiles and extraordinary geometric patterns caught the sunlight, gleaming in the dun roads as splashes of colour. Hulegu knew the Moslems were forbidden from using human forms in their art, so they made patterns of reflected and interwoven shapes. It was said their mathematics had grown out of the art, from men forced to consider angles and symmetry to worship their god. To his surprise, Hulegu found he enjoyed the style far more than the battle scenes Ogedai had commissioned in Karakorum. There was something almost soothing about the repeated shapes and lines that covered vast walls and courtyards. Above the city, minarets and towers loomed, more splashes of colour. When Hulegu looked up, he could see the distant figures of men watching from the heights.

No doubt they could see his army outside the city as they stared into the distance.

He passed the famous House of Wisdom and ducked down in his saddle to peer through an archway into the dark blue courtyard there. Nervous scholars peeped out of every window and he recalled that they were said to possess the greatest library in the region. If Kublai had been present, Hulegu knew his brother would have been salivating to get in, but he had other things to see. His minghaan followed a small group of the caliph's guards through the city, passing over the Tigris at one point on a bridge of white marble. Baghdad was larger than Hulegu had realised, the sheer scale of it only truly visible from inside the walls.

The sun was high by the time he reached the caliph's gated palace and passed through into sheltered green gardens. Hulegu snorted at the sight of a peacock, running from the armed men with its tail quivering.

Most of the minghaan stayed outside the caliph's residence, with orders to visit all the banks in the city. Hulegu cared little for what the caliph thought of him. Even as he dismounted, a full tuman of ten thousand was entering the city in slow procession, disciplined men who would seek out its hidden wealth without touching off another riot.

Hulegu was in good spirits as the caliph's servants led him through cool rooms and down steps to where their master waited. He knew he could be ambushed, but he depended on the threat of his men to keep him safe. The caliph would have to be insane to take him with so many Mongols already in the city – and so few weapons to fight them. Hulegu was certain there were still caches of blades in Baghdad. It was almost impossible to find every knife, sword and bow in a population with basements and hidden rooms. It had been a symbolic act for the most part, though it increased the sense of helplessness in the city as they waited for him to keep his word and leave.

Caliph al-Mustasim was waiting at the bottom of a flight of stone steps that led on from two more above it, so that the treasure rooms were deep into the bedrock and lit only by lamps. No sunlight reached so far down, but it was dusty and cool rather than damp. Even in his soiled clothes, the leader of the city looked far more confident than he had in the Mongol camp. Hulegu watched for some sign of deceit as the caliph's guards removed a heavy locking bar, a piece of iron so massive that two of them could barely lift it out of its brackets. Al-Mustasim then stepped in and pressed his hands on the doors, heaving at them until they swung open noiselessly. Unable to help himself, Hulegu edged forward to the threshold to get the first sight of what lay within. He was watched in turn by the caliph, who saw greed kindle in his eyes.

The treasure rooms must once have been a natural cave under the city. The walls were still rough in places, stretching far away. The servants of the caliph had obviously gone in before, as the place was well lit with lamps hanging from the ceiling. Hulegu smiled as he realised the grand opening of the doors had been staged for his benefit alone.

It had been worth the wait. Gold gleamed its unique colour in stacks of bars as thick as a man's finger, but that was just a small part of the whole. Hulegu swallowed drily as he saw the extent of the cave, every corner of it packed with statuary and shelves. He could not help but wonder how much had been removed before that day. The caliph would want to keep some portion of his wealth back and Hulegu knew he would have a struggle finding the other rooms and chests, wherever they were hidden. Still, it was an impressive sight. Just that one room was equal to or greater than all Mongke's vaults. Though Hulegu knew he would have to hand over at least half of it to his brother, he realised that at a stroke he had become one of the richest men in the world. He laughed as he stood there, seeing the wealth of ancient nations.

The caliph smiled nervously at the sound.

'When you check the lists I gave you, you will see I have accounted for it all. I have dealt honourably for my city.'

Hulegu turned to him and laid a hand on his shoulder. One of the caliph's guards bristled and found a sword laid across his throat in an instant. Hulegu ignored them.

'You have shown me the visible treasures, yes. They are magnificent. Now show me the rest, the true wealth of Baghdad.'

The caliph looked at the smiling man in horror. He shook his head wordlessly.

'Please, there is nothing else.'

Hulegu reached out and took a firm grip on one of the caliph's jowls, shaking him gently.

'Are you certain?' he asked.

'I swear it,' the caliph responded. He stepped away from the insulting grip as Hulegu spoke again to one of the Mongol warriors.

'Tell General Kitbuqa to begin burning the city,' he said. The man ran back up the steps and al-Mustasim watched him go, his face twisting in panic.

'No! Very well, there is a store of gold hidden in the garden ponds. That is all. I give you my word.'

'It is too late for that now,' Hulegu said regretfully. 'I asked you to make an accurate tally of the tribute and you did not. You have brought this on yourself, O caliph, and upon your city.'

The caliph drew a dagger from the folds of his robe and tried to attack, but Hulegu merely stepped aside and let his guards intervene, knocking the weapon from the man's fleshy fingers. Hulegu picked it up, nodding to himself.

'I asked you to disarm and you did not,' he said. 'Take him to a small room and keep him prisoner while we work. I am tired of his wind and promises.'

It was no easy task to drag the caliph's bulk up the stairs, so Hulegu left his guards to it while he walked inside the vault to inspect what he had won. Kitbuqa knew what to do. He and Hulegu had set their plans weeks before. The only difficulty had been in securing Baghdad's treasures before they destroyed the city.

The winter was mild in that region and Kublai's tumans settled in around their new lands, secure in their gers. From records of Tsubodai's Russian campaigns, Kublai knew winter was the best time to launch an attack, but so far to the south the natural Mongol advantage in cold-weather fighting was almost nullified. Armies still moved through the cold seasons and he could not be assured of a respite from warfare. His enemies must have known the same discomfort. The Mongols had entered their lands and no one knew where they would strike next.

Kublai had expected to fight for every step across Sung territory, but after the first battle, it almost seemed as if he were being ignored. Kunming city had opened its gates to him without a struggle, then Qujing and Qianxinan. He wondered if a sense of shock and effrontery had paralysed the Sung emperor. It had been centuries since anyone had last launched a conquest of their lands, but the lessons of the Chin would surely have been hard to ignore. If Kublai had been in power, he would have armed his entire population for all-out war, forcing millions of men against the Mongol war machine until it was ground down to nothing. He still feared exactly that. His only comfort was that the Yunnan region was isolated by a vast range of hills and mountains from the rest of Sung territory. To reach a major Sung city, his maps revealed broken land for two hundred miles, with no detail. Kublai fretted at every passing week as he sent men and money to locate the silver mines of the Sung emperor. It took far longer than he had hoped. Many of his scouts came in empty-handed, or with false leads that wasted time and energy. As two months passed without success, he was forced to head east into the first hills, leaving small groups of warriors in his pacified cities to ensure supplies continued to flow.

Ten tumans and his host of camp followers moved slowly across the land. Kublai had given Uriang-Khadai standing orders to buy food rather than take it, but the result was that his small treasury dwindled visibly. The orlok had insisted on a meeting to point out the idiocy in leaving Chin silver with peasant villages, but Kublai refused to discuss it and sent him back to the tumans without satisfaction. He knew he took too much pleasure in baiting the older man, but he would not explain himself to one who would never understand what he was trying to do. Mountain towns large and small were left intact behind the Mongol ranks and the coins had begun to flow month by month, so that the lowest unranked warrior could be heard to jingle when he trotted his mount. They carried the Chin coins on leather thongs around their necks or hanging from their belts like ornaments. The novelty of it had kept them quiet while they waited to see what such coins would buy them in the Sung cities. Only Uriang-Khadai refused his monthly payment, saying that Kublai would not make a merchant of him, not while he kept his rank. Under the orlok's angry stare, Kublai had been tempted to strip that rank from him, but he had resisted, knowing it would have been from spite. Uriang-Khadai was a competent commander and Kublai needed all the ones he had.

The going was slow, though there were paths through the

hills. There were no great mountains, just a distant horizon of peaks and troughs made green with heavy rain. The drizzle lasted for days at a time, turning the clay into sticky clods that slowed them all further and bogged down the carts. They trudged and rode onwards, the women and children growing thin as the herds were butchered to keep the men strong. The grazing was the only good thing about the trek and Kublai spent his evenings in a leaking ger with Chabi and Zhenjin, listening to Yao Shu reading aloud from the poetry of Omar Khayyam. At every town, Kublai asked for news of soldiers or mines. Such remote places rarely had anyone who had been to the cities and he was relieved when his scouts called him to the farm of a retired Sung soldier named Ong Chiang. Faced with armed warriors, Ong Chiang had discovered he knew a great deal. The ex-soldier told Kublai of the city of Guiyang, which was barely forty miles from an imperial barracks and a silver mine. It was not a coincidence that the two things went together, he said. A thousand soldiers lived and worked in a town which existed only to support the local mines. Ong Chiang had been stationed there for part of his career and he spoke with relish of the harsh discipline, showing them a hand with just two fingers and thumb left on it to make his point. To be born in the towns around Guiyang was to die in the mines, he said. It was a poor place to live, but it produced great wealth. It was just possible that in all his life Ong Chiang had never had such an attentive audience. He settled back in his small home, while Kublai listened to every word.

'You saw the soil being brought to the surface, then heated?'

'In huge furnaces,' Ong Chiang replied, lighting his pipe as he spoke and sucking appreciatively at the long stem. 'Furnaces that roar all day so that the workers go deaf after just a few years. I never wanted to get close to those things, but I was just there to guard them.'

'And you said they dig up lead . . .'

'Lead ore, mixed with the silver. They're found together, though I don't know why. The silver is a pure metal and the lead can be melted off. I saw them pouring ingots of silver at the site and we had to work to make sure the miners didn't steal even a few shavings of it.'

He launched into an anecdote about a man trying to swallow sharp pieces of silver that made Kublai feel ill. He suspected the Sung veteran knew little more than he did himself about the actual process, but in his rambling speech, he gave away many useful details. The mine at Guiyang was clearly a massive undertaking, a town that existed only for the purpose of digging ore. Kublai had been imagining something on a smaller scale, but Ong Chiang talked of thousands of workers, hammering and shovelling day and night to feed the emperor's coffers. He boasted of at least seven other mines in Sung lands, which Kublai had to dismiss as fantasy. His own people worked two rich seams, but Kublai had never visited the sites. To think of eight of them being hollowed out, their ores made into precious coins, was a vision of wealth and power he could hardly take in.

At last the man ran out of wind and settled into silence, made all the more comfortable by a flask of airag Kublai had produced from his deel robe. He rose and Ong Chiang smiled toothlessly at him.

'You have silver enough to pay a guide?' he said. Kublai nodded and the man rose with him, reaching out to jerk his arm up and down. 'I'll do it then. You won't find the mine without a guide.'

'What about your farm, your family?' Kublai said.

'The land is shit here and they know it. Nothing but chalk and stones. A man has to earn money and I can smell it on you.'

Ong Chiang's gaze travelled up and down Kublai's clean deel robe and his mutilated hand twitched as if he wanted to touch the finely woven cloth. Kublai was amused despite himself. He became aware of the farmer's wife glowering at him from the doorway. Kublai met her eyes for a moment and she looked down immediately, terrified of the armed men around her home.

'How will I know if I can trust you?' Kublai said.

'I am Ong Chiang the farmer now, but I was once Ong Chiang the officer in charge of eight men, before I lost my fingers to some fool with a spade. They told me to hand back my armour and my sword and they gave me my pay, then that was it. Twenty years and I was sent away with nothing. Don't think I'll cause you any trouble. I can't hold a sword, but I will show you the way. I'd like to see their faces when they see your men riding in.' Ong began to cackle and wheeze and he sucked on his pipe again, like a teat that gave him comfort. His wheezing became gurgles and finally settled, leaving him red-faced.

'I pay my men four silver pieces a month,' Kublai said. 'You will earn an extra payment when you find me a silver mine.'

Ong Chiang's face lit up. 'Four! For that much, I'll walk night and day, anywhere you want.'

Kublai hoped Yao Shu hadn't overdone his estimates of a soldier's pay. It was one area where the Buddhist monk lacked experience. Kublai was losing half a million silver coins each month from his campaign funds and though Mongke had been more than generous, he had at best six months before the problem of looting was back. Kublai was still struggling to understand the impact of such a simple decision, but he had a vision of his men descending on a peaceful city with too much wealth in their pouches. Prices would soar. They would drink it dry, argue over the local whores and then fight until they were unconscious.

He winced at the thought. Far to the north, Xanadu was being built by Chin workers who assumed he would return with their back pay. The new capital he imagined would be left as ruins if he didn't find a new source of silver.

'Very well. From this day, you are Ong Chiang the guide. Do I need to warn you what will happen if you lead us wrong?'

'I don't think you do,' the man said, showing his withered gums again.

CHAPTER TWENTY-ONE

The caliph wept as the House of Wisdom burned. The science and philosophy of ages had been tinder dry and the flames spread with a whoosh, quickly becoming an inferno and spreading to the close-packed buildings around it. His Mongol guards had left him alone, keen to take part in the looting of the ancient city. Al-Mustasim had waited for a time, then walked out of his palace, stepping over bodies and past the pools in the courtyards, where bars of gold had been hidden in the mud. The pools were brown and the fish all dead, choked in filth or speared for fun as the bars were dragged out.

He walked on, through streets that were marked with spattered blood trails. More than once, some Mongol warrior came charging out of a side street with a red sword. They recognised his bulk and ignored him, lending an odd feeling of nightmare to his progress. No one would touch the caliph, on Hulegu's orders. The rest of the city did not enjoy the same protection and he began to weep as he saw the dead and smelled the smoke on the breeze. The House of Wisdom was only one of many fires, though he lingered there for a time, his eyes red in the bitter smoke.

Perhaps a million people lived in Baghdad at the time Hulegu's tumans had surrounded it. There were whole districts devoted to perfumes, others to alchemy and artisans of a thousand different kinds. One area had been built around dye baths large enough for men to stand in and plunge their feet into the bright coloured liquids. Flames had burnt out there and Al-Mustasim stood for a time looking over hundreds of the stone bowls. Some of them contained drowned men and women, their faces stained by the dyes, their eyes still open. The caliph walked on, his mind numb. He tried to accept the will of Allah; he knew that men with free will could cause great evil, but the reality of it, the sheer scale, rendered him mute and blank, like a staggering beggar in his own streets. The dead were everywhere, the stench of blood and fire mingling across the city. Still there was screaming: it was not over. He could not imagine the mind of a man like Hulegu, who could order the slaughter of a city with no feeling of shame. Al-Mustasim knew by then that Hulegu had intended the destruction from the beginning, that all their negotiations had been just a game to him. It was an evil so colossal that the caliph could not take it in. He stumbled for miles across the city, losing his sandals as he climbed a pile of bodies and going on barefoot. As the day wore on, he saw so many scenes of pain and torture that he thought he was in hell. His feet were bloody and torn from sharp stones, but he could not feel the pain. The words of the Koran came to him then: 'Garments of fire have been prepared for the unbelievers. Scalding water shall be poured on their heads, melting their skins and that which is in their bellies. They shall be lashed with rods of iron.' The Mongols were neither Christian, Hindu nor Jew, but they too would suffer in time, as the people of his city had suffered. It was his only comfort.

On a bridge of white marble, al-Mustasim looked down on the river that ran through the city. He rested his arms on the stone and saw hundreds of bodies tumbling past, locked together in the red water, their mouths open like fish as they were washed away. Their suffering was at an end, but his anguish only intensified until he thought his heart would burst in his chest.

He was still there as the sun set, locked in his despair, so that General Kitbuqa had to shake him to bring him back to understanding. Al-Mustasim stared blearily into the eyes of the Mongol officer. He could not understand his words, but the gestures were clear as Kitbuqa tugged him into movement. They headed back to the palace, where lamps had been lit. Al-Mustasim wished only for death to take him. He dared not think of the women of his harem, or his children. The smell of blood grew stronger in the air and, without warning, he bent over and vomited a flood of water. He was prodded on, his feet leaving bloody prints on the marble floor.

Hulegu was in a main chamber, drinking from a gold cup. Some of the caliph's slaves were attending him, their faces growing pale as they recognised the man who had been their master.

'I told you to stay in the palace . . . and you did not,' Hulegu said, shaking his head. 'I will enter your harem tonight. I am told the door to that part of the palace is known as the gate of pleasure.'

Al-Mustasim looked up dully. His wives and children still lived and hope kindled in him.

'Please,' he said softly. 'Please let them live.'

'How many women are there?' Hulegu said with interest. His men had begun the labour of emptying the vaulted basement, stacking artwork like firewood alongside treasures of the ages. Beyond that, the main palace had been left untouched.

'Seven hundred women, many of them mothers, or with child,' al-Mustasim replied.

Hulegu thought for a time.

'You may keep a hundred of the women. The rest will be

given to my officers. They have worked hard and they deserve a reward.'

The men around Hulegu looked pleased and their master stood up, throwing the cup of wine to the ground so that it clattered noisily.

Hulegu led the way through corridors and halls, coming finally to the locked door that hid the gardens of the harem from view. He looked expectantly at al-Mustasim but the caliph no longer had the key, or knew where it was. Hulegu gestured to the door and in moments his men had kicked it in.

'Just a hundred, caliph. It is too generous, but I am in a fine mood tonight.'

Al-Mustasim hardened his soul, blinking back the tears that threatened. The women screamed when they saw who had come into the private gardens, but the caliph calmed them. They stood with their heads bowed and Hulegu inspected their lines like cattle, enjoying himself. He allowed al-Mustasim to pick a hundred of the weeping women, then sent the others out to his waiting men, who greeted them with cries of excitement. The children remained behind, clinging to women they knew, or wailing as their mothers were taken away.

Hulegu nodded to al-Mustasim.

'You have made some fine choices. I will take this hundred as my own. I do not need the children.'

He spoke in his guttural language to the guards and they began to pull the women out of the gardens one by one, knocking the children down if they tried to hang on. Al-Mustasim cringed at this final betrayal, though part of him had expected it. He called out words from the Koran to his wives and children. He could not look at them, but he promised them all a place in heaven, with the prophet and the love of Allah for all eternity.

Hulegu waited until he was finished.

'There is nothing more here. Take the fat man out and hang him.'

'And the children, lord?' one of his men asked.

Hulegu looked at the caliph.

'I asked you to surrender and you did not,' he said. 'Perhaps I would have been merciful then. Kill the children first, then hang him. I have squeezed Baghdad dry. There is nothing more worth having.'

Kublai lay on his stomach and cursed softly to himself. He had sent out his scouts looking for silver, paying men for information for hundreds of miles, without considering that the Sung emperor would eventually hear of his interest and respond. It was an error and, though he could curse his own naivety, he could not wish away the army encamped around the Guiyang mines. His own tumans were still twenty miles or more to the west and he had come forward with just Ong Chiang, the newly fledged guide, and two scouts to see the details. Kublai grimaced as he kept low and stared across the hills at the mass of men and machines. This was no guard regiment sent to protect the silver, but a massive force, complete with cannon and pike, lancers and crossbowmen by the tens of thousand. They could not be surprised or ambushed and yet he still needed the silver that lay at the heart of them all. Even then, Kublai doubted the emperor had left much of value beyond the raw ore. He considered abandoning the attack, and only the thought that Mongke would eventually hear he had retreated kept him planning.

The mine was in a shallow valley, which would lend speed to his charging warriors. His cannon teams would be firing down, if they could get their weapons to the edge, whereas the Sung soldiers would have to fire upwards into them. No advantage was too small to consider against so many. Kublai stared with a surveyor's intensity, taking in every feature of the terrain that he might use. The cannon would be crucial, he realised. He had never yet seen them used in a fixed battle, at least in daylight, but the Sung commanders would surely have more experience of that than he had. He could not assume the officers had won their commissions with connections to the imperial court, or in examinations, no matter what he had heard. He thought back over everything he had read of Sung warfare, how even more than the Chin, battles took place in a ritualistic fashion, with strike and counter-strike. They rarely fought to annihilation, only until one side was satisfied. That too would be an advantage. His tumans fought to destroy, to shatter and break the will of an enemy until he was dust under their feet.

Kublai looked across the thick grass at Ong Chiang, who had been staring down at the Sung lines with just as much intensity. When the farmer felt Kublai's gaze on him, he looked up and shrugged.

'There was talk of an extra payment when I found the mine, my lord,' he said. As he spoke, he began to search his pockets for his pipe and Kublai reached across and stopped his hand. It would not do to have a thin trail of smoke rising from their position.

'I have a battle to plan, Ong the suddenly wealthy,' Kublai whispered to him. 'See me after that and I'll give you a token to take to my quartermaster.'

Ong Chiang looked once again at the massive camp around the mining town and chewed his lips a little, wishing for his pipe.

'I think I would prefer it before the battle, my lord. In case it does not go so well for you.' He saw Kublai's expression and carried on quickly. 'I'm sure it will go well, but if you could let me take my payment now, I'll start back to my family.'

Kublai raised his eyes for a moment. With Ong Chiang and

the scouts, he crept back on his stomach until he was sure none of the Sung scouts could see them. He had not spotted any watchers during his careful approach and he did not know if that was because they had not been placed, or because they were simply much better than he was at remaining unseen. He wore no signs of rank, knowing that if they recognised him for who he was, they would hunt him down. Just riding the twenty miles to the site had been a risk, but he had needed to see.

When he returned to the tumans, Kublai paid Ong Chiang well, giving him a fat pouch of silver that had the man beaming. The farmer used two of the coins to buy the old mare he had been lent and was soon on his way, without looking back. Kublai smiled as he watched him go. The silver was an investment that would repay itself many times over, if he could win the mine.

The morning was fine and clear as he gathered his generals. Uriang-Khadai had lost some of his usual sourness at the prospect of a battle. Bayar too was pleased, hanging on every word Kublai uttered as he described the scene in incredible detail.

'So many soldiers must be fed,' Kublai said, 'and the farms in the area cannot possibly support such an army. Bayar, send a minghaan out in a wide line around the site. Find their supply line, or wherever they cache their food. Destroy it all. They will not fight so well on an empty stomach.'

Bayar nodded, but stayed where he was.

'They outnumber us,' Kublai went on, 'but if they have been told to protect the mine, they will fight defensively, rather than coming out when they are attacked. That is to our advantage. Uriang-Khadai, you will place our cannon in tight ranks, to pour fire into them. Begin with a ranging shot from the ridge, then move the cannon quickly to where we can reach their position. If anyone comes against our cannon, they must be destroyed. It will allow me to remove almost all the men behind and use them to charge the flanks.'

Uriang-Khadai nodded grudgingly. 'How many horsemen do they have?' he asked.

'I saw at least ten thousand horses. I do not know how many were remounts. It could be five thousand cavalry. They must not be allowed to pin us from the sides, but we have enough good archers to keep them back.' Kublai took a deep breath, feeling his stomach tighten in anticipation and nervousness.

'Remember that they have not known war for generations, whereas our warriors have fought all their lives. That will make a difference. For now, your task is to get the tumans into strike range as quickly as possible, bringing the cannons up as fast as we have ever moved them before. The families will remain here with heavy carts and supplies. I need rapid movement, to appear against them before they know we are coming. I need that solid front if I am to hammer them on the wing.' He looked at his two most senior men and knew they were both different characters, but men on whom he could depend. 'I will give you new orders as we engage. Until then, pray it does not rain.'

As one, they looked up, but there were few clouds and those were high above, white wisps in a spring sky.

Mongke threw a sheaf of reports onto a pile almost as large as his chair and rubbed his eyes wearily. He had put on weight since becoming khan and he knew he was no longer as fit as he had once been. For years he had taken his body's massive strength for granted, but time stole away all things, changing men in such small ways that they hardly noticed until it was too late. He pulled in his stomach as he sat there, telling himself for the hundredth time that he would have to practise more with the sword and bow if he were not to lose all traces of his strength and vitality.

The problems of a vast khanate were nothing like those he had known as an officer. The Great Trek west with Tsubodai had been a simpler life, with more basic obstacles to overcome. He could not have dreamed back then that he would be trying to settle a complicated dispute between the Taoists and Buddhists, or that silver coins would become such an important part of his life. The yam lines kept him informed in a flood of information that almost overwhelmed him, despite the cadre of Mongol scribes who worked in the city. Mongke would deal with a hundred small problems each morning and read as many reports, making decisions that would affect the lives of men he would never see or know. In the sheaf he had thrown down was a request from Arik-Boke for funds, a few million silver coins that had to be dug out and smelted from the mines. Mongke might envy his youngest brother the simple life in the homeland, but the truth he had discovered about himself was that he loved the work. It was satisfying to solve problems for other men, to be the one they came to with their questions and catastrophes. As far away as Syria and Korea, they looked to Karakorum, as Ogedai Khan had once hoped they would. Bankers could cash drafts for silver in different countries because of the peace Mongke had fostered. If there were bandits or thieves, he had a wide net to catch them, thousands of families devoted to running the khan's lands, in his name, with his authority backing them. He patted his stomach ruefully. As with all things, peace had its price.

His knees cracked as he stood up. He groaned softly as his chief adviser, Urigh, came trotting in with more papers.

'It is almost noon. I will see those when I have eaten,' Mongke said. He would enjoy an hour with his children when they had run home from their school in the city. They would speak Mandarin and Persian as well as their own language. He would see his sons as khans when they were grown, just as his mother had worked to raise her eldest over the rest.

Urigh put down most of the papers he carried, a bundle of scrolls bound in twine. He held just one and Mongke sighed, knowing the man too well.

'All right, tell me, but be quick.'

'It is a report from your brother Kublai's domain in Chin lands,' Urigh said. 'The costs of his new city have become immense. I have the figures here.' He handed over the scroll and Mongke sat down again to read it, frowning to himself.

'When he runs out of money, he will have to stop,' he said with a shrug.

Urigh looked uncomfortable discussing the brother of the khan. Mongke's feelings for Hulegu, Arik-Boke and Kublai were complex and no man wanted to come between them, no matter how Mongke complained.

'You can see he has spent almost all you gave him for the campaign, my lord. I have reports that he has been seeking out silver mines on Sung land. Could he have found one and not declared it to you?'

'I would know,' Mongke said. 'I have men close to him who report every movement. The last message was a week ago on the yam lines and he had not found a mine yet. It cannot be that. What about these new farms of his? He leased thousands of plots two years ago. They will have been ploughed and planted twice by now, more if they are growing rice in the flood plains. In Chin markets, that will have brought in enough silver to keep building his palaces.' Mongke frowned as he considered his own words, checking through the details of the accounting in Xanadu. Huge stocks of marble had been ordered, enough to build a palace to equal his own in Karakorum. He felt a seed of distrust grow in him.

'I have not interfered with his campaign, or Hulegu's.'

'Hulegu has sent back vast revenues, my lord. Baghdad alone has brought in gold and silver to keep Karakorum for a century.'

'And how much have we had from Kublai?' Mongke asked.

Urigh bit his lip. 'Nothing so far, my lord. I assumed it was with your permission that he put the funds into his new city.'

'I did not forbid it,' Mongke conceded. 'But the Sung lands are wealthy. Perhaps he has forgotten he acts for the khan.'

'I am sure that is not true, my lord,' Urigh said, trying to walk a careful line. He could not criticise the khan's brother, but the lack of proper accounting from Sung lands had troubled him for months.

'Perhaps I should see this Xanadu myself, Urigh. I have grown fat in peace and it may be my brothers have grown too sure of themselves without feeling my eye on them. Kublai has done enough, I think.' He fell silent and thought for a time. 'No, that is unfair. He has done well with what I gave him, better than I dared to hope. By now, he will have discovered he needs me to finish the Sung. He may even have learned a little humility, a little of what it takes to lead tumans into battle. I have been patient, Urigh, but perhaps it is time for the khan to take the field.' He patted his belly with a rueful smile. 'Send your men to me when they come back with their report. It will do me good to ride again.'

CHAPTER TWENTY-TWO

Kublai watched as the Chin regiments ran from their tents, forming up into well-disciplined lines. He could still hardly believe how close his tumans had got to the mine before the alarm horns sounded. At less than two miles, a distant blare of brass had begun to wail, muffled by the fall of the land. The Sung officer should have had more scouts further out, regularly relieved by men from the main camp. Kublai prayed silently for it to be the first of many mistakes they would make.

Kublai took strength from the long line of horsemen on either side of him as they trotted forward. Bayar's minghaan had cut the Sung supply lines four days before, then waited to ambush whoever they sent. Not a single man of a hundred had made it back to the Sung camp. Kublai hoped they were getting hungry. He needed every edge he could find.

The bowl of land that led down to the mine ended on a flat field some miles across. Kublai tried to put himself in the place of the Sung general. The site was not a good one for a defensive battle. No leader would choose a spot where he could not command the closest heights. Yet it was exactly the sort of battle that came when an emperor thousands of miles away ordered one of his senior men to hold a position, no matter who came against it or how strong they were. There would be no retreat, Kublai was certain. He raised his fist and the Mongol ranks halted, curving slightly as they met the line of the valley ridge. The sun was high above them and the day was warm. He could see a long way, beyond the mine itself to the shantytown that fed it with workers each morning. The air itself shimmered over part of the sprawling site, revealing the location of the smelting furnaces. Kublai took heart from the fact that they were still working. Perhaps there would be silver in the warehouses after all. He could see a stream of workers leaving the site and as he waited for his cannons to come up, the distant shimmering ceased. The mine shut down and the air was very still.

Behind him, the cannon teams whipped horses dragging the heavy cannon, straining for the last burst of speed up the ridge. Kublai and Bayar had experimented with oxen and horses, even camels, trying to find the best combination of speed and stamina. Oxen were painfully slow, so he had left them in camp with the families and used teams of four horses. Once the guns were rolling, they could triple the speed to the front, though the cost in horses was enormous. Hundreds of them would be lame or have had their wind broken pulling the guns, as well as the carts full of shot and gunpowder.

Kublai readied his orders in his head. The Sung had formed quickly on the valley plain and he saw the dark shapes of their own cannons dragged to the front, ready with braziers to light the black powder. To charge that camp would be to ride through a hail of shot, and Kublai felt his gut tighten in fear at the thought. He scowled as he saw that the Sung regiments were holding their ground, certain that he had to come to them.

Kublai sent single warriors out ahead of the tumans. Thousands of eyes on both sides watched them walk their mounts down the gentle slope. The Mongol warriors waited to see if they found hidden trenches or spikes in the grass, while the Sung regiments tensed at what could have been the first outriders of a suicidal charge. The braziers by the Sung cannon smoked furiously as their tenders fed in fresh coal, keeping them hot. Kublai could feel his heart thumping as he waited for one of the riders to fall. His emotions were mixed when they reached the bottom safely and rode on to the edge of arrow range. They were young men and he was not surprised when they stopped to jeer at the enemy. It was more worrying that the Sung commander had not set traps. The man wanted them to ride in fast and hard, where he could destroy them. It was either justified confidence or complete foolishness and Kublai sweated without knowing which. His riders returned to the ranks amidst shouts and laughter from those that knew them. The tension had been unbearable, but with a glance Kublai saw four of his own cannon were ready, their braziers lit and smoking, well clear of the piles of powder bags and shot balls. The rest were still hitched to the teams that dragged them, poised to move closer once they saw the range. He told himself the Sung could not have expected so many of the heavy weapons.

He still hoped to surprise them. The Persian chemists working in Karakorum had produced a finer powder, with more saltpetre than the Chin mixture. Kublai understood little of the science, but smaller grains burned faster and threw the ball with more force. The concept was clear enough to anyone who had ever fried a slab of meat, or seen it cut into small pieces for cooking. He watched anxiously as the four cannon were hammered loose from their mountings and fresh wooden blocks put in to raise the black muzzles to the maximum elevation. The blocks often shattered on firing and the teams drew them from sacks of spares, each one hand-cut from birch. Powder bags were shoved down the iron tubes and on each team a powerfully built man lifted a stone ball, straddling it as if he were giving birth. With a massive heave, the balls were raised to the lip and another of the team made sure it did not fall back. For an instant, Kublai had almost ordered a second powder bag, but he dared not risk the guns exploding as they fired. He would need every one.

Three-quarters of a mile below and across the valley floor, the Sung regiments waited in perfect, shining ranks. They could see what was happening on the ridge, but they stood like statues, their flags and banners flapping. Kublai heard his gun teams shout instructions, using those same flags to judge the wind. They began to chant, with an emphasis on the fourth beat. Almost as one, the iron weapons were heaved around, lifted by main force and groaning men. The shots would fire straight until the wind changed.

Kublai raised his hand and four tapers were lit and shielded from the breeze as the officers readied themselves to touch the reed filled with the same black powder, the spark that pierced the bag within and slammed the balls out into the air.

Kublai dropped his arm, almost flinching in anticipation. The sound that followed had no comparisons. Even thunder seemed less terrible. Smoke and flame spurted from each of the iron holes and blurs vanished upwards. Kublai could see the curving lines and his heart raced faster as he saw they would surely reach the Sung. His mouth fell open as the cannonballs soared over the regiments, striking too far back for their damage to be seen.

There was a moment of stillness, then every man who could see suddenly roared and the rest of the cannon teams lashed their horses with fresh urgency, bringing them up. They could hit the enemy. Either the Sung had misjudged the benefit of the ridge, or the Mongol gunpowder was much better than their own.

Kublai shouted fresh orders, overcome with a sense of urgency to use his sudden advantage. He watched the painfully slow adjustment as the teams grabbed up heavy hammers and began to bang out the blocks while others lifted the iron barrels to make a space.

On the valley floor, horns wailed and conflicting orders were given in sudden confusion. Kublai could see that some of the Sung officers thought they merely had to pull back closer to the mine. Others who had seen the balls pass right overhead were shouting angrily and pointing up at the ridge. There was no safe spot for them to stand. They would either have to attack or abandon the mine and move out of range, in which case Kublai decided he would take the tumans in quickly and capture their guns. He tensed as his gun teams readied all the cannon for a massive volley.

When it came, the balls of polished stone skipped and bounced their way through the Sung ranks. Horses and men crumpled as if a point of hot iron had been laid onto them. Two of the Sung cannon were struck, flipping over and crushing men underneath. Kublai exulted and his teams worked on, pouring with sweat.

The shots came faster, rippling along the line as they sought to outdo each other. Kublai looked round in shock when one of the iron weapons burst its barrel, killing the men at the muzzle. Another man was killed when his companion failed to cool the barrel quickly enough with the long rammer and sponge. The powder bag went up while he was still pushing it down, tearing it open in his enthusiasm. The rush of flame could only find a path past him and he burned in an instant. The mad pace slackened slightly after that, the lesson not lost on the other teams.

Kublai was too far away to see Bayar's expression, though he could imagine it. He had weapons designed to pulverise a city wall and the chance to use them against standing enemy ranks. The warriors around him were still stunned by the damage the cannons could inflict and Kublai wondered if they would be as fast to ride against the Sung weapons, now that they had seen in daylight what cannons could do.

The Sung lines re-formed over their dead, but Kublai did not think they would stand for long in the face of such murderous fire. He did not envy the Sung commander, whoever he was. He waited for the Sung to pull back, but they stood their ground while red claws sank into their ranks. Kublai glanced at the pile of stone balls nearest to him and bit his lip as he saw it was down to barely a dozen. Sheer weight made it as difficult to move the shot as the guns themselves and some of the carts had broken on the trip. He watched almost mesmerised as the pile dwindled until the final ball lay on its own. The barrel was sponged out for the last time. A billow of steam hissed and crackled over the men around them, part of a greater cloud that hid the entire ridge. It irritated Kublai by drifting across his sight, making him blind for long moments until the air cleared. He heard the cannon team fire the last shot, and by then most of the thundering guns had fallen silent, their teams standing proudly to attention. A few more shots sounded from slower teams and they were done at last, suddenly useless after the carnage and destruction.

Kublai felt the wrench to his emotions as his power to reach out and strike suddenly vanished. The air was thick with sulphur and steam and he had to wait while the breeze tore it into wisps and he could see again.

When they were revealed, the Sung regiments had taken a vicious battering. Thousands of men were clearing the dead and the officers rode up and down the lines, exhorting them, pointing up to the ridge and no doubt shouting that the worst was already over. Kublai swallowed drily. They had not broken. As he stared into the distance, he saw their own cannon teams swarm around their weapons. Time slowed down for him and he could hear every beat of his heart as he raised his hand. His men had to cross half a mile of land, one hundred and twenty to one hundred and eighty heartbeats. He would feel every one of them. He roared the orders and his tumans came over the ridge, kicking their mounts into a gallop. Kublai remained still as they flowed past him, knowing he had to be the calm centre, the eye above them that could read the battle and react to it, as the men below could not.

They poured down towards the Sung lines and a great shout of anger and challenge went up from those who had been forced to stand through the most terrifying moments of their lives. Kublai barked at his bannermen and they raised the flags that would send Uriang-Khadai and Bayar out wide against the flanks.

He could not trust his heartbeat to judge the time. When he held a finger to his neck, he could not find it at first, then felt such a rapid pulse that he gave up. The tumans hit full gallop on the short plain below the bowl and he could see the black needles of arrows fly before them, a different kind of terror for those Sung who still stood and dared them to come in close.

He winced as the first Sung cannons fired. Below, he could see the paths of the balls, chopping through the galloping ranks. The tumans covered the ground at reckless speed and as the Sung teams reloaded, his men sent arrow shafts whining in among them, so that the Sung gunners fell faster than they could be replaced. On the wings, Uriang-Khadai and Bayar had ridden in close, then halted at two hundred paces. From each ten thousand, arrows soared, punched out from bows too strong for other men to draw. There were no cannons on the wings, but most of Kublai's archers could hit an egg at fifty paces. They could hit a man at two hundred and the very best of them could pick the spot.

On the ridge, thousands of warriors still poured past him. An entire tuman was pressing on, desperate not to be left out of the battle. The resting gun teams shouted encouragement, knowing they could play no further part. Kublai found himself trembling as the last warrior rode over the ridge. He had a mere twenty men left as a personal guard and a drummer boy on a camel to give signals. Every officer below could see him and he was the only one able to judge the entire battlefield. He wrestled with the urge to give new orders, but at that point it would have been more likely to hamper his officers.

For a time, he raised himself up, standing on his saddle so that he could see exactly what was happening. His mind still ticked away with ideas and plans and he knew he would have to set forges to make iron balls for the cannons. It was difficult work to make a true sphere with no imperfections that might snag on a barrel and burst it or send the ball slicing off in the wrong direction. Iron had to be heated until it ran like water, and the temperatures were far beyond the portable forges he had. Lead balls were a possibility, but the soft metal was too prone to becoming misshapen. Kublai wondered for a moment if the smelter of the mine could be used. It was far easier to polish stone, but the labour took weeks and, as he had seen, he could lose the best part of a year's supplies in a morning.

He shook his head to clear it of the endless spinning thoughts. The Sung regiments were falling back on themselves, assaulted on all sides. More than half their number lay dead and anyone with an officer's armour was already cold, fat with arrows. As Kublai watched, his two wings used the last of their shafts. The rear ranks passed lances forward and they kicked into a gallop, lowering the long weapons to open holes into the enemy that they could follow. Those behind drew swords and even at a distance Kublai could hear their battle cry.

*　*　*

Hulegu was tired. In the months since he had burnt Baghdad, he had been busy with the administration of a vast area. He had entered Syria and taken the city of Aleppo, smashing a small army and slaughtering three tribes of Kurds who preyed on the local towns as bandits. The nobles of Damascus had come to him long before he attacked their city. The example of Baghdad had not been lost on them and they surrendered before they could even be threatened. He had a new governor there in his name, and beyond a few token executions, the city lay untouched.

He had been surprised to learn that Kitbuqa was a Christian, though it seemed not to blunt his righteous rage against the Moslem cities. Kitbuqa had begun holding Mass in captured mosques before burning them, a deliberate insult. Hulegu smiled at the memory. Together, they had captured more wealth than Tsubodai, Genghis or Ogedai had ever seen, sending much of it back to his brother in Karakorum. More was used to rebuild the cities he had taken under new governors. Hulegu shook his head in amusement at the thought, still surprised that he could earn gratitude in such a way. Memories were short, or perhaps it worked because he had killed everyone who might object. Baghdad was being rebuilt with a tiny part of the caliph's own treasury, made new under a Mongol governor. Merchant families came in daily to find homes in the city, where land and houses were suddenly cheap. Business was already growing and the first taxes were being collected, though the city was not a fraction yet of what it had been.

Hulegu rested for that night in a roadside inn, chewing his food slowly and wishing only that the Moslems would turn their considerable ingenuity to alcohol. He had tasted their coffee and found it bitter in comparison, not a drink for a man at all. His stocks of wine and airag had long gone and until they found a new supply, his army was running dry, making the men irritable and short-tempered. Hulegu knew he would have to import a few hundred families to make the fiery spirit he had enjoyed from childhood. With that small reservation, he was pleased with the lands he had won for himself. His sons would have a khanate and Mongke would honour him. Hulegu chuckled wearily to himself as he ate. It was strange how he still looked for Mongke's approval. At their age, a difference of just a few years should not have mattered, but somehow it did. He emptied a glass of some fruit drink, grimacing at the sickly sweetness, with an after-taste of metal.

'A little more, master?' the servant asked, holding up a jug.

Hulegu waved him away, trying not to think of how good airag would cut the sweetness and make his throat burn. He felt an ache begin in his abdomen and he massaged it with short, blunt fingers. He strained for a time, but there was no wind and the pain increased, sweat breaking out on his face.

'Bring me water,' he said, scowling.

The servant smiled. 'It is too late for that, master. Instead, I have brought you a greeting from Alamut and a peace you surely do not deserve.'

Hulegu gaped at him, then tried to rise. His legs felt weak and he staggered, but he had the strength to shout.

'Guards! To me!'

He slumped against the table. The door slammed open and two of his men entered with their swords drawn.

'Hold him,' Hulegu snarled.

A wave of weakness washed over him and he slid to his knees, pushing two of his fingers deep into his throat. As his men watched in horrified confusion, Hulegu vomited up the contents of his stomach in a great flood. He had eaten well and he heaved again and again, the bitter smell filling the room. Still the pain increased, but his head cleared a little. The servant had not resisted and merely stood between the warriors, watching closely with a worried frown.

Hulegu was a bull of a man, but his heart was pounding and his face poured with sweat as if he had run all day. It dripped off his nose onto the wooden floor as he sagged.

'Charcoal,' he growled. 'Grind up as much as you can find . . . in water. Take it from the fireplaces. Fetch my shaman . . .' He struggled through a wave of dizziness before he could speak again. 'If I pass out, force charcoal slurry into me, as much as you can.' He saw the guards hesitate, neither man willing to let go of the servant. Hulegu snapped, anger rising in him with the pain.

'Kill him and go,' he shouted, falling back.

He heard a choking sound as they cut the man's throat and then raced out of the room. Hulegu tried to vomit again, but his stomach was empty and every dry heave made lights flash before his eyes. His head felt enormous, fat with pounding blood. His heart was racing too fast, making him dizzy and weak. He was dimly aware of men clattering into the room and a wooden bowl being pressed to his lips, full of swirling blackness that he took in and immediately vomited in a gritty flood over his clothes. He forced himself to drink again, bowl after bowl until he felt his stomach would burst. His teeth grated against each other as he tried to clear his mouth and throat, gasping between gulps. There were a dozen men in the room by then, all working to reduce chips of charred wood to dust with any tool they could find. After a time, he fell into blackness, covered in his own bitter acids.

When he woke again, it was dark. His eyes were covered in something, so that his eyelids stuck together. He reached up and rubbed one of them, feeling his eyelashes tear away. The gesture was noticed and voices called that he was awake. Hulegu groaned, but the biting pain was gone from his stomach. His mouth felt raw and he could still feel the grit between his teeth from the charcoal that had saved him. The same filth had once saved Genghis and Hulegu gave silent thanks to the old man's spirit for lending him the knowledge he needed. The Assassin had been confident at first, he recalled. It would have been a close thing, a certain death without the charcoal to soak it up. If the man had kept silent, Hulegu would have died without knowing why.

He could not believe how weak he felt. General Kitbuqa was looming over him, but Hulegu could not rise. He felt himself lifted up and saw he was in another room of the roadhouse, propped up on thick blankets under his head and shoulders.

'You were lucky,' Kitbuqa said.

Hulegu grunted, unwilling even to think back to the appalling moments before unconsciousness. It had come so suddenly: from eating a good meal to fighting for his life with his killer watching him complacently. He thought his hands were still trembling and he bunched his massive fists in the blankets so that Kitbuqa would not see.

'The charcoal worked, then,' he muttered.

'You are too stubborn to die, I think,' Kitbuqa said. 'Your shaman tells me you will be shitting black for a few days, but, yes, you gave the right orders.'

'Have you been praying for me?'

Kitbuqa heard the mockery and ignored it.

'I have, of course. You are alive, are you not?'

Hulegu tried again to sit up straight, his thoughts suddenly sharpening.

'You must warn my brothers, especially Mongke. Send a dozen fast scouts along the yam lines.'

'They have already gone,' Kitbuqa said. 'It happened yesterday, my lord. You have slept since then.'

Hulegu slumped back. The effort of rising and thinking had

exhausted him, but he was alive and he had expected death. He shuddered as he lay there, flashing memories disturbing his peace. Had the leader in Alamut sent men to kill him even before he saw the fortress? It was possible. Yet it was more likely that he had men out already doing their work, men who would have returned to Alamut and found it in ruins. Hulegu could imagine them swearing vengeance against those who had broken their sect and killed its leaders. He closed his eyes, feeling sleep come swiftly. How many more could there be? Perhaps there was only one, now just another corpse in the road.

Kitbuqa looked down, pleased to see some colour return to his friend's face. He could only hope that the attack had been the last spasm of a dying clan. Even so, he knew it would be years before Hulegu went anywhere without a troop of guards around him. If even one Assassin still survived, there would always be danger. Kitbuqa only wished the poisoner had lived, so that he could have taken him out into the woods and questioned him with fire and iron.

CHAPTER TWENTY-THREE

Kublai had given strict orders that the workers in the mine town were not to be touched. For once, Uriang-Khadai had nothing to say on the subject. Someone had to continue to drag the ore out of the ground and none of Kublai's men understood the processes involved, even when they had seen the smelters and the sacks of strange powders in the buildings around it. A huge heap of black lead and slag metal was part of the sprawling site and the smell of bitter chemicals was always in the air, somehow drying the throat so that warriors coughed and spat as they searched it.

Bayar brought the news himself when they found the silver ready to be taken out. Kublai had seen from his face that it had been worthwhile and the reality astonished him. Refined metal filled a long stone building, behind an iron door that had to be broken in when no one could find the key. Inside, slender bars were set out on trestle tables, black with tarnish and ready to be loaded into carts and taken to the emperor's capital city.

Bayar had not even counted them and Kublai had the pleasure of making the first estimate. He counted two hundred and forty on a table, then multiplied it by eighty tables to reach a total that was dizzying. Each bar could be melted and pressed into at least five hundred small coins if he found the right

272

equipment. For a time, Kublai just stood in the silent room, then a smile appeared and Bayar laughed. The contents of the room came to almost ten million coins, enough to pay his army at their current rate for two years in the field. He frowned at the thought of sending a tithe back to Mongke in Karakorum, but it was long overdue. Bearing in mind Ong Chiang's response to his offer, Kublai wondered if there was a way of reducing the monthly pay without losing the trust of his men. He could hardly claim hardship after such a find. The news would already be winging its way around the camp.

'Find the most senior man in the town, whoever runs the mine,' he said to Bayar. 'I need to know if this is the product of a month or a year. I'll need to leave men to defend this place and keep it working.'

'The emperor will fight to get the mine back, if it's worth this much,' Bayar replied, still looking around him in a kind of awe.

'I hope so. I want him to send his best, general. At the rate I've been going, I'll be an old man by the time I reach his capital. Let them come and we will add rich new lands to the khanate.'

For a moment, he felt a pang that everything he won, everything he accomplished, would be for the glory of Mongke in Karakorum, but he stifled the thought. Mongke had been generous: with men, with his generals, with cannon and even with lands. Kublai realised he no longer missed the life of a scholar in Karakorum. Mongke had set out to change him and in one important way he had been successful. Kublai could not go back to the man he had been. He had even grown used to the scale armour. He found he looked forward to the battles to come, the tests and trials that he would face with the elite tumans of his nation. Kublai clapped Bayar on the shoulder.

'A mining town will have something to drink, I am certain. We had better move quickly before the men run it dry.'

'I put guards on the inns in town, first thing,' Bayar said.

Kublai grinned at him. 'Of course you did. Very well, show me.'

Both men turned at the sound of running footsteps. Kublai felt his mouth go dry at the sight of one of his scouts, sweat-stained and dusty. The man was close to collapse and he leaned on one of the tables, barely noticing the wealth it held as he gasped out his message.

'There is a Sung army, my lord, force-marching in this direction.' He went white for a moment as if he might vomit. Kublai gripped him by the shoulder.

'How far away?' he demanded.

The scout took gulping breaths, his body shuddering under Kublai's touch.

'Maybe fifty miles, maybe less. I did it in one long reach.'

'How many?'

'More than the tumans. I don't know for certain. I caught sight of them and then rode clear as fast as I could.' His eyes looked for approval, worried that he should have stayed longer.

'You did well,' Kublai assured him. 'Get yourself food and find a place on a cart to sleep. We won't be staying here.' He turned to Bayar, all the lightness gone from his manner. 'It won't stop now, general. I'd hoped for a little more time, but we have stuck a hand into the wasp nest and they will throw everything they have at us, every army they can raise and march.'

'We'll destroy them,' Bayar said.

Kublai nodded, but his eyes were shadowed. 'We have to win every battle. They only have to win one.'

'I've known worse situations,' Bayar said with a shrug.

Kublai blinked at him and then laughed, some of the tension going out of him.

'We have entered the heartland of the Sung, Bayar. You have *not* known worse situations.'

'Our people beat the Chin emperor,' Bayar replied, unabashed. 'City by city, army by army. Have faith in your men, my lord. We will not let you down.'

For a moment, Kublai was unable to speak. He had led the tumans at first as an intellectual exercise, enjoying the challenge of manoeuvres and tactics, of finding ways to confound his enemies. Bayar's words made him think it all through again. He would ask them to die for him, for his family. It was madness of a sort that they would follow him at all. Kublai found himself touched by what he saw in the faces of Bayar and the scout. He stopped himself from explaining, remembering almost too late that he had to keep a distance. He had not yet managed to codify the skill of leading men. It happened around him like a strange form of alchemy. It was more than rank or discipline, more than the structure of the army his family had built, more even than the legend of his grandfather. Some of them followed for those things, or just because they enjoyed the life of the tumans. Others, the best of them, would risk it all for Kublai because they knew him. They had measured him and gave their lives freely into his hands. For once, Kublai was unable to express what it meant to him and he chose refuge in gruff orders.

'Get the silver packed up, general. I will send scouts back to the camp to let them know they are on their own for a while longer. Have your men find a good place for us to stand and face these Sung. We will walk over them all.'

Bayar grinned, seeing the fire kindle in Kublai once again.

Chabi was outside her ger as Kublai came riding in. She put down the goatskins she had been cutting and sewing when she saw him. Zhenjin spotted his father at the same moment and darted to the wall of the ger, where he had placed a stool. As Kublai reined in and dismounted, his son climbed onto the felt roof and clung precariously over the door. All around them, women were gathering for news. They would not interrupt the khan's brother, but Chabi knew they would press in with questions the moment he left.

'Another army on the way,' Kublai said. He was panting slightly as she handed him a skin of airag and he took a long pull at it. 'I need to change clothes and it's time to break camp.'

'There's a threat to us?' Chabi asked, trying to remain calm. Kublai shook his head.

'Not so far, but if the tumans have to move fast, I don't want to leave you vulnerable. I must keep the families in range.'

Chabi looked up as a ger suddenly collapsed nearby, going from a home to spars and felt rolls in an instant. Kublai had not come in alone and she could hear shouts all over the camp as it went from peaceful stillness to rapid dismantling. Everything was designed to be moved quickly and she had servants for the task. She saw two of them coming with reins and harness over their shoulders for the ox-cart.

'Come down, Zhenjin,' Kublai called to his son. He knew the boy had been waiting to jump on him as he passed, but there was no time for games. Zhenjin scowled at him, but clambered down.

'You look worried,' Chabi said softly.

Kublai shrugged and smiled at her.

'We have better men, but the numbers, Chabi! If the Sung lords band together, they can put an army in the field that makes mine look like a raiding group.'

'They don't have anyone like you,' she said. He nodded.

'There is that,' he replied with a smile. 'I am an unusual man.'

Chabi could sense his distraction as Kublai's gaze flickered around the camp, taking in every detail.

'You don't have to worry about us,' she said.

Kublai turned slowly, trying to listen to his wife at the same time as solving some other problem and failing at both.

'Hmm?'

'We are not defenceless, Kublai. There are, what, three hundred thousand in the camp? It's a *city*, Kublai, and *everyone* is armed.' She drew a long blade from her belt. 'Including me. There must be enough maimed men to make a few tumans more. Many of them can still ride or use a bow.'

Kublai dragged his attention back to his wife. He saw she was trying to ease his mind and stifled his irritable impulse to describe the savage terror of an attack on a camp. It would do no good to make her afraid. Thousands of lives rested on his ability to protect them. Words and promises meant nothing in the face of such a burden. In the end, he just nodded and she seemed relieved.

'There's cold mutton and some spring onions in the pot. I'll cut you some slices. I have flatbread you can use to wrap it and eat it as you go.'

'And garlic,' he said.

'I'll get it, while you talk to your son. He's been waiting to jump on you for three days. A man can't ride past the ger without him scampering up the roof to be ready.'

Kublai sighed.

'Zhenjin! Come out here.'

The boy reappeared, still sulking. Kublai gestured at the ger.

'Go on then, I don't have long.'

Chabi snorted with laughter as Zhenjin's face lit up. The boy scrambled up the felt wall and once again waited like a spider above the door.

'I thought I could see my son,' Kublai said. 'Perhaps he is

inside.' He ducked to enter and Zhenjin leapt at him, his weight sending Kublai staggering backwards as Kublai roared in mock surprise. After a moment, he let the boy down to the ground.

'That's enough now. Help your mother and the servants. We're moving camp.'

'Can I come with you?' Zhenjin asked.

'Not this time. When you're older, I promise.'

'I'm older now.'

'That's true, but older still.'

Zhenjin began to complain in a high voice as Chabi came out with two wrapped packages of food. In the time since his arrival, hundreds of gers had come down and been loaded onto carts, as far as they could see in any direction.

'You will beat them all, Kublai. I know it. You will show your brother he was right to send you against the Sung.' She reached up and kissed her husband on the neck.

Kublai watched in strained silence as his tumans formed up ahead of him. The Sung would seek him out wherever he chose to stand, so he picked a grassy plain overlooked by a small hill and watched the gleaming regiments crawl across the land towards his men. Every one of his warriors knew he was there, the hand that held a sword over them. They would fight well in his sight.

The sun was shining, but his mood remained sour. He could not fathom the enemy tactics. His scouts reported more than one army heading towards his main camp, but they did not join together. Each one came in as if they were not part of a greater nation. He thanked the sky father for it, even as he cursed the numbers they could bring against him.

Kublai nodded to a boy seated on a camel near him, watching as the lad raised a long brass horn to his lips and blew a wailing note. It was answered by Bayar and Uriang-Khadai, taking four tumans each and advancing on the enemy squares. Twenty thousand men remained behind as the reserve, mounted and patient as they strained their eyes into the distance. Kublai took a stone from his pocket and rubbed his thumb along the curved lines. Yao Shu had said it would relax him.

His generals split up to ride along the flanks of the Sung force, finding the perfect distance just outside the range of crossbows. As Kublai watched, a sudden blur of shafts crossed the open air between the forces, like a cloud shadow moving across the open land.

The first arrows were followed by crushing volleys, loosed every six or eight heartbeats. The Sung foot soldiers compressed as their flanks jerked inwards. The pace slowed and they left a trail of screaming men and the dead as they marched. They could not answer the tumans and Kublai clenched his fists as he saw sword regiments try to push through the terrible thorns that came punching into their shields and armour. Uriang-Khadai drew back as they charged, but the arrow-storm didn't falter and the rush of swordsmen collapsed. The orlok's tumans came back into a straight firing line.

Kublai waited, his heart thumping. The last few shafts soared into the Chin and almost before the final one had landed, they were kicking their mounts into a gallop. Lances came down, but the Sung lowered their pikes and jammed the butts into the ground. The tumans hit like closing jaws, mirrored in Bayar's men on the other flank. Kublai shook his head at the thought of men and horses running onto the vicious metal weapons, but there seemed to be no hesitation. They were close enough by then for him to see bright red slashes as horses and men were impaled.

'Send in the reserve,' he said clearly.

The drummer boy was staring at the battle with his mouth

open and Kublai had to repeat the order before he raised his horn once again. Two more tumans began to trot and then canter towards the enemy. The lances worked well against the pikes bristling along the Sung front line, but Kublai had to struggle not to flinch in anticipation. He did not envy his men at that moment.

From the small hill, he saw the Sung regiments boxed in, still held on the flanks as their forward progress was halted by the new attack. He could not see as far as their rear, but he hoped some of them would be streaming away in terror.

He looked round at the sound of horses and his eyes widened. Some forty horsemen came galloping out of the woods at the bottom of the hill. He could see the heads of the animals lunging as they thundered up the gentle rise.

His guards were not idle. Before Kublai could give the order, all twenty of them were racing to meet the threat, galloping down the slope with bows bending as they went. Kublai jerked around in the saddle, looking for other threats. The battle went on ahead of him, barely eight hundred paces from his position, but he was suddenly alone with the drummer boy, who had gone as white as new felt. Kublai drew his sword, furious with himself for not scouting the copse. Humiliation burned in him as he thought of his confidence that morning, picking the best spot to secure a good view. Some Sung officer had guessed where he would stand and hidden men to wait for the right moment. Kublai flushed to have been out-thought in such a way. He saw the first arrows soar, many of them caught on shields by the Sung horsemen. Even so, three of the horses fell in a spasm of kicking hooves, whinnying in pain.

The Mongol guards heaved back again, sending more of the Sung crashing down. They had left it late and barely had time to throw down the bows and draw swords before they were together, their speed combining so that men and animals crunched and fell stunned or dead. Kublai could hear high screams and fresh sweat broke out on him. He glanced at the battle still going on, but there was no signal to call reinforcements to his own position.

Barely a hundred paces along the slope, his guards were fighting like maniacs to stop the enemy getting closer. Kublai swallowed, feeling a heaviness in his limbs. It was fear, he realised. The Sung commander would have sent the best he had for such a task. They did not expect to live through it, but they would reach him.

His guards were swordsmen and archers from boyhood and they did not fall easily. Kublai stared as five of the enemy broke around his men and kicked their mounts on. Their swords were bloody and they yelled at the sight of him on his horse, with just one camel boy.

One of the guards threw his sword with vicious strength. It plunged into a Sung back, making the man cry out in agony. He fell with his arms tight in the reins, bringing the mount down with him. Kublai saw the guard cut down, suddenly defenceless. He had given his life by the act, but it would not be enough. Four Sung horsemen reached the crest and accelerated, holding their blades ready for the strike that would take his head. Kublai watched them, terror making him numb. He could not run. Some part of him knew his best chance of survival was to gallop away from them, but he would never recover from it. Cowardice was the least forgivable sin and if he ran he knew he would never command tumans again.

Some of his guards were still struggling with the enemy below, but two of them had seen the threat to him and cut their way free. Kublai saw them surging up the hill after the four enemy soldiers. He could feel every heartbeat as his mind worked clearly, assessing the chances. He shook his head, seeing his own death in the men who were coming for him. He raised his sword and the fear suddenly vanished, leaving him almost dizzy. He breathed again, aware only then that he had been holding it. It was almost a moment of joy to have the crippling terror leave him. He could move and the sound of the battle came back to him as his senses woke.

The four horsemen bore down on him and the drummer boy suddenly moved, yelling and digging in his heels. The camel lurched forward with a groaning bray of sound, directly into the path of the enemy. With a thump, the man in the lead struck the shaggy side of the animal and went flying over the boy. His horse smashed the camel to its knees and it bellowed, stretching its neck as it fell.

The men on Kublai's left yanked their reins savagely, cursing as they missed the chance to strike. Kublai faced only one and his arm moved without thought to meet the blade he saw as a grey blur coming at his face. There was a clang as the man galloped past and Kublai felt the shock of it ripple up into his shoulder. Whoever the man was, he kept control of his snorting mount, reining in fast and turning to hack down in a wild blow. Kublai met it calmly. He was strong and his senses were all burning, giving him speed. It was not a conscious decision to counter, but his body moved from thousands of hours of training. As soon as the blades touched, he knew instinctively to slide the blade into a straight lunge. The Sung soldier jerked as the tip of Kublai's blade sank into his throat and snagged on the cartilage. Blood sprayed and Kublai blinked through the sting.

The camel lurched to its feet with an unearthly noise, kicking out in panic and making Kublai's horse skitter sideways. Another of the riders came in as the first slumped and slid away. Kublai felt his confidence swell as he turned a lunge to the side and reached out as Yao Shu had once taught him, half-opening his sword hand to grab the man's sleeve and yank him off balance.

His horse moved at the wrong moment then, walking backwards as Kublai pulled. Instead of landing a punch on the exposed chin as the soldier's head came forward, Kublai could only hang on and pull the man free of his saddle. He saw the man's foot caught in a stirrup and as Kublai let go, the leg twisted and snapped. The soldier screamed and flailed as he hung helplessly with his head close to the ground, every movement wrenching the splintered bone.

Kublai grunted in pain as something striped his arm and he turned to see the one who had struck the camel's shaggy side raising his sword for another blow. The man's face was a bloody mess from hitting the ground and he staggered as he drew back. Kublai took his feet from the stirrups and kicked out, hitting the man in the jaw. As he moved, he felt a thump across his chest armour as someone strained to reach him. Kublai reeled in the saddle, swinging his sword desperately. He had a glimpse of his attacker snatched away as someone on the ground dragged him down and Kublai stared as one of his guards smashed savagely with his boots, over and over until the man's ribs gave way.

Panting as if he had run for miles, Kublai met the eyes of the guard. The man nodded to him, not as a warrior to his officer, but as two men who had just survived a fight. Kublai blew air out slowly, looking around him. The Sung were all dead, but just four of his guards were still on their feet. Three of them stalked among the bodies down the hill, bringing their swords down in sharp blows at the slightest movement of wounded men. They were still raging and Kublai was alone with the last one standing, the man who had saved him.

The camel bellowed again in pain and Kublai saw its leg was broken, hanging as if only stretching skin kept it attached. His mind cleared and he looked around for the drummer boy who had thrown himself at the attackers. Kublai closed his eyes for a moment as he saw a sprawled figure on the ground. He dismounted, growling as his bruises made themselves known. The cut on his arm would have to be stitched. He could feel something dripping from his fingers and he raised his hand in surprise to look. There should have been more pain to produce so much bright red blood.

The boy had been knocked senseless, a large lump visible on his forehead. Kublai opened one of his eyes with a rough thumb and saw it twitch at the light. He was about to speak when he froze and remembered the battle he was meant to be commanding. His legs and back protested as he stood again. He did not try to mount, instead shading his eyes as he stared out.

The Sung had broken. Thousands of them stood in dejected silence, holding their hands up to show they had laid down their weapons. Many of them had already been bound and knelt with their head down in exhaustion. In the distance, a few were racing away from the bloody field, hunted down in twos or threes by Mongol warriors. Kublai let go of his held breath, desperately relieved. The boy groaned and Kublai went back to him as he stirred.

'What is your name?' Kublai asked. He should have known it, but his mind felt thick and slow.

'Beran, my lord,' the boy replied, his voice weak. One of his eyes was red as blood seeped into it, but he would live.

'Your bravery saved me. I will not forget it. When you are old enough, come to me and I will give you command of a hundred men.'

The boy blinked through his pain and a smile began to spread before he turned to one side and vomited onto the grass.

Kublai helped him up and watched as Beran staggered to the camel, the boy's swollen face distraught at what he saw.

'I will find you another mount, lad. That one is finished.'

The boy winced, though he understood. For a moment, Kublai met the gaze of the guard standing near him, the man's expression somehow out of place. He too had been battered in the fight and Kublai could hardly find words to express his thanks. He wanted to reward him, but at the same time, the man had done nothing more than his duty.

'Come and find me tonight, in my ger,' Kublai said. 'I think I have a sword you'll like. Something to remember our little fight on the hill.'

The guard grinned at him, revealing a bloody mouth and more than one missing tooth.

'Thank you, my lord. With your permission, I'd like to take my son back to his mother. She'll be worrying.'

Kublai nodded stiffly, his mouth slightly open in surprise as the guard tapped the staggering drummer boy on the shoulder and walked him away down the hill. He could not help wonder if the man would have fought with such berserk energy if he had not seen his son knocked down, but it did not matter. Alone, Kublai sagged against the flank of his horse. He had survived. His hands began to shake and he held them up, seeing the sword calluses that ridged each finger of his bloody right hand. They were no longer ink-stained. For the first time, Kublai felt truly comfortable in the armour that had certainly saved his life. He began to laugh as he leaned against his mount, reaching out to rub its muzzle and leaving a bright smear of blood that the animal licked away.

CHAPTER TWENTY-FOUR

Xuan, Son of Heaven and heir to the Chin empire, looked over the glassy surface of Hangzhou lake and listened to his children laughing as they splashed one another in the sun. He could see the ripples they made in the shallows spreading out over the deeper water, where a boatman fished for trout and stared too obviously in the direction of the Chin emperor's family. Xuan sighed to himself. It was unlikely so lowly a man was a spy for the Sung court, but you never knew. In his years of peaceful captivity, Xuan had learned to trust no one outside his wife and children. There was always someone watching and reporting his every word and action. He had thought once that he would grow used to it in time, but in fact the opposite was true. Whenever he felt eyes on him, it was like already tender skin being prodded again and again until he wanted to rail and shout at them. He had done so once and the unlucky scribe who had made him angry had been quietly removed from his post, only to be replaced by another before the day was out. There was no true privacy. Xuan had come into Sung lands to escape a Mongol army and they had never been quite sure what to do with him. He was a cousin of the Sung emperor by blood and had to be treated with respect. At the same time, the twin branches of the family had not been friends or allies for centuries, and more importantly, he had lost his lands, his wealth and power – a sure sign that bad luck stalked his house. The truth was that luck had played a very small part in the tragedies he had known. The armies of Genghis had taken Yenking, his capital city. Xuan had been betrayed by his own generals and forced to kneel to the khan. Even decades later, the memories stirred restlessly beneath the calm face he showed the world. Yenking had burned, but the wolves of Genghis had still hunted him, relentless and savage. He had spent his youth running from them, city by city, year by year. The sons and brothers of Genghis had torn his lands apart until the only safe place was across the Sung border. It had been the worst of all choices, but the only one left to him.

Xuan had expected to be assassinated at first. As he was moved around the Sung regions from noble to noble, he used to jump up from his bed at every creak in the night, convinced they had come to end it. He had been certain they would stage his death to look like a robbery and hang a few peasants afterwards for show. Yet the first decade had passed without him ever feeling a knife at his throat. The old Sung emperor had died and Xuan was not even sure the man's son still remembered his existence. He looked at the wrinkled skin on the backs of his hands and made fists, smoothing them. Had it truly been sixteen years since he had crossed the border with the last of his army? He was forty-nine years old and he could still remember the proud little boy he had been, kneeling to Genghis in front of his capital city. He still remembered the words the khan had said to him: 'All great men have enemies, emperor. Yours will hear that you stood with my sword at your neck and not all the armies and cities of the Chin could remove the blade.'

The memories seemed part of another age, another lifetime. Xuan's best years had vanished while he remained a captive, a slave, waiting to be remembered and quietly killed. He had seen his youth wither, blown away on silent winds.

Once again, he looked to the lake, seeing the young men and women bathing there. His sons and daughters, grown to adulthood. The figures were blurred, his eyes no longer sharp. Xuan sighed to himself, lost in melancholy that seemed to spin the days away from him, so that he was rarely *in* the world and sometimes only dimly aware of it. Their fates saddened him more than his own. After all, he had known freedom, at least for a time. His eldest son, Liao-Jin, was a bitter young man, petty in his moods and a trial to his brother and sisters. Xuan did not blame Liao-Jin for his weaknesses. He remembered how his own frustration had gnawed at him, before he managed at last to become numb to the passing seasons. It helped to read. He had found a fresh copied scroll of the *Meditations* of Marcus Aurelius in a library. Though he did not understand all of it, there was something about its message of accepting fate that fitted his situation.

Xuan still missed his wife, dead these ten years of some disease that ate her up from the inside. He had written many letters then, breaking his silence to beg the Sung court for doctors to save her. No one had come and each time he had been allowed to visit, she had grown a little weaker. His mind skittered away from the topic as it did with so many things. He dared not let his thoughts drift into the angry roads within.

A flight of ducks passed over his head and Xuan looked up at them, envying them their ability to fly and land wherever they wanted. It was such a simple thing, freedom, and so completely unappreciated by those who had it. Xuan was given a stipend each month for clothes and living expenses. He had servants to tend him and his rooms were always well furnished, though he was rarely allowed to stay in one place for more than a year. He had even been allowed to live with his children after the death of his wife, though he had discovered that was a mixed blessing at best. Yet he knew nothing of the outside world, or the politics of the Sung court. He lived in almost complete isolation.

Liao-Jin came out of the lake, dripping water from his lean body. His chest was bare and finely muscled, with his lower half covered in belted linen trousers that clung to him. The young man's skin roughened in the breeze as he shivered and shook his long black hair. He towelled himself dry with brisk efficiency, looking over at his father and resuming his habitual scowl. At twenty, he was the oldest of the children, one of three Xuan had brought across the Sung border so many years before. The last, now a girl of twelve, had been born knowing no other way of life. Xuan smiled at her as she waved to him from the water. He was a doting father to his girls in a way that he found difficult with his two sons.

Liao-Jin pulled a simple shift over his head and tied his hair back. He could have been a young fisherman, without any sign of rank or wealth. Xuan watched him, wondering what sort of mood he would be in after the swim. Out of the corner of his eye, he watched his son walk up the small pebbly beach towards him. Sometimes, he could hardly recall the bright, cheerful boy Liao-Jin had once been. Xuan could still remember when his son had truly understood their situation for the first time. There had been tears and rages and sulky silences almost ever since. Xuan never knew what to expect from him.

Liao-Jin sat on the pebbles and pulled his knees up, clasping his hands around them to keep warm.

'Did you write to the prefect, as you said you would?' he asked suddenly.

Xuan closed his eyes for a moment, weary of the conversation even before it had begun.

'I did not say I would. He has not answered me for a long time.'

Liao-Jin's mouth twisted unpleasantly.

'Well, why would he? What *good* are you?'

The young man gripped a handful of pebbles and threw them into the water in a jerky motion. One of his sisters yelped, though she had not been hit. When she saw who had thrown the stones, she shook her head in admonishment and waded out deeper.

When Liao-Jin spoke again, the tone was almost a whine.

'You know, there is no law to prevent me joining the Sung army, father. Whatever they think of you, I could rise. In time, perhaps I could have a house of my own. I could take a wife.'

'I would like that for you,' Xuan agreed distantly.

'Would you? You haven't written to the one man who might agree. You have done *nothing*, as usual, while every day passes so slowly I can't bear it. If my mother was alive . . .'

'She is not,' Xuan said, his own voice hardening to match his son's. 'And there is nothing I can do until this prefect moves on to another post, or dies. I do not believe he even reads my letters any longer. He has not replied to one for eight, no ten years!' His mood was spoiled, the peace of the day gone under his son's fierce glare.

'I would rather be in prison than here with you,' Liao-Jin hissed at him. 'At least there, I might dream of being released. Here, I have no hope at all. Shall I grow old? Do you expect me to tend you when your mind is gone and I am wrinkled and useless? I won't. I'll walk into the lake first, or put a rope around my neck. Or yours, father. Perhaps then they would let me walk away from my captivity.'

'There are servants to tend me, if I grow ill,' Xuan said weakly.

He hated to hear the bitterness in his son, but he understood it well enough. He had felt the same for a long time; part of him still did. Liao-Jin was like a stick stirring the muddy depths of his soul and he resisted, pulling away physically and coming to his feet rather than listen to any more. He raised his head to call his other children and paused. The distant towers of Hangzhou could be seen around them, the lake a creation of some ancient dynasty more than a thousand years before. On the rare days he was allowed there, he was rarely bothered by anyone, yet he saw a troop of cavalry trotting down from the road onto the shores of the lake. As he watched in vague interest, they turned in his direction. Xuan came to himself with a start.

'Out of the water, all of you,' he called. 'Quickly now, there are men coming.'

His daughters squawked and Liao-Jin's brother Chiun came out at a rush, spattering droplets onto the dry stones. The riders rode around the curving shore and Xuan became more and more certain they were coming for him. He could not help the spasm of fear that touched his heart. Even Liao-Jin had fallen silent, his face set in stern lines. It was not impossible that the soldiers had been told to make them disappear at last and both of them knew it.

'Did you write to anyone on your own?' Xuan asked his son, without looking away from the strangers riding in. Liao-Jin hesitated long enough for him to know he had. Xuan cursed softly to himself.

'I hope you have not drawn the attention of someone who might wish ill on us, Liao-Jin. We have never been among friends.'

The soldiers drew to a halt just twenty paces from the shivering girls as they moved back to stand close to their father and brothers. Xuan hid his fear as the officer dismounted, a short stocky figure with grey hair and a wide, almost square face that was ruddy with health. The man flicked his reins over his horse's head and strode to the small group watching him.

Xuan noted the small lion symbol etched into the officer's scaled armour as he bowed. He did not know every rank of the Sung military, but he knew the man had proven himself

291

as an archer and swordsman, as well as passing an exam on tactics in one of the city barracks.

'This humble soldier is Hong Tsaio-Wen,' the man said. 'I have orders to escort his majesty Xuan, Son of Heaven, to the Leopard barracks to be fitted with armour.'

'What? What is this?' Xuan demanded incredulously.

Tsaio-Wen stared at him with unblinking eyes. 'His majesty's men have been assembled there,' he replied, stiff with the formal idiom that would not allow him to address Xuan directly. 'His majesty will want to join them there.' He raised an arm to gesture to his men and Xuan saw they had brought a spare horse, saddled and waiting. 'His majesty will desire to come with me now.'

Xuan felt ice touch his heart and he wondered if the moment had come when the Sung emperor had finally tired of his existence. It was possible that he would be taken to a place of execution and quietly made to vanish. He knew better than to argue. Xuan had known many Sung soldiers and officials in the sixteen years of his captivity. If he demanded reasons or explanation, Tsaio-Wen would simply repeat his orders with placid indifference, never less than polite. Xuan had grown used to the stone walls of Sung manners.

To his surprise, it was his son who spoke.

'I would like to come with you, father,' Liao-Jin said softly.

Xuan winced. If this was an order for his execution, his son's presence would only mean one more body at sunset. He shook his head, hoping it was answer enough. Instead, Liao-Jin stepped around to face him.

'They have allowed your men to assemble, after how long? This is important, father. Let me come with you, whatever it turns out to be.'

The Sung officer could have been made of stone as he stood there, giving Xuan no sign he had even heard. Despite himself, Xuan looked past his son and spoke.

'Why am I needed now, after so long?'

The soldier remained silent, his eyes like black glass. Yet there was no aggression in his stance. It had been a long time since Xuan had judged the mood of fighting men, but he sensed no violence from the rest of the small troop. He made his decision.

'Liao-Jin, I commission you as yinzhan junior officer. I will explain your duties and responsibilities at a later time.'

His son flushed with pleasure and he went down on one knee, bowing his head. Xuan rested his hand on the back of his son's neck for a moment. Years before, he might have resisted any sign of affection, but he did not care if some honourless Sung soldiers saw it.

'We are ready,' Xuan said to Tsaio-Wen.

The officer shook his head slightly before speaking.

'I have only one spare horse and orders to bring his majesty to the barracks. I have no orders about any other.'

The man's tone was sour and Xuan felt an old anger stir in him, one he had not allowed himself to feel in years. A man in his position could have no honour, could allow himself no pride. Yet he stepped closer to the soldier and leaned in, his eyes bright with rage.

'Who are you to speak to me in such a way? You, a dog-meat soldier of no family? What I choose to do is no concern of yours. Tell one of your men to dismount and walk back, or give up your own mount.'

Hong Tsaio-Wen had lived his life in a rigid hierarchy. He responded to Xuan's certainty as he would have to any other senior officer. His head dipped and his eyes no longer challenged. Xuan was certain then that this was no execution detail. His thoughts whirled as Tsaio-Wen snapped orders to his men and one of them dismounted.

'Tell your brother to take your sisters home,' Xuan said loudly to Liao-Jin. 'You will accompany me to the barracks. We will see then what is so important that I must be disturbed.'

Liao-Jin could hardly hide his mingled delight and panic as he passed on the word to his siblings. He had ridden a few times in his life, but never a trained warhorse. He dreaded embarrassing his father as he ran to the mount and leapt up into the saddle. The animal snorted at the unfamiliar rider and Xuan's head snapped round, suddenly thoughtful.

'Wait,' he said. He passed his eyes over the other horses and found one that stood placidly, without any of the bunched tension of the first mount. Xuan looked across at Tsaio-Wen and saw the man's hidden anger. Perhaps the officer had not deliberately chosen the most unruly mount in his troop, but he doubted it. It had been many years since Xuan had managed soldiers, but the old habits came back to him. He strode across to another rider and looked up at him with complete certainty that he would be obeyed.

'Get down,' he said.

The soldier barely looked at Tsaio-Wen before he swung his leg over and jumped to the shingle.

'This one,' Xuan called to his son.

Liao-Jin had not understood what his father was doing, but he too dismounted and came over, taking the reins.

Xuan nodded to him without explanation, then raised his hand briefly to the rest of his family. They stood forlorn, watching as their father and brother mounted up and rode away along the shore of the lake, heading back into the city of Hangzhou.

CHAPTER TWENTY-FIVE

Hangzhou had many barracks for the emperor's armies. The best of them enclosed training grounds and even baths, where the soldiers could learn their trade, strengthen their bodies and then sleep and eat in huge dormitories.

The Leopard barracks showed signs of having been abandoned for many years. The roofs sagged and the training ground was overgrown with weeds poking through the sand and stones. Xuan rode under an archway covered in lichen and drew to a halt with Tsaio-Wen's men in an open courtyard. He was flushed from the ride, long-unused muscles complaining in his legs and back. Yet he felt better than he had in years at just that taste of freedom and command.

Tsaio-Wen dismounted without a word or a glance at the two men he had brought with him. Xuan could see the traces of anger in the man's walk as he strode into the first building. Xuan looked over to his son and jerked his head for him to get down from his borrowed horse. He did not know what to expect, but there had been so little novelty in recent years that almost anything would be welcome.

The troop of riders stood in silence and waited. After a time, Tsaio-Wen came out and took his reins. To Xuan's surprise, he mounted, turning his horse back to the gate. Two of his men gathered the reins of the horses Xuan and his son had ridden and began to lead them away.

'What is this?' Xuan said. He knew Tsaio-Wen had heard him from the way the man stiffened. The officer chose to have his revenge in impoliteness and there was no reply.

A loud cry sounded from close by and Xuan spun round. Running towards him, he saw faces he knew, memories of a different life. Liao-Jin tensed as if they were about to be attacked, but his father laid a hand on his arm. When he spoke, his eyes were bright with tears.

'I know these men, Liao-Jin. They are my people.' He smiled, realising that his son would not recognise any of the men coming out and crowding around them. 'They are *your* people.'

Xuan had to work hard to keep the smile on his face as he began to recognise men he had not seen for sixteen years. Time was never kind. Age had never made a man stronger, or faster, or more vital. He felt wrenched within, shocked over and over. He kept seeing faces he remembered as young, unlined, and somehow they were still there, but become wrinkled and weary. Perhaps at home they would have been less marked by the years. He doubted they had ever been well fed or allowed to stay fit.

They pressed in close and some of them even reached out to touch his clothes, almost to reassure themselves he was real. Then voices he had not heard for too long shouted orders and they fell back. The courtyard continued to fill as more and more came out from the dormitories, but those who had been officers were snapping orders at them to form ranks for an inspection. They smiled as they did so and there were many questions called from their number. Xuan could not answer them. He could hardly speak for the swelling emotions that filled him. He stood straight, his eyes shining as they made ragged groups of a hundred and marched out to take position on the weed-strewn parade ground.

It was not long before he realised the numbers coming out were thinning. Xuan's heart sank. He had brought some forty thousand men into Sung lands. Some would always have died – the oldest among them would have been close to seventy by then. Natural causes would have taken a toll, but when he counted the silent squares, the total was only eight thousand men.

'Where did you all go?' he murmured to himself.

One man who had been shouting orders was dressed in little more than filthy rags. He was emaciated and where his skin showed it was marked in dirt that had almost been tattooed into him. It was pitiful to see such a figure trying to stand tall. Xuan did not recognise him, but he walked over and met the man's eyes. They searched his, glimmering with hope where there should have been none.

'It has been a long time,' Xuan said. He was about to ask the man's name when it came to him, with the rank first, flashing into his head from over the years. 'Shao Xiao Bohai.'

Xuan blinked back pain as Bohai smiled to reveal just a couple of long yellow teeth in an empty jaw. The man had once commanded thousands, one of his experienced sword officers, but it was almost impossible to reconcile the memories with the skeletal figure who stood before him.

'Is this *all* the men?' Xuan asked.

Bohai dipped his head, then dropped prostrate on the ground. The rest of them followed on the instant, so that only Xuan and his son remained standing.

'Up, all of you,' Xuan ordered. His eyes had dried and he knew he could show no more emotion to these men. They needed more than that from him.

'Well, Shao Xiao Bohai? You have not answered my question. You may speak freely to me.'

The man's voice only creaked at first. He wet his lips and gums with his tongue until he could shape words.

'Some of us ran. Most were brought back and killed in front of us. Others never returned.'

'But so many?' Xuan said, shaking his head.

'His majesty will not want to hear the complaints of soldiers,' Bohai said, staring off into the middle distance.

'I order you to tell me,' Xuan replied softly. He waited while the man wet his lips once more.

'There were fevers each summer and some died from bad food. One year, some six thousand of us were taken away to work in a coal mine. They did not return. Each month, we lose a few to the guards they set, or Sung nobles looking for entertainment. We do not always know the fates of those who are taken away. They don't come back. Your majesty, I have not seen the whole group together for sixteen years. I did not know until three days ago that we had lost so many.' A spark appeared in the man's dull eyes. 'We endured in the hope of seeing his majesty one last time before death. That has been granted. If there is to be no rescue, no release, it will be enough.'

Xuan turned and saw his son standing with an expression of horror on his face.

'Close your mouth, my son,' he said softly. 'These are good men, of your blood. Do not shame them for what they cannot control.' His voice rose in volume, so that Bohai and those close by heard his words.

'They are filthy because they have not been given water. They are starved because they have not been given food. See beyond the rags, my son. They are men of honour and strength, proven in their endurance. They are your people and they fought for me once.'

Xuan had not heard the Sung officer Tsaio-Wen approach behind him until the man spoke.

'How touching. I wonder if their emperor will embrace them in their shit and lice?'

Xuan spun round and stepped very close to Tsaio-Wen. He seemed oblivious to the sword that hung from Tsaio-Wen's belt.

'You again? Have I not yet taught you humility?' To Tsaio-Wen's astonishment, Xuan prodded him in the chest with a stiffened finger. 'These men were allies to your emperor, but how have they been treated? Starved, left in their own dirt without proper food? My enemies would have treated them better than you.'

Sheer surprise held Tsaio-Wen still for a moment. When his hand dropped to his sword, Xuan stepped even closer, so that their noses came together and angry spittle touched Tsaio-Wen's face.

'I have lived long enough, dog-meat. Show a blade to me and see what these unarmed men will do to you with their bare hands.'

Tsaio-Wen looked past him and was suddenly aware of all the ranks of furious men watching the scene. Carefully, he stepped back. Xuan was pleased to see a line of sweat along his forehead.

'Personally, I would let you all starve,' Tsaio-Wen said. 'But instead, you are to be sent out against the Mongol tumans. No doubt the emperor would rather see Mongol swords blunted on your skulls than on Sung soldiers.'

He handed over a package of orders and Xuan took them, trying to hide his astonishment. He broke the imperial seal he knew so well and read quickly as Tsaio-Wen turned away. The Sung officer managed to cross some forty paces of the parade ground before Xuan raised his head.

'Stop,' he shouted. The soldier marched on, his stiff back showing his anger. Xuan raised his voice to a bellow. 'You are mentioned in these orders, Hong Tsaio-Wen.'

The Sung officer scraped to a halt. His face red with rage,

he came back. Xuan ignored him, continuing to read while the man stood quivering in indignation.

'It seems my cousin the emperor is not a complete fool,' Xuan said. Tsaio-Wen hissed at the insult, but he did not move. 'He has recalled that there is only one group in his lands who have faced the Mongols before – and held them off. You see those men before you, Tsaio-Wen.' To his pleasure, the closest ranks pulled their shoulders back as they heard. 'It says that I should expect armourers and trainers to fit them once more for war. Where are these men?'

'On their way,' Tsaio-Wen grated through a clenched jaw. 'Where is my name mentioned?'

'Here,' Xuan said, showing him the page of thick vellum covered in tiny black characters. It surprised him that the officer could read. Things had changed since his day.

'I do not see it,' Tsaio-Wen said, squinting at the page.

'There. Where it says I may choose Sung officers to help with the supplies and training. I choose you, Tsaio-Wen. I enjoy your company too much to let you go.'

'You *can't*,' Tsaio-Wen replied. Once again his hand fell to the sword and then dropped away at a guttural snarl from the closest men.

'Your emperor has written that I can, Tsaio-Wen. Choose to obey me or choose to hang, I do not care which. The emperor has said we will march again. Perhaps we will be destroyed, I do not know. Perhaps we will triumph. It will be easier to decide when we have eaten well and grown strong, I know that. Have you made your decision, Hong Tsaio-Wen?'

'I will obey the orders of my emperor,' the man said, promising death with his eyes.

'You are a wise man to show such obedience and humility,' Xuan said. 'You will be a lesson to all of us. Now it says here that there are funds available, so send runners into the city for food. My men are hungry. Send for doctors to tend the weak and sick. Employ servants to clean the barracks and painters to make it fresh. Find roofers to repair broken tiles, carpenters to rebuild the stables, butchers and ice men to fill the basements with meat. You will be busy, Tsaio-Wen, but do not despair. Your work benefits the last Chin army and there is no better cause.'

Tsaio-Wen's eyes drifted to the papers Xuan held in his hand. Whatever the injustice or humiliation, he dared not refuse. Just a word from one of his senior officers that he had baulked at a lawful order and he would be finished. He bowed his head as if he had to break bones to do it, then turned on his heel and walked away.

Xuan turned to the incredulous smiles on the faces of his men. His son could only stare and shake his head in amazement.

'None of us thought today would end like this,' Xuan said. 'We will grow strong in the months to come. We will eat well and train again with sword, pike and bow. It will be hard. None of us are young men any longer. When we are ready, we will leave this place for the last time. It does not matter whether we ride against the Mongols. It does not matter if we ride into hell. What matters . . . is that we will *leave*.'

His voice broke as he said the last words and they cheered him, their voices growing stronger and louder until they echoed across the parade ground and the barracks beyond.

In the gers of the camp healers, Kublai sat in grim silence as the wound on his arm was bandaged by a harried shaman. The man's hands were deft and practised, working by instinct. Kublai grimaced in pain as the shaman tied off the knot and bowed briefly before moving on. General Bayar was just two cots down, wearing the cold face of indifference as another shaman worked to sew a gash on his leg that slowly dripped dark red blood.

Yao Shu approached, bearing a sheaf of paper with hastily scrawled figures.

'Where are the Sung guns?' Kublai asked Bayar suddenly. He did not want to hear the numbers of maimed and dead from Yao Shu, not then. He was still shaking slightly from his own fight on the hill, a quivering deep inside him that had lasted far longer than the swift struggle itself. Bayar stood to answer him, flexed his leg with a wince.

'We found them still being brought up, my lord, a mile or so back. I have our own men looking them over.'

'How many cannon?'

'Only forty, but enough powder and balls for a dozen shots each. Smaller shot than the ones we had.'

'Then abandon our own. Have oil wiped over them and cover them with oiled linen, but leave them where they are until we have a respite or we make more shot and powder.'

Bayar looked wearily at him. They had received news of two more armies approaching the area, marching hard and fast to support the ones that had gone before. Their only chance was to ride to the first and smash it before they faced a battle on two fronts.

'Have you retrieved the arrows?' Kublai asked.

Bayar was swaying as he stood, utterly exhausted. Kublai saw him summon his will to answer, a visible effort that reduced him to awe.

'I have a minghaan out among the dead, collecting any that can be re-used. We'll get perhaps half of them back. I'll have more sent to the camp to be repaired. They'll bring them up to us when the work is done.'

'Send them with the wounded men who can't fight,' Kublai

said. 'And check the stocks in the camp. I need the fletchers working day and night. We can't run out.' He clenched his fist and looked at Yao Shu, waiting patiently. 'All right. How many men have we lost?'

The old man did not need to consult his lists for the total.

'Nine thousand and some hundreds. Six thousand of those dead and the rest too badly cut to go on. The shamans say we'll lose another thousand by morning, more over the next week.'

Bayar swore under his breath and Kublai shuddered, his arm throbbing in time with his pulse. A tenth of his force had gone. He was sore and tired, but he knew the dawn would bring another fight against fresher soldiers. He could only hope the long march had taken the edge off the Sung troops.

'Tell the men to eat and sleep as best they can. I need them ready before dawn for whatever comes. Send Uriang-Khadai to me.'

'Lord, you have been wounded. You should rest.'

'I will, when I am certain the scouts are all out and the wounded are being taken back to the main camp. It will be a cold meal tonight.'

Bayar bit his lip, then decided to speak again.

'You need to be alert for tomorrow, my lord. Uriang-Khadai and I have everything else in hand. Please rest.'

Kublai stared at him. Though his body ached and his legs felt weak with weariness, he could not imagine sleeping. There was too much to do.

'I'll try,' he promised. 'When I have spoken to the orlok.'

'Yes, my lord,' Bayar said.

A scout came through the camp, searching the wounded and those tending them. Kublai saw him first and his heart sank. He watched the man out of the corner of his eye, seeing him ask someone who pointed in Kublai's direction. As the scout came up, Kublai glared at him.

'What is it?'

'A third army, my lord. Coming from the east.'

'Are you sure this isn't the same report I had before?' Kublai demanded. The man paled to see him angry and Kublai tried to get a hold of himself.

'No, my lord. They have been marked. This is a new one, around sixty thousand strong.'

'The wasp nest,' Bayar murmured at Kublai's side. He nodded.

Kublai wanted to ride again immediately, but Uriang-Khadai came to him as he was spooning a bowl of cold stew into his mouth and chewing, his eyes glazed.

The orlok had a strange expression on his face as he stood before Kublai. In less than a week, they had survived two major battles, each time outnumbered. Uriang-Khadai had expected the younger man to falter a hundred times, but he had always been there, giving calm orders, shoring up a failing line, sending in reinforcements as necessary. The orlok saw exhaustion in the khan's brother, but he had not broken under the strain, at least not yet.

'My lord, the third army is smaller and won't be in range until tomorrow or the day after. If we ride towards them now, we can rest before the battle. The men will be fresher and if we have to fight twice tomorrow, they have a better chance of living through it.'

Uriang-Khadai was tense as he waited for an answer. He had grown used to the younger man ignoring his advice, but out of a sense of duty, he still gave it. He was ready to be rebuffed.

'All right,' Kublai said, surprising him. 'We'll ride east and break contact with the large force.'

'Yes, my lord,' Uriang-Khadai said, almost stammering his answer. It did not seem enough. 'Thank you,' he said.

Kublai put down the empty bowl and rubbed his face with

both hands. Apart from being unconscious for a time, he could not remember when he had last slept. He felt dizzy and ill.

'I may not always listen, orlok. But you have more experience than me. I don't forget that. We'll move the main camp out of their range as well. I need to find a safe place for them, a forest or a valley where they can rest. We have to keep moving and they can't match our pace.'

Uriang-Khadai murmured a response and unbent enough to bow. He wanted to say something to raise the spirits of the young man who sat with his legs sprawled, too tired to move. Nothing came to mind and he bowed again as he withdrew.

Bayar had seen the exchange and strolled over, his mouth quirking as he watched Uriang-Khadai begin to issue the new orders.

'He likes you, you know,' Bayar said.

'He thinks I am a fool,' Kublai said without thinking, then chewed his lips irritably. Tiredness made it hard to keep his mouth shut. He had to lead without any show of weakness, not invite confidences.

'No, he doesn't,' Bayar replied. He nodded to himself, still watching Uriang-Khadai. 'Did you see him this morning when the Sung overran the wing? He didn't panic, just pulled back, re-formed the men and shored up his position. It was good work.'

Kublai wished Bayar would stop talking. The last thing he wanted was to invite one officer to comment on another.

'He isn't a natural leader, Uriang-Khadai,' Bayar said.

Kublai closed his eyes with a sigh, seeing green lights flash across the darkness.

'The men respect him,' Bayar went on. 'They have seen his competence. They don't worship him, but they know he won't throw them away for nothing. That means a great deal to the ranks.'

'Enough, general. He's a good man and so are you. We all are. Now get on your horse and drag the tumans twenty more miles so we can intercept a Sung lord.'

Bayar laughed at the tone, but he ran to his horse and was wheeling the mount and giving orders before Kublai dragged his eyes open again.

In the years since Mongke had become khan, the numbers in the nation had grown beyond anything Genghis would have recognised. His brother Arik-Boke had benefited from peace on the plains of home and the birth rate had soared. Karakorum had become a settled city, with a growing population outside the walls in new districts of stone and wood, so that the original city was hidden from view. The soil was good and Mongke had encouraged large families, knowing that they would swell the armies of the khan. When he rode out in spring, he took with him twenty-eight tumans, more than quarter of a million men, travelling light and fast. They took no cannon and only the minimum of supplies. With horsemen just like those, Genghis and Tsubodai had swept across continents. Mongke was ready to do the same.

He had tried to be a modern khan, to continue the work Ogedai had begun in making a stable civilisation across the vast territories of his khanate. For years, he had struggled with the urge to be in the field, to ride, to conquer. Every instinct had pulled his mind away from the petty rule of cities, but he had strangled all his doubts, forcing himself to rule while his generals, princes and brothers cut the new paths. The great khanate had been won quickly, in just three generations. He could not escape a sense that it could be lost even faster unless he built and made laws to last. He had fostered trade links and yam stations, strings across the land that bound men together, so that the poorest sheep farmer knew there was a khan as his lord. Mongke had seen to it that each vast region had its khanate government reporting to him, so that those who had suffered could make their complaint and perhaps even see warriors come to answer for them. At times, he thought it was too big, too complicated for anyone to understand, but somehow it worked. Where there was obvious corruption, it was rooted out by his scribes and those responsible were removed from their high positions. The governors of his cities knew they answered to a higher authority than their own and it kept them quiet, whether from fear or security, he did not know. The taxes came in a flood, and rather than bury them in vaults, he used them to build schools, roads and new towns for the nation.

Peace was more effort than war, Mongke had realised early on in his time as khan. Peace wore a man down, where war could give him life and strength. There had been times when he thought his brothers would return to Karakorum to find him a withered husk, ground to nothing under the great stone of responsibility that was always turning above his head.

As he rode with his tumans, Mongke felt himself shedding the weight of the years. It was hard not to think of his trek with Tsubodai, facing Christian knights and battering foreign armies into submission. Tsubodai would have given fingers from his right hand for such an army as the one Mongke now commanded. Mongke had been young then and being back in the saddle with armed ranks before and behind was rejuvenating, an echo of his youth that filled him with joy. His horizons had been too small for too long. Chin lands lay to the south and he would see this new city Kublai had created on the good black soil. He would see Xanadu and decide for himself if Kublai had overstepped his authority. He could not imagine Hulegu ever turning away from the great khan, his brother, but Kublai had always been independent, a man who needed to know he was watched. Mongke could not shake the suspicion that he had better not leave Kublai too long alone.

Hulegu's letter to him under personal seal had been the only sour moment in months of preparation. Mongke told himself he did not fear the Assassins his brother had stirred from their apathy, but what man would not? He knew he could hold his nerve in a battle, with everything going wrong around him. He could lead a charge and face men. His courage was a proven thing. Yet the thought of some masked murderer pressing a knife to his throat as he slept made him shudder. If there were Assassins dedicated to his death, he had surely left them behind for another year or two.

Arik-Boke had come to Karakorum to take over the administration while he was away. Mongke had made sure he too understood the risk, but his youngest brother had laughed, pointing to the guards and servants that scurried everywhere in the palace and the city. No one could get in unseen. It had eased Mongke's mind to know his brother would be safe – and to leave the city behind him.

In just fourteen days, his tumans were in range of Xanadu, less than two hundred miles north of Yenking and the northern Chin lands. Half his army were barely twenty years old and they rode the distances easily, while Mongke suffered from lack of fitness. Only his pride kept him going when his muscles were ropes of pain, but the worst days came early and his body began to remember its old strength after nine or ten in the saddle.

Mongke shook his head in silent awe at the sight of a new city growing on the horizon. His brother had created something on the grand scale, turning fantasies into reality. Mongke found he was proud of Kublai and he wondered what changes he would see when they met again. He could not deny his own sense of satisfaction in bringing it about. He had sent Kublai into the world, forcing his younger brother to look beyond his dusty books. He knew Kublai was unlikely to be grateful, but that was the way of things.

They stopped in Xanadu long enough for Mongke to tour the city and work his way through the dozens of yam messages that had gone ahead or reached him while he travelled. He grumbled as he dealt with them, but there were few places he could ride where the yam riders couldn't find him eventually. The khanates did not remain still simply because Mongke was in the field. On some days, he found himself working as hard as he had in Karakorum and enjoying it about as much.

He stripped Xanadu of food, salt and tea in the short time he was there. The inhabitants would go hungry for a while, but his was the greater need. So many tumans could not scavenge as they went. For the first time in his memory, Mongke had to keep a supply line open behind him, so that there were always hundreds of carts coming slowly south in the wake of his warriors. The supplies backed up while he rested in Xanadu, but when he left, they spread out again, paid for thousands of miles away in Karakorum and the northern Chin cities. Mongke grinned at the thought of his shadow stretching so far. Their food would catch them up whenever they stopped and he thought bandits were unlikely to risk raiding his carts, with the khan's scouts never too far away.

He pushed the tumans south, revelling in the distances they could travel, faster than anyone but a yam rider able to change horses at every station. For the great khan, the tumans would ride to the end of the world without complaint. On minimum rations, he had already lost some of the flesh that clung to his waist and his stamina was increasing, adding to his sense of well-being.

Mongke crossed the northern Sung border on a cold autumn day, with the wind blustering along the lines of horsemen.

Hangzhou lay five hundred miles to the south, but there were at least thirty cities between the tumans and the emperor's capital, each well garrisoned. Mongke smiled as he rode, kicking in his heels and enjoying the rush of air past his face. He had given Kublai a simple task, but his brother could never have succeeded on his own. The twenty-eight tumans Mongke had brought would be the hammer that crushed the Sung emperor. It was an army greater than any Genghis had ever put in the field and as he galloped along a dusty road, Mongke felt his years in Karakorum slowly tear into dusty rags, leaving him fresh and unencumbered. For once, the yam riders were behind. Without the staging posts, they could make no better time than his own men and he felt truly free for the first time in years. He understood at last the truth of Genghis' words. There was no better way to spend a life than this.

CHAPTER TWENTY-SIX

Kublai and Bayar sat with their backs against the same massive boulder of whitish grey stone. Uriang-Khadai watched them, his face unreadable. The twin of the huge stone loomed nearby, so that between them was a sheltered area that local sheep must have used every time it rained. The ground there was so thick with droppings that no grass showed at all and everyone who walked through it found their boots getting heavier and heavier as they went.

The sheep had gone, of course. Kublai's tumans had rounded up eighty or so, and for some lucky warriors there would be hot meat that night. The rest would have to make do with blood from their spare mounts, along with a little mare's milk or cheese, whatever they had.

Ponies grazed all around them, whickering and snorting as they cropped grass that grew in clumps so thick that it made progress slow over the hills. They could not even trot on such an uneven surface. The horses had to be walked slowly, their heads drooping with weariness.

'We could circle back to the last site,' Bayar said. 'They won't expect that and we need those arrows.'

Uriang-Khadai nodded wearily. Though he had gone with Tsubodai into the west, he had never known such a constant run of battles before. There had been a time when he had scorned reports of swarming Sung cities, but the reality was every bit as bad as he had been told. Kublai's tumans had run out of gunpowder, shot and arrows, the sheer numbers of the enemy overwhelming them. Uriang-Khadai could still hardly believe they had been forced to retreat, but he had lost track of the armies they had beaten, and the one struggling to reach them was fresh and well armed. The tumans were down to swords for the most part, with even their lances broken and thrown away. Faced with new regiments racing towards them, Kublai had withdrawn at speed, seeking out the high ground.

'Are they still there?' Kublai asked.

Bayar stood up with a groan on aching legs, peering past the boulder. Below, he could see Sung regiments in ragged squares, seeming to inch their way up the slopes of the mountain.

'Still coming,' Bayar said, slumping back. Kublai swore, though it was no more than he had expected. 'We can't fight on this ground, you know that?'

'I know, but we can stay ahead of them,' Kublai said. 'We'll find a way out of the hills and when it's dark, we'll ride clear of them. They won't catch up, not today anyway.'

'I don't like leaving the main camp unprotected for this long,' Uriang-Khadai said. 'If one of those armies comes across them, they'll be slaughtered.'

Kublai tensed his jaw, irritated at Uriang-Khadai for reminding him. Chabi and Zhenjin were safe, he told himself again. His scouts had found a forest that stretched for hundreds of miles. The families and camp followers would have headed for the deepest part of it, as far from a road as they could get. Yet it only took one enemy tracker to spot smoke from a fire or hear the bleating of the herds. They would fight, of course. Chabi's calm courage made his chest grow tight in memory, but he agreed with Uriang-Khadai about the outcome. A small voice within him worried as much about the stocks of arrows

312

held in the camp. Without them, his tumans were a wolf whose teeth had been drawn.

'You find me a way to make this Sung bastard vanish and I'll ride back and see how they are getting on,' Kublai said irritably. 'Until then, we'll just stay ahead of them and hope we aren't riding into the arms of another noble out hunting for us.'

'I would like to send a small, fast group for arrows,' Uriang-Khadai said. 'Even a few thousand shafts would make a difference at this point. Twenty scouts riding fast should be able to get past the Sung forces.'

Kublai multiplied numbers in his head and blew air out slowly. He didn't doubt his scouts could survive the ride out, but coming back, with a quiver under each arm, one on their back, two tied to the saddle? They would be defenceless, easy prey for the first Sung cavalry to spot them. He needed more than two thousand arrows. He needed half a million at a minimum. The best stocks of fletched birch shafts lay on battle-fields for fifty miles behind them, already warping from damp and exposure. It was infuriating. He had prided himself on his organisation, but the Sung armies had just kept coming, giving his men no time to rest.

'We need to find another city, one with an imperial barracks,' he said. 'They have what we need. Where are the maps?'

Bayar reached inside his tunic and pulled out a sweat-stained sheet of goatskin, dark yellow and folded many times, so that whitish lines showed as he opened it out. There were dozens of cities shown on the map, marked in characters painted by some long-dead scribe. Bayar pointed to one that lay beyond the range of mountains where the tumans sprawled in exhaustion.

'Shaoyang,' he said, jabbing a finger at it. Sweat dripped as he leaned over, so that dark spots appeared on the material. With a curse, he wiped his face with both hands.

'That's clear then,' Kublai said. 'We need to reach this city, overcome their garrison and somehow get to their stores of weaponry before the army behind catches up, or the population turns out and finishes us.' He laughed bitterly to himself.

Uriang-Khadai spoke as Kublai leaned back. 'There is a chance the garrison is already out,' he said thoughtfully. 'For all we know, we may have already beaten them. Or they could be out looking for us, like every other Sung soldier in the region.'

Kublai sat up, struggling to think through his exhaustion.

'If they're in place, we could draw them away. If we sent a few men into the markets with information to sell, maybe. Rumours of a Mongol army fifty miles in the wrong direction would surely bring the garrison out. We know by now there are standing orders to attack us on sight. They could not remain in the city with the right bait.'

'If they are there at all,' Uriang-Khadai agreed.

'If they ignore the news, we will be waiting to enter a hostile city, with another army coming up fast behind us,' Bayar pointed out. He was surprised to be the one urging caution, but Uriang-Khadai seemed to be caught up in the idea.

Kublai stood up, stretching his aching legs and looking down the mountain to the Sung regiments plodding after them. The ground was so broken with its clumps and hillocks of grass that they could not move any faster than those they chased. He could be thankful for that at least. He felt his head clear with the movement and gave a low whistle to the closest minghaan officers, jerking his head in the direction of travel. It was time to move on again.

'You know I'd love to get into their stores,' he said, 'but even if the garrison is already out, the prefect of the city won't let us just walk in and take what we need.'

'The citizens of Shaoyang won't know how the war is going,'

Uriang-Khadai said. 'If you gave them the chance, he might surrender to you.'

Kublai looked closely for some sign of mockery, but Uriang-Khadai's face was like stone. Kublai grinned for a moment.

'He might,' he agreed. 'I'll think about it as we go. Come on, the ones following are getting too close. What do you say to a fast ten miles over the peak to put some distance between us?'

All those who heard made some groaning noise at the prospect, but they lurched to their feet. With the ground so broken, it was all they could do to stop the Sung regiments below snapping at their heels.

Mongke hated sieges, but without a massive force of catapults and cannon, he faced the same problems Genghis had once known. Cities were designed to keep out marauding armies such as his, though for once they were not his main objective. Somewhere to the south, Kublai was engaging the Sung armies. Mongke would have liked to smash down the walls of the cities he passed, but his primary aim was to reach Kublai. It suited his purposes well enough if every city barred its gates against him – and the garrisons stayed safely inside. His problem lay in the supply line, which grew more and more vulnerable with every mile he rode south. Cities who hid from a quarter of a million warriors would not mind sallying out against a long line of carts, guarded by just a few thousand. When the line broke somewhere behind him, he had been forced to reduce the rations. He had sent scouts out for well over a hundred miles to report any herds he might snap up. It was one resource the Sung cities could not protect behind their walls, and as he entered a region of rich grassland Mongke saw so many cattle that his supply lines became unnecessary. For a glorious few days, his men feasted on charred beef still dripping with blood, putting back some of the body fat they had lost in hard riding. In its way, the problems of a campaign were equal to anything Mongke had dealt with in Karakorum, but he took more satisfaction in simple obstacles he could face and overcome.

As he went on, Mongke noted the cities he would return to when he had finished sweeping through the south with Kublai. He looked forward to seeing his brother more and more, imagining Kublai's face when he saw the host Mongke had brought to support him.

Towns were easy prey compared to the great cities. Mongke's tumans could fell trees and leave stubs of branches in just a morning, using them as rough ladders to climb lesser walls. Yet even then, Mongke had let hundreds of towns survive intact while his tumans swept on. They would keep until his return.

A little more than a month had passed since entering Sung lands when his outlying scouts reported a huge Sung army marching south with banners flying. The news spread through the tumans as fast as Mongke heard it himself, so they were ready to move when he raced to his horse. No infantry alive could stay ahead of them for long and his tumans were eager to fight.

His twenty-eight tumans followed the scout's directions at full speed, sighting the enemy at evening three days later. Mongke was pleased to see they were less than half the size of his force. For once his generals would not have to think their way around an army that outnumbered them. It had always been his plan to bring a bigger hammer to the Sung than anyone had managed before. The Sung emperors had survived Genghis, Ogedai and Guyuk. They would not survive his own khanate.

As night fell, the tumans herded their spare mounts behind them. If the enemy attacked in the dark, the animals were likely to panic and stampede, or at the least get in the way of a counter-charge. They chewed sticks of dried beef to a soft mush and washed it down with airag or water, whichever they had to hand. The warriors wrapped reins around their boots and lay down on the damp grass to sleep. Every man there knew they would be off before dawn and fighting at first light.

As the camp settled, Mongke's servants created a ger for him, taking the felt and spars from half a dozen packs. While they worked in the moonlight, he lay out a thin blanket and knelt on it, pulling his deel robe closer over his armour to keep him warm. He could see his breath as mist and he slowed his heart, letting the cares of the day ease from him. With the stars achingly clear overhead, he spent a moment praying to the sky father for the battle to go well, for Kublai to be safe, for the nation to prosper. Even in his private prayers, he thought as a khan.

He did not want to enter the ger they had prepared for him. Sleep was very far away and he felt strong and at peace. The dew had frozen on the grass so that he could hear every whispering footstep from his guards as they walked their shift. Mongke was surrounded by his people. He could hear them snoring, calling out in their sleep and mumbling to themselves. He chuckled as he stretched out on the blanket, deciding to spend the night under the stars like the rest of the warriors.

He woke in silence, with his head hidden in the crook of his arm. The cold ground seemed to have reached into him so that he could hardly move for stiffness. He felt his neck crunch as he sat up and rubbed his hands over his face. A shadow moved nearby and Mongke's right hand darted for his sword in the scabbard, half-drawing the blade before he realised whoever it was held out a bowl of tea to him.

He smiled ruefully at his own nerves. The camp was coming to life around him, though dawn was still some way off. Horses suckled waterskins held high for them, though they would have found moisture in the frozen dew. There was movement everywhere and Mongke sipped his tea, letting the anticipation grow within him. He could not leave anyone alive from the Sung force marching ahead of his tumans. As tempting as it was to spread terror with a few survivors, he needed to use the speed he could bring to the battlefield. His task was to push the men and animals to their limits, crushing a vast track south and running ahead of the news until he had Hangzhou in sight. The Sung would have no time to entrench and prepare for him. Kublai had cannon, two hundred good iron weapons. Mongke would use those to smash down the emperor's city.

He rose to his feet and stretched, wondering at the strange mood that had led him to sleep on the frozen grass. There was still frost in his hair and he rubbed at the strands with one hand while he finished the tea. He could feel the salt and heat hit his empty stomach and he sighed at the thought of cold meat to break his fast.

His horse was made ready by servants, already fed and watered with its coat brushed to a gleam. Mongke walked over to inspect the animal's hooves, though it was just old habit. Some of the men were already mounted and waiting, sitting idly in the saddle and talking to their friends around them. Mongke accepted a thick wedge of stale bread and cold lamb, with a skin of airag to wash it down his throat.

'Do you want to discuss tactics, my lord khan, or shall we just ride right over them?'

His orlok, Seriankh, was smiling as he spoke. Mongke chuckled through a mouthful. He looked up at the brightening sky and breathed deeply.

'It will be a fine morning, Seriankh. Tell me what you have in mind.'

As befitted a senior officer, Seriankh responded without hesitation, long used to making quick decisions.

'We'll ride their flanks at the limit of their arrow range. I don't want to surround them and make them dig in. With your permission, I'll make a three-sided box and match their pace. The Sung cavalry will try to break out and stay mobile, so we'll take them first with lances. For the infantry, we can cut them from behind, working our way up to the front.'

Mongke nodded. 'That will do. Use the bows first, before the young men go in hand-to-hand. Keep the hotheads back until the enemy is reeling. There aren't so many of them. We should be finished with this by noon.'

Seriankh smiled at that. It was not so long ago that a force of a hundred thousand would have been a battle to the last man, a bloody and desperate struggle. The force of tumans Mongke had brought had never been seen before and all the senior men were enjoying themselves with such strength at their backs.

Somewhere nearby, Mongke heard a jingle of saddle bells and he cursed softly. Another yam rider had caught up. Without the way stations to change his horse, he would have ridden to exhaustion to bring his letters.

'I am never left alone,' Mongke muttered.

Seriankh heard.

'I could lose a yam rider at the rear until the battle is over,' he said.

Mongke shook his head. 'No. The khan never sleeps, apparently. Isn't that what they say? I know *I* sleep, so it is a mystery to me. Form the ranks, orlok. Command is yours.'

Seriankh bowed deeply and strode away, already issuing orders to his staff that would ripple down to every warrior in the tumans.

The yam rider was so caked in dust and mud as to appear almost one with his horse. As he dismounted, fresh cracks appeared in the muck that covered him. He wore only a small

319

leather pack across his shoulders and he was very thin. Mongke wondered when the man had last eaten, without yam stations to keep him going in Sung lands. There would have been little or nothing to scavenge in the wake of the tumans, that much was certain.

Two of the khan's guards approached the rider. He looked surprised, but stood with his arms outstretched and his palms visible as they searched him thoroughly. Even the leather pack was opened, its sheaf of yellow papers handed to the rider before it was tossed down. He rolled his eyes at such caution, clearly amused. At last they were finished and turned away to mount with the rest. Mongke waited patiently, his hand outstretched for the messages.

The yam rider was older than most, he saw, perhaps approaching the end of his career. He did indeed look exhausted through the grime of hard riding. Mongke took the sheaf from him and began to read, his brow creasing in puzzlement.

'These are stock lists from Xanadu,' he said. 'Have you brought me the wrong pack?'

The rider stepped closer, peering at the pages. He reached for them and Mongke didn't see the thin razor he had kept concealed between his outstretched fingers. It was no wider than a finger itself, so that just the very edge of it glinted as he drew it sharply across Mongke's throat, forward then back. The flesh opened like a seam under tension, a white-lipped mouth that spattered them both with blood.

Mongke choked and raised his right hand to the wound. With his left, he shoved the man away so he fell sprawling. Shouts of rage and horror went up and a warrior threw himself from the saddle at the khan's attacker as he tried to scramble up, pinning him to the ground.

Mongke felt the warmth pouring out of him, leaving his flesh like stone. He stood, his legs locked and braced against the earth. His fingers could not hold the wound closed and his eyes were desperate. Men were shouting everywhere, racing back and forth and calling for Seriankh and the khan's shaman. He could see their open mouths, but Mongke could not hear them, just a drum pulsing in his ears and a rushing sound like water. He eased himself down to a sitting position, showing his teeth as the pain grew. He was aware of someone binding a strip of cloth around his neck and hand, pressing hard on the wound so that he could not breathe. He tried to fight them off, but his great strength had deserted him. His vision began to constrict and he still could not believe it was truly happening. Someone would stop it. Someone would help him. His skin grew pale as blood left him in a pulsing stream. He sagged to one side, his eyes growing dull.

Seriankh stood over him, his eyes wide with shock. He had spoken to the khan only moments before and he stared in disbelief at the twisted figure with the right hand bound into bloody bandages tied tightly around the throat. Blood was sinking into the grass, making it black and wet.

Seriankh turned slowly to see the yam rider. His face had been smashed in by fists while Mongke died. His teeth and nose were broken and one of his eyes had been speared by a thumb. Even so, he laughed at Seriankh and spoke in a language the orlok did not know, his slurred speech sounding triumphant. His cheeks were pale under the dirt, Seriankh saw, as if he had shaved a beard and revealed skin long hidden from the sun. The Assassin was still laughing as Seriankh had him bound for torture. The Sung army was forgotten as Seriankh ordered braziers and iron tools made ready. The Mongols understood both suffering and punishment. They would keep him alive as long as they could.

CHAPTER TWENTY-SEVEN

Kublai stared as he trotted along the road to Shaoyang. The city was deep into the Sung heartland and he suspected it had not been attacked in centuries. Instead of a solid outer wall, it sprawled over square miles, a central hub surrounded by smaller towns that had grown together over centuries. It made Xanadu look like a provincial town and even Karakorum would have been lost in it. He tried to make an estimate of the numbers of people who must live in such a vast landscape of buildings, shops and temples, but it was too much to take in.

His tumans were drooping with exhaustion, having forced themselves to trot and walk, trot and walk for seventy miles or more, leaving their pursuers as far behind as possible. He had sent light scouts to the city, but he doubted they were more than a day ahead of him, such was the pace he had set. Both his men and their mounts were close to collapse. They needed a month of rest, good food and grazing before they went back to the fighting, but they would not find it in Shaoyang, with enemies all around.

As the first of the tumans walked their horses into an open street, there was no sign of the inhabitants. Such a place could not be defended and he could only wonder at a society where walls had been torn down to build new districts. It was hard even to imagine such a settled life.

There was no sign of a garrison riding out to meet them. Kublai's scouts had already questioned the inhabitants, alternating between bribery and threats. He had been lucky, but after months of hard fighting, he was due a little luck. The garrison was apparently in the field, ten thousand of the Sung emperor's finest sword and crossbowmen. Kublai wished them a long hunt, many, many miles away.

He heard Uriang-Khadai give a horn signal that sent two groups of three tumans on wider paths to the centre of the city, so that they would not all approach along the same road. Kublai supposed Shaoyang had a centre, that its oldest places would have been swallowed in the rambling districts. He did not enjoy riding along streets where the roofs loomed over him. It was too easy to imagine archers appearing suddenly, shooting down into men who had little room to manoeuvre. Once again, he was glad of the armour Mongke had made him wear.

Shaoyang seemed deserted, but Kublai felt eyes on him in the silence and he could see the closest officers were nervous, jerking their heads at the slightest hint of movement. They almost drew swords when a high voice sounded nearby, but it was just a child crying behind closed doors.

The tumans who rode with Kublai carried his banners, hanging limp in the windless roads. He was marked by them as leader for anyone who might have been watching and he felt his heart beating faster, convincing himself in the silence that it was a trap. As he passed each side street, he tensed, craning his neck to see down it, past the stone gutters and roadways to shuttered shops and tall stone buildings, sometimes three or four storeys high. No one came rushing out to drag his men from their horses. When he heard hooves clattering ahead, he assumed the sound came from some of his own men. He had single warriors out as scouts, but the streets were a

323

labyrinth and there was no sign of them as he saw a small group of horsemen ahead.

The strangers were not armoured. They wore simple leggings and tunics and two of them were bare-armed, guiding their horses easily. Kublai took in the details as he looked around him once again for an ambush. The roofs remained clear and nothing moved. The Sung horsemen just sat and stared at them, then one of them spoke to the others and they began to walk their mounts slowly forward.

Around Kublai, swords came out of scabbards with a silk whisper. Bows creaked as they were made ready. The strangers moved stiffly under that close attention, very aware that the street could become their place of death with just one wrong step.

'Let them come,' Kublai murmured to those near him. 'I can't see any weapons.'

The tension grew as the small group closed on the line of Mongol warriors. One of the Sung men sought out Kublai in the ranks, assuming his identity from the bannermen on both sides of him. As if he had heard Kublai's voice, he raised his arms very slowly and twisted in the saddle, first one way and then the next so they could see there was nothing on his back.

'Ease off,' Kublai said to the warriors.

Arms grew tired holding drawn bows; fingers could slip. He did not want the man killed when he had gone to so much trouble to speak to him. Around Kublai, bows and swords lowered reluctantly and the Sung men began to breathe again.

'That's near enough,' Kublai said when they were just a dozen paces away.

The Sung group looked to the one who had ridden closest. His bare arms were heavy with muscle though his cropped hair was white and his face was deeply seamed.

'My name is Liu Yin-San,' the man said. 'I am prefect of Shaoyang. I am the one who met your scouts.'

'Then you are the one who will surrender Shaoyang to me,' Kublai replied.

To his surprise, Liu Yin-San shook his head, as if he were not facing thousands of armed men stretching from that point to the outer towns of the city. Kublai had a sudden vision of a knife plunged into Shaoyang, with himself at the head. No, three knives, with Bayar and Uriang-Khadai. At the edges behind him, there would be warriors who had yet to enter, waiting impatiently for news from the front.

'I have come unarmed to say I cannot,' Liu Yin-San said. 'The emperor has given orders to all his cities. If I surrender to you, Shaoyang will be burnt as a lesson to the others.'

'You have met this emperor?' Kublai asked.

'He has not visited Shaoyang,' Liu Yin-San replied.

'Then how does he command your loyalty?'

The man frowned, wondering if he could explain the concept of fealty to men he had been told were little better than wild animals. He took hope from the fact that Kublai spoke in perfect Mandarin to him, the language and dialect of the Chin noble classes.

'I took an oath when I was made prefect of the city,' he said. 'My orders are clear. I cannot give you what you want.'

The man was sweating and Kublai saw his dilemma clearly. If he surrendered, the city would be destroyed by a furious master. If he resisted, he expected Shaoyang to suffer the same fate from the tumans. Kublai wondered if Liu Yin-San had a solution, or whether he had ridden towards them expecting to be cut down.

'If I became the emperor, would your oath of loyalty extend to me?' he asked.

Liu Yin-San sat very still as he considered it.

'It is possible. But, my lord . . . you are *not* my emperor.'

He tensed as he spoke, aware that his life hung in the balance. Kublai fought not to smile at his reaction. The prefect would have made different decisions if he'd known a Sung army was marching towards the city as they spoke. Kublai would not allow himself to be trapped in Shaoyang. He glanced up at the sun and thought he would have to ride clear soon.

'You leave me with few choices, Liu Yin-San,' he said. The man paled slightly, understanding his own death in the words. Kublai went on before he could reply. 'I did not intend to stop in Shaoyang. I have other battles. From you, I merely needed supplies for my men, but if you will not surrender the city, you force me to give this order.'

Kublai turned in the saddle and raised his hand. Once more his men drew swords and raised their bows.

'Wait!' Liu Yin-San called, his voice strained. 'I can . . .' He hesitated, making some inner decision. 'I can*not* lead you to the barracks that lie less than a mile down this very road.'

Kublai turned slowly back to him, raising an eyebrow in silent question.

'I will not surrender Shaoyang,' Liu Yin-San said. Sweat was pouring from him, Kublai noticed. 'I will order my people to barricade themselves in their homes. I will pray that the storm passes the city without bloodshed, that you take whatever you need and leave.'

Kublai smiled. 'That would be a wise decision, prefect. Ride home past the barracks and be sure to fight if you are attacked. I do not think you will be, not today.'

Liu Yin-San's hands were trembling as he turned his horse and began to walk it away. His men were driven before the Mongol army so that they rode awkwardly, expecting arrows in their backs at any moment. Kublai grinned, but he followed closely, taking his column in further until they reached the barracks of the city garrison. An open square eased some of the tension in the Mongol warriors. At the edges, double-storey buildings stretched, enough to house thousands of men.

Liu Yin-San halted then and Kublai could see the prefect was still expecting to be cut down.

'There will come a time,' Kublai said, 'when I stand again before you and ask you to surrender Shaoyang. You will not refuse me then. Now go home. No one will die today.'

Liu Yin-San left with his small group, many of them looking back over and over as they dwindled into the distance, finally vanishing into the streets of the city. No one else was in sight, Kublai realised. The people of Shaoyang had indeed hidden themselves behind locked doors rather than face the invader.

His men began throwing open the buildings of the Shaoyang garrison, revealing vast stables, armouries, dormitories and kitchens. One of them put his fingers to his mouth and whistled sharply, drawing Kublai's attention. He walked his horse over the training ground and saw Uriang-Khadai's column enter the other side as he went. Kublai turned to the scouts that were always at his side.

'One of you run to the orlok and tell him to report to me. Another to general Bayar, wherever he has gone to.'

They galloped away over the stones, a pleasant clattering that echoed back from the buildings around the open space. Kublai dismounted and walked into a long hall that had him grinning in the first few steps. He could see pikes by the thousand in racks, then as he walked further, he found shields stacked against each other in wooden frames. He walked past bows that could not match the range of his own. Rooms opened onto rooms and by the time Uriang-Khadai had reached the outer ones, Kublai was standing in a fletchers' hall, with the smell of glue and wood and feather strong in the air. Dozens of benches showed where men worked each day and the results could be seen in the stacks of perfect quivers on every side. He pulled out a shaft and inspected it, rubbing the flights with his thumb. The Sung regiments were served by master craftsmen.

Kublai removed his bow from its loop over his back and strung it with quick movements. He heard someone enter behind him and he turned to see Uriang-Khadai standing with a rare expression of satisfaction on his face. Kublai nodded to him and drew the bow, sending an arrow at the far wall. It punched through the wood and vanished beyond it, leaving a visible spot of light as the flights fell to the wooden floor. For the first time in days, Kublai felt his weariness lift.

'Have your men gather them up quickly, Uriang-Khadai. Get the scouts out looking for a place where we can sleep and eat, somewhere clear of the city. Tomorrow is soon enough to begin fighting our way clear.'

Kublai smiled as he looked around the hall. Someone would have to work it out, but there had to be a million shafts in new quivers, perhaps even more.

'We have teeth again, orlok. Let's use them.'

Xuan, Son of Heaven, had never seen the Sung at war. The sheer scale of it was impressive, but he thought the pace was dangerously slow. It had taken them a month to escort him to a meeting of Sung lords in the city. More than a hundred had been in attendance, placed according to their ranks in tiered seating, so that the most powerful had positions on the actual debating floor and the least were leaning over the upper balconies to listen. They had fallen silent as he'd walked in, flanked by Sung officials.

His initial impression had been of a mass of colour, staring eyes and stiff robes of green and red and orange. There were as many different styles as men in the room. Some wore simple tunics beaded in pearls, while others sweltered in high collars and headgear decorated with anything from peacock feathers to enormous jewels. A few of the younger ones looked like warriors, but many more resembled ornate birds, hardly able to move for the layers of silk and finery.

Xuan's presence had flustered servants with no clear instructions. In terms of his nobility, he outranked all the men in the room, but he was the nominal ruler of a foreign nation and commanded a tiny force of ageing soldiers. The servants had found him a place on the lower floor, but towards the back, a typical compromise.

At first, Xuan was content merely to watch and listen, learning the personalities and politics as he suffered through another month of detailed talks. He recognised few faces or names from his time in Sung lands, but he knew the lords in that room could put a million men in the field if they chose to do so or were given a direct order by the emperor. Xuan had yet to see his cousin. The elderly emperor rarely left his palace and the actual business of the war was the concern of the lords. Yet the emperor had insisted Xuan attend the council, as one of the few men who had faced Mongol hordes and survived. His presence was tolerated, though he was not exactly welcomed as a long-lost son. Proud Sung nobles stopped just short of snubbing him completely. They had to endure his presence, but when he did not put his name down as a speaker, many of them were privately pleased, assuming he was intimidated by the powerful assembly.

They met twice every month, though it was rare for the seats to be filled as they had been on his first entrance. Through more regular attendance than half the lords there, Xuan learned of the second massive army Mongke Khan had brought into their lands. For a morning, the threat had almost swept aside the petty politics of the court. Two lords whose lands adjoined each other spoke without their usual barely concealed bitterness. It had not lasted beyond that first sense of truce and by the afternoon one of them had stormed out with his trail of servants and the other was frozen in rage at whatever insult he had perceived to his house and rank.

Despite the chaotic lack of leadership, actual fighting did take place. Xuan learned that in the south, the tumans with Kublai had smashed eleven armies, some three-quarters of a million men. Rather than allow them to grow strong on captured weapons, the only choice had been to throw regiment after regiment at the Mongols, forcing Kublai to keep moving and fighting, wearing him down. In his time in the debating chamber, Xuan had seen four nobles stand and make their farewells to take the field. None of them had returned and, as the news came in, their names were added to a scroll of the honoured dead.

As the third month began, Xuan entered the chamber with a lighter step. It was barely half full, but more were coming in behind him and taking their accustomed places. Xuan made his way to one of the scribes who reported the debates and stood in front of him until the man looked up.

'I will speak today,' Xuan said.

The scribe's eyes widened slightly, but he nodded, bowing his head as he added Xuan's formal name with his brushes and ink. It took some time for him to complete it but the scribe knew his business and did not have to check his records. The gathering lords had not missed the event. Many of them were staring at him as he returned to his seat and others sent runners to their allies. While Xuan waited patiently, more and more lords came from their homes in the city until the room was as packed as it had been on his first day.

Xuan wondered if any of them knew he had been summoned to the emperor's palace the night before, taken from the barracks where he stayed with his men. It had been a short meeting, but he had been pleased to find his elderly cousin was not unaware of the war, or its lack of progress. The emperor of the Sung was just as frustrated as Xuan himself and had left him with one command – to shake the lords out of their complacency. The rest of the night had been spent with Sung scribes, and for once Xuan had been allowed to see any record he wanted. He had given up sleep to learn everything he could and as he sat peacefully in the debating chamber, his mind twitched with facts and stratagems.

He waited through the ritual opening of the council, though the formalities took an age. Two other men spoke before him and he listened politely until they were finished and minor votes took place. One of them appeared to know the assembled lords were waiting for Xuan and hurried his presentation, while the other was oblivious and rambled on for an hour about iron ore supplies in the eastern provinces.

When they sat down, the emperor's chancellor spoke his name and Xuan stood. Heads craned to see him and on a whim he walked forward to the centre of the room, so that he faced them all in half-circles rising up to the balconies above. No one whispered or shuffled. He had their complete attention.

'According to the imperial records in Hangzhou, more than two million trained soldiers are under arms, not counting the losses to date. The honourable lords in this room have eleven thousand cannon between them. Yet a Mongol force of barely a hundred thousand has made them look like children.'

A ripple of outrage ran around the room, but the calculated reference to records had not been lost on them. Only the emperor had such information and it silenced those who might have shouted him down. Xuan ignored the murmuring and went on.

'In time, I believe sheer numbers would have brought success

331

despite the lack of a unified command. Mistakes have been made, not least the assumption that the army of Kublai is in the field and must eventually return home to resupply. They have no need to do so, my lords. They are not in the field. They are merely in a new *place*, as all places are new to them. They cannot be waited out, as I have heard so eloquently argued in this chamber. If they are not destroyed, they will come to Hangzhou in a year, or two years, or ten. It took them longer than that to take control of Chin lands in the north, lands far larger than those of the Sung.'

He had to wait as voices spoke over him, but the majority wanted to hear what he had to say and the fiery arguments died for lack of support.

'Even so, they would eventually have failed against the Sung regiments. But now the Mongol khan has brought a new army to the Sung, greater than any he has wielded before. The reports give the numbers as more than a quarter of a million men – this time without their camps. They have no cannon and so their strategy becomes clear.'

The silence was total then, as every lord strained to hear. Xuan deliberately dropped his voice so that no one would dare to interrupt him again.

'He ignores Sung cities and moves incredible distances. If I had not read the scout reports in the emperor's offices, I would not have believed it, but they are crossing vast stretches of land each day, heading south. Their intention is clearly to join up with Kublai's tumans, clearing the field of any army in their way. It is a bold strategy, one that shows contempt for the armies of the Sung. Mongke Khan will destroy the men in the field and then take the cities at his leisure, either using captured cannon, or by siege. Unless he is stopped, he will be at the gates of Hangzhou in less than a year.'

As one, the lords began to shout indignantly at the slur on

their courage and strength. To be lectured in such a way by a failed emperor was too much, insufferable. Cooler heads considered once again that he had the ear of the emperor, his cousin by blood. The noise died down to just a few, who eventually subsided back to their seats with angry expressions. Xuan continued as if there had been no interruption.

'There must be no more personal actions by individual lords. Those have failed to end the threat – a threat which has now grown. Nothing less than the complete mobilisation of Sung forces is necessary.' Two Sung lords rose from their seats in silence, indicating to the emperor's chancellor that they wished to speak. 'This is the moment to strike,' Xuan went on. 'The Mongol khan is with his armies. If he can be stopped, there will be a period of time when both Chin and Mongol lands can be conquered.' Four more stood to speak. 'It will no longer be a mere defensive war, my lords. If you gather your armies under a single leader, we have a chance to unite Chin and Sung once again.'

He paused. A dozen Sung lords had risen, their eyes moving from him to the emperor's chancellor, whose task it was to impose some order to debates. Until Xuan sat down, he could not be formally interrupted, though the rule was often ignored. For once, they waited, aware of the importance of the debate to come. Xuan frowned, knowing the men who would speak were not those likely to add to a clear resolution.

'This war can no longer be fought as individuals. Appoint a leader who will command complete authority. Send half a million men against Kublai and as many against the Mongol khan. Surround their small armies and crush them. In that way, you will be spared the sight of Hangzhou in flames. I have seen Yenking burn, my lords. That is enough.'

He sat down under the silent pressure of so many eyes, wondering if he had reached anyone in the room.

The voice of the emperor's chancellor rang out.

'The chamber recognises Lord Sung Win.'

Xuan hid his grimace at the name and waited. He had a right to reply before the end.

'My lords, I have just two questions for the esteemed speaker,' Lord Sung Win said. 'Do you have the emperor's direct order to unite the armies? And is it your intention that the command of the Sung should fall to your hands?'

A roar of derision went up from the rest of the men in the room and Xuan frowned more deeply. He recalled the watery eyes of his cousin at their brief meeting. The emperor was a weak man and Xuan could still feel the clutch of his hand on his sleeve. He had asked for a letter of authority, an imperial mandate, but the man had waved his hand in dismissal. Authority lay in what the lords would accept and Xuan had known then that his cousin feared to give such an order. Why else would he have summoned an old enemy to his private rooms? If the emperor ordered it and they refused, his weakness would be exposed and the empire would fall apart into armed factions. Civil war would accomplish everything the Mongols could not.

All this flashed through Xuan's mind as he stood stiffly once more.

'I have the emperor's confidence that you will listen, Lord Sung Win. I have his faith that you will not allow the Sung to be destroyed for petty politics, that loyal Sung lords will recognise the true threat. And I am not the one to lead you against the Mongols, my lord. Whoever does so must command complete confidence from this chamber. If you will take the responsibility, my lord, I will support you.'

Lord Sung Win blinked as he rose again, clearly wondering if Xuan had just ruined his chance to do exactly that. The Chin emperor was a thorn in the side of the lords there and his support was worthless.

'I had hoped to see the emperor's personal seal,' Lord Sung Win said, his eyes bright with dislike. 'Instead, I hear vague words with no substance, no opportunity to verify their accuracy.'

The chamber grew hushed and Lord Sung Win realised he had gone too far in almost accusing Xuan of lying. He recalled Xuan's lack of status and grew calm once again. There would be no demand for reparation or punishment from such a fallen power.

Sung Win's hesitation cost him with the imperial chancellor, who knew better than most what had gone on the night before between his master and the Chin cousin.

'The chamber recognises Lord Jin An,' he bellowed.

Sung Win closed his mouth with a snap and took his seat with bad grace as a younger lord nodded to the chancellor.

'Does anyone here deny the existence of the khan's army and its smaller brother in the south and west?' Lord Jin An said, his voice clear and confident. 'Will they refuse to accept the threat to us all, until those armies are battering at Hangzhou gates? Let us move to a vote at once. I put my name forward to lead one of the two armies we must send.'

For a moment, Xuan lost his frown and looked up, but the young lord's voice was lost in the uproar. Even the number of armies was in dispute and Xuan felt his heart sink as he realised they could not be shaken from their apathy. In moments, Lord Jin An was angrily vowing that he would take his own men against Kublai, that he would act alone if no one else had the good sense to see the need. Xuan rubbed his eyes as the lack of sleep caught up with him. He had seen it four times before, when young lords set out to battle the tumans. Their martial fervour had not been enough. Accusations and threats were thrown back and forth across the chamber, as each of the lords shouted over their neighbours. There would be no resolution that day, if at all, and all the time the Mongol armies grew closer. Xuan shook his head at the insanity of it. He could try to reach the emperor once again, but the man was surrounded by thousands of courtiers who would consider such a request and whether they should even pass it on. Xuan had seen too much of Sung bureaucracy in his years as a captive and he did not have much hope.

When the meeting broke up at noon, Xuan approached the young lord, still talking furiously to two others. They fell silent at his presence and Lord Jin An turned to him, bowing instinctively to his rank.

'I had hoped for a better outcome,' Xuan said.

Lord Jin An nodded ruefully.

'I have forty thousand, Son of Heaven, and the promise of support from a cousin.' He sighed. 'I have good reports this Kublai has been seen around Shaoyang. I should not even be here in this chamber, arguing with cowards. My place is there, against the weaker of the two armies. Forty thousand would be lost against the khan's army in the north.' His mouth twisted in irritation and he swept his arm across to indicate the last of the departing lords. 'Perhaps when these fools see him riding through Hangzhou's streets, they will see the need to work together.'

Xuan smiled at the younger man's indignant expression.

'Perhaps not even then,' he said. 'I wish I had a strong army to send with you, Lord Jin An. Yet my eight thousand are yours to command, if you will have us.'

Lord Jin An waved his hand, as if at a trifle. In truth, Xuan's force would make little difference and both men knew it. In their prime, they would have been valuable, but after years of poor food and worse conditions, a few months had barely begun to restore them. Nonetheless, the young lord was gracious.

'I will leave on the first of the month,' he said. 'It would be an honour to be accompanied by such men. I hope you will be available to advise me.'

Xuan's smile widened in genuine pleasure. It had been a long time since he had been treated graciously by any Sung lord.

'Whatever service I can provide is yours, Lord Jin An. Perhaps by the time we leave, you will have found other lords who might share your views.'

Lord Jin An looked back at the empty chamber.

'Perhaps,' he murmured, looking doubtful.

Orlok Seriankh paced as he addressed his assembled officers. Twenty-eight tuman generals stood before him. At their backs, two hundred and eighty minghaan officers stood in ranks.

'I have sent scouts north to join the yam lines,' Seriankh said. His voice was hoarse from giving a thousand orders, keeping the army from falling into chaos as a thousand voices argued over what to do. Mongke Khan lay dead, wrapped in cloth inside a lone ger. The rest of the army had packed up and were ready to move in any direction as soon as Seriankh gave the order.

'Lord Hulegu will be informed of the khan's death in a month, two at most. He will return. The khan's brother, Arik-Boke, will get the news faster still, in Karakorum. There will be another quiriltai, a gathering, and the next khan will be chosen. I have a dozen men riding south to find Kublai and pass on the news. He too will come home. Our time here is at an end until there is a new great khan.'

His most senior general, Salsanan, stepped forward and the orlok turned to acknowledge him.

'Orlok Seriankh, I will volunteer to lead a force to Kublai, to support his withdrawal. He will not thank us for abandoning him in the field.' The man paused and then continued. 'He may be the next khan.'

'Guard your mouth, general,' Seriankh snapped. 'It is not your place to guess and spread rumours.' He hesitated, thinking it through. Mongke had many sons, but the succession of khans had never been smooth since the death of Genghis.

'To support his withdrawal, very well. We have lost a khan, but Lord Kublai has lost a brother. Take eight tumans and bring him safely out of Sung territory. I will take the khan home.'

CHAPTER TWENTY-EIGHT

With ancient oaks overhead, Kublai sat out in the open air. He bore the pain in silence as Chabi washed a cut on his right hand with a skin of airag, taking pulls from it himself to keep him warm. They had both known men who walked away from battles with just a gash, then died in feverish delirium days or weeks later. Humming to herself, Chabi sniffed at his hand and wrinkled her nose. Kublai hissed through his teeth as she squeezed the livid edges, making a thin stream of pus dribble down to his fingers.

'I do have shamans for this, you know,' he said affectionately.

She snorted. 'They're busy and you wouldn't bother them with it until your arm was green.'

She gave his skin another sharp pinch, making him jerk. The flow of pus grew red and she nodded, satisfied, resting one hand on the curve of her belly as new life grew within. Kublai reached out and patted the bulge affectionately as she rewrapped the cut with a clean strip of cloth.

The families and followers had moved deeper into the forest while he had been fighting the Sung, obscuring all signs that might be found by enemies looking for them. Kublai had been forced to send hundreds of his men into the green depths.

Just to reach the area, he had fought his way back past two Sung armies and seen his stocks of arrows and lances dwindle once again, though he salvaged as many as he could. Without healers and rest, some of his wounded men had died each day.

He looked overhead, oddly uncomfortable as the thick branches reduced the forest floor to gloom. At least they were hidden. The families and camp followers had been kept safe by the dense forest, but he couldn't shake the fear that they could also hide an enemy creeping up. Even for a man of Karakorum, the forest felt stifling compared to the open plains.

He looked closer at his wife as she stood, seeing dark smudges under her eyes. She looked thin and he cursed himself for not having made better preparations. He should have known the families would be forced to butcher the flocks while they waited for him to return. The vast herds usually replenished themselves each spring, but the one thing the forest did not have was good grazing. The ground was covered in rotting leaves and what little greenery there was had been stripped down to bare earth in the first month. The families had eaten deer and rabbits, even wolves when they found them, but it had not been long before the forest was trapped out for fifty miles. The herds of sheep and goats had shrunk to the point where everyone was on a meal a day and not much meat in that.

When Kublai had ridden in at last, the sight of his people had not been inspiring. They had rallied around as the tumans came in and he made a point of praising them for their survival, even as he seethed at how badly they had done without him. It was possible to count the ribs on the precious oxen and he wondered how many would have the strength to pull carts when the time came to move. His son and pregnant wife had been given barely enough meat to survive and Kublai wanted to lash out in rage at the rest of them. He would have done if they hadn't been just as thin and pale as Chabi.

'We have to move the camp,' Chabi said softly. 'I don't want to think what would have happened if you'd stayed out much longer.'

'I can't take you out. They just keep coming,' he said. 'You've never seen anything like it, Chabi. There isn't any end to them.'

Her mouth firmed as he spoke.

'Even so, we can't stay here. There isn't a rabbit for twenty miles and when the last of the flocks are gone, we'll starve. Some of the men were saying they'd strike out on their own if you didn't come back soon.'

'Who?' he demanded.

Chabi shook her head. 'Men with families of their own. Can you blame them? We knew we were in trouble, Kublai.'

'I'll drive herds back from the Sung hills and villages. I'll get new animals to pull the carts.'

He swore under his breath, knowing it wouldn't work. Even if he could drive a herd towards the forest, the marks of their passing would be there for any Sung scout to read. He had already endangered the position by bringing his tumans back to the camp. To do it again would leave a wide road through the forest. He pushed his fingers into the corners of his eyes, easing away some of the tiredness. The camp supported the warriors with everything from arrow shafts to shelter and hot food, but he had reached an impossible position.

'I can send out the tumans to gather food and draft beasts to be butchered, or replace the weakest of our stock . . .' He swore under his breath. 'I can't be thinking of this, Chabi! I have made tracks into the Sung, but I need to keep going, or everything I've done will have been wasted.'

'Is it so terrible to rest up for the winter? You'll be here when the child is born, Kublai. Send out your men to bring back anything that lives, raid the local towns and you'll be ready to go out again in the spring.'

341

Kublai groaned at the thought. Part of him ached at the idea of simply stopping to rest. He had never felt so tired.

'I've cleared a route as far as Shaoyang and beyond, Chabi. If I can keep moving, I'll be able to reach their capital by spring or summer. If I stop now, I'll see another dozen armies coming out against me, fresh and strong.'

'And you will lose the camp if you go on,' she snapped. 'You will lose the fletchers, the tanners and saddlers, the hard-working wives and men who keep you in the field. Will the tumans still fight well while their families starve behind them?'

'You will not starve,' Kublai said.

'Saying it does not make it so. It was getting ugly before your scouts found us, husband. Some of the men were talking about taking the last food stocks for themselves and letting the weakest ones die from hunger.'

Kublai grew still, his eyes hard.

'This time you *will* tell me their names, Chabi. I'll hang them from the branches.'

'That is a distraction! It doesn't matter now. Find a way to solve the problem, husband. I know the pressure on you, or I think I do. I know you will work it out.'

He walked a few paces away from her, staring into the green undergrowth all around.

'This land is rich, Chabi,' he said after a time. 'I can take a month to raid new flocks. We can drive them back here, but then I'm sending half the camp home to Karakorum.' He held up a hand to forestall her as she opened her mouth. 'These aren't the battles Genghis knew, where he could take the entire nation and raid with tumans from the centre. The Sung are like ants in their numbers, army after army. I need to think like a raider, with the bare minimum of supplies. The women and children can go home, with enough warriors to keep them safe. You and Zhenjin will leave with them. There. You asked for a decision and that's it. I can take a month, I think.'

'You can, but I am not going. I won't lose another child on a hard journey home, Kublai. I'm staying with the camp until the birth.'

He saw the resolution in her face and sighed.

'I'm too tired to argue with you, woman.'

'Good,' she said.

Kublai begrudged every day lost as his tumans scoured the land for herds for a hundred miles and more. In the winter, it took longer than he hoped and he saw the full moon twice before he brought the families out of the forest. The dark months were colder than the previous year. Ice crackled in the boughs of the forest, beautiful and dead at the same time. There was always wood for the stoves and the gers were surrounded by firewood piled higher than a man's head.

The ground was still frozen when they began to pack up and leave the forest depths. Behind them, they left the usual marks, from black circles of ground under dismantled gers, to the graves of those who had died. Most were wounded men the shamans could not save, but there were many smaller graves as well, of children who had not lived through their first year. There were no mountains to lay them out for sky burial, where the carrion birds would feast. Cremation fires were too likely to spread or be seen by an enemy, so the frozen ground was broken just deep enough to cover them.

Kublai gathered the camp on an open plain. Hundreds of oxen had been yoked and they were better fed than when he had come upon them. Grain from Sung towns had been brought back with the herds and the massive animals were glossy with care, their muzzles wet and pink. He had ordered two hundred thousand of his people home, mostly the wives and children. Ten thousand men would go with them, those who had been wounded, or maimed in some old war. They could still fight if they had to.

His men griped out of habit at the order, but they too had seen the Sung armies and there was relief amidst the final embraces. The families would go fast to the Chin border, crossing in the spring to safer lands. From there, Kublai had sent scouts to his own estates. They would be safe on their journey north. He had kept only the most skilful craftsmen and herders, the metalsmiths, rope-makers and leather-workers. Most of the gers would go, so the tumans would sleep uncovered in the rain and frost.

Kublai had to keep some carts for the forges and equipment supplies – his silver would go with him into the east. He knew the camp would be less cheerful from that point. It was no longer a moving nation but a war camp, with every man there dedicated to the tumans they supported.

The two massive groups slowly drew apart, with many shouting last words. The mounted tumans watched grimly as their families grew smaller in the distance. Chabi and Zhenjin remained with her servants, but no one dared object to the decisions of the khan's own brother. They had scouted to the Chin border and there were no armies in that direction. The danger lay only in the east and every man in the tumans knew the work was not finished. It was hard to be cheerful on such a day.

It was still a host that trundled deeper into Sung lands, but there was already a sense of having cut away the fat. They kept a good pace and if there was no singing in the camps at night, at least the men were quietly determined. Without the individual wives, the warriors were fed from communal pots, filled to the brim with a thick broth each night.

As the days began to lengthen, Kublai passed sites of his own battles. He rode in sick horror through fields of rotting corpses. Foxes, wolves and birds had feasted and flesh sloughed off the bones, enemies and friends sliding into one another as they were made soft in sun and rain. His tumans rode through with utter indifference, making Kublai wonder how they could keep their food in their stomachs. His imagination forced him to consider his own death, left in a foreign field. He did not know whether such concerns troubled men like Uriang-Khadai, or whether they would admit the truth if he asked.

His scouts reported contact with a force of cavalry forty miles shy of Shaoyang, but whoever it was retreated at speed before the tumans, staying out of range and riding as if all hell was on their heels. Without an order being given, Kublai's warriors began to increase their pace each day. The carts in the reduced camp fell back to the maximum range of twenty miles, within reach of a sudden assault if they came under attack. During the cold days, the men drank warm blood from the mares, sharing the slight wounds between three or four spare mounts so that none of the animals grew too weak. They were in their own battle trail and there were no fresh supplies to be had until they passed Shaoyang. Kublai wondered how the prefect there would react when he saw them return. He would survive their passing for a second time, something few men could say.

Kublai had understood at last that he had too few warriors to smash their heads against Sung walls. Eventually, the swarming enemy would grind his tumans into dust. He had made his decision and wondered if he was even the same man who had entered Sung lands with such youthful confidence. He could not have gambled it all back then. Now, he would drive them on to the heart of the empire in one great push.

He would not stop for Shaoyang. He would not stop for anything.

His tumans could see men on the roofs of the sprawling city as they rode past. Kublai raised a hand to them, in greeting or farewell, he did not know. He would cut the heart out of the Sung dragon in one strike. The other cities had nothing to fear from him.

Past Shaoyang, the land had not been stripped of everything that might feed a hungry soldier. The first small towns were looted for food, though Kublai forbade their destruction. Back in the forest camp, his men had seen the great store of silver he had taken, handed down from a thousand horses, the bars passing from man to man and then placed in piles on the wet leaves. Though the tumans had not been paid in months, they knew at least that it existed and did not grumble too loudly or too often.

He did not expect yam riders, so far to the south. The lines of way stations had ended in Chin lands and when he saw not one but two of the men, they barely resembled the fast-moving endurance riders he knew. His scouts brought the pair in together and Kublai drew to a halt on a wide plain as he heard the jingle of bells from their saddle cloths. He nodded to Uriang-Khadai and the orlok bellowed orders to dismount and rest.

'They look half dead,' Bayar murmured to Kublai as the men rode up with his scouts on either side.

It was true enough and Kublai wondered how the men had been finding food without the yam stations to feed them or give them fresh mounts. Both were unkempt and one of them moved with obvious pain, grunting at every step of his horse. They came to a halt and Bayar told them to dismount. The first one slid from the saddle, staggering slightly as he landed.

While he was searched, Bayar looked up into the grey face of his companion.

'I have an arrow somewhere in my back,' the yam rider said weakly. 'It's broken off, but I don't think I can get down.' Bayar saw how his right hand hung limp, flopping in the reins that were wrapped around it. He called one of his men and together they pulled the rider clear of his saddle. He tried not to cry out, but the strangled sound of agony he made was worse.

On the ground, Bayar lowered the man to his knees and looked at the arrow stump sticking out high on his shoulders. Every breath would have hurt and Bayar whistled softly. He reached down and prodded the stub, making the rider jerk away with a stifled curse.

'It's rotting the flesh,' Bayar said. 'I can smell it from here. I'll have a shaman cut it out and seal it with fire. You've done well.'

'Did anyone else reach you?' the man said. He leaned forward on his locked arms, panting like a dog. Bayar shook his head and the yam rider swore and spat. 'There were twelve of us. I've been searching and riding for a long time.' The eyes were angry and Bayar bristled in response.

'We were enjoying ourselves, seeing a bit of the local country. You found us in the end. Now would you like to deliver your message, or shall I have that arrow cut out first?'

The second rider had been searched and allowed to approach Kublai, opening his leather bag and handing over a folded sheet sealed with Mongke's mark in wax. Bayar and the wounded man watched in silence as Kublai broke the seal and read.

'No need now. He already knows.'

The wounded yam rider sagged and Bayar took him under the arms, ignoring the stink of sweat and urine. He could feel heat radiating from the flesh, a sure sign of fever. Even then,

Bayar was surprised at the lack of weight. The young man had almost starved to bring the message and he wondered what could have been so important as to send twelve riders with the same message. Bayar knew enough to suspect no good news ever arrived in that way. He called one of his officers over.

'Fetch a shaman. If he's to live, the arrowhead will have to be dug out and the wound cleaned. Take him from me.' He passed the dazed rider over and stood, unconsciously wiping his hands down his leggings.

Kublai had grown pale as he read. The sheet with its broken seal hung forgotten from his hand. He stared into the distance, his eyes like dull glass. Bayar's mood sank further as he walked across to him.

'As bad as that?' the general said quietly.

'As bad as that,' Kublai confirmed, his voice hoarse with grief.

Xuan felt alive for the first time in years as he rode west. The old skills were still there, long dormant, like seeds beneath the autumn leaves. He could see his men felt the same. They had grown old in captivity, their best years wasted and thrown away, but with every mile they rode from Hangzhou, the past was further behind. More important than that was the news that had come as they left the city. Mongol scouts had been captured as they came south. Each carried an identical message written in the script of their homeland.

Xuan had seen one of the originals, still stained with the blood of its owner. Only a suspicious mind could have seen the benefits of announcing the khan's death as he rode south. Xuan had that mind, made so by years of captivity. Even so, he longed for the news to be true. He knew the traditions the Mongols followed so slavishly. If they returned home, it would be an answer to his prayers, indeed the prayers of the Sung nation.

He shook his head in the wind, clearing his thoughts with the physical movement. Whether Mongke Khan was truly dead or engaged in some dark game did not matter to him. Xuan did not know if he would live when they found Kublai's tumans, but he was certain he would never return to Hangzhou.

He looked across at his eldest son, riding on his right hand. Liao-Jin was still swept up in the sheer ecstasy of freedom, no matter where they rode or who might face them. He had thrown himself into the training with all the energy of his youth. Xuan smiled to himself. The men liked him. He would have made a fine emperor, if there had been an empire for him to rule. None of that mattered. They were free. The word was like sweet summer to every man there.

In the chaotic activity of preparing eight thousand men to ride with Sung regiments, it had not been hard to bring Xuan's other children out of captivity. Xuan had simply sent two of his men on horseback through the city streets, with orders in his own hand. No one had dared to question his new authority, or if they had, the responses had been too slow to stop them. Xuan had even hired servants for them with his Sung cousin's silver. Given just one moonless night, he would send them north with a few of the best Chin men remaining to him. They would survive in their old lands, somehow. He had not yet told Liao-Jin that his son would travel with them, away from the Mongol tumans coming east.

On either side of the Chin force, Sung lords rode. Lord Jin An had been as good as his word and provided almost fifty thousand soldiers, half of them cavalry. Xuan had not known the young lord was a man of such power, but it seemed his clan had been leaders in the field of war for many generations. Lord Jin An had managed to persuade one other to join him, a cousin who brought another forty thousand to the ranks. To Xuan, it felt like a huge host, though both the Sung lords still seethed at the lack of support from the council, or the emperor himself.

They had brought hundreds of cannon that cut their pace down to a third of what it could have been, but Xuan took heart from the sight of those black tubes trundling along good Sung roads. There were times when Xuan could even dream of futures where he destroyed the Mongol army that was cutting its way through the Sung territories. A solid victory would unite even the council of lords, so that they would move as one against the greater threat in the north. On his most optimistic days, Xuan allowed himself to imagine his old lands returned to him. It was a good thought, but he smiled at his own foolishness. The Mongols had not been beaten for generations. He only wished Tsaio-Wen was there to see Chin soldiers riding with pride. The surly Sung officer had managed to vanish at the same time as the orders for him to report to the barracks had been sent. A coward at the last, Xuan thought. That too did not matter.

Shaoyang was not many miles ahead and the scouts were out, watching for the first sign of Kublai's tumans. The Mongols had been in the area months before and Xuan did not expect them to be close, but he would find them. He would run them down. Xuan reached out and patted his horse's neck, feeling again the exultation of being out at last. He turned to Liao-Jin and shouted above the noise of horses and men.

'Take out the banners, Liao-Jin. Show the Sung who we are.'

He saw the flash of white teeth from his son as he passed on the orders to bannermen on either side. In its way, it had been the hardest task of the previous few months. Finding cloth had not been difficult, but Xuan had been forced to give the task to his own men, in case the news reached the lords or his emperor cousin and was forbidden before he could ride. They had shaped and sewed and cut the long banners, marking yellow silk with the painted chop of Xuan's noble house. Xuan found he was holding his breath as the bannermen unfurled the cloth. The streaming banners fluttered in the wind, stretching out in lines of gold.

The last Chin army raised their heads. Many of them grew bright-eyed with tears at a sight they had never expected to see again. They cheered the banners of a Chin emperor and Xuan felt his throat grow thick with pride and grief and joy.

CHAPTER TWENTY-NINE

As the afternoon wore on, the tumans remained in the same place, just a few miles east of Shaoyang. The warriors saw that Kublai's ger was being assembled and the constant, slight tension vanished. There would be no sudden order to mount and ride while the white ger was up. Between them, the eighty thousand men had three hundred thousand spare horses that ran together in a herd like the leaves of a forest, brown and grey and black and dun. As well as providing blood and milk for their riders, the ponies all carried some item of kit, from spare armour scales, ropes and glue, to hard blocks of cheese. It was the secret of their success that alone of all nations they could raid for hundreds of miles from the main camp.

Kublai seemed almost in a trance as he stood on the empty grassland, surrounded by the sea of horses and men. The carts of his camp could be seen in the distance, slowly coming up behind them. He was aware of Bayar walking over again to speak to him, but he did not reply, just stood in silence, drawn utterly into himself.

It had been Bayar's order to raise the ger. The general was filled with apprehension. Whatever Kublai had read had left him pale and dumbstruck on the grassy plain. It was a crime punishable by flogging for a man to question a yam rider about his messages, but even so, Bayar watched closely as the man accepted tea and a pouch of bread and meat. The rider chewed with the same long stare that Bayar saw in Kublai and the general itched to take him for a walk and discover the truth.

The carts arrived without fanfare or any great welcome, now that the wives and children had gone. Oxen and camels were turned loose to graze. Forges were set up on the grass and fed with charcoal until the heavy iron glowed red. Warriors who needed something strolled in with no great urgency. All over the plain, others sat down to ease their legs and backs. Many of them took the chance to defecate in a place where they would not stay, or urinate into the grass. Others sharpened weapons and checked their bows and shafts as they liked to do at every opportunity. Some of them ate, others talked, but the strange stillness at the heart of the tumans was spreading out, so that more and more of them knew something was wrong.

When the ger was complete, Bayar approached Kublai again.

'There is a place to rest, my lord,' he said.

Kublai dragged his gaze back from very far away.

'Bring my packs to me,' he said softly. 'There are things I need in them.'

Bayar bowed and trotted away. The strangeness of the day made him want to return to Kublai as soon as possible. He sent four scouts into the baggage carts to bring back the great rolls, tied with rope.

'Put them inside,' Bayar ordered the men. Kublai had not moved. 'My lord, is the news so terrible? Will you tell me what's wrong?'

'The khan is dead, general,' Kublai replied, his voice barely a whisper. 'My *brother* is dead. I will not see him again.'

Bayar recoiled in shock. He shook his head as if he could deny the words. He watched as Kublai ducked into the ger, disappearing in the gloom within. Bayar felt as if he had been kicked in the chest, the air hammered out of him. He leaned forward, placing his hands on his knees as he tried to think.

Uriang-Khadai was close enough to see Bayar rocked by whatever Kublai had said to him. He approached the younger general with a wary expression, needing to hear, but at the same time deeply worried about what he might be told.

Bayar saw that there were many men nearby who had witnessed his reaction to the news. They had almost abandoned the pretence of not listening. Regardless of the penalties, he doubted the two yam riders would be left alone for long. The news could not be contained. Bayar found himself sweating at the thought. It would spread across the world. Campaigns would come to a halt, cities would grow still as they heard. The men of power in the khanates would know they were thrown back into the maelstrom once again. Some of them would fear the future; others would be sharpening their swords.

'Mongke Khan is dead,' Bayar told his superior.

Uriang-Khadai blanched, but gathered himself quickly.

'How did it happen?' he said.

Bayar raised his hands helplessly. Everything Kublai had achieved in Sung lands was thrown into chaos by a single message. He could hardly think. Watching him, Uriang-Khadai's lips thinned to a seam of pale flesh.

'Get a hold of yourself, general. We have lost khans before. The nation goes on. Come with me to speak to the yam riders. They will know more than we have been told.'

Bayar stared. He followed as Uriang-Khadai strode away, heading to the unwounded rider who stared at him like a rabbit faced with a wolf.

'You. Tell me what you know.'

The yam rider swallowed a mouthful of bread and meat painfully, then stood.

'It was an assassin, general.'

'*Orlok*,' Uriang-Khadai snapped.

The man was trembling as he repeated the title.

'Orlok. I was sent out with a dozen others. More went north to the Chin yam lines.'

'What?' Uriang-Khadai stepped closer to him. 'You were in *Sung* territory?'

'The khan was coming south, orlok,' the man stammered, his nervousness growing. He knew yam riders were meant to be untouchable, but sooner or later, he was going to have to tell the manner of the khan's death. It struck at the heart of every yam rider in the khanates. They would never be as trusted again.

'How far away are they?' Uriang-Khadai demanded. 'How many men? Must I ask for every detail before it spills from your mouth?'

'I . . . I'm sorry, orlok. Twenty-eight tumans, but they will not come further. Orlok Seriankh is taking them back to Karakorum. The khan's other brothers will have heard by now, certainly Lord Arik-Boke as he was in the capital. Lord Hulegu may hear any day now, if he has not already.' The scout searched for something else to say under Uriang-Khadai's cold stare. 'I was there when the body of Guyuk Khan was found, orlok. The nation will pull back to Karakorum until there is a new khan.'

'*I* was there when Tsubodai had the news of *Ogedai's* death, young man. Do not tell me what I already know.'

'No, orlok, I'm sorry.'

Uriang-Khadai turned to Bayar, frustrated with the yam rider and his nervousness.

'Do you have questions for him?'

'Only one,' Bayar replied. 'How did an assassin reach the khan in the middle of such an army?'

The exhausted young man looked as if his bread and meat had lodged in his throat.

'He . . . dressed as a yam rider. He was let through. He was searched, but I heard he kept a razor hidden.'

'Jesus *Christ*,' Uriang-Khadai growled.

Bayar looked at him in surprise, though the Christian curses were spreading even to those who had no knowledge of the faith itself.

Kublai stood inside the ger without moving for a long time. He wanted Chabi to come to him, but he could not summon the energy to send for her. He could hear the noises of his people around him, but at least the small space kept out their stares. It was a relief to be apart from them, though he did not weep. His thoughts moved sluggishly. As a boy, he had once swum in a frozen river and felt his arms and legs become numb, helpless, so that he thought he might drown. It had been Mongke who pulled him out, the older brother who laughed as he shivered and curled up on the bank.

He had a hundred memories, a thousand conversations vying for space in his mind. He remembered Mongke sending him out to hammer the Sung, but he also remembered the old ger they had found in a valley when they were fifteen or so. While the rest of their family slept, Kublai and Mongke had taken iron bars and destroyed it. The rotting wood and felt had collapsed on itself as they flailed and swung, lucky not to hit each other in their enthusiasm.

It was not a grand tale of the sort to tell at a khan's funeral, just two boys doing something stupid one night, for fun. They had discovered later that the ger had not been abandoned at all. When its owner had returned, he had been incandescent with rage and vowed to find the ones who had done it. He never had. Despite all the adult years that had passed since that day, Kublai smiled at the memory. He had lost friends before, but he had thought his brothers would always be there, in good times and bad. To lose Mongke was to take an axe to the foundations of everything he was.

Kublai was barely aware of falling as his legs gave way. He found himself sprawled on thick rolls of carpet, dust rising into the air around him. He felt choked and his hands moved unconsciously to the leather ties of his armour, tugging them loose until the lacquered chest-plate of scales yawned open. He snapped the last tie in a spasm of anger, throwing it down. The motion spurred him on and he pulled off his helmet and thigh-plates in rough movements, tossing them aside to clang against the other pieces on the canvas floor. It was not long before the last of the armour was on the pile and he sat in simple leggings and a stiff silk tunic with long sleeves that reached past his hands and had been folded into cuffs. He felt better without the armour and sat with his arms around his knees, thinking through what he must do.

Bayar saw the galloping scout before Uriang-Khadai. He tapped the older man on the shoulder and they both turned to watch as the scout angled his mount towards the only ger he could see in the assembly of grazing horses and resting men.

The scout dismounted at the ger, but Bayar intercepted him, taking him by the arm and walking him away until he could be sure Kublai would not hear the interruption.

'Report,' Bayar said.

The scout was flushed and his face gleamed with sweat. He had ridden far and fast. With only a glance at the ger, he bowed to both men.

'Orlok, general. There is a Sung army in range. Ten foot regiments or more. Five of horse and many cannon. They have their own riders out and I only had time to make a rough estimate before I came back.'

'How far?' Uriang-Khadai said. His gaze fell on the ger that sat alone.

'Thirty miles east, about.' The scout made a gesture showing a movement of the sun in the sky.

'With cannon, they won't be here until tomorrow,' Bayar said in relief.

'Unless they react to contact and push on without the guns,' Uriang-Khadai replied sourly. 'Either way, it does not matter. We must withdraw.'

The scout looked from man to man in surprise. He had been riding out far ahead of the tumans and had no idea of the news that had come in his absence. Neither of them chose to inform him.

'Change mounts and get back out as soon as you can,' Uriang-Khadai said to the scout. 'I need eyes close to them. Better still, take three others and place them at the quarter points so they can relay whatever you see to me quickly.'

The scout bowed and jogged away.

Whatever Bayar might have said next was lost when Kublai walked out of the ger. He had left his armour inside and both men gaped at the change in him. He wore a robe of gold silk with a wide belt of dark red. The chest was embroidered with a dark green dragon, the highest symbol of Chin nobility. He held a long sword, his knuckles white on the scabbard as he looked over and approached his two most senior men.

Bayar and Uriang-Khadai went down on one knee, bowing their heads.

'My lord, I am sorry to hear such news,' Uriang-Khadai said. He saw Kublai look up as four scouts mounted nearby and began to gallop away to the east. Uriang-Khadai chose to explain before he could be asked.

'There is a Sung army coming west, my lord. They will not be here in time to prevent our withdrawal.'

'Our withdrawal,' Kublai echoed, sounding as if he did not understand. Uriang-Khadai faltered under the yellow gaze.

'My lord, we can stay ahead of them. We can be back in Chin lands by spring. The yam rider said your brothers will have received the news already. They will be making their way home.'

'Orlok, you do not understand me at all,' Kublai said softly. 'I *am* home. This is my khanate. I will not abandon it.'

Uriang-Khadai's eyes widened as he understood the significance of Kublai's Chin robes.

'My lord, there will be a quiriltai, a gathering of princes. Your brothers . . .'

'My brothers have no say in what happens here,' Kublai interrupted. His voice grew hard. 'I will *finish* what I have begun. I have said it. This is my khanate.' He spoke the words with a kind of wonder, as if he had only then understood the turmoil inside him. His eyes were chips of bright gold in the sun as he continued.

'No, this is my *empire*, Uriang-Khadai. I will not be made to leave. Ready the tumans for battle, orlok. I will face my enemies and I will destroy them.'

Xuan paced in the darkness. His mind buzzed too loudly to rest, stinging him with questions and memories. Armies were strange things, sometimes far greater than the individual strengths of the soldiers in them. Men who might have run on their own would stand with their friends and their leaders. Yet they all had to sleep and they all had to eat. Xuan had camped near to an enemy before and it remained one of the oddest experiences of his life. The armies were so close that he could see the Mongol campfires as points of light on the darkling plain. The two Sung lords had guards and scouts at all points around the camp, but no one expected the Mongols to attempt a night attack. Their strength was in speed and manoeuvres, strengths which would vanish in the blind dark. Xuan smiled at the thought of men sleeping peacefully next to those they would try to kill in daylight. Only humanity could have conceived such a strange and artificial way to die. Wolves might tear the flesh of deer, but they never slept and dreamed near their quarry.

Somewhere close, Xuan could hear the deep snoring of some soldier lying flat on his back. It made him chuckle, though he wished he too could find the balm of sleep. He was no longer young and he knew he would feel it tomorrow, when the horns sounded. He could only hope the battle would not last long enough for his weariness to get him killed. It was one of the great truths of battle, that *nothing* exhausted a man as quickly as the rush and struggle of fighting hand to hand.

Shadows moved in the darkness and Xuan raised his head, suddenly panicky. He heard his son's voice and relaxed.

'I am here, Liao-Jin,' he whispered.

The small group came to him and though it was dark he knew each one of them. His four children were all the mark he had made on the world. Lord Jin An had understood that. Xuan thought with affection of the young Sung noble. He might have spirited his children away without speaking to Jin An, but it was just as likely they would have been discovered. Xuan had taken a risk in speaking honestly to him, but he had not misjudged his man. Lord Jin An had understood immediately.

Xuan pressed a bag of coins into his son's hand. Liao-Jin looked at him in surprise, straining to see his father's features in the starlight.

'What is this?' he said softly.

'A gift from a friend,' Xuan replied. 'Enough to keep you all for a time. You will survive and you will be among your own people. I do not doubt you will find others willing to help you, but no matter what happens, you have a chance at a life and children of your own. Isn't that what you wanted, Liao-Jin? Someone was listening, perhaps. Go now. I have given you horses and only two men to accompany you, my son. They are loyal and they want to go home, but I did not want to send so many that they might think of robbing you.' Xuan sighed. 'I have learned not to trust. It shames me.'

'*I* am not going!' Liao-Jin said, his voice too loud. His sisters shushed him, but he passed the bag of coins into their hands and stood close to his father, bending his head to speak into Xuan's ear.

'The others should go. But I am an officer in your regiment, father. Let me stay. Let me stand with you.'

'I would rather see you live,' Xuan said curtly. 'There will be many here who die tomorrow. I may be one of them. If it happens, let me know my sons, my daughters are safe and free. As your commander, I order you to go with them, Liao-Jin, with my love and my blessing.'

Liao-Jin did not reply. Instead, he waited while his sisters and brother embraced their father for the last time, standing aloof from them all. Without another word, Liao-Jin walked them away into the darkness, to where the horses waited. Xuan could see little, but he listened as they mounted and his youngest girl sobbed for her father. His heart broke at the sound.

The small group moved away through the camp and once again Xuan was pleased he had thought to seek permission from Lord Jin An. There would be no startled cries from Sung sentries in the night. Jin An had enjoyed the idea of it all and had even signed papers for Xuan that would help them if they were stopped in Sung lands. Everything else was down to fate. Xuan had done his best to give them a chance.

Footsteps approached and his heart sank with heavy knowledge. He was not surprised when the dark figure spoke with Liao-Jin's voice.

'They are gone. If you are to die tomorrow, I will be at your side,' his son said.

'You should not have disobeyed me, my son,' Xuan said. His voice grew less harsh as he went on. 'But as you have, stay with me as I walk the camp. I won't sleep now.'

To his surprise, Liao-Jin reached out and touched him on the shoulder. They had never been a family given to open displays of affection, which made it worth all the more. Xuan smiled in the dark as they began walking.

'Let me tell you about the enemy, Liao-Jin. I have known them all my life.'

Karakorum was full of warriors, the plains before the city once again filled with tumans and every room in the city housing at least a family. Two hundred thousand of them had come home and the land was hunted out for a hundred miles around the city. In the cramped camps, the talk was often of Xanadu in the east, apparently crying out for citizens.

Arik-Boke stood in the deepest basements of the palace, with all life and movement far above his head. It was cold in that place and he shivered, rubbing at bumps on his arms. His brother's body lay there and Arik-Boke could not look away. Traditionalist to the end, Mongke had left instructions for his death, that he should be taken to the same mountain as his grandfather and buried with him. When he was ready, Arik-Boke would take him there himself. The homeland would swallow his brother into the earth.

The corpse had been wrapped and the terrible white-lipped gash across the throat had been sewn shut. Even so, it made

Arik-Boke shudder to be alone in the dimly lit room with a pale mockery of the brother he had known and loved. Mongke had trusted him to rule Karakorum in his absence. He had given him the ancestral homeland as his own. Mongke had understood that blood and brotherhood was a force too strong to break, even in death.

'I have done what you wanted, my brother,' Arik-Boke told the body. 'You trusted me with your capital and I have not let you down. Hulegu is on his way, to honour you and everything you did for us.'

Arik-Boke did not weep. He knew Mongke would have scorned the idea of red-eyed brothers growing maudlin. He intended to drink himself unconscious, to walk among the warriors as they did the same, to sing and be sick and drink again. Perhaps then he would shed tears without shame.

'Kublai will be home soon, brother,' Arik-Boke said. He sighed to himself. He would have to go back to the funeral feast above soon enough. He had just wanted to say a few words to his brother. It was almost as hard as if Mongke had been there alive and listening.

'I wish I had been there when our father gave his life for Ogedai Khan. I wish I could have given my life to save you. That would have been my purpose in the world. I would have done it, Mongke, I swear it.'

He became aware of the echo in the basements and Arik-Boke reached out and took Mongke's hand, surprised at the weight of it.

'Goodbye, my brother. I will try to be the man you wanted. I can do that much for your memory.'

CHAPTER THIRTY

Before the sun rose, before even the grey light that heralded the dawn, both camps began to wake and get ready. Tea was brewed in ten thousand pots and a solid meal eaten. Men emptied their bladders, often more than once as internal muscles tightened with nerves. On the Sung side, the cannon teams looked over their precious weapons for the thousandth time, rubbing down the polished shot balls and checking that the powder bags had not grown damp and useless.

When the pale light known as the wolf dawn came, both armies could see each other. The Mongols were already mounted, forming up into minghaans of a thousand that would act independently in the battle to come. Men eased tight backs as they rode up and down the lines. Many of them tested the strings on their bows by pulling back without a shaft, loosening the heavy muscles of their shoulders.

Some things had to wait for light, but as soon as he could tell a white thread from a black one, Lord Jin An had the cannon teams pulled into position on the front rank. Others went to the sides, where they would present their black mouths to any flanking attack. He could see Mongol officers staring over at his regiments, noting their positions and pointing out features of the formation to others like them. Lord Jin An smiled. No matter how brave or how fast the Mongols were, they would have to ride through roaring shot to reach his ranks. He had learned from the defeats of other men. He tried to put himself in the Mongols' position, to see how they might counter such a display of force, but he could not. They were lice-ridden tribesmen, while he was of the noble class of an ancient empire.

The Sung regiments formed up behind the lines of cannon. Lord Jin An sat on his horse and watched as his subordinates assembled the gun soldiers in the first ranks back. Their heavy hand-cannon were slow to reload and notoriously inaccurate, but they would hardly be able to miss as they poured fire alongside the cannon. When the shot and powder was all spent, his cavalry ranks could ride out. Deeper still behind the guns, swordsmen waited in their lacquered armour of iron and wood, standing in disciplined silence. Lord Jin An had placed the Chin contingent there, behind the protection of his guns.

He liked the man who had once been an emperor. Lord Jin An had expected Xuan to be one of those obsessed with his status, having lost so much of it. Yet Xuan reminded the Sung lord of his own father, dead for almost a decade. He had found the same world-weariness in both men, tempered with a dry humour and the sense that they had seen more than they cared to remember. Lord Jin An did not think the Chin soldiers would run, but at the same time, he dared not trust his strategy to such elderly men. They were keen enough at dawn, but if the fighting went on all day, they would not be able to keep up with those half their age. Lord Jin An made a mental note to keep an eye on them through the fighting, to be sure a weakness in the lines did not develop.

The sun seemed to take for ever to creep above the eastern horizon. Jin An imagined it showing its face to the citizens of Hangzhou and to the lords who still disdained the threat to their culture and the emperor. They were fools. Before it set, he hoped to have broken the foreign army that had dared to enter Sung lands. With such a victory behind him, a man might rise far indeed. It was just one day, he told himself, feeling sweat break out on his skin. Just one, long day.

Kublai sat his horse, with Bayar and Uriang-Khadai on either side of him. The other officers had formed the tumans, though they remained ready for any orders from the three men watching the Sung positions.

'I do not understand how imperial Chin banners can be flying there,' Kublai said, frowning into the distance. 'Is it mockery to present the colours of men we have defeated? If so, they are fools. We beat the Chin. They hold no fear for us.'

'My lord, it is more important that the cannon ranks reduce their ability to manoeuvre,' Uriang-Khadai said. He was flushed with a slow-burning indignation over Kublai's refusal to listen to any idea of a retreat. In his frustration, he became ever more stilted in his manner, his tone lecturing. 'They put too much faith in the heavy weapons, my lord, but we can still move. With respect, I must point out that I have been against engaging them from the beginning. This formation only reinforces my view. Why commit suicide against their guns?'

It irritated Kublai that Uriang-Khadai was so obviously right. Before hearing the news of his brother's death, he knew he would have ridden round the Sung regiments, forcing them to come after him and leave their guns behind, or make such slow progress with them that they would never catch up. He could then choose the best ground to attack.

It was the merest common sense not to let an enemy have his main advantage. All Kublai's cannon, both captured and brought from home, lay rusting on fields hundreds of miles away. The weapons were terrifyingly powerful in the right place and time, but until someone found a way to move them quickly, they were more often a hindrance to fast-moving cavalry. The Sung commander did not seem to understand that, at all.

Yet under the stillness, Kublai felt a part of him clamouring and clawing its way out. It was red-mouthed in savagery, demanding that he attack just where the enemy were strong. He wanted to take all the grief and pain of his brother's death and dash it out against those iron guns. He wanted to show Mongke that he had courage, whether his brother's spirit knew it or not.

'Sun Tzu said there are seven conditions for victory,' Kublai said. 'Shall I list them for you?'

'Sun Tzu never saw gunpowder used in war, my lord,' Uriang-Khadai said stubbornly.

'One. Which of the two sovereigns is imbued with Moral Law? Who is in the right, orlok? It matters to the men. The Sung are defending their lands, so perhaps they must take that first point. Yet I am the grandson of Genghis Khan and all lands are mine.'

Uriang-Khadai stared at him in worried silence. He had never seen Kublai so intensely focused. The scholar had been burnt out of him and Uriang-Khadai feared the effects of his grief.

'Two. Which of the generals has most ability? I give you that one, Uriang-Khadai, and you also, Bayar. These Sung have made a house that cannot move, with walls of guns. Three. With whom lie the advantages of Heaven and Earth? I call that equal, as the land is flat and the skies are clear.'

'My lord . . .' Uriang-Khadai tried to interrupt.

'*Four*. On which side is discipline most rigorously enforced? That would be ours, orlok, men who live hard lives from birth, men who endure. They have not grown soft in Sung cities. Five. Which army is stronger? In numbers, perhaps the Sung, but we have beaten their armies before. I will have that one, I think.

Six. On which side are the officers and men more highly trained? That is ours. Every man here has fought and won many times. We are veteran soldiers, Uriang-Khadai. We are the elite tumans of the nation. The Sung have had peace for too long.' He paused. 'The last is a strange one. Which army is most constant in reward and punishment? Sun Tzu valued good leadership, I think, if I have understood it correctly. Without knowing the Sung, I cannot be certain, so I will call that one equal. The balance is with us, orlok.'

'My lord, the guns . . .'

'The guns must be swabbed down between shots,' Kublai snapped. 'The barrels must be cleaned of burning scraps of cloth or embers. A new powder bag must be jammed down and carefully pierced by a hollow reed filled with black powder. The ball must be lifted into the barrel and shoved down. It all takes time, orlok, and we will not give them time. They will have one shot and then we will be in range to kill the cannon teams. We can face one shot.'

He had been staring out to the Sung regiment waiting for them, but he turned to face Uriang-Khadai, his yellow eyes blazing.

'Should I treat them with respect, these Sung men who know nothing of war? Should I fear their weapons, their black powder? I do not, orlok. I *will* not.'

'My lord, please reconsider. Let them stand and run dry for a few days without water. Let them grow hungry while we forage the land and remain strong. They cannot remain for ever in one place, leaving us to ride unchecked around them. Let me burn the closest towns to us and they will be forced to answer, to come out.'

'And by then, there will be another Sung army on its way to support them,' Kublai said bitterly. 'Have you not learned yet that there is no end to these people? Today, I think I will answer their arrogance with arrogance of my own. I will ride down the mouths of their guns.'

Uriang-Khadai was horror-struck.

'My lord, you must stay clear of the battle. The men look to you. If you are killed . . .'

'Then I will be killed. I have made my decision, orlok. Stand with me, or join the ranks under the orders of others.'

Uriang-Khadai slowly bowed his head, understanding at last that he would not move the younger man from his choice. He looked again at the Sung guns, in the new light of knowing he would ride into them.

'Then, my lord, I suggest wide-spaced ranks as we go in, coming back after the first shot for massed arrow volleys and a lance charge. If I may, my lord, I would also hold back two groups of five hundred heavily armoured riders to strike as gaps appear in their lines.'

Kublai grinned suddenly.

'You are an interesting man, Orlok Uriang-Khadai. I hope you live through today.'

Uriang-Khadai grimaced.

'As do I, my lord. With your permission, I will pass on those orders to the minghaans, telling them to target the cannon teams first.' When Kublai nodded, he went on. 'The Sung have not placed as many cannon at their rear, my lord. General Bayar is reasonably competent. He should swing out with a tuman and attack them from behind.'

Bayar chuckled at the grudging description of him.

'Very well,' Kublai replied. He felt lighter now he had made the decision. It was done. He would ride against the guns with his men, the bones of his fate tossed high into the air.

Uriang-Khadai passed on the new orders to the minghaan officers. Through them, the news reached the jagun commanders of a hundred and the most junior officers in charge of just ten men. The sun had hardly moved before every warrior there understood what Kublai intended them to do. He made no speeches to them. Even if he had, only a small number would have heard the words. Though he watched them, they seemed unsurprised by the orders and simply readied themselves, checking their mounts and weapons one last time. Kublai sent a silent prayer to his brother's spirit. Men would die that day who might have lived if he had made different choices.

He stopped, the moment stretching in his head. It felt as if a veil had lifted, as if the sun shone through his grief for the first time. He could almost hear Mongke's voice speaking in anger or mockery. For just an instant, it was as if his brother was standing behind him. Kublai dug in his heels and rode to where Uriang-Khadai and Bayar were discussing the battle plan with a group of other men. Kublai did not dismount.

'I have new orders, Orlok Uriang-Khadai. We will ride round this army and head for Hangzhou. If the enemy leave their guns to chase, we will turn and tear them to pieces. If they bring them, we will attack while the cannon are still attached to oxen.'

'Thank *God*,' Uriang-Khadai said.

The men around him were grinning and Kublai could suddenly see how much strain they had been under before. Yet they had not baulked at what he had asked of them. His heart filled with pride.

'We are the tumans of Mongke Khan,' Kublai said. 'We move, we strike and we move on again. Mount up. Let us leave these Sung fools behind.'

There was laughter in the ranks as the news spread and Kublai's words were repeated hundreds of times. The tumans surged forward into a trot and the Sung regiments less than a mile away watched in confusion as they swung clear of the battlefield, leaving only dust, manure and cropped grass in their wake.

General Salsanan had not expected it to be such a task when he volunteered to leave the khan's tumans and come south. Though he did not know exactly where Kublai was, he expected to track him down by following a trail of burnt towns and cities. Instead, the Sung countryside seemed hardly to have been affected by the passage of armies. It was true that there were few animals grazing and the peasants ran to hide from his soldiers as they searched for anything they could eat. Even so, it was a far cry from the trail of devastation he had thought to see.

His eighty thousand had not even brought the usual supplies. Each man had only two spare mounts, and as they pushed on, Salsanan's tumans lost a few ponies each day to lameness. Unable to keep up, the mounts were quickly butchered, providing enough meat to give two hundred men a hot meal. The tumans left only bones and often split those for the rich marrow before moving on.

After a month of searching, Salsanan would spend much of each day wishing Mongke Khan was still alive. The land was wide and the endless stream of small towns tempted him to stop and loot. Only his sense of duty kept him going. His men were disciplined, but he was beginning to wonder where Kublai had gone. It seemed impossible to lose a hundred thousand men, even in the vastness of Sung territories. He questioned every village leader and town official who trembled before him, but it was not until he reached the city of Shaoyang that the prefect gave him a solid lead. As he rode, Salsanan reminded himself that the man he went to fetch home could be the next khan. He would have to tread carefully with the scholar prince.

On the road east, Salsanan's scouts had him riding up ahead of the tumans to confirm the strange sight they reported. Hundreds of heavy cannon lay overturned in the road, their draught animals slaughtered. The carcases had been expertly butchered, with most of the meat taken. In many cases, flies swarmed over just a head and hooves and bloody ground. There were dead men with them, unarmed peasants with dead hands still clutching at whips and reins. Salsanan smiled to see it, recognising the work of his own people.

Just a few miles further on, he found the first remnants of a shattered army, bodies lying in the dusty road. Over the crest of a hill, the corpses grew thicker, as if a stand had been made on that spot. Salsanan walked his mount slowly through them, then reined in as the full battle site was revealed. Dead men lay everywhere, scattered in heaps like shrivelled insects.

Salsanan saw distant figures walking amongst the dead, stopping and staring in terror as his warriors came into sight. He knew some men always survive a battle. In the chaos of fighting, they are knocked unconscious, or pass out from a wound. There will always be a few to rise the following day, limping home while armies and the war move on without them. As he rode further through the field of the dead, Salsanan watched battered Sung survivors raise their hands, their faces slack as his men began to round them up.

He nodded in fascination as he read the battle that had taken place. It had been hard. There were many Mongol bodies and he could discern the pattern of their charges in the corpses and broken lances. Kublai's tumans had been beaten back more than once, he could see, perhaps almost flanked. The Sung commander had known their tactics and answered them without panic.

Salsanan picked up a broken arrow and scratched his head with the tip. He would speak to the bruised and battered survivors, but first he walked the field, learning from the bloody script the sort of man who might one day rule the nation.

He found a place where the grass had been churned into mud, just a short way from the main battle lines. A tuman had been rallied there and sent back in. Salsanan could almost see the line of their attack in his mind's eye. He frowned as he walked through the echoes of the battle, revising his opinion of Mongke Khan's brother. The charge had been tight, discipline excellent. The Sung lines had bowed back and Salsanan could see the broken and bloody spears where they had tried to stand. His years of training made him look right and left for the second charge that he would have sent in at the right moment. There. He led his horse by the reins over the corpses, moving carefully as they slid and shifted under his boots.

He found the spot where the battle had been decided. Crossbow bolts and pitted iron balls littered the ground and there was still a taste of gunpowder in the air. Kublai's men had ridden through heavy fire to circle out and back at full gallop. Salsanan could read their confidence and he nodded, satisfied. There had been no hesitation, no doubts from the man who commanded them.

One of Salsanan's men signalled and he mounted to ride over to another section.

'What is it?' he said as he rode up.

His man gestured to the bodies that lay all around them. The smell of spilt guts was appalling and flies buzzed into Salsanan's face, making him wave them off. Even so, he bent to look.

'They are so *old*,' the scout said.

Salsanan stared around him, confirming it. All the faces were lined and the dead men closest to him looked thin and wasted.

'Why would the Sung go to battle with such elderly soldiers?' he muttered. His foot was on a yellow banner and he reached down and picked up the torn cloth. Part of a painted symbol was revealed, but Salsanan did not recognise it. He let the crumpled cloth fall.

'Whoever they were, they should not have fought against us.'

His gaze fell on the centre of the dead, a corpse with short-cropped grey hair surrounded by a ring of many others, as if they had died trying to protect him. A much younger man lay almost across the body, the only youthful face Salsanan could see. Arrow and sword wounds marked them all, the shafts themselves wrenched out from their flesh.

Salsanan shrugged, letting the small mystery go. 'We cannot be far behind them now. Tell the men to make a good pace. And make sure the scouts show themselves early. I do not want to be attacked by my own people.'

Salsanan caught up with Kublai's tumans on the outskirts of Changsha city. Like wolves entering another's territory, both sides were cautious at first. The outer scouts overlapped and raced back with messages for those who led them on both sides. The armies halted far enough away for there to be no sense of threat. Kublai rode out with Bayar and Uriang-Khadai, breaking off his negotiations with the prefect of Changsha almost in mid-sentence when he heard.

He and General Salsanan met on a spring afternoon, with just a few mare's tails of cloud in the sky above and a warm breeze blowing. Between them, sixteen tumans faced each other. On Kublai's side, they were veterans, fierce and grubby with old blood and dirt. On the other, they were fresh, their armour shining. Both forces looked at the other side in astonishment and there were many jeering calls.

Kublai was flushed with pleasure at the sight of so many tumans of the nation. He let Salsanan dismount first and bow before he climbed down from his horse.

'You do not know how welcome you are,' Kublai said.

'My lord, it seems to have fallen to me to bring the worst news,' Salsanan said.

Kublai's smile vanished. 'I already know my brother is dead. Yam riders found me, two of them.'

A crease appeared on Salsanan's brow.

'Then I do not understand, my lord. If they found you, why have you not begun the journey home? The nation is gathering at Karakorum. The funeral of the khan . . .'

'My brother Mongke gave me a task, general. I have made the decision to finish it.'

Salsanan did not respond at first. He was a man used to authority and comfortable in a chain of command. With the khan dead, it was as if a vital support beam had been removed and his habitual certainty was gone. He stammered slightly as he tried again, unnerved under the pale stare of the khan's brother.

'My lord, I was given the task of escorting you home. Those are my only orders. Are you saying you will not come?'

'I am saying I *cannot*,' Kublai snapped, 'until I have brought the Sung to heel. The sky father has sent you to me, Salsanan. Your tumans are a gift, when I thought there could be none.'

Salsanan saw Kublai's assumption and spoke quickly to head him off before he gave orders that could not be undone.

'We are not reinforcements, my lord. My orders were to bring you home to Karakorum. Tell me where your camp is and I will begin the preparations. The khan is dead. There will be a gathering in Karakorum . . .'

Kublai had flushed again as he spoke, this time in anger.

'Are you deaf? I have said I will not come back until my work is finished. Until I have the Sung emperor's head. Whatever your orders were, I countermand them. You *are* my reinforcements, sorely needed. With you, I will complete the khan's wishes.'

Salsanan clenched his jaw, seeking for calm and finding it difficult to grasp. He found his own anger rising and his voice hardened as he replied.

'With respect, I am not yours to command, my lord. Neither are the tumans under me. If you will not come home, I must leave you here and make my way back. I will carry whatever messages you want me to take to Karakorum.'

Kublai turned away, taking a moment to wrap his reins around his hand. He could see Salsanan's tumans in silent ranks stretching into the distance. He hungered to have them with him, doubling his forces at a stroke. At his back, his veterans were waiting in good spirits, certain that this new army had come to bolster their strength. To see them march away would be a small death, abandoned at the moment of triumph. Kublai shook his head. He could not allow it. Every mile to the east had brought a greater density of towns, better roads and teeming people. Hangzhou was barely five hundred miles on, but already he could see the wealth and strength of the outlying cities. He *needed* Salsanan's men. They were the answer to prayers, the sign of benevolent spirits bringing him aid when he needed it most.

'You leave me no choice, general,' Kublai said, his eyes glinting with anger. He mounted his horse easily, leaping into the saddle. 'General Bayar, Orlok Uriang-Khadai, bear witness.' Kublai raised his voice, making it carry to both sides of waiting warriors.

'I am Kublai of the Borjigin. I am grandson to Genghis Khan. I am eldest brother to Mongke Khan.'

'My lord!' Salsanan said in shock, as he realised what was happening. 'You can't do this!'

Kublai went on as if he had not spoken.

'Before you all, in the lands of my enemies, I declare myself great khan of the nation, of the khanates under my brothers Hulegu and Arik-Boke, of the Chagatai khanate and all others. I declare myself great khan of the Chin lands and the Sung. I have spoken and my word is iron!'

Deep silence followed his words for a beat, then his tumans bellowed in joy, raising their weapons. On the other side, Salsanan's men responded in a great roar of acclamation.

Salsanan tried to speak again, but his voice was lost in the tumult. Kublai drew his sword and held it high. The noise seemed to double in volume, crashing against them.

Kublai looked down at Salsanan as he sheathed his sword.

'Tell me *again* what I can't do, general,' he said. 'Well? I have the right. I claim it by blood. Now I will take your oath, or I will have your head.' He shrugged. 'It is nothing to me.'

Salsanan stared, slack-jawed at what he had witnessed. He looked around at his cheering men and the last of his resistance faded. Slowly, he knelt on the grass, looking up at the khan of the nation.

'I offer you gers, horses, salt and blood, my lord khan,' he said, glassy-eyed.

CHAPTER THIRTY-ONE

At dawn, Arik-Boke stood on the plains before Karakorum. Mongke's two oldest sons had been granted a place close by their uncle. Asutai was sixteen and Urung Tash fourteen, but in their wide shoulders they showed signs of what would become their father's massive strength. They were still red-eyed from grief. Arik-Boke had been kind to them in the days after the terrible news had come home and both young men looked up to him in simple hero worship.

Hulegu stood at his brother's right hand, still darkly tanned from his time in Persia and Syria. He had left only a small force behind with General Kitbuqa to guard the new cities, the new khanate he had won there. Arik-Boke could practically feel his brother's pride. Hulegu had done well with Baghdad, but the region was far from pacified. He could not stay long in Karakorum.

Arik-Boke rubbed the scar across his ruined nose. He caught himself in the habit and took his hand away, determined to be dignified on this of all days. He looked out at the massed tumans of the nation, the princes who had crossed half the world to be there when they heard of the khan's death. They had come a long, long way from the fledgling nation Genghis had created from far-flung tribes. It showed in their numbers and in their obvious wealth.

The body of Mongke Khan lay hidden in a huge covered cart, specially built for that task, for that day. It was to be drawn by forty white horses and followed on foot by thousands of men and women. Their tears would salt the ground as they returned to the last resting place of Mongke's grandfather. Proud princes would walk in its wake, putting aside the signs of their rank as they mourned the father of the nation.

Arik-Boke watched as the sun began to set. In the dark, torches would be lit along a path that stretched away from the city and they would begin. Before that, they waited for him. He turned to Hulegu and his brother nodded to him. Arik-Boke smiled, recalling the first tense meeting after Hulegu's return. For the first time in years, they had walked out of the city like a pair of poor herdsmen, bearing skins of airag on their shoulders. There were many fires around the city, many men and women huddling around them against the cold. Hulegu and Arik-Boke had sat down to join the vigil, talking all the while of the khan and brother they had lost. They had honoured Mongke with mouthfuls of airag spat into the air and both of them had drunk themselves into a bleary stupor.

Hulegu had been burnt dark under a harsh sun. He even smelled different, an odour of cloves and strange spices coming off his skin. As that first night had gone on, his eyes were bright as he described the lands he had seen, with sunlit mountains and ancient secrets. He told Arik-Boke of kohl-eyed Persian women he had seen dance to exhaustion, flinging sweat like bright jewels in the light of feast fires. He spoke of the great markets; of snakes and magicians, of brass and of gold. His voice had grown hoarse with recollection and awe.

Before the sun had risen, Arik-Boke had understood that Hulegu did not want the empire of the great khan. His brother had fallen in love with the desert lands and itched even then to return to them, begrudging every day spent on the cold plains of home. In the morning, they had risen to their feet with groans and creaking joints, but they were at peace with each other.

Arik-Boke breathed slowly, forcing himself to relax. It was time: the nation waited for him to speak. He took a deep breath, filling his lungs with the incense that lay strongly on the air.

'My brother Mongke entrusted the homeland to me, the plains where Genghis himself was born. In his absence, he entrusted Karakorum to my hands. I will continue his work, his ambitions, his vision for the small khanates. The nations cannot be left unattended, this we have agreed.' His heart pounded and he took another breath.

'I will be great khan, in the line of Genghis, in the line of Ogedai, Guyuk and my brother Mongke. Speak your oaths to me and honour my brother's wishes.'

Hulegu knelt first at his side and Arik-Boke rested a hand on his shoulder. Mongke's sons followed, for all to witness. Arik-Boke had offered them lands and wealth and had hardly needed to explain the alternative. After such a public display, there would be no one whispering to them that they could have taken the khanate.

As far as the eye could see, the tumans followed suit. In a ripple like a rock dropping into a still pond, the assembled princes knelt and offered gers, horses, salt and blood. Arik-Boke shuddered slightly, closing his eyes. Only Kublai was missing from the great host before Karakorum. His brother would hear the news from the yam riders waiting to gallop away, but by then the whole world would know there was a new khan. At least Kublai was not a man of great ambition, or he would surely have challenged Mongke when they were all still young. Arik-Boke tried to ignore the itch of his doubts. Kublai should have come home when he heard Mongke had died, but he had not. He was a dreamer, more suited to libraries and scrolls than leadership of the nation. If his older brother chose to challenge him, Arik-Boke would answer with all the force of the risen nation.

Arik-Boke smiled at the thought of the scholar riding to war. Kublai had sent home the women and children of his tumans. They too had given their oaths to him, kneeling in the dust before Karakorum. As Mongke's sons had chosen their path, Kublai would be forced to accept the new order. He sighed with pleasure at the sight of so many tens of thousands on their knees before him. The youngest son of Tolui and Sorhatani had dared to stretch out his hand when the people needed a khan. It was Arik-Boke's day and the sun was still rising.

PART THREE

AD 1260

CHAPTER THIRTY-TWO

The imperial meeting chamber at the heart of Hangzhou was in uproar. Sung lords had gathered without being called, as the sense grew that they must not miss whatever was happening. As the morning wore on, runners and servants constantly reported to those in their city houses outside the grounds. More and more made the decision and summoned their bearers and palanquins. Younger lords came on horseback, wearing swords on their waists and surrounded by loyal guards. There was no sense of peace or security in the hall. The tension and noise rose by the hour.

They had travelled in from their estates to the old emperor's funeral, but when it was over, they remained in their city houses, waiting to be summoned to council. The Mongol armies had come within striking distance of the capital city. There was fear in Hangzhou, a febrile tension in the air. Soldiers on the walls strained their eyes into the distance as if Mongol outriders could appear out of the morning mist with no warning at all. Information changed hands for strings of silver coins as the rumour-mongers parlayed small knowledge into the highest profits.

The conclave that day had begun from a rumour that the new emperor was ready to call them. No one knew who had begun it, but the news spread to every noble house before dawn. Daylight brought no formal summons and barely a dozen lords had come to the imperial precinct and taken places. Word went out that they were there and as the morning passed the number doubled and then doubled again, as senior lords worried they were being excluded from some important event. The tipping point came in the early afternoon. Independently, the last eight heads of Sung houses decided they could wait no longer for the new emperor to call them. They entered the meeting hall together with swordsmen and servants, so that every seat and balcony was packed as the sun began to ease towards the west.

Lord Sung Win was at the centre of it all, tall and thin in robes of mourning white. Many of the others wore less traditional dark blue to mark the passing of the emperor, but there was no sense of funereal calm. The gong that usually rang to announce the conclave was silent and many eyes glanced towards it, still expecting the booming note that would restore order. It could not be struck without the emperor's command to gather, yet they were there, waiting for some act or voice. No one knew how to begin.

As the day waned, Lord Sung Win had taken a central position on the open floor, letting others come to him. Through his servants and vassal lords, he brokered information, observing the factions that gathered briefly and then drifted apart like silkworm husks in the wind. He showed no sign of weariness through the long hours and in fact seemed to grow in energy, his height and confidence commanding the room. The numbers swelled around him and the level of noise became almost painful to the ear. Food and drink were brought and consumed without anyone leaving their place.

There was tension and even fear in the faces of those who came. It was forbidden for them to assemble without the emperor's order and for many the decision to do so risked their names and estates. They would not have dared to come if Emperor Lizong still lived. The heir to the dragon throne was unknown to them, a boy of only eleven years. It was that fact above all else that allowed them to join the throng in the hall. The light of heaven had been extinguished, the empire left suddenly adrift. In the face of such an omen, there was a fragile consensus. They could not ignore the enemy any longer.

Lord Sung Win felt the chaos like strong drink in his blood. Everyone who entered could see him there, representing one of the oldest houses in the empire. He spoke softly to his vassals, a centre of calm and tradition in a growing gale. The smell of opium was pungent and he watched in amusement as lords set out ornate trays, soothing their nerves with the ritual process that began with rolling soft pills on bronze vessels and ended with them sitting back, drawing deeply on the pipes and wreathing themselves in bitter smoke. His own fingers twitched with the urge, but he controlled it. The meeting was a new thing and he dared not lose even some part of his wits.

As the sun began to set, many of the lords present lowered themselves onto porcelain pots carried in by their servants. Their robes hid everything from view as they emptied long-held bladders and bowels, the steaming contents borne away quickly so that the lords could stay in place. Sung Win waited for the right moment. There were at least two other groups who might yet open the conclave. One could be dismissed as lacking support, but the young man at the centre of the other faction was flushed with his own sudden rise to power. Lord Jin Feng's brother had been killed in the most recent attack on the Mongol forces. It should have left his house weak for a season, but the new lord had taken on the responsibilities with skill.

Sung Win frowned at the memory of a trade agreement he had tried to force through with the family. It had looked like the support of a friend, a financial gift with few conditions to tide them through difficult times until the house was stable. A single clause would have allowed him to annex part of their land if they had defaulted. It had been perfect, both subtle and powerful. They would have given him insult if they had refused and he had waited for the sealed document to be sent back to him. When it had arrived, he had been delighted to see the perfect lines of the house chop on the thick parchment. He had let his eyes drift down to the single line that made the agreement a weapon as sharp as any dagger. It had not been there.

Sung Win shook his head in irritated memory as Lord Jin Feng clapped some supporter on the shoulder. To copy a document and its seals so perfectly, even to the handwriting of Sung Win's own scribe, was ingenious. He could hardly complain. The choice had been his to accept the altered agreement or let it accidentally be destroyed in a fire and send his regrets. He had accepted, acknowledging a fine stroke.

Sung Win watched his neighbour from under lowered lids, wondering if it would be best to let Jin Feng bear the brunt of imperial disapproval. The first to speak formally took the greatest risk, but it was not an advantage he felt he could give up. Sung Win smiled to himself, enjoying the tension across his shoulders and the way his pulse beat in his veins. All life involved risk.

He stood slowly in the tumult and his vassals fell silent, turning towards him. In such a tense crowd, that simple action was enough. The pool of stillness was noticed and spread quickly across the hall. Men broke off from whispers or open arguments, craning their necks without dignity to see who would dare to speak first without the emperor's formal command.

Lord Sung Win glanced at the entrance arch for the last time that day, looking for the emperor's herald, or his chancellor. He did not doubt the boy Huaizong had heard of the conclave by then. The old emperor's spies would be in that room for their new master, ready to report every word and who had said them. Lord Sung Win took a deep breath. Nonetheless, the moment was upon him and silence had spread across the hall. More than a hundred lords watched him with eyes that gleamed in the light of the evening lamps. Most were too weak to affect the outcome of the day, but there were thirty-two others who held power in the nation, Lord Jin Feng among them. It may have been Sung Win's imagination, but they seemed to stand out from the crowd. Though every man there wore white or dark blue, he could almost sense the points in the room where power lay.

'My lords,' he said. The silence was so profound he hardly needed to raise his voice at all. 'Your presence reveals your understanding. Let us go forward in the knowledge that Emperor Lizong would not have wished us to sit idly while our lands are savaged and destroyed by an invader. We are in the crucible, my lords, knowing that we face a terrible enemy. Great and ancient houses have been lost to us. Others have passed to new heirs while the true bloodlines are broken.'

Whispers could be heard and he spoke louder, holding them. He had planned every word during the long hours of that day.

'I accept my part of the guilt we share, that we have indulged ourselves in games of power while the empire suffered. I have watched lords leave this chamber and seen their names cut into the honour stone as men who have fallen to protect our freedoms.'

He looked to Lord Jin Feng and the young man nodded reluctantly to him.

'Through our weakness, through our mistrust of one another, we have allowed an enemy to creep closer to the imperial capital than anyone has ever come. We have thrown mere straws into the wind to stop him and wasted our energies on politics and personal vengeance. The price has been high. My lords, the favour of heaven has been withdrawn from us. The emperor has gone from this world. At this moment of weakness, of chaos, the enemy comes, the wolf with bloody jaws. You know this.'

Once more he took a deep breath. Lord Jin Feng could have spoken then. There was no imperial chancellor to order the speakers or control the debate. The young man remained silent, waiting.

'Without the emperor's voice,' Sung Win went on, 'we do not have the power to put the empire under arms as one. I know this. I accept this. I have tried to reach Emperor Huaizong and heard nothing from the court. I know many of you have been rebuffed by ignorant courtiers. That is why we are here, my lords. We know the wolf is coming to Hangzhou and we know what must be done. He must be fought, or he must be paid tribute to leave our lands. There is no third choice. If we do nothing, we have failed in our duty and our honour is as dust. If we do nothing, we will deserve the destruction that will surely come.'

Lord Sung Win paused, knowing that his next words would take him into treason. His life, his house, his history would be forfeit if the boy emperor chose to make an example of him. Yet if he could break the Mongol armies, he would earn the gratitude of the imperial house. He would be beyond punishment, untouchable. Sung Win dared not dream of his sons rising to become emperor in turn, but his actions that day would put him closer to the dragon throne than any of his ancestors. Or they would get him killed.

'I have come to see that we must act. Therefore I call the council. I call all Sung lords to defend the empire. Thirty-three noble houses are here today. Between us, and our vassals, we control more than a million soldiers. I call a vote in conclave.'

One of his servants went to the wooden case that stood against the far wall. Inlaid with ivory, it was an ancient and beautiful thing. The servant held an iron rod and at the last moment he looked back at Lord Sung Win, hesitating. Sung Win nodded and the servant inserted the rod and yanked back, breaking the lock.

There was a gasp across the chamber. Every lord stared in fascination and dread as Sung Win's servant brought out a deep glass bowl, larger than his head. He held it up as he walked back to the centre. Other servants reached into the cabinet and withdrew marbles of black and clear glass from the shelves where they lay in neat rows. The men moved through the crowd, handing them in pairs to the most powerful houses of the empire. The crowd of lords began to speak in louder voices and Lord Sung Win strained his eyes and ears to gain a sense of the room. He could not judge the mood at that moment and it frustrated him. Some of them would be too terrified of the emperor's disapproval to vote. They would abstain in their cowardice and weakness. He could not know how Jin Feng would act. His brother's army had been torn apart by the Mongol invader, but the house was ancient and his decision would matter.

Lord Sung Win raised his hands to show them the two marbles he held, one black and one clear.

'Let the neutral colour be for tribute,' he said, raising the black ball. 'Let clear water be for war.' He dropped the clear ball into the glass sphere, so that it rang out a note across the hall, whirring around in slow circles before it rested. 'That is my vote, with my vassal houses. That is my pledge of ninety-two thousand soldiers, horses, all the equipment and accoutrements of war at my command. Let us destroy the enemy before us, in the name of the Lord Perpetual Nation, the Son of Heaven. In the name of Emperor Huaizong and the dragon throne.'

Up to that point, Lord Sung Win had dominated the room. As the clear glass ball rattled to a stop, the realisation flashed round the hall that they were expected to respond. Sung Win felt a prickle of sweat begin at his brow and held himself very still so they would not see it run down his face and know the strain he felt.

The head of the most ancient house in the empire was seated in one of the first rows around the central space. Lord Hong was a large man, made wider by his formal robes. He sat with his legs braced before him and one hand resting on each knee. His right hand clicked in the silence as he rubbed two of the marbles together. Sung Win waited for him to move and so he was startled when Lord Jin Feng stood up at the edge of his vision and came forward to the servant with the glass bowl. Lord Hong watched warily, only his hand moving.

'This is a day of new things,' Jin Feng said. 'My brother Lord Jin An gave his life to protect our lands and honour. Xuan, Son of Heaven, died with him, the end of a noble Chin line. In defence of the empire, can I offer less than my own life?' He looked around at the gathered nobles and nodded as if he understood them. 'We have a duty to burn thorns in our fields. My vassals and I vote for war.'

He dropped another clear ball into the bowl and it rattled around, holding the gaze of every man in the meeting place. Jin Feng bowed briefly to Sung Win. He neither liked nor trusted the older man and as their eyes met, Jin Feng could not help the suspicions that flared in him. Yet for once, Lord Sung Win was on the side of right. Jin Feng handed the black ball to a servant and returned to his place as two more lords stepped up. Both of them placed clear marbles in the bowl and passed back the others.

Sung Win began to relax as three more men came and added clear balls. He saw Lord Hong rise from his seat. The man moved easily, with grace and strength. Lord Hong was one of the few in the hall who did not neglect his training with sword and bow each day.

Lord Hong held both marbles above the bowl.

'I see no emperor's chancellor here,' he said, his voice deep. 'I have heard no gong summoning us to this council, this conclave.'

Lord Sung Win began to sweat again at the words. Though a distant cousin of the old emperor, Lord Hong was still a member of the imperial family. He could yet sway the gathering if he chose to exert his influence.

Lord Hong flashed a gaze around the chamber.

'My heart rebels at the idea of paying tribute to this enemy, but it will buy us time for Emperor Huaizong to bring order. I would wish to lead an army if the vote goes for war, but without imperial approval, I cannot add the fate of my house to that decision. Therefore, I choose tribute.'

He dropped a black ball into the bowl and Sung Win struggled not to scowl at the man. Lord Hong had revealed only weakness with his speech, as if he could keep himself safe from imperial anger, yet still expect to lead if the vote went against him. It was infuriating, but typical of the politics in that chamber. Lord Hong had reminded them of the prospect of the emperor's disapproval and the ripples had begun to spread. Sung Win showed no reaction as four more lords added black marbles to the bowl. Internally, he seethed.

The lamps burned down to dark yellow flickers with no imperial servants to replenish the oil. Lord Sung Win stood straight and tall as the lords of the Sung empire came up one by one. Few of them spoke, though the first to abstain explained his decision in words that demonstrated only cowardice in Sung Win's assessment. Even so, seven others abstained from the vote, handing back both marbles to the servants.

The damage had been done by Lord Hong, just enough to frighten the weak men and make the strong cautious. Sung Win could feel the mood in the chamber shift as they chose the safer path of tribute over war. He clenched his jaw, feeling his teeth grate as the black balls were dropped in, one after the other. When the vote stood against him at eleven to seven, he thought of speaking again, but it would have meant another breach of tradition. His chance had come and gone. He allowed himself a glare at those who abstained, but kept his silence as the glass bowl filled. Two more black marbles went in and then two more clear ones. A distant hope formed in Lord Sung Win's icy thoughts. Another vote for tribute and two abstentions followed, men who would not even meet his eyes as they shuffled back to their seats.

When the thirty-three great houses had all voted or abstained, the glass bowl was almost full. Sung Win had kept count in his mind, but he showed no emotion as the results were tallied, watched by all.

'Ten have abstained. There are fourteen votes for tribute, nine for war,' he announced in a voice as clear and loud as any imperial herald. He breathed in relief. 'The vote is carried for war.'

Sung Win smiled, feeling dizzy from the strain. Fourteen was the unluckiest number possible, a number that sounded like the words 'Want to die' in both Cantonese and Mandarin. Nine was a number of strength, associated with the emperor himself. The result could not have been clearer and many of the men in the room relaxed visibly at the sign of heavenly favour. To go forward under nine was a blessing. No one would dare to move under fourteen, for fear of utter disaster.

A low note boomed across the room, interrupting the excited conversations that had sprung up over the meeting hall at the announcement. Lord Sung Win jerked his head around, his mouth dropping slightly open. The imperial chancellor stood by the gong, holding the rod he had used to strike. The man was red-faced, as if he had run a long way. He wore a tunic and trousers of white silk, and in his right hand he held his staff of office. A yellow-dyed yak tail spilled over his fist as he stood and glared in fury at the assembled lords.

'Rise for Emperor Huaizong, Lord Perpetual Nation, ruler of the middle kingdom. Make obeisance for the Son of Heaven!'

A ripple of shock snapped across the hall. Every man there stumbled to his feet as if yanked up. The emperor did *not* attend the conclave of lords. Though they met at his order, the imperial will had always been carried out by his representatives in that chamber. Of the hundred lords present, barely three or four would have found themselves in the imperial presence before and a sense of awe overwhelmed them as the gong rang out again.

There was no order in the way they knelt. The lords' delicate appreciation of status and hierarchy vanished as their faces and minds blanked in terror. Lord Sung Win knelt as if his legs had given way, his kneecaps striking sharply on the floor. Around the chamber, the other lords followed suit, some of them struggling to get down in the press of their servants. Sung Win had a glimpse of a boy in a white tunic decorated with gold dragons before he dropped his head and brought his damp brow down to the ancient wood three times. All his plans and stratagems tore to rags in his mind as he rose briefly and then dipped again, knocking his head on the floor three more times. Before he had completed the third kowtow of the ritual, Emperor

Huaizong was among them with his guards, walking confidently towards the centre of the floor.

Lord Sung Win struggled to his feet, though he kept his head bowed with the rest. He struggled against confusion, trying to understand what it might mean to have the new emperor enter the chamber. Huaizong was a small figure, fragile against the hulking swordsmen who surrounded him. It was not necessary to clear the floor. The imperial presence had every lord pushing back to give him space, Sung Win among them.

Silence fell again and Sung Win had to repress the mad urge to smile. A memory came to him of his father's anger when he had discovered a young Sung Win stealing dried apples. It was ridiculous to feel the same way in the presence of a young boy, but Sung Win could see many other faces flushed in hot embarrassment, their dignity forgotten.

Emperor Huaizong stood straight and unafraid before them all, perhaps aware that he could have ordered any of them killed with a single word. They would not resist the order. Obedience was too ingrained in them. Lord Sung Win thought furiously as he waited for the boy to speak. The emperor looked almost like an animated doll, his shaven head gleaming in the lamplight. Sung Win realised the imperial servants were replenishing the oil as the light grew around the hall, bathing them all in gold. He could see the nine yellow dragons that twined on Huaizong's tunic, symbols of his authority and bloodline. He repressed a sigh. If Huaizong denied the vote they had taken, Sung Win knew his life was forfeit. He felt himself tremble to have his house waiting on the words of one he did not know.

When Huaizong spoke, his voice was high and clear, unbroken.

'Who summoned this meeting?'

Sung Win's stomach clenched as fear rose in him. He did not need to look to know every eye in the chamber had turned to him. With his head bowed, he felt his mouth twitch in spasm. The silence stretched and he nodded to himself, gathering his dignity. The boy had broken traditions by entering the chamber. It was the one act he could not have foreseen and Sung Win clenched his fists behind his back as he raised his head. He knew better than to look into the boy's eyes and kept his own gaze on the floor.

'Son of Heaven, we gathered to answer the enemies who threaten us.'

'Who are you?' the boy asked.

'This humble servant is Sung Win, Son of Heaven, House of . . .'

'You speak for these others, Sung Win? You take responsibility for them?'

Rather than condemn himself by answering, Sung Win dropped again to the kneeling position and tapped his head on the warm wood.

'Get up, Sung Win. You were asked a question.'

Sung Win risked a glance around the chamber, certain he could feel the stares of the lords. Not a head was raised. To a man, they were standing in abject terror at the presence of the emperor. For all Huaizong was a young boy, he represented heaven itself, the divine in that room of mere men. Sung Win sighed softly. He had wanted to see the new foals born on his estate, the result of carefully chosen bloodlines. He had put as much time and effort into that as anything else in his life. He felt a pang at the thought of his wives and sons. If the emperor chose to make an example of his house, their deaths would come in orders tied with yellow silk ribbons. His daughters would be executed, his family estate burnt.

'I speak for them, Son of Heaven. I called the vote today.'

He shut his mouth hard as his treacherous fear threatened to begin babbling excuses.

'And so you did your duty, Lord Sung Win. Did my lords vote to raise the banners?'

Sung Win blinked and gulped visibly as he tried to understand.

'Y-yes, Son of Heaven.'

'Then feel pride, Lord Sung Win. You have acted with the emperor today.'

Sung Win stammered a response, overcome as the boy faced the assembled lords.

'Before his death, my uncle told me that you were a nest of vipers,' the boy said to them. 'He told me that you would rather see Hangzhou in flames than risk your dignity and honour. I see that he was mistaken.'

Sung Win had the intense pleasure of watching those who had voted for tribute shift uncomfortably, Lord Hong among them. The emperor went on, his voice confident.

'I will not begin my reign under threat, my lords. You will go from this place and summon your regiments. Your personal guards will march with them. I lay my peace on the houses, with the promise that they will not be left vulnerable in your absence. I will act to destroy the line of any noble house who seeks advantage.'

He turned to Sung Win once more.

'You have done well, my lord. In peace, perhaps I would have found fault with your judgement. However, we are not at peace. I will make some appointment honouring your house when we return.'

'When we return, Son of Heaven?' Sung Win said, his eyes widening.

'Of course. I am not an old man, Lord Sung Win. I wish to see war.'

For an instant, Sung Win saw a gleam in the boy's eyes. He shuddered, hiding it with a deep bow.

'Lord Hong, you will lead the host,' Emperor Huaizong said. The big man knelt and touched his head to the floor. 'How much time do you need before I may leave Hangzhou?'

Lord Hong sat back on his heels, his face a sickly colour. Sung Win smiled to see him so uncomfortable. Moving a million men needed supplies, arms, weapons, a city of equipment.

'A month, Son of Heaven. If I have the authority, I can be ready by the new moon.'

'You have whatever authority you need,' Huaizong replied, his voice hardening. 'Let those who can hear understand that he speaks with my voice in this. Move quickly, my lords.'

Turning on the spot, the boy strode out. As the others averted their gaze, perhaps only Sung Win saw how the slight figure trembled as he went.

CHAPTER THIRTY-THREE

Heavy rain hissed onto the roof of the house Kublai had borrowed. The man who owned it waited out in the fields with a crowd of villagers and his family. Kublai had passed them as he rode in. They had looked like half-drowned puppies as he trotted past. At least they would be left alive. Kublai only needed the stockade village for a night.

A huge fire crackled in the grate and he stood close to it, letting the heat dry his clothes so that steam came off him in wisps. At intervals, he would pace back and forth across the fireplace, talking and gesturing as he discussed the future.

'How can I stop now?' he demanded.

His wife Chabi stretched out on an ancient couch, much patched and restuffed. The baby girl was asleep in her arms, but still fussing and likely to wake at any moment. Chabi looked wearily at her husband, seeing how the years in Sung lands had worn him almost down to bone. He would not have recognised his old scholar self at that moment. It was more than a physical change, though he had earned the muscle and sinew that gave grace to his movements. The true change had come in the battles he had won as well as the tactics he had used to win them. Chabi loved him desperately, but she feared for him as well. Whatever had been his intention, Mongke had hardened her husband, changed him. Though the old khan was dead, she could still hate him for that, at least. She could not remember the last time Kublai had opened a book. His collection sat on carts under greased linen, too valuable to be abandoned, but growing green with mildew in the spring rains.

'Is she asleep?' Kublai said, his voice still rough with anger.

'She is at last, but I am listening. You said you had made the decision. Why are you still struggling with this?'

'Because I am so *close*, Chabi! I could *reach* Hangzhou, do you understand? Everything I have done for the last five years has brought me to this point and then my bastard brother declares himself khan! Am I supposed to leave everything we have accomplished and go home, crawling on my stomach like a dog? How can I leave now?'

'How can you *not*? Please, keep your voice down, or you can settle her again,' Chabi replied. She was exhausted from lack of sleep. Her nipples ached from feeding, but she could not leave Kublai to work himself into a panic or drink himself unconscious.

'When Tsubodai was called home from the west, he never went back,' Kublai said, beginning to pace again. 'Do you understand? This is *my* chance, *my* time. If I vanish, the Sung will not fall so easily again, even if I do manage to return. They will learn from this and we will have to fight for every bloody step. If I come back at all. If I'm not killed on some distant battlefield fighting my own brother! How could he do this to me, Chabi? The useless, arrogant . . .'

'Don't curse in front of the child,' Chabi said warningly. He frowned at her.

'She can't understand anything, woman.'

'Don't "woman" me, husband. You wanted me to listen, so I'm listening, but you said you had made the decision to go home. Why have we stopped here in this cold place? Why is nothing resolved?'

'Because it's not a simple question!' he snapped. His wife began to rise. 'Where are you going?'

'To bed.'

His mood changed and he went to her, kneeling by the couch.

'I'm sorry. It's just that I thought I didn't have to watch my back from my own brother. Not from him. I thought Arik-Boke would always support me.'

Chabi ran her hand along his jaw in a caress.

'Do you know how you've changed since you left Karakorum? Perhaps he has as well. Five years is a long time, Kublai. He probably still thinks of you as his scholar brother, more in love with books and strange ideas than anyone else in your family. He does not know you now. And you don't know him, not any more.'

'I have a letter from him,' he said, wearily. His wife sat up, looking deep into his eyes.

'So that is why you are so angry. What did it say?'

Kublai sighed. 'Some part of me hoped it was all a mistake. Arik-Boke declared himself khan at almost the same time I did. He had no idea what I was doing out here. I hoped he would understand I had the right over him, but instead he wrote to me as if what he did was already set in stone.' His temper grew again as he recalled his brother's words, written in the hand of some distant scribe. 'He ordered me home, Chabi. My youngest fool of a brother, writing as if he were my equal.'

'You are not boys any longer, Kublai,' Chabi said softly. 'It doesn't matter now who was born first. He has grown to manhood and he has been a khan of the homeland, your own mother's inheritance and Mongke's gift. He is used to leading a nation. I don't doubt he considered your reaction, but your experience has been in the field, against enemies.'

'A trial he will come to understand, if I face him in battle,' Kublai said, clenching his right hand into a fist. He took a deep breath, controlling the rage that flooded through him. 'You're not saying he's right?' he demanded.

She shook her head. 'Of course not, husband. He should have put it before the princes and senior men. He should have considered you might challenge for the great khanate before he declared. But that is in the past. It is pointless to argue what he should have done. He declared himself khan. You have to see him as a man now, not the boy you once picked up when he fell, or you told stories to. He had the same mother in Sorhatani, who practically ruled the nation for years. He had the same father, who gave his life for a khan. You both had Genghis for a grandfather. If you keep thinking of Arik-Boke as a weakling or an idiot, he could destroy you.'

'I'll *kill* him first,' Kublai said. 'I did not expect to be khan, Chabi. Mongke had a dozen sons. If he'd lived just a few years longer, he would have named an heir and the line would have passed smoothly. But he did not and now he is gone and instead, *instead* . . .' He could not express the fury that filled him and only clasped at the empty air.

'You need to find calm,' Chabi said. 'You need to put aside your anger and betrayal and think as a khan.' She shook her head. 'And you need to make the decision. Either treat him as your enemy, or give up the khanate and swear an oath of loyalty to Arik-Boke. One or the other. There is no point driving yourself to madness with this. Either way, you cannot remain in Sung lands.'

In an instant, the anger went out of her husband and he slumped as he stood before her, his shoulders drooping.

'It's just such a *waste*,' he said softly. 'I've lost good men. We've all suffered to carry out the orders Mongke gave me. I don't know if he expected me to succeed or not. Maybe it's

403

true that he thought I'd fail and he would have to ride in and rescue me. But I am here, still standing. I could take their capital, Chabi.'

'And you would lose the world if you do,' she murmured wearily. 'You've said all this before. Even if you win against the Sung, even if you become emperor here, you will still have to face Arik-Boke. You will have taken a khanate for the greater nation, but you will be your brother's vassal. You would still have to go to Karakorum and swear loyalty to him.' She sighed as the baby started to squeak and wriggle, gently putting her little finger in its mouth. Still asleep, the baby sucked greedily on it.

'I cannot do that,' he said, staring into the distance as if he could see all the way to the homeland. 'I *am* khan, Chabi. I have the right and I will not give it up. What was he thinking to call himself khan? Do you see what he's done to me? He had no right, Chabi. No right at all.' He shook his head, turning again to stare into the fire.

'When I was young, I used to dream of following in the path Ogedai laid out, but it was just a fantasy. His son Guyuk would inherit. I knew that. I understood that. When Guyuk died, Mongke was the obvious choice. He was older, respected. He'd ridden with Tsubodai into the west – he was everything I was not, Chabi. I wasn't ready then. He used to sneer at me for the way I dressed and spoke, the books I read.'

'I remember,' Chabi said softly.

'But he was right, Chabi! The things I've seen . . . no, the things I've *done*.' He shuddered slightly as memories flashed into his mind. 'I was an innocent. I thought I understood the world, but I was little more than a child.'

Kublai took up an iron poker and began to thrust it at the burning logs, causing a stream of bright sparks to fly into the room. Chabi shielded the little girl from the heat with her hand.

'But I am no longer a child,' he said, his voice grown low and hoarse. He put the poker down and faced her.

'We were so young then, but by the sky father, I am not that young man who had never seen the swollen dead. I am khan. It is done and I would not change it.' He clenched his fist, taking pleasure in his own strength. 'I will not let another stand in my place.'

Both of them turned their heads as a man cleared his throat at the outer door. One of Kublai's guards stood there, rain streaming off his oiled cloak and puddling around his boots.

'Orlok Uriang-Khadai is here to see you, my lord khan,' he said bowing deeply.

No one reached Kublai without being checked for weapons and passing at least two guards. Even yam riders were forced to strip to bare skin before being allowed to dress and enter his presence. Those few who had reached him had been forced to remain with his tumans, rather than have them carry back the news of his declaration. The lessons of Mongke's death were still rippling through the nation. It explained why Uriang-Khadai was flushed with indignation as he came in out of the rain.

'You asked to see me, my lord khan,' the orlok said, his mouth a thin, pale line. He spotted Chabi at that moment and bowed to her, unbending enough to smile at the child in her arms.

'My lady, I did not see you there. Is your daughter well?'

'She sleeps all day and keeps me awake all night, but yes, she is well. It's time for me to wake and feed her.'

Uriang-Khadai nodded, almost amiable. Kublai watched him in surprise, seeing a side of the man he had not witnessed before. Uriang-Khadai had not brought his wives or children on the campaign and it had simply not occurred to Kublai that the stern officer might be a doting father as well.

Kublai cleared his throat and Uriang-Khadai bowed again to Chabi before approaching her husband at the great fire. Kublai gestured for him to warm himself and the orlok stood with his palms outstretched, gazing into the flames.

'You were my brother Mongke's man, Uriang-Khadai. I know it and it does not trouble me.' He glanced at the orlok, but Uriang-Khadai said nothing.

'You have proved yourself to me against the Sung . . .' Kublai went on. 'But that is past. It seems I must take my tumans home. If it comes to battle, we will face Mongol tumans on their own land. We will face our own people, men that perhaps you know and respect.'

Uriang-Khadai turned from the flames, his eyes and the planes of his face in shadow. He nodded briefly.

'And you wish to know if I can be trusted, my lord. I understand.' He thought for a time, wiping some of the droplets of rain from his face. 'I do not see how I can make you certain, my lord. It is true that your brother Mongke chose me to lead your armies, but I have obeyed every order from you. I have been loyal and I gave my oath with the rest when you declared yourself khan. If that is not enough, I do not know what else I can offer you.'

'Your family is in Karakorum,' Kublai said softly.

Uriang-Khadai nodded, the muscles in his jaw tensing.

'That is true. It is true for most of the men, the new tumans and the old. If your brother Arik-Boke uses my family as hostages, there is nothing I can do to save them. I *will* expect to avenge them.'

For an instant, his eyes revealed a flash of raw anger and Kublai had a sudden insight that brought something like shame. His family had manipulated this man for years. Kublai looked away first. He had sent the women and children of his tumans back to Karakorum and he would have given his right hand to undo that innocent decision. It gave Arik-Boke a piece to play that would cut to the heart of those who fought with Kublai. He did not know yet if Arik-Boke would use the threat, but as Chabi had said, he no longer knew his brother.

'I must plan a campaign against the homeland,' Kublai said, almost in wonder. 'Will you help me in this?'

'Of course, my lord. You are the khan. My loyalty is yours.' Uriang-Khadai spoke each word with such quiet certainty that Kublai felt his doubts vanish.

'How would you begin?' he said.

Uriang-Khadai smiled, aware that the crisis had passed.

'I would withdraw immediately from Sung lands, my lord. I would make my base in the Chin territory, around Xanadu. There is food enough there to keep us in the field. Your brother has to bring in grain and meat from the Chagatai khanate and Russian lands, so I would move to cut those lines. Supply will play a part in this war.' The orlok began to pace in unconscious mimicry of Kublai's movements before he had entered. 'Your brother will have vassal princes, personally sworn to him. You must break the strongest of those quickly, to send a message to the rest. Take your brother's power, his support, and when you face him in battle, he will collapse.'

'You have thought about it,' Kublai said with a smile.

'Ever since the news came in, my lord. You must return home and if you have to, you must tear down Karakorum. You are the khan. You cannot allow another to claim the title.'

'You are not troubled at the thought of facing our own people in war?' Kublai asked.

Uriang-Khadai shrugged.

'We have fought almost continuously for five years, my lord. The tumans under you were the best Mongke could give you, but they have become far stronger. I do not flatter them when I say that. No one your brother can field could stand against

407

us. So no, I am not troubled. If they choose to draw a line in the ground, we will step right over it and gut them.'

Uriang-Khadai paused, weighing his next words.

'I do not know what you intend for your brother. You should know that if Arik-Boke threatens the families of our tumans, you may not be able to spare his life at the end. I have seen you grant mercy to entire cities, but your warriors lost only silver and loot when you did. If your brother has blood on his hands when we meet him . . .' He broke off as Kublai grimaced.

'I understand,' Kublai said. The older man was watching him closely. 'If this begins, I will end it. I do not want to kill him, orlok, but as you say, there are some things I will not ignore.'

Uriang-Khadai nodded, satisfied at what he saw in Kublai's face.

'Good. It is important to understand the stakes. This is not a game, or a family feud that can be settled with a good argument and strong drink. This will get bloody, my lord. I take it you have not informed your brother of your intentions? I saw you were holding the yam riders prisoner.'

Kublai shook his head.

'That is something, at least,' Uriang-Khadai said. 'We will be able to surprise him and that is worth half a dozen tumans. I suggest you make Xanadu your stronghold, my lord. It is within striking range of your brother and we can leave the remaining camp followers there. Moving fast, we can break his supply lines and take the lands of whichever princes support him. We need information on those men, but with a little luck, the war could be over before your brother realises what is happening.'

Kublai felt the older man's confidence lift him. He thought of the letter from Arik-Boke once again. His brother had boasted of the princes who had given their oath to him.

'I believe I may have a list, orlok. My brother was kind enough to give me the names of his most prominent supporters.'

Uriang-Khadai blinked and then smiled slowly.

'There were no yam lines when you made yourself khan, my lord. He may not hear for months yet what you have done. We can stay ahead of the news and be welcomed by the princes before they have any idea of our intentions.'

Kublai's mouth tightened at the thought. He did not enjoy the idea of approaching men who thought of him as an ally and then destroying them, but his brother had left him with few choices.

'If that is how it must be,' he said. 'Mongke's two oldest sons declared for my brother, Asutai and Urung Tash. Do you know them?'

'No, my lord. They will have been given lands in exchange for their support. Who else?'

'Chagatai's grandson, Alghu; Jochi's son, Batu. Those are the most powerful of his new allies.'

'Then we will take them first. I am not worried about Mongke's sons, my lord. They will be minor players and they have not yet made their names. Batu will control the supplies of food and equipment coming from the north. He is the one we must attack first, then Alghu.'

Kublai thought for a moment.

'Batu . . . owes me a great deal. Perhaps we can bring him to our side.' Uriang-Khadai looked at him questioningly but he shook his head, unwilling to discuss it. 'Even so, it means going around the homeland. Thousands of miles.'

'Tsubodai managed three times the distance, my lord. Send a small force, two or three tumans to make the raid. General Bayar would bite your hand off if you offered him the chance to act for you. You and I will assault the Chagatai territory to the west.'

'My brother Hulegu has a new khanate around Damascus. I will send someone to him there. Then Karakorum,' Kublai said softly. 'Each one in a season, orlok. I will not spend years on this. I want this finished quickly, so that I may return to the Sung.'

'As you will, my lord khan,' Uriang-Khadai said, bowing.

Arik-Boke opened the door and leaned against the frame as he stared into the palace hall. The room was large enough to echo at the slightest noise, but the host of scribes seated at desks were almost silent. Only the scratch of quills and the gentle thump of ink-stamps could be heard. They sat with their heads bowed, writing and reading. Occasionally, one of them would rise from his seat with a scroll in hand and cross the room to check it in whispers with his superior.

Batu peered through the open doorway. He was much older than Arik-Boke, though he too was a grandson of Genghis, descended through the line of Jochi, the first-born son to the great khan. His black hair was shot through with grey and his face was as weathered as any herdsman who spent his days in wind and rain. Only his paler skin showed his lands lay in the Russian north. He raised his eyebrows at the sight of the scribes and Arik-Boke chuckled.

'You wanted to see the beating heart of the empire, Batu. This is it. I admit, it is not what I imagined when I became khan.'

'I think I would go mad if I had to work in such a room,' Batu replied seriously. He shrugged. 'But it is necessary. I can only imagine the weight of information that must pass through Karakorum.'

'It is the new world,' Arik-Boke replied, closing the door softly behind them. 'I think Genghis would not have understood it.'

Batu grinned, looking suddenly boyish.

'He would have hated it, I know that much.'

'I am not one to dwell too long in the past, Batu. That is why I invited you to Karakorum. You are my cousin and men speak well of you. We should not be strangers.'

'You honour me,' Batu said lightly. 'Though I am comfortable enough on my lands. My tribute is a burden, of course, but I have not failed to make the payments yet.'

The hint was obvious enough and Arik-Boke nodded. 'I will send a scribe to you to review the amounts. Perhaps some new arrangement should be worked out, for my khanate. All things can be remade, Batu. I have spent months simply learning the extent of my influence and power, but it is not all work. I see no reason why I should not reward those loyal to me.'

'It is better to lead than to follow,' Batu said. 'It's more tiring, but the rewards . . .'

Arik-Boke smiled slyly. 'Let me show you the rewards,' he said, gesturing for Batu to follow. 'My brother Hulegu described a seraglio in Baghdad. I have begun something similar here.'

'A seraglio?' Batu replied, pronouncing the strange word carefully.

'A gathering of beautiful young women, dedicated to me. I have men in the slave markets with my funds, looking only for the youngest and best. Come, I will give you your choice, any of them that takes your eye. Or more than one, if you wish.'

He led Batu down a series of corridors, until they came to a door and two heavyset guards. Both men stood rigidly in the presence of the khan and Arik-Boke swept past them, opening the door onto sounds of laughter and running water. Batu followed him in, his interest growing.

A small courtyard was revealed beyond, set with lush plants and with a covered walkway running around it. Batu saw six or seven young women and he noted Arik-Boke's wolfish smile

411

broaden. Around the courtyard were simple chambers with beds and a few ornaments.

'I keep them here until they are pregnant, then move them out to other rooms in the palace to have the children.'

'They are . . . wives?' Batu asked.

Already the women were scrambling up at the khan's presence, some of them kneeling on the polished stones. Arik-Boke laughed.

'I have four wives, cousin. I do not need more of those.'

He gestured to one young woman and she came forward with fear in her eyes. Arik-Boke raised her chin with his outstretched hand, turning her head to the right and left so that Batu could see her beauty. She stood very still as he dropped his hand past her neck and opened her robe, revealing her breasts. He lifted one with rough fingers and the girl tensed. When Arik-Boke spoke again, his voice had roughened.

'What a delicious weight on my hand. No, Batu, these are for pleasure and children. I will have a thousand heirs. Why not? A khan should have a strong line. Choose any of them. They will give you a night to remember.'

Batu had seen the girl's wide pupils and understood the sweetish smell in the air was from opium. He showed Arik-Boke nothing as he nodded pleasantly.

'My own wives are not so forgiving as yours, my lord khan. I think they would take a knife to my manhood if I took up your offer.'

Arik-Boke snorted, waving the girl away.

'What nonsense, cousin! Every man should be khan in his own home.'

Batu smiled ruefully, struggling to find a way through that would not give offence. He did not want Arik-Boke's women.

'Every man has to sleep, my lord. I prefer to wake up with everything still attached.'

412

He chuckled and Arik-Boke responded, some of the tension easing out of him. He continued to fondle the girl's breasts, distracted.

'My brother Hulegu described rooms dedicated to pleasures of the flesh,' Arik-Boke said. 'With costumes and strange chairs and tools; hundreds of beautiful women, all for the shah.'

Batu grimaced, unseen. The girl stared with dull eyes as Arik-Boke pawed her. Her lips looked bruised and swollen, and in truth Batu found her intensely attractive. Yet, as Ogedai Khan had once told him, everything was about power. Batu did not want to put himself in Arik-Boke's debt. He could sense the small man's arousal coming off him in waves, almost like heat. Arik-Boke snuffled as he breathed through his mouth, the scarred face ugly in lust. Batu struggled with nausea as he kept his smile in place.

'And Kublai, lord? I have not seen him in years. Is he returning to Karakorum?'

Arik-Boke lost some of his flush at the mention of his brother. He shrugged deliberately.

'At his best speed, cousin. I have ordered him home.'

'I would like to see him again, my lord,' Batu said innocently. 'He and I were friends, once.'

CHAPTER THIRTY-FOUR

'Be silent for the Son of Heaven, Emperor of the Sung, Lord Perpetual Nation,' announced the imperial chancellor. His master raised a hand in greeting to Lords Hong and Sung Win as he came to the front ranks. Huaizong's young face was flushed with excitement to be riding with such a host. He rode an elderly gelding as wide as a table. The amiable mount had been considered suitable for an eleven-year-old who could *not* be thrown. It had to be flogged mercilessly to do anything but walk, but it didn't dampen the young emperor's enthusiasm.

'See how they run before us!' he called to his lords. Huaizong had come from the safety of the centre to the front lines to confirm the news his imperial messengers had brought. In the far distance, he could see the Mongol tumans riding north to the Chin border. The sight of it made him want to laugh in joy. His first act as emperor had been to drive them forth from his lands. Truly, heaven smiled on a reign that began in such a way.

It did not matter that his lords had been forced to push hard just to bring the enemy in sight. Emperor Huaizong was by then aware that the Mongols had begun to withdraw before his vast army was in range.

'They are going home,' he said. None of the closest lords chose to answer what was not a clear question.

Huaizong climbed up onto his saddle, so that he stood there with the careless balance of the very young. His horse ambled along beneath him, keeping pace with the multitude of soldiers and horsemen that stretched on either side and behind for as far as he could see. When he turned to look over his shoulder, Huaizong could only shake his head in wonder at the strength of the nation he had inherited. Soldiers marched in perfect lines, coloured banners fluttering. Those nearby averted their gaze from the emperor, while those further back marched stolidly, too far to see the small figure staring over their heads. Still further he looked, until the colours darkened and the marching lines resembled the distant waves of some dun sea, rippling across the land under the wide, blue sky. A host of peasants trudged behind on foot and in carts, carrying the food and equipment to support the soldiers. Huaizong did not heed those. His towns and cities teemed with them. When he noticed them at all, it was only as beasts of burden, to be used and discarded at will.

Huaizong turned back and dropped into his saddle with a pleased grunt as Lord Sung Win brought his horse alongside.

'They will not stand to face us?' Huaizong asked, craning to see the Mongol tumans over the land ahead. His voice was sour.

Lord Sung Win shook his head.

'Perhaps they know the Son of Heaven rides with us today,' he said, not above flattering the boy who held power over his house and line. 'They have showed no sign of stopping for days now.'

'I am only disappointed not to have seen a battle, Lord Sung Win,' Huaizong said.

Sung Win glanced sharply at him, worrying that the boy would order them across the border into Chin lands just to slake his immature desire to see blood. The older man had a fair idea of the costs involved. As with most men who had known battle in their youth, he was quite happy to see an enemy retreat and to leave them to it. He spoke before the boy could throw away the lives of thousands.

'The reign of Emperor Huaizong has begun well,' he said. 'You have driven out the enemy and you will have time now to secure your position and complete your training.'

It was perhaps the wrong thing to say to an eleven-year-old. Lord Sung Win frowned as the boy's mouth turned into a sneer.

'You think I should return to my dusty tutors? They are not here, Lord Sung Win. I am free of them! My army is marching. Shall I stop now? I could drive them from Chin lands. I could drive them right back to their home.'

'The Son of Heaven knows our cities lie defenceless behind us,' Lord Sung Win said, searching for the right words. 'In normal times, we have strong garrisons, but they have either been lost to the enemy or they are here with us. I'm sure the Son of Heaven knows the tales of armies who drove too far into the lands of their enemies and were cut off from behind, then lost.'

Emperor Huaizong looked at him in irritation, but lapsed into silence, biting his lip as he thought. Lord Sung Win prayed silently that the boy would not begin his reign with an unplanned campaign. Warily, he chose to speak again.

'The Son of Heaven knows they are well supplied on their own land, while we must bring in food and equipment for hundreds of miles. Such a campaign is worthy for the second or third years of a reign, but not in the first, not without planning. The Son of Heaven knows this much better than his humble servants.'

The boy made a sulky noise in his throat.

'Very well, Lord Sung Win. Begin work on such a campaign. We will chase these men to the border, but you will lead the war next year. I am not a sick old man, Sung Win. I will take back the lands of my ancestors.'

Sung Win bowed deeply as best he could in the saddle.

'The Son of Heaven honours me in sharing his great wisdom,' he said. A bead of sweat ran down his nose and he rubbed it discreetly. It was like the village boys who played with snakes, laughing wildly at the danger as a cobra lunged for them. A single mistake would mean death, but they still did it, gathering around in a circle whenever they found one. Sung Win felt like one of those boys as he stared at the ground passing underneath him, not daring to raise his eyes.

Kublai's neck hurt from staring over his shoulder as he rode, his frustration clear to see. He felt Uriang-Khadai's gaze on him and his frown eased.

'Don't worry, I'm not going to turn the tumans around and charge them. I've never seen so many soldiers on the move. With Bayar gone ahead, we have what, a tenth of their numbers? A twentieth? I've learned enough to know when to attack and when to tuck in my tail and run.'

He spoke lightly, but Uriang-Khadai could see the glances back were calculating, watching for flaws in the Sung lines. They were too far off to read accurately, but Kublai had spent a long time facing those very soldiers. He knew their strengths and weaknesses as well as his own.

'Do you see how the centre is protected?' Kublai said. 'That formation is new. So many, orlok! It has to be the emperor, or at the least one of his relatives. Yet I must leave them behind to fight my own brother.' He leaned over in the saddle and spat as if he wanted to rid himself of the taste of the words.

'Still, we go on,' he said. 'Do you think they will stop at the border?' His question was almost hopeful, but Uriang-Khadai answered quickly.

'Unless they are led by a man like your grandfather, almost certainly. They have put everything they had into a short campaign in their own lands. I doubt they have food enough to feed so many for more than a few weeks.'

'If they cross the border, I will be forced to take them on,' Kublai said, watching the older man closely. He laughed as Uriang-Khadai winced. 'Well, it's true, isn't it? I'll fight a running battle back to Xanadu and wear them down in my lands. I'll scour the ground before me and keep them hungry and on the move. We could do it, orlok. What are tenfold odds to us?'

'Destruction, I suspect, my lord khan,' Uriang-Khadai said. He thought Kublai was only teasing him, but there was an underlying hunger in the younger man. He had given much of his prime to the task of defeating the Sung. It had hurt Kublai deeply to break off, and for all his banter, the orlok thought he might welcome the chance to end it against the emperor himself.

As they crossed the border into Chin lands, marked by a series of small white temples, more and more of the men began looking back to see if the pursuing forces would follow. It was a bitter-sweet moment for Kublai when he saw the Sung vanguard halt. He had deliberately slowed his pace by then, so that they were barely a mile behind. He could see the front ranks standing in perfect stillness as they watched the Mongols depart and he imagined their jubilation. The border darkened with standing men and horses for miles to the east and west, a clear statement of strength and confidence. We are here, they were saying. We are not afraid to face you.

'I will have to leave tumans here with such an army this close,' Kublai said to Uriang-Khadai.

'There is no point. No small part of our forces could resist such a host,' Uriang-Khadai replied. 'The Chin dominion has its own tumans. You are now their khan, my lord. They are yours to use. Yet if the Sung invade while we are riding against your brother, your cities could be sacked. You could lose Xanadu and Yenking.'

'I am too old to do it all again! What do you suggest?'

'Make Salsanan your orlok for Chin lands. Give him the task of defending the territory and your authority to raise and lead armies in your name. You have ten times the land of this Sung emperor. He will not find it easy, even if he is foolish enough to enter your domain.'

Kublai nodded, making a quick decision.

'Very well. I will also leave one tuman here, to patrol the border and make it look as if we are ready for them.'

'Or to carry the news if the attack begins,' Uriang-Khadai said, refusing to give up his dour tone.

Kublai sighed as he rode further and further away from the border. It was the end of his campaign against the Sung. He prayed to the sky father that he would see the southlands again before he died.

By crossing, Kublai knew he had passed into territory that linked right back to Karakorum. He would not have been able to move his tumans without yam riders reporting it, galloping off on the first leg of a journey that would take them into Arik-Boke's presence. There had been only one way around the problem and he had discussed it with General Bayar as well as Uriang-Khadai. Only Salsanan had spoken against the idea and Kublai had ignored him. Salsanan had not been there for the years of war among the Sung and he had not yet earned the respect of the others. Kublai was satisfied at the idea of giving the man orders to defend the Chin khanate.

They found the first yam station on a crossroads some ten

miles in from the border. It had been looted, the riders taken as warriors for Bayar, the stables empty. Kublai rode past the way station with a sense of misgiving. It would be the first of many as his general broke yam lines right across Chin territory. In that single act, Kublai knew he had declared war on his brother. It could not be taken back. He had set a path that would end with his death or in Karakorum. He clenched his jaw as he rode on and a sense of relief swept over him. Xanadu lay north, where he would leave the rest of his camp followers, as well as Chabi and his baby daughter. His son Zhenjin would stay with him, strong enough at last to endure the distances. Kublai nodded to himself. From Xanadu, his warriors would ride with just spare horses and provisions, enough to last a month. They would go out almost as raiders, moving as fast as any force Genghis had commanded. It felt good to take his own fate in his hands. The choice was made; the doubts were past.

Arik-Boke drew his bow back to his lips, letting the feathers touch him before he loosed. The arrow soared where he had aimed, taking a fallow deer buck through the neck and sending it tumbling, its hooves kicking wildly. His bearers whooped at the shot, kicking their mounts forward and jumping down to cut the animal's throat. One of them raised the buck by its horns, the long neck arching as he showed Arik-Boke the spread. It was a fine animal, but Arik-Boke was already moving on. The circle hunt arranged by Lord Alghu was at its zenith, with animals driven to the centre over dozens of miles. It had begun before dawn, as the heat of the region around Samarkand and Bukhara made the afternoon a time of quiet and rest. The sun was high overhead and Arik-Boke was sweating in streams. Everything from snorting hogs to a carpet of sprinting hares ran under the hooves of his mount, but the khan ignored them all when he heard the coughing roar of a leopard somewhere close. He spun in the saddle and cursed under his breath as he saw Alghu's daughter already on the charge, her lance held low and loose in her hand. The girl Aigiarn had a name that meant beautiful moon, but in private, Arik-Boke thought of her as the hainag, a muscular yak with a short temper and thick, matted hair. She was a freak of a woman, so large and bulky across the shoulders that her breasts were mere flat sacks on muscles.

Arik-Boke shouted for her to ride clear as he saw a flash of dark yellow in the press of animals. Only a Persian leopard could move so swiftly and he felt his heart leap at the glimpse. He lunged forward and almost collided with Aigiarn as her mount danced in front of him, spoiling his shot. The noise of roaring men and screaming animals was all around them and she had not reacted to his shout. As he yelled again, she lowered her lance and leaned into a blow as a flash of gold and black tried to dart under the hooves of her horse. The leopard snarled and yowled, seeming to curl around the long birch spear as it punched into its chest. Algiarn cried out in triumph, her voice as ugly to Arik-Boke's ear as the rest of her. While he swore, she leapt down, drawing a short sword that resembled a cleaver as much as anything. Even with the lance through its chest, the leopard was still dangerous and Arik-Boke shouted again for her to stand clear for his shot. She either ignored him or didn't hear and he muttered in anger, easing the bow. He was tempted to send a shaft into the young yak herself for her impudence, but he had travelled a long way to flatter her father and he restrained himself. In disgust, he saw her cut the leopard's throat as he turned his mount away.

With the burning sun so high, the circle hunt was almost at an end and there were no great prizes left in the swarming mass of fur and claw all round the riders. Arik-Boke dropped a warthog with a neatly aimed shaft behind its shoulder, cutting into its lungs so the animal sprayed red mist with every breath. Two more deer fell to him, though neither had the spread of horns he wanted. His mood was still sour as a shout went up and children ran in among the warriors, killing hares and finishing off the wounded beasts. Their laughter only served to irritate him further and he passed over his bow to his servants before dismounting and leading his horse out of the bloody ring.

Lord Alghu had known better than to take the best animals. His servants were already dressing the carcases of deer for the night's feast, but none of them had a great spread of antlers. The only leopard had fallen to his daughter, Arik-Boke noted. She had waved away the servants and taken a seat on a pile of saddles to begin skinning the animal with her own knife. Arik-Boke paused as he walked past her.

'I thought the shot was mine, for the leopard,' he said. 'I called it loud enough.'

'My lord?' she replied. She was already bloody to the elbows and once again Arik-Boke was struck by the sheer size of her. In build, she reminded him almost of his brother Mongke.

'I didn't hear you, my lord khan,' she went on. 'I haven't taken a leopard pelt before.'

'Yes, well . . .' Arik-Boke broke off as her father strode across the bloody grass, looking worried.

'Did you enjoy the hunt, my lord?' Alghu asked. His eyes flickered to his daughter, clearly nervous that she had managed to offend his guest. Arik-Boke sniffed.

'I did, Lord Alghu. I was just saying to your daughter that she came across my shot as I was lining up on the leopard.'

Lord Alghu paled slightly, though whether it was anger or fear, Arik-Boke could not tell.

'You must take the pelt, my lord. My daughter can be blind and deaf in a hunt. I'm sure she meant no insult by it.'

Arik-Boke looked up, realising the man was genuinely afraid he would demand some punishment. Not for the first time, he felt the thrill of his new power. He saw Aigiarn look up in dismay, her mouth opening to reply before her father's glare made her drop her head.

'That is generous of you, Lord Alghu. It is a particularly fine pelt. Perhaps when your daughter has finished skinning the animal, it could be brought to my quarters.'

'Of course, my lord khan. I will see to it myself.'

Arik-Boke walked on, satisfied. He too had been one of many princes in the nation, each with their own small khanates. Perhaps he'd had a greater status than most as the brother of the khan, but he had not enjoyed instant obedience then. It was intoxicating. He glanced back to find the daughter glaring at him, then quickly looking away as she realised she had been seen. Arik-Boke smiled to himself. He would have the skin tanned into softness, then make a gift of it to her as he left. He needed her father and the small gift would reap much greater rewards. The man obviously doted on his yak of a daughter and Arik-Boke needed the food his khanate produced.

He rubbed his hands together, ridding himself of flakes of dried blood. It had been a good day, the end of months touring the small principalities that made up the greater khanate. He had been feted wherever he went and his baggage train groaned under the weight of gifts in gold and silver. Even his brother Hulegu had put aside the strife of his new lands, though General Kitbuqa had been slaughtered there by Islamic soldiers when Hulegu came back to Karakorum for the funeral of Mongke. His brother had carved a difficult khanate for himself, but he had paraded his men for Arik-Boke and given him a suit of armour shaped from precious jade as a gift and token of affection.

In the company of Lord Alghu's court, Arik-Boke entered the palace grounds in Samarkand, walking under the shadow of a wide gate. On all sides were carts covered in the heaped carcases of animals they had taken that day. Women came out to greet them from the palace kitchens, laughing and joking as they stropped their knives.

Arik-Boke nodded and smiled to them, but his thoughts were far away. Kublai had not yet replied to him. His older brother's absence was like a thorn in his tunic, pricking him with every movement. It was not enough to have men like Alghu bowing to him. Arik-Boke knew the continuing absence of Kublai was being discussed all over the small khanates. He had an army with him that had not sworn allegiance to the new khan. Until they did, Arik-Boke's position remained uncertain. The yam lines were silent. He considered sending another set of orders to his brother, but then shook his head, dismissing the idea as weakness. He would not plead with Kublai to come home. A khan did not ask. He demanded – and it was done. He wondered if his brother had lost himself in some Chin ruins, oblivious to the concerns of the khanate. It would not have surprised Arik-Boke.

CHAPTER THIRTY-FIVE

Kublai rode in pouring rain, his horse labouring and snorting as it plunged through thick mud. Whenever they stopped, he would change to a spare horse. The sturdy animals were the secret of his army's power and he never envied the much larger Arab stallions, or the Russian plough horses with shoulders higher than his head. The Mongol ponies could ride to the horizon, then do it again the next day. He was not so sure about himself. His numb hands shook in the cold and he coughed constantly, sipping airag from a skin to ease his throat and let a trickle of warmth spread down his chest. He did not need to be sober to ride and it was a small comfort.

Twelve tumans rode with him, including the eight who had fought their way to within reach of Hangzhou. There was no road wide enough for such a horde and they left a trail of churned fields half a mile wide. Far ahead, his scouts rode without armour or equipment, taking over the yam stations and holding the riders there long enough for the tumans to arrive and swallow them up. He was able to judge the distance they travelled each day by the number of them he passed – the regular spacing set by the laws of Genghis himself. Passing two meant he had ridden fifty miles, but on a good day, when the ground was firm and the sun shone, they could pass three.

This was not that day. The front ranks did better, but by the time the second or third tuman rode over the same ground, it had become deep, churned clods that wearied the mounts and cut the distance they could travel.

Kublai raised his hand to signal one of his personal bondsmen. The drummer boys on camels could not have kept up the pace of the previous fifteen days of hard riding. No camel alive could run fifty or seventy miles a day over rough terrain. Kublai grinned at the sight of the man. His bondsman was so spattered with mud that his face, legs and chest were almost completely black, his eyes showing as red-rimmed holes. The bondsman saw the gesture and raised a horn to his lips, sounding a low note that was immediately echoed by others down the lines.

It took time to stop so many, or even for them to hear the order. Kublai waited patiently as the lines ahead and behind began to slow to a walk, and finally he was able to dismount, grunting in discomfort as tired muscles creaked. He had been riding at speed for a morning and if his men felt half as tired as he did, it was time to rest and eat.

Three hundred thousand horses needed to graze for hours each day to keep up the pace. Kublai always chose stopping points by rivers and good grass, but they had been hard to find as they pushed into the west. Xanadu was over a thousand miles behind him, his half-built city showing clearly what it would become in a few more years. The wide streets had been laid in fine, smooth stone, perfect and ready to be worn down by his people. Great sections were finished and he had brought life to silent streets with his people. The excitement on their faces had pleased him as they claimed empty houses and moved in together, chattering at every new wonder. He smiled as his mind embellished the memories, making parks and avenues where there were still pegs and saplings. Yet it was real and it would grow. If he left nothing else behind, he would have made a city from nothing.

Since then, the terrain had changed many times, from wet river plains to rough hills with nothing but scrub thorn bushes. They had passed a hundred small towns, with the inhabitants hiding themselves away. That was one thing about riding with twelve tumans – Kublai had nothing to fear from bandits or scavengers. They rode through an empty landscape as every potential enemy vanished at the sight of them.

Each group of ten warriors had two or three whose job it was to lead thirty horses to water and grass. They carried grain, but problems of weight meant they could take only enough for an emergency supply. Kublai handed over his reins to another and stretched his back with a groan. In the downpour, he hadn't bothered looking for woodland to provide fuel. It would be a cold meal of stale bread and meat scraps for most of the men. Xanadu had provided enough salted lamb and goat to last a month, an amount that had left the entire population on half-rations behind them until the herds replenished themselves. They were not yet at the point of drinking mare's blood from the living animals, but it was not far away.

Kublai sighed, taking pleasure in watching the routines around him, enjoying the lessening of eye strain as he focused on something close instead of miles ahead. He missed his wife, though he had learned not to grow too attached to a baby until he was sure it would survive. His son Zhenjin rode with the bondsmen, white with fatigue by the end of a day, but doggedly determined not to let his father down. He was on the edge of true manhood, but thin and wiry like his father. There were worse ways to grow into a man – and worse companions than the tumans around him.

As Kublai stretched, Uriang-Khadai walked over to him, shaking clods of mud from his feet as he went. They were all covered in the muck that spattered up from hooves and Kublai had to grin at the sight of the dignified orlok made to look as

427

if he'd rolled down a wet hill. The force of the rain increased suddenly, washing away the worst of it as they stood and stared at each other. It made a dull thunder as it hammered down and somewhere close lightning cracked across the sky, a dim flash behind the heavy clouds. Kublai began to laugh.

'I thought we were going to cross deserts, orlok. A man could drown standing up here.'

'I prefer it to heat, my lord, but I can't get the maps out in this. We've taken two yam stations today. I suggest we let the horses and men rest until tomorrow. I doubt it will last much longer.'

'How far to Samarkand now?' Kublai asked. He saw the older man raise his eyes to heaven and recalled he'd asked the same question many times.

'Some seven hundred miles, my lord. About fifty less than this morning.'

Kublai ignored the orlok's sour tone and worked it out. Twelve more days, maybe ten if he forced the men to the edge of ragged exhaustion and changed mounts more often. He had been careful with his resources to that point, but perhaps it was time to push for their highest possible speed.

The Chagatai khanate was well established and there would be yam lines running right through it in all directions. Though he took the riders from each one, he still worried that someone would get ahead of him. It would take a superb rider to stay in front of his tumans, but a man without armour on a fresh horse only had to reach one station ahead and then change horses at every point. It could be done and he dreaded the news that someone had already gone racing through.

Uriang-Khadai had waited patiently while the khan thought, knowing Kublai well.

'What can you tell me about the land to come?' Kublai asked. The orlok shrugged, glancing south. If it had not been for the rain, he would have seen the white-capped mountain peaks that led down into India. They were skirting the edges of the range, taking a path almost straight south-west that would lead them into the heart of the Chagatai khanate and its most prosperous cities.

'The maps show a pass through the final range of mountains. I do not know how high we must go to get over it. Beyond the peaks, the land is flat enough to make up whatever time we lose there.'

Kublai closed his eyes for a moment. His men could endure the cold far better than heat and he had spare deel robes on the packhorses. The problem was always food, for so many men and animals. They were already on short rations and he did not want to arrive in the Chagatai khanate like refugees from some disaster. They had to come fresh enough to fight and win quickly.

'Fifteen days then. In fifteen, I want to see Samarkand's walls before me. We'll stop for the night here, where the grass is good, to let the horses fill their bellies. Tell the men to go out and seek firewood; we have almost nothing left.'

It had become his practice to carry enough old wood for a fire each night, if he could. Even that was in short supply. Kublai wondered if Tsubodai had faced the same problems as he drove north and west beyond the boundaries of the nation of Genghis.

He stretched again as his men erected a basic awning held with poles. It would keep the rain off long enough to make a fire from the dry wood they unwrapped. Who would have known what a precious resource a few sticks and logs would become? Kublai's mouth filled with saliva at the thought of hot food. Most of the men would eat the cheese slop they made by mixing the iron-hard blocks with water. A few dried sticks of meat would give them strength, though it was never enough.

They would go on. They would endure anything while they rode with their khan.

General Bayar loved the cold north. From his youth, he had dreamed of what it must have been like to ride with Tsubodai into the white vastness, the land without end. In fact, he had been surprised how green the Russian steppes were in spring, at least the lowlands. His mother had brought him up with stories of Tsubodai's victories, how he took Moscow and Kiev, how he broke the knights of Christ in their shining armour. To ride in those footsteps was a joy. Bayar knew Christians and Moslems visited holy places as part of their faith. It amused Bayar to think of his journey into Batu's lands as his own pilgrimage. The rashes and infections that had plagued his men in the humid south slowly vanished, finally able to scar once the pus dried. Even lice and fleas were less active in the cold and many of the men smoked their clothes over open fires to give them relief while they could find it.

Bayar understood he had to be a stern leader for his men. He knew he faced battle ahead and the warriors of three tumans looked to him for leadership. Yet he wanted to whoop like a little boy as his horse plunged through snow, with white hills all around him.

At that height, it was always winter, though the steppes stretched into a green and dun horizon far below. It was open land, without the trappings of civilisation he had come to loathe among the Sung. There were no roads to follow there and his tumans cut their own path. The cold made his bones ache and each breath bit into him, but he felt alive, as if the years in Sung lands had been under a blanket of warm moistness that he was only then clearing from his lungs. He had never been fitter and he rose each day with fresh energy, leaping into his saddle and shouting to his officers. Kublai depended on him and Bayar would not let him down while he lived.

His tumans had not been with Kublai in the south. All of them were warriors Mongke had been bringing against the Sung. They did not have the lean look of those who had been at war for years, but Bayar was satisfied. They had given their oath to the khan and he did not worry about their loyalty beyond that. Part of him exulted at being in sole command of so many, a force to strike terror into Kublai's enemies. This was the nation: the raiding force of ruthless warriors, armed with sword, lance and bow.

Batu's khanate was part of the history, its story told around fires a thousand times since. His father Jochi had rebelled against Genghis, the only man ever to do so. It had cost him his life, but the man's khanate remained, given to Batu by the hand of Ogedai Khan. Bayar had to struggle not to grin at the thought of meeting a grandson of Genghis, first-born to first-born. Batu was one among many who could have been khan, with more right than most. Instead, the line had passed to Ogedai, Guyuk and then Mongke, descendants of different sons. Bayar hoped to see some trace of the Genghis bloodline in the man he would meet. He hoped he would not have to destroy him. He had come to declare Kublai's khanate and demand obedience. If Batu refused, Bayar knew what he would have to do. He would make his own mark in the history of the nation, as a man who ended a noble line from the great khan himself. It was a bitter thought and he did not dwell on it. Kublai was khan, his brother a weak pretender. There was no other way to see it.

In the cold months, Batu could not have had scouts out for weeks at a time without them losing fingers and toes to the frost. Bayar was not surprised to see isolated stone houses as he led his men down from the high hills. From a great distance, he could see smoke drifting up from dwellings with thick walls and sharply angled roofs, designed to let the snow fall rather than build up a crushing weight. He could also see riders galloping away from them as they caught sight of the tumans, no doubt to inform Batu of the threat. Bayar had broken his last yam station some miles before, taking the furious riders with him. Kublai's orders no longer applied, now that he had made contact. Arik-Boke would soon hear, as they wanted him to hear, and he would know his northern lands were cut off. Bayar hoped Kublai and Uriang-Khadai had reached Samarkand. Between them, they would isolate Karakorum, snatching away the two great suppliers of grain and herds to the capital.

With battle horns droning, Bayar picked up the pace, his thirty thousand men moving well as they dragged the tail of spare horses behind them. At the far rear, he had men with long sticks to force the herds on when they wanted to stop and graze. They would get a chance to rest and eat when he was done with Lord Batu.

Bayar was able to judge the man he would face by the speed of his response to the incursion. He had to admit it was impressive how fast Batu's tumans appeared. Even without the warning from yam lines, in a long-settled land with no close enemies, Bayar made barely ten miles across a valley of ice-rimed grass before he heard distant horns and saw black lines of galloping horses coming in fast. Kublai's general watched in fascination as the numbers visible kept growing, pouring into the valley from two or three different directions. The Batu khanate was barely a generation old and he had no idea how many men could take the field against his incursion. He had planned for a single tuman of warriors, possibly two. By the time they had formed up in sold ranks, blocking his path, he suspected they almost equalled his force – some thirty thousand men ready to defend their master's lands and people.

Kublai had been away from home too long, Bayar realised. When he had left for Sung lands, Batu's khanate had barely registered in the politics of Karakorum. Yet Batu's people had bred and taken in many more over the years. For the first time, Bayar considered that he might not be able to bring crushing force against the man. He had seen the way the tumans moved, recognising the shifting patterns of smaller jaguns and minghaans in the host. It was no wild horde he faced, but trained men, with bows and swords just like his own.

Bayar halted his tumans with a raised fist. He had been given a free hand by Kublai, but for the first time in years he felt his inexperience. These were his own people and he did not know instantly how to approach them as a hostile commander. He waited for a time in the front rank, then breathed in relief as a group detached on the other side and rode into a middle ground. They bore the red flags of the Golden Horde khanate, but also pure white banners. There was no one symbol for truce among the khanates, but white was gaining ascendancy and he could only hope they thought it meant the same as he did. Bayar gestured to his bondsmen.

'Raise white banners. Two jaguns forward with me,' he said, digging in his heels before they could move. He focused on the others as he rode forward – wondering if he could think of them yet as the enemy. There was an older man at their centre, surrounded by warriors in full armour with bows in their hands. Bayar headed for him, knowing his men would be forming behind him without further orders.

The tension seemed to swell in the air as his two hundred closed on the detachment. Bayar felt himself shudder slightly as he passed the point where he knew he was in arrow range. He wore layered scale armour in the Chin style, but he knew as well as any man alive that the long Mongol arrows could pierce it. He felt sweat trickle from his armpits and showed them only the cold face. Kublai depended on him.

At a hundred yards, Bayar wanted to call a halt, but it was too far to speak with whoever led them and he forced himself to ride on as if he didn't face armed men able to send shafts down his throat at that distance. Batu's detachment watched him come with no expression, though they shifted their bows in growing tension as he came to barely twenty paces. In the sudden silence, he could hear the banners in the wind, furling and snapping. He took a deep breath, controlling his nerves so his voice would be strong and steady.

'Under flags of truce, I seek Lord Batu Borjigin,' he shouted.

'You have found him,' the man at the centre responded. 'Now why have you come onto my lands with tumans? Has the great khan declared war on my people?'

For an instant, Bayar fought not to smile. He faced death in a heartbeat and his physical reaction was to grin.

'I do not know what the pretender is doing, my lord. I know Kublai Khan offers you peace in exchange for loyalty.'

Batu's mouth fell slightly open. He spluttered as he spoke, his dignity forgotten.

'What? Kublai Khan? Who are you to come here and talk of Kublai?'

Bayar laughed at the man's confusion, finally letting out some of the tension in him.

'Offer me guest rights in your camp, my lord. I have ridden a long way and my throat is dry.'

Batu stared at him for a moment that seemed endless, until Bayar's threatening laughter grew still in him. The man was around fifty, Bayar judged, with hair that had gone dark grey and heavy lines around his mouth and eyes. He wondered if he resembled Genghis as he waited, memorising the face.

434

'Very well, I grant you guest rights for this evening and no longer. Until I have heard what you have to say to me.'

Bayar relaxed slightly. He would never be completely safe, even after such an offer, but it was never given lightly. Until the following morning, Batu would be his host, even to the point of defending him if he were attacked. He dismounted and nodded to his men to do the same. Batu followed the action and came stalking over the frozen grass, his face full of curiosity.

'Who are you?' Batu demanded.

'General Bayar, my lord. Officer to Kublai Khan.'

Batu shook his head in confusion.

'Send your men away and have them camp in the valley two miles to the east. I won't have them frightening my villages. There will be no looting, or contact with my people, general. Is that clear?'

'I will give the orders, my lord,' Bayar replied.

The older man seemed to be studying him, his expression still astonished. Bayar watched as felt rugs were laid out on the grass and tea put on to boil. He sent word back to his tumans and then settled himself. He only hoped he could find the right words to impress the man who sat across from him.

Batu waited until Bayar had taken a bowl of tea in his right hand and sipped it, tasting the salt.

'Now explain, general. You know, I almost hope you are a madman. That would be a better thing than the news I think you have brought.'

CHAPTER THIRTY-SIX

Samarkand was a beautiful city, with white mountains in the distance and walls so thick that three horsemen could ride abreast on the crown. Blue towers showed over the sand-coloured walls, but the great gates were closed. Kublai's tumans had driven farmers and villagers ahead of them like geese, the crowd growing as they rode the last few miles. Unable to enter the city, they sat and wailed in front of it, raising their hands to those within. Kublai's warriors ignored them.

All along the walls, armoured Mongols and Persians looked down in stupefaction. No army had besieged Samarkand since Genghis. Yet there were many still alive who remembered the horrors of that time. Hundreds, then thousands of the inhabitants climbed steps on the inside to stare at the tumans.

Kublai looked up at them, sitting comfortably on a thin horse as it nuzzled the ground for anything worth eating. His face and fingers still ached from the cold he had endured in the mountain passes. Though the sun was strong, he knew he would lose skin on his cheeks, already darker than the rest of his face as it began to peel and crack.

Zhenjin trotted his mount over to his father, though he did not speak as he too looked up at the great walls. Kublai smiled to see his son's expression.

'My grandfather took this city once, Zhenjin,' he said.

'*How?*' the boy replied, in awe. He barely remembered Karakorum, and Samarkand was designed to impress exactly the sort of force Kublai commanded.

'Catapults and siege,' Kublai replied. 'He did not have cannon then.'

'We have no cannon, father,' Zhenjin replied.

'No, but if I must, I will have the men build heavy machines to break the walls. It will not be quick, but the city *will* fall. That is not why I came here though, Zhenjin. I have no interest in killing my own people, unless they force my hand. There are faster ways, if they know their history.'

He signalled to Uriang-Khadai and in turn the man snapped an order to two of the warriors. They leapt from their saddles and began to unpack equipment from spare horses. Zhenjin watched as they took rolls of material and spars onto their shoulders, grunting at the weight.

'What do they have there?' he asked.

'You will see,' Kublai replied, smiling strangely to himself. The scholar he had been was very far away at that moment, though he took joy in the story of his family and the history of the city. History was more than just stories, he reminded himself as the men walked forward with their burdens. It taught lessons as well.

Under the eye of their khan, the men worked quickly, heaving layers of cloth onto a wooden frame and hammering pegs and ropes into the stony ground. They had walked into arrow range and their stiff backs showed how they tried to resist the fear that someone would put a shaft into them as they worked.

When they stood back, the tumans broke into a roar of challenge, unplanned, a crash of sound that echoed back to them from the walls. A white tent stood before Samarkand.

'I do not understand,' Zhenjin said, shouting to be heard over the noise.

'The senior men in the city will,' Kublai replied. 'The white tent is a demand for surrender, a sign to them that the khan's tumans have declared war. As the sun sets, if their gates remain closed to me, a red tent will follow. It will stand for a day before their walls. If they ignore that, I will raise a black tent before them.'

'What do the red and black tents mean?' Zhenjin asked.

'They mean death, my son, though it will not come to that.'

Even as he spoke, the huge gates began to swing open. A cry of hope went up from the crowd of terrified refugees around the walls. They streamed to that one point as if a dam had burst, pushing each other in desperation and getting in the way of riders trying to leave the city. Kublai grinned at his son.

'They remember Genghis still, at least in Samarkand. See there, my son. They come.'

Lord Alghu was sweating heavily, though he had bathed in cool waters as the sun rose. He had been called from his palace rooms by senior men, their faces white with fear. He could still hardly believe the sheer size of the army that had gathered before Samarkand. For the first time in his life, he understood how it must have been for the enemies of the nation to wake and see tumans waiting for them. He wished his father Baidur still lived. He would have known what to do in the face of such a threat.

Alghu had rushed up to the crest of the wall, sagging against a stone pillar as he stared out into the distance. Had he offended Arik-Boke in some way? Lord Alghu swallowed painfully, his throat dry in the breeze. If the khan chose to make an example of him, his beloved cities would be burnt, his people slaughtered. Alghu had no illusions about the destructive strength of a Mongol army in the field. The tumans before Samarkand would tear through the Chagatai khanate like an unstoppable plague. He saw his own death in the fluttering banners.

His senior men had climbed the sandstone steps to see and they looked to him to give orders. Lord Alghu summoned his will, forcing himself to think. He led them all and their lives were in his hands. He did not blame his daughter. Aigiarn was young and headstrong, but whatever insult Arik-Boke believed he had been given did not warrant sending an army. He would send her away from the city so that Arik-Boke's malice would not fall on her. Lord Alghu shuddered at the thought.

'My lord, I cannot see the khan's banners out there,' one of his men said suddenly.

Lord Alghu had been turning to the steps to go down. He stopped.

'What do you mean?' he said, coming back and peering out again. The day was clear and he could see a long way from the height of the walls.

'I don't understand,' Alghu muttered as he confirmed it with his own eyes. Arik-Boke's banners were missing, but he did not recognise the others flying there. They seemed to have some animal embroidered on yellow silk. It was too far to be certain, but Lord Alghu knew he had never seen those flags before.

'Perhaps I should go out and ask them what they want,' he said to his men, smiling tightly.

Their expressions didn't ease in reply. All of them had family in Samarkand or the cities around it. The Chagatai khanate had not been attacked for decades and yet they all knew the stories of slaughter and destruction that had come with Genghis. It was impossible to live in the khanate and not hear them.

A small group of warriors walked forward from the tumans in front of his city, each man bearing rolls of cloth. Alghu stared down in confusion as they approached the walls. One of his soldiers began to bend a bow nearby, but he snapped an order to be still.

Thousands watched curiously as the white tent began to take shape, the men below hammering pegs and stretching ropes to hold it. It was not as solid as a ger and its sides fluttered in the breeze. When Lord Alghu recognised it, he fell back a step, shaking his head.

'It can't be,' he whispered. Those who remembered stood in shock, while their friends demanded to know what it meant.

'Ready the gates!' Lord Alghu shouted suddenly. 'I will go out to them.' He turned to his men, his expression sick with worry.

'This has to be a mistake. I do not understand it, but the khan would not destroy Samarkand.'

He almost fell as he ran down the steps, his legs weak under him. His horse was on the main street into the city, waiting with his personal guards. They knew nothing of what he had seen and he did not enlighten them. The white tent was a demand for total surrender and it had to be answered before the red tent rose. As he mounted, Alghu told himself he had a day, but he could hardly think for fear. The red tent would mean the death of every male of fighting age in the city. The black tent was a promise to slaughter every living thing, including women and children. The city of Herat had ignored Genghis when he threatened them in such a way. Only lizards and scorpions lived in that place when he had finished.

'Open the gates!' Lord Alghu roared. He had to answer the demand immediately. His soldiers removed the great bar of oak and iron and began to heave them apart. As a line of light showed, their lord turned to one of his most trusted men.

'Go to my sons, my daughter. Take them safely to . . .' He hesitated. If the khan had decided to destroy his line, there *was* no safe place in the world. Arik-Boke would hunt them down

440

and no one would dare give them shelter for fear of the khan's vengeance.

'My lord, the village of Harethm is a hundred miles to the north and west,' the bondsman said. 'I lived there once and it lies within the borders of the Hulegu khanate. No one will know they are there but you. I will protect them with my life.'

'Very well,' Alghu replied, breathing in relief. 'Go now, from another gate. I will send for them if I can.'

As the gates opened further, Lord Alghu saw a crowd of men and women pressing in, their hands outstretched in panic. His soldiers began to shove them back to let their master pass. Lord Alghu had no eyes for them as they streamed around his men. The city was no safer than their place outside it.

He stared out at the dark lines of the tumans waiting for him. Fear was a knot in his stomach as he dug in his heels and began to trot forward. As he passed under the shadow of the arch, he saw his bannermen begin to unfurl his personal flags.

'White banners,' he snapped, close to panic. 'We go out under truce.'

His men stared at him, seeing his fear. They had no white flags, but one of the refugees wore a white robe. In an instant, the unfortunate man had been clubbed to the ground and stripped, his garment raised to flutter on a spear as Lord Alghu rode out.

'Would you like to come with me?' Kublai asked his son. Zhenjin grinned, showing white teeth. In answer, he dug in his heels and his horse lunged forward. Kublai nodded to Uriang-Khadai and the orlok whistled to the closest jagun of a hundred warriors. They detached from the ranks, forming up on both sides of the two senior men. Kublai's bannermen came with

441

them, carrying yellow flags with Chinese dragons on them that caught the sun and glittered.

'Be silent and listen,' Kublai murmured to Zhenjin at his side as they closed on the force from the city.

'Are we going to kill them?' Zhenjin asked. The idea did not seem to trouble him particularly and Kublai smiled. He had seen the white flag flapping above them.

'Not unless I have to. I need this khanate on my side.'

They halted together, demonstrating their discipline to those who watched from the walls. Lord Alghu's men pulled up with less precision, the sort of sloppy display Kublai's tumans expected from city soldiers.

Lord Alghu came out with his most senior man and Kublai matched him with Uriang-Khadai. The two smaller groups faced each other in the bright sunlight, casting long shadows on the sandy ground. Kublai waited, standing on his dignity for once and forcing them to speak first.

The silence lasted only moments before Lord Alghu cleared his throat.

'Who are you to raise a white tent before my city?' he demanded.

'I am Kublai Borjigin, grandson of Genghis, great khan of the risen nation. Give me your name and acknowledge me as your lord and we have no quarrel.'

Lord Alghu gaped, slumping in the saddle. He had met Kublai as a boy, but the years had changed him beyond all recognition. The man he faced wore a Chin silk robe over a tunic, with dragons embroidered on the material. Yet there was a sword at his hip and he looked strong and dangerous. Lord Alghu peered into the sunlight and saw the light gold eyes that so often marked the line of Genghis. He swallowed.

'I am Alghu Borjigin,' he stammered, 'khan of the Chagatai territory. If you are . . .' He hesitated, having been about to say words that suggested he doubted Kublai's claim. He could not afford to insult a man with twelve tumans. 'I am your cousin, son to Baidur, son to Chagatai, son to Genghis.'

'I met you when I was young, did I not? Before Guyuk was made khan in Karakorum?'

Lord Alghu nodded, trying to reconcile the memory of the thin boy with the man he faced.

'I remember you. You have returned from the Sung lands, then?'

Kublai chuckled. 'You are a man of rare insight, with me standing before you. Now surrender your city, Lord Alghu. I will not ask again.'

The older man's mouth opened, but no sound came out. He shook his head, simply unable to take in what he had been told.

'Arik-Boke is khan,' he stammered at last. To his horror, Kublai's expression turned cold and the yellow eyes seemed to gleam with anger.

'No, Lord Alghu. No, he is not. I claim the khanate and all the nations within it. My brother will bow the knee to me or fall. But that is for another day. Give me your answer or I will take this city and put another in your place.' Kublai turned to Uriang-Khadai, his voice light. 'Would you be interested in ruling Samarkand, orlok?'

'If it is your will, my lord khan,' Uriang-Khadai replied. 'But I would rather ride with you against the usurper.'

'Very well. I will find another.' He turned back to Lord Alghu, still watching with a slightly open mouth. 'Your answer, Lord Alghu?'

'I . . . I gave my oath to Arik-Boke. To your brother, my lord. I cannot take the words back.'

'I release you from your oath,' Kublai replied immediately. 'Now . . .'

'It is not as simple as that!' Alghu snapped, anger finally breaking through his shock.

'No? Who else has the authority to release your oath, if not your khan?'

'My lord, this is . . . I need time to think. Will you enter the city in peace for a night? I grant guest rights to you and your men.'

For an instant, Kublai felt for the man he had put in an impossible position. Twelve tumans faced his city, promising certain destruction. He could not break his oath to Arik-Boke, but Kublai was giving him no choice. His will hardened.

'No, Lord Alghu. You will make a decision here and now. You have chosen to give oath to the usurper, but I do not hold you responsible for his crimes. I am the rightful khan of the nation. I am the gur-khan. My word is iron and my word is law. I tell you again that you are released from your oath, your vow. It is done. At this moment, you call no man lord. Do you understand what I have said to you?'

Lord Alghu had grown pale. He nodded.

'Then, as a free man, you must make your decision. My place is not here. I have other concerns than this khanate, but I cannot leave an enemy behind me while I seek out my foolish brother. I cannot leave a supply line into Karakorum, when I will bring that city under siege. Do you understand *that*?'

Lord Alghu nodded again, unable to reply. Kublai's voice softened, almost to friendliness.

'Then choose, Lord Alghu. We have so few real choices in our lives. I will have no choice but to destroy Samarkand if you make the wrong decision here, this morning, but I do not wish to threaten you. The nation is in error, Lord Alghu. I have merely to put right what has gone wrong.'

Alghu thought of his children, already on their way to a safe village. He had no illusions about what Kublai was describing.

Arik-Boke had a vast army and he would never surrender to his brother, not now he was khan. No Mongol force had *ever* fought against their own people in battle, but it would come, and it would bring destruction on a scale he could hardly imagine.

Slowly, carefully, under the watchful eye of Kublai's orlok, Lord Alghu dismounted and stood by his horse, looking up at the man who claimed to rule the world. The Chagatai khanate was just a small part of that, he told himself. Yet if he gave a new oath, Arik-Boke would send his own tumans in reprisal. There would be no mercy, no quarter for an oath-breaker lord. Lord Alghu closed his eyes for an instant, caught between impossible forces.

At last, he spoke.

'My lord,' he said, 'if I give you my oath, my cities lie within reach of Karakorum. It will be an act of war with the great khanate.' He blinked as he realised the words he had used, but Kublai only laughed.

'I cannot promise you safety, Lord Alghu. There is no safety in this world. I can say that I will keep my brother's attention on me for this summer. After that, the khanate will be restored and I will look kindly on your cities.'

'If you lose, my lord . . .'

'If I lose? I do not fear some weakling brother who thinks he can stand in my place. The sun is hot, Lord Alghu, and I have been patient with you. I understand your fears, but if I stood in your place, I would know what to do.'

Lord Alghu stepped clear of his horse. On the dusty ground, he lowered himself to both knees.

'I offer you gers, horses, salt and blood, my lord khan,' he said, his voice almost a whisper. 'You have my oath.'

The tension went out of Kublai's frame as he spoke.

'The right decision, Lord Alghu. Now welcome my men

445

into your city, that we may rest and drink the dust from our throats.'

'Very well, my lord khan,' Lord Alghu said, wondering if he had just thrown away his honour, as well as his life. He had been considering bringing his children back to the city, but it would do them no harm to spend a season with the villagers, as safe from harm as anyone could be with the khanates about to erupt into civil war.

General Bayar watched sourly as Batu paced up and down in the wooden house. The man had not taken the news well and Bayar was still searching for the right words to convince him. He knew most of Kublai's plan and part of it was making certain the princes of the nation stayed out of the struggle between brothers. It was a difficult request that struck at the root of their honour and their oaths, but Kublai had been clear in his instructions.

'There has never been civil war in the nation,' Kublai had told him. 'Make sure Batu understands the normal rules are suspended until my family have made an ending. His oath is to the office of the great khan. Until this is settled, until only one man is khan, he *cannot* honour his oath. Tell him to stay in his lands and we will have no quarrel.'

Bayar thought back over the words for the hundredth time as Batu sat down at his great oak table and nodded to the servants bringing steaming platters of meat and vegetables in butter.

'Join me, general,' Batu said as he pulled out a bench. 'This is beef from my own herd.'

Bayar looked at the bloody slices and his mouth watered. He shrugged, then sat down, pulling pieces towards him with his fingers and chewing so that the juices ran down his chin.

'It's good,' Bayar said, suppressing a groan of satisfaction. The meat came apart in his mouth almost without chewing and he pulled more into reach, leaving a pink trail on the old wood.

'You'll never taste anything better,' Batu replied. 'I am hoping to sell the meat to the khan's cities in a few years, when I've built the herd up.'

'You'll make a fortune,' Bayar said, 'but not while the fighting goes on. I still need an answer from you, my lord.'

Batu chewed slowly, savouring each mouthful, but always watching the man who sat across from him. At length, he cleared his throat with a long draught of pale wine, then sat back.

'Very well. I have three choices, general, as I see it. I can let you go, do as Kublai wants and stay out of the fighting, tending to my own lands and my own people until it is done. If he loses, I will have the khan . . .' He raised a hand as Bayar opened his mouth. 'I will have Arik-Boke riding here in a fury, asking why I kept my head down while my rightful lord was under attack. If that is the result, I could lose everything.'

Bayar didn't reply. Neither he nor Batu knew for certain what would happen if Kublai lost. Arik-Boke might well exact some kind of vengeance. A sensible man might declare an amnesty for the small khanates, but nothing in the bloodline suggested Arik-Boke would be sensible.

'My second choice is to mount up with my tumans and ride in support of my lawful khan. I suspect you would oppose me in that, so the first thing would be to slaughter your men.'

'If you think . . .' Bayar began.

Once again, Batu stopped him with a raised palm.

'You are in my land, general. My people are serving yours with fine meat and drink every day. I could give a single order and see an end to it before sundown. That is my second choice.'

'Just tell me what you have decided,' Bayar said irritably.

Batu grinned at him.

'You are not a patient man, general. My third choice is to do nothing and keep you here with me. If Kublai wins, I have done nothing to injure him. If Arik-Boke triumphs, I have held three tumans from joining the fight. It would allow me to keep my life and lands, at least.'

Bayar paled slightly as the other man spoke. He had already wasted too much time in Batu's khanate. Kublai had made him repeat his orders to ride for Karakorum and Bayar had some idea of his place in the khan's plans. If he was held prisoner for months, it would mean the difference between success and disaster.

Batu had been watching his reactions closely.

'I see that does not find favour with you, general. The best choice for my people is perhaps your worst.'

Bayar stared at him in sullen anger. Everything Kublai planned would come down to a battle before Karakorum. Bayar's tumans were the final bone to throw, the reserve that would hit the enemy rear at exactly the right moment. He swallowed painfully, the rich meat feeling like a stone in his stomach. Kublai would look for him when the time came. If he was not there, his friend would be cut down.

Slowly, Bayar stood up.

'I will leave now,' he said. 'You will make whatever choice you think is best, but you will not hold me here.'

He turned sharply at the sound of swords being drawn behind him. Two of Batu's bondsmen were watching him with grim expressions, blocking the door to the sunlight and open air.

'Sit down, general. I have not finished with you yet,' Batu said, leaning back from the table. He saw the general's eye drop to the heavy knife that had been used to cut the meat. Batu chuckled as he picked it up and used it to spear another thick slice.

'I told you to sit down,' he said.

CHAPTER THIRTY-SEVEN

Arik-Boke drew back his bow and tried again to bring his heartbeat and breathing under control. He couldn't do it. Whenever he felt the beginning of calm, spiking fury would make his pulse race and his hands tremble.

He loosed with a shout of frustration and saw the shaft strike high on the straw target. In disgust, he threw the bow down, ignoring the wince of his arms master at the treatment of such a valuable weapon. Tellan was in his sixties and had served three khans before Arik-Boke, one of them in the field. There were three boys working brooms around the perimeter of the training square and they all froze in shock to see an act that would have earned any one of them a whipping.

Tellan showed no expression as he gathered up the precious bow and stood patiently, though his hands ran down the length without conscious thought, searching for cracks or damage. When he was satisfied, he held it out again. Arik-Boke waved it away.

'No more now. I can't keep my mind clear,' he said.

At his side, the orlok of his armies had been in the process of drawing his own bow. Alandar was faced with a delicate choice. His own heart thumped slowly and his hands and arms were like hardwood. He could have placed the shaft anywhere he chose, but under the khan's glare, Alandar decided not to take the shot. He released the tension slowly, feeling muscles twitch uncomfortably across his chest.

Alandar untied the quiver from his shoulder and handed the equipment to the arms master of Karakorum's training ground. He had thought Arik-Boke might benefit from a morning of sweat and practice, but the khan only seemed to grow in anger with every poor shot.

'Would you prefer to work with swords, my lord khan?' he asked.

Arik-Boke snorted. He wanted to hack someone to death, not go through routines and stances until his muscles ached. He nodded with bad grace.

'Very well,' he said.

'Fetch the khan's training swords, Tellan.'

As the arms master turned, Arik-Boke raised his head in inspiration.

'Bring the wolf's-head blade as well,' he muttered. 'And fetch the training suit.'

Tellan trotted off with the bows into the buildings around the training square. He returned with two swords in scabbards and an armful of stiff leather. Arik-Boke took the swords and felt the heft of each one.

'Put the suit on, Tellan. I'm in the mood to cut something.'

The arms master was a veteran warrior. He had fought alongside Tsubodai and earned his position at the khan's court. His brows lowered slightly and his expression grew stern. For one of his trainees, it would have been a sign of gathering storm clouds, but Arik-Boke was oblivious.

'Shall I have one of the boys put it on, my lord khan?' Tellan said.

Arik-Boke barely glanced at him.

'Did I ask you to fetch one of the boys?' he snapped.

'No, my lord.'

'Then do as you are told.'

Tellan began to buckle the leather straps around himself. The practice suit had begun life as a blacksmith's apron with long sleeves, the layers of sewn leather so stiff that it would hardly bend at the waist. To that had been added a padded helmet with neck-pieces and heavy guards that buckled under the sleeves and onto the shins. Tellan heaved the main part over his head and stood still as Alandar began to fasten the buckles.

Arik-Boke drew a practice sword and swung it through the air. It was heavier than a normal blade, weighted with lead so that a warrior's wrist and forearms could develop strength. It lacked much of an edge and the point was rounded. He frowned at it and drew his personal blade, recovered from Mongke's body.

The eyes of both Alandar and Tellan slid over to him as they heard the sound of shining steel being drawn. It was not just that both men were veterans. The sword had been in the khan's family for generations. The hilt had been cast in the shape of a stylised wolf's head and, in its own way, it was one of the most potent symbols of the risen nation. Genghis had carried it, as had his father before him. The sword was polished and viciously sharp, with every chip or dent smoothed out of it. It looked exactly what it was, a length of sharp metal designed to cut flesh. Arik-Boke swished it through the air with a grunt.

Alandar met Tellan's eyes and smiled wryly at the man's expression. He liked Tellan and had spent a few evenings drinking with him. The arms master was not one to faint at a little blood or the prospect of a battering, but he did not look happy. Alandar finished the buckles and stepped away.

'Shall I give him a sword?' he asked.

Arik-Boke nodded. 'Give him yours.'

All three of them knew it would make little difference. The suit had been designed for multiple attacks, to let a young warrior try to remain calm and focused as half a dozen of his friends worked him over. It would not let Tellan move quickly enough to defend himself.

Alandar handed his blade to the arms master and grinned as he stood for an instant with his back to the khan. Tellan rolled his eyes in answer, but he took the weapon.

As Alandar stepped clear, Arik-Boke stepped in and swung at Tellan's neck with everything he had. Alandar's smile vanished as Tellan staggered backwards. The headgear for the suit had heavy pieces overlapping the neck area, but the wolf's-head sword had almost cut through and one of them hung by a few threads.

The arms master blocked the next strike with a huge effort, using all his strength to make the leather arms bend fast enough. Arik-Boke grunted as sweat appeared on his face, but he moved forward, hitting high and low, groin and neck. His sword left bright slashes in the suit and mouths opened in it so that Alandar could see Tellan's clothing beneath. The orlok considered making a comment, but chose to remain silent. Arik-Boke was khan.

Tellan seemed to realise he was in a fight and when Arik-Boke stepped too close he reversed his backwards motion, using the bulk of the suit to throw his hip into the khan and make him stagger. The reply was another flat blow to the neck, tearing the leather free so that it fell. Tellan's veined throat was exposed and he knew it, feeling the air on his flesh as soon as it happened. He tried to step aside and back, but Arik-Boke pressed him at every step, swinging the sword as if it were a club rather than a blade. More than one of his wild strikes were turned aside on the leather, wrenching his fingers and making him hiss in pain.

It seemed an age before Arik-Boke paused. The leather suit was in tatters, half of it hanging loose and the rest on the ground at Tellan's feet. Blood dripped down the man's legs and slowly pooled as Arik-Boke panted, watching him for a sudden move. To the equal horror of the arms master and Alandar, Arik-Boke rested the point of his sword on the ground, putting his weight on it as if it were a simple stick and not the most famous blade in the history of the nation. Sweat poured from the khan and he breathed in great, rasping breaths.

'That will do,' he said, straightening with an effort and tossing the blade to Alandar, who caught it easily. 'Have my shaman look at your cuts, Tellan. Alandar, with me.'

Without another word, he strode off the training square. Alandar collected the scabbard and barely had time to dart a quick look of apology to Tellan before he went after him.

The arms master stood alone and panting in the centre of the square. He had not moved for some time when one of the sweeping boys dared to approach him.

'Are you all right, master?' the boy said, peering round the torn remnants of the headgear.

Tellan's lips were bloody and he showed his teeth to the boy as he tried to take a step.

'Take my arm and help me, boy. I can't walk back on my own.'

The admission hurt him as much as the wounds he had taken, but his pride wouldn't let him fall. The boy called a friend and between them they helped Tellan stagger out of the sun.

Arik-Boke strode quickly down the corridors of the palace. The tightness of his rage felt as if it had eased slightly and he rolled his shoulders as he walked. He had been imagining Kublai before him as he had battered the arms master and for a time it had taken the edge off his anger. As he walked, it swelled again within him, a red coil that made him want to strike out.

He came to polished copper doors and shoved them open without acknowledging the guards who stood there. Alandar followed him into the meeting room, seeing his most senior men rise to their feet as if jerked up by strings. Since the khan had stormed out hours earlier, they had been waiting for him to return, unable to leave without his permission. They showed no sign of impatience as they bowed. Alandar noticed the single jug of wine had been drunk dry, but there was nothing else to indicate Arik-Boke had kept a dozen men waiting for the best part of a morning.

Arik-Boke walked through them to the table and cursed when he saw the jug was empty. He grabbed it and took it to the copper doors, shoving it into the hands of one of his Day Guards.

'Bring more wine,' he said, ignoring the man as he tried to bow and keep hold of the jug at the same time. When he turned to his officers once more, his eyes glittered with simmering fury and no one would meet his gaze.

'Now, gentlemen,' he grated. 'You have had time to think. You know the stakes involved.' He waited for barely a beat before going on. 'My scouts find broken yam stations. My orders go unanswered. Supplies have stopped from the north and if my spies have not been turned against me, my brother Kublai has made war on a khanate. My own *blood* has turned his tumans against his lawful ruler.' He paused, his eyes raking them.

'The world has gone quiet as rabbits with a snake in their hole and you have nothing to offer your khan? *Nothing*?' He roared the last word, spraying spit. The men in the room were seasoned warriors, but they pulled back from him. His snuffling breath was loud in the room and the scar that ran across the ruined bridge of his nose had grown red.

'Tell me how it is possible for an army to ride into my khan-ates without us becoming aware of it before this. Did my grandfather set up the yam lines for nothing? For months, I have been asking my advisers why the letters have stopped coming, why the reports are late. I asked my senior officers what fault there could be that might result in Karakorum being cut off from the rest of the world in such a way. Now you tell

455

me how such a thing could happen within a thousand miles of this city and have us know nothing about it.'

His guard returned with two brimming jugs of wine, erring on the side of caution. Arik-Boke waited while a cup was poured for him and drained it in quick gulps. When he had finished a second, he seemed calmer, though a heavy flush was stealing up his neck, where the veins were clearly visible.

'That is past. When this is over, I will have the heads of those men who told me that the yam lines could never be broken, that they gave me a security and an early warning that no other khan had ever known. I will have the head of Lord Alghu and give his daughter to my bondsmen for their sport.' He took a deep breath, aware that simply ranting at his men would produce no good result.

'I want them rebuilt. Orlok Alandar will come to you for your best scouts and have them man the lines. I need to know where my brother's tumans are, so that I can answer their betrayal with the greatest possible force.'

He faced the men in the room, making sure they saw his contempt.

'Alandar, give me a tally of our strength,' he said at last.

'Without the tumans of the Russian khanate, or the Chagatai . . .' he began.

'Tell me what I have, orlok, not what I don't have.'

'Twenty tumans, my lord khan. Leaving only the Guards to keep peace in the city.'

'And my brother?'

Alandar hesitated, knowing it would be at best a guess.

'He may have as many as eighteen tumans, my lord, though he has been at war with the Sung for years and he will have lost many, perhaps six or seven of them.'

'Or more, orlok. My scholar brother could easily have lost

half his force while he was reading his Chin books, while he was learning to dress like a Chin whore.'

'As you say, my lord. We cannot know for certain until the yam lines are re-established.'

'He did not beat the Sung, Orlok Alandar. He merely held his place for five years, waiting for Mongke Khan to ride to his aid. That is the sort of man we face. That is the false khan, my *brother*, who has broken our supply lines and rides the world in careless confidence, while the khan of the nation of Genghis can only react. No more, Alandar! I have had enough of these ragged riders terrified to tell me the khanates are falling apart. We will go out and meet this scholar brother. And I will have him crawling at my feet before we are done.'

'Your will, my lord,' Alandar said, bowing his head.

'We can place the traitor at Samarkand two months ago.' Arik-Boke gestured to one of the twenty generals who waited in nervous tension for their orders. 'Bring me my maps, gentlemen. We will see how far he could have run in the time.'

Some of the men exchanged glances, knowing from experience that a fresh Mongol tuman could have covered a thousand miles or more since then. Alandar chose to speak, knowing that of all of them, he was most immune to Arik-Boke's anger.

'My lord, he could be almost anywhere. We suspect he sent tumans against Batu in the north, so it is likely he has already split his forces. But we *know* he will come to Karakorum.'

'This is just a city,' Arik-Boke said.

'It is a city with the women and children of his tumans, my lord. Kublai will come for them. What choice does he have?'

Arik-Boke grew still, thinking. At last, he nodded.

'Yes, we have that at least. We know where he will come and we have something precious to him. That will do as a starting place, orlok. But I do not want to fight a defensive battle. Our strength is in movement, in speed. He will not pin me down.

457

Do you understand? That is the thinking of our enemies. I want to get out of Karakorum and find him while he moves. I want to run him down like a circle hunt, closing slowly on his men until there is nowhere left to run.'

'The closest yam stations are already working, my lord,' Alandar replied. 'We are restocking a dozen each day, now that we know what happened to them. We will have warning as soon as they sight his tumans.'

'I was told that before, Alandar. I will not rely on them again.' He took a deep breath. 'Send the tumans towards the Chagatai khanate, with scouts running between them. Five battle groups of forty thousand to cover the ground. Keep the scouts out, ready for the first touch. When they sight the enemy . . .' He paused, savouring the word in relation to his foolish brother. 'When they see him, they will not engage until the full force has gathered. We will strike him down, this false khan. And I will be there to see it.'

'Your will, my lord. I will leave a thousand men to patrol the camps and Karakorum and establish the yam stations first between the city and the Chagatai lines.' It was an interpretation of the orders he had been given and Arik-Boke bristled immediately.

'This is just a city, orlok. I have said it. I am khan of the nation. One city means nothing to me.'

Alandar hesitated. The khan was in no mood to hear an argument, but he had to speak. His position demanded it, to temper the khan's righteous anger with tactical sense.

'My lord, if your brother sent tumans into the north, they would be behind us as we move against his main force. Karakorum could be destroyed . . .'

'I have hostages to keep them peaceful, Alandar. I will have knives at the throats of their women and children if they touch the first stone of Karakorum. Does that satisfy you? What general of my brother's would give *that* order? They will not move against the city for fear of the slaughter that will follow.'

Alandar swallowed uncomfortably. He was not certain that Arik-Boke would go through with the threat and he knew better than to press him on it. No khan had ever considered butchering his own people, but then there had never been a war amongst their own, not since Jochi had betrayed Genghis. That was nothing compared to what Arik-Boke faced and the orlok voiced none of his misgivings, choosing to remain silent.

Arik-Boke nodded as if he had received assent.

'I will leave enough men to carry out my orders, orlok, sworn men who understand the meaning of their oath. That is enough now. My blood cries out to answer these insults. Send messengers to Hulegu. Tell him I call his oath. And gather my tumans on the plain. I will ride to find my brother Kublai and I will choose the manner of his death when we have him.'

Alandar bowed his head. He could not shake the sense that the khan was underestimating the enemy tumans. They were as fast as his own men and, for all Arik-Boke's bluster, he could not make himself believe they were led by a fool, a scholar. A fool would not have cut the supplies into Karakorum before the attack. A scholar would not have removed the most powerful lords from Arik-Boke's side before the true fighting even began. Even so, he had learned obedience from a young age.

'Your will, my lord khan,' he said.

CHAPTER THIRTY-EIGHT

Hulegu cursed his general's memory as he galloped along the fighting line. Kitbuqa had been killed years before, but his legacy lived on in the Moslems who had vowed never to accept his khanate. Holding Christian Mass in mosques had turned out to be a terrible idea when it came to pacifying the region, though it was true that many of the tribes also screamed the name of Baghdad as he caught and punished them.

He had never known such a cauldron of trouble as the khanate he had chosen. From the destruction of the city on, men had drifted in from thousands of miles away to fight for the land he had taken. He grinned as he rode. His grandfather had said there was no better way to spend a life and the khanate was never still, never peaceful, as it vomited up new enemies each year. It was good for the tumans he commanded. His men kept themselves sharp against the dark-skinned madmen who died screaming the name of a city or their god.

Hulegu ducked as an arrow whirred somewhere close. The line of enemy horsemen blurred as he ran down its flank. He had only heartbeats before they began to react to his sudden manoeuvre. He could hear their roaring voices and the air was thick with dust and sweat and the taint of garlic under a battering sun.

Hulegu barely gestured and his galloping line angled into the enemy flank, raising lances at the last moment. They plunged through horses and men, spearing a hundred paces into the crush as if they were a knife sinking into flesh. The Persians crumpled before them and Hulegu cut down on his left and right, each blow aimed to break and blind, to leave falling men behind him.

He heard the snap of crossbow bolts and something struck him high in the chest, piercing his armour and thumping his collarbone. He groaned, hoping it had not broken again. As he punched through the lines, he felt only numbness from the area, but the pain would come. His tumans were outnumbered, but they were still fresh and strong and the day had barely begun. His charge had sliced away a great section of their lines and he signalled to his minghaan officers to enclose and cut it free. It was shepherd's work, separating young rams from a flock and cutting them down. The main force of horsemen and foot soldiers moved on to face the Mongol shafts ahead and there was space for a time.

Hulegu wiped sweat from his face with a damp hand, blinking as his eyes stung with salt. He was thirsty, but as he looked around, there was no sign of his camel boys with waterskins.

Movement drew his attention and Hulegu stared as a dark mass of soldiers came jogging over the crest of a hill. They moved quickly and lightly despite the heat and he could see they were armed with bows and swords. Hulegu trotted out from the main battle for twenty or thirty paces, judging the best response. All his tumans were engaged by then and he had no separate reserves. He began to frown as the Persian soldiers kept coming, as if there were no end to them. They gleamed in the sun, wearing armour of brass and iron. As he

461

watched, horsemen appeared on their flanks, overtaking the walking men.

He had missed an army, hiding in the hills. Whichever local leader had brought them in and hidden them had chosen his moment with care. Hulegu wet his dry lips with his tongue, looking around him and trying to keep a sense of the battle. He would have to detach a full tuman to meet and prevent them from joining up with their brothers.

Sweat ran into his eyes as the men around him finished butchering the hundreds they had cut out from the main force. It was work they knew well and his warriors were confident in their power, well used to battle after years spent fighting.

The flow of men over the hill-crest kept coming, like a spread of oil. Hulegu looked for a tuman he could disengage, but they were all in the thick of the fighting. The Afghans and Persians raised their heads as they saw the reinforcements and fought with more energy, knowing they could waste their strength and fall gasping because the Mongols would have to answer the threat. One of the tumans was pushed back by yelling thousands, forcing them to break free and gain space around them for another charge.

Hulegu cursed. He would have to take the opportunity, but he saw the danger if he pulled them out. The men they had been killing would surge after them and in doing so flank the tuman next in line. For an instant, he pictured the threat.

'God's blood,' he muttered. Kitbuqa's old habit of blaspheming had rubbed off on him. Hulegu knew he could have done with his friend on the field that day. It had been poor fortune that Kitbuqa had faced a huge army while Hulegu was in Karakorum to see his brother made khan. At least the tribes had paid a harsh price for the life of a Mongol general. He had seen to that in massive organised reprisals.

Hulegu signalled to his bannerman and watched the result as the tuman flag went up and was swung in a great circle, flapping. The tuman answered its personal flag in moments, halting almost as they began to charge back in. Hulegu could see the faces turned towards his position and he tried to ignore the feeling of panic as the enemy began to surge forward.

'Second flag. Engage enemy,' he snapped to his bannerman. There were too few signals and he had nothing to point to the new force coming over the hills. Yet his men were experienced and they would know he wouldn't stop them only to order them back in.

They whirled their horses and began cantering up the rising ground. Hulegu grunted in relief, then his breath caught as he saw the enemy were still coming. Thousands more of them had appeared and he cursed the labyrinth of valleys all around that could hide so many from his scouts.

The Persian lines below ran forward, howling in glee as they appeared to chase the tuman from the field. Their momentum took them along a wing of his personal tuman as he had feared. Hulegu took a deep breath to shout new orders to the single minghaan of a thousand who had come with him.

'Back in support!' he bellowed. 'To the Brass tuman line, in support!' He repeated the order as he dug in his heels. There were too many of the enemy, but he was not ready to retreat, not from those. The battle could yet turn and they could break. He would wait for the moment, pray for it. The Brass tuman was under pressure at the front and side, close to being overwhelmed. For the first time that day, Hulegu felt a worm of doubt in his stomach. He had never lost a fixed battle against the wild tribesmen, though they challenged him each year with increasing numbers, crying 'Baghdad' and 'Allahu Akbar' as they came. He showed his teeth as he rode to support his tuman. His men would not break against dog-raping farmers. They could be defeated, but never made to run.

The thousand with him stretched out to a full gallop. Many of them had lost their lances and emptied their quivers in the fighting, but they drew swords and struck into the enemy, seeking to cut through the chaos, roaring their battle cries. Hulegu laid on around him with all his strength, smashing his sword down on helmets as shields were raised against him. From horseback, he could still see the fresh soldiers meet his tuman on the rising ground. The tuman had slid into a wide charging line with lowered lances, but even as Hulegu watched, it began to falter against the sheer numbers. Like a broken fishing net, the charging line was sundered in a dozen places. They could not hold and the screaming Persians were flowing around and through them, losing hundreds of men to reach the main battle.

Hulegu swore, turning his anger into a quick chopping blow that cracked the skull of a bearded man as he showed his red mouth in a wild yell. It was his task to keep a feel for the battle and never to lose himself in the pain and fury. The ranks on the hill were still coming and Hulegu felt a cold chill, despite the heat. The shahs had caught him neatly, making him commit his forces and then springing the ambush with everything they had.

Hulegu had cut himself a space and he was gathering the minghaan back to him for another charge at a weak point when he saw his scouts racing over the bloody grass. They were already pointing into a shadowed valley on his right hand and Hulegu groaned to himself. If there was another army there, he was done.

Even as he formed the thought, the first ranks came out of the shadowed hills, not far from the heels of the scouts they followed. Hulegu rubbed sweat from his eyes, gaping. What he saw was impossible, but he felt his heart lift even so. Solid ranks of Mongol warriors came surging out, lances standing upright like a forest of thorns. He knew them from their banners and he shook his head in a sort of wonder before turning back to see the enemy. Slowly, his lips pulled back to reveal his teeth. It was not a smile.

The tumans in the hills had been riding close, pressed in by the narrow valleys all around. As they hit the open space, they fanned out and Hulegu shouted in joy to see manoeuvres he knew as well as his own body. Two entire tumans jerked into a new path, heading for the force sliding over the hill-crest. Two more increased their speed on the flat ground and came at his position like a hammer swinging down on the Persian ranks.

Hulegu saw arrows soar out from them, bows thrumming their deep note over and over, shafts by the tens of thousand filling the air as the forces closed. The Persian ranks crumpled under the new assault, their battered shields saving only a few. Hulegu stood in his stirrups to see the lances come down. A rank five hundred wide struck his enemies and went over them, crushing and cutting. He bellowed in excitement and snapped new orders to his officers. He had the Persians on two sides, as neat a trap as if he had planned it. One last glance up the hill let him see the new tumans were butchering the Persian reserve, taking on their cavalry and sweeping across their face with black arrows, again and again.

The battle was over, but the slaughter had barely begun. Many of the Persians threw down their weapons and tried to run, or simply held bare hands up to the sky and prayed their last. They were cut down as the tumans rode around them, accepting no surrender and sending arrows in to pick them off at close range.

Hulegu's tumans lifted their heads, putting aside the weariness they felt as their pride forced them to stand tall in the presence of their own people. They had been hard-pressed and they were merciless as the enemy fell back. The killing went on and on as the sun began to set and the enemy were herded into smaller groups. Wounded men stood among the dead and Hulegu used a broken lance as a club as he rode past one man, snapping his neck with the force of the blow and sending him tumbling.

The single minghaans rode the battlefield like stinging ants, lunging across to find new targets until the last of the enemy were running in terror, hoping only for darkness to hide them. The heat of the sun began to wane and Hulegu removed his helmet, rubbing his wet scalp. It had been a good day. A warm breeze picked up, carrying the smell of blood. Hulegu closed his eyes in relief, turning into it. He thanked the sky father for his deliverance and then on a whim thanked the Christian God as well. Kitbuqa would have enjoyed the scene around him and Hulegu was only sorry he had not lived to see it.

He opened his eyes as Mongol horns sounded victory across the open ground, a low drone that was quickly echoed by every tuman who heard. The sound raised gooseflesh on Hulegu's arms. He whistled between his teeth to catch the attention of his officers and watched as his banners went up, bringing the senior men to him. The droning noise of victory went on and on, filling the valleys and echoing back from all directions. It was a good sound.

Hulegu's tumans began to loot the dead, and in the distance more than one scuffle broke out as they disputed their rights over weapons and armour with the newcomers. Hulegu laughed at the sight of men rolling on the ground who had been fighting as brothers just moments before. His people were fierce, wolves all.

As his officers gathered, he saw a group of a few dozen riders detach from one of the tumans and come trotting over to him. Banners fluttered in the breeze as they came, taking their mounts carefully around the dead.

Uriang-Khadai had read the battle as he entered it. As he met Hulegu's gaze, both men knew Hulegu owed him. Though Hulegu was a prince of the nation and a khan in his own right, he spoke first to honour the older man.

'I was beginning to think I'd have to take another day to finish them, orlok,' Hulegu said. 'You are welcome here. I grant you guest rights and I hope you will eat with me this evening.'

'I am pleased to be of service, my lord. I do not doubt you would have called the victory in the end, but if I saved you even half a day, that is good.'

Both men smiled and Hulegu wiped sweat from his face once again.

'Where is my brother Kublai, orlok? Is he with you?'

'Not today, my lord, though I am his man. I will be happy to explain as we eat.'

The sun had set by the time the tumans left the battlefield. Metal armour long heated in the sun tended to creak as it cooled and bodies twitched, sometimes hours after death. Experienced men could all tell tales of how they had seen dead warriors belch and even sit up in a spasm before they fell back. It was not a place to spend the night and Hulegu knew he would have to send men back to complete the looting. He led Uriang-Khadai and his warriors to a grassy plain a few miles to the west, almost at the edge of the hills. He had a basic camp there and before the moon rose to its highest point, there was simmering stew for them all, with bread hard enough to use as a spoon until it dissolved.

Hulegu was in ebullient mood as Uriang-Khadai's senior men removed their armour and tended to their horses. His tunic was sweat-stained, but it had been a relief to get out of the armour and feel the night cool on his bare arms and face. He sat opposite Kublai's orlok, burning with curiosity, but willing to let the man eat and drink before he demanded answers. Nothing tired a man more than fighting and the tumans never missed a chance to eat well after a battle, if they had the opportunity. They were professional men, unlike the dead Persians behind them.

When Uriang-Khadai was finished, he handed his bowl to a servant and wiped his fingers on his leggings, adding to an old patch of dark grease.

'My lord, I am a blunt man. Let me speak bluntly,' he said. Hulegu nodded at him. 'Your brother Kublai asks that you step aside from the battles to come. He has declared himself khan and he will fight Lord Arik-Boke. All he asks is that you remain in your khanate and take no part.'

Hulegu's eyes widened as the older man spoke. He shook his head in dull amazement.

'Arik-Boke is khan,' he said hoarsely, trying to take it in. 'I was there, orlok. I gave my oath.'

'I have been told to say this, my lord. Your brother Kublai calls on you to stay away while he settles this with his younger brother. He has no grievance with you, but he would not have you choose between blood brothers in a time of war.'

Uriang-Khadai watched the other man in silent hope. Kublai had given no orders to attack, but Uriang-Khadai's tumans were already among Hulegu's forces. At his shout, they could kill thousands. With Hulegu's men smiling and relaxed among them, Uriang-Khadai knew he could win.

Hulegu's eyes drifted out over the camp and perhaps he too

saw the threat. He shook his head again, his expression hardening.

'You were useful to me today, orlok. For that I am grateful. I gave you guest rights in my camp, but that does not give you the right to tell me my oath. When the sun rises . . .' He stopped, his anger dwindling as confusion swelled in him.

'How is this even possible?' he said. 'Kublai has not been back to Karakorum. I would have heard.'

Uriang-Khadai shrugged. 'My master is khan, my lord. Your brother Arik-Boke should not have declared. This will be settled in a season and the nation will go on – under its rightful khan.'

'Why has Kublai not come to me himself? Why did he send you, Uriang-Khadai?'

'He has a war to fight, my lord. I cannot tell you all his plans. I speak with his voice and everything I have said is true. He does not ask you to break your oath. Out of love for you, he asks only that you remain until it is settled.'

Hulegu rested his head on his hands in thought. Both Arik-Boke and Kublai were his brothers. He wanted to gather them both by their necks and shake them. For the thousandth time he wished Mongke were still alive, to tell him what to do. He had given his oath, but what if Arik-Boke had been wrong to take the khanate? There had been talk even back then, voices wondering why he had not waited for Kublai to come home. This was the result. Hulegu could hardly take it in as the potential for disaster spread and spread in his mind.

At best, he would lose one of his brothers, a pain like a knife in his chest so soon after losing Mongke. At worst, the nation would tear itself apart in the conflict, leaving them vulnerable to the enemies all around. Everything Genghis had created would be destroyed in a single generation. There was no right and wrong to it, no claim that stood above the other in clear sunlight. Yet Arik-Boke was khan. No matter what Kublai said, that stood in stone, unchangeable. Hulegu slumped further.

'This is my khanate,' he muttered, almost to himself.

Uriang-Khadai bowed his head. 'It will remain so, my lord. You conquered it and it will not be taken from you. My master knew you would be troubled. Your pain is his, multiplied a thousandfold. He wishes only for a quick settlement.'

'He could stand aside,' Hulegu said, barely whispering.

'He cannot, my lord. He *is* khan.'

'What does that matter to me, orlok?' Hulegu demanded, his head rising. 'There are no rules in life. Whether it is written down, or spoken by shamans, nothing binds a man beyond himself. Nothing, save the chains he accepts for himself. Laws and traditions mean nothing, if you have the strength.'

'Kublai has the strength, my lord. Even as I speak to you here, he will be moving towards Karakorum. It will be settled before winter comes, one way or the other.'

Hulegu made his decision, his mouth becoming a firm line.

'My brothers are at play, orlok. I want no part of it. There are cities to my north that still hold out against me. I will spend a season bringing them to siege. When that is done, I will come east to Karakorum and see who rules.'

Uriang-Khadai felt a tension leave him at the words.

'That is wise, my lord. I am sorry to have brought you pain.'

Hulegu grunted in irritation. 'Find another fire, orlok. I am weary of your face. As the sun rises, you will go from here. You have your answer. I will abide.'

Uriang-Khadai rose to his feet, wincing as his knees protested. He was no longer young and he wondered if he could trust the word of a man who acknowledged no power in the world beyond his own ability to destroy and lead. The honest answer was that he could not.

For an instant, Uriang-Khadai considered shouting his order to the waiting men. They were all ready. At a stroke, he could remove a man of power from the struggle.

He sighed briefly. Or he could accept the words he had been given and perhaps regret it later. Kublai had already lost one brother. Uriang-Khadai bowed and walked to another fire. He would not sleep that night, he knew.

CHAPTER THIRTY-NINE

High in the grey-green hills, Kublai could not rest. He stood and looked out over a wide plains valley, deceptively still and peaceful from such a height. Water trickled from a stream close by his right hand, so that he could reach out and cup freezing water to drink when he felt the urge. The day was hot and the sky was baked blue and empty of clouds. It was land he knew, and after so long in the Sung territories, it still touched some deep part of him to be home.

He could hear one of his men cursing behind him as the warrior clambered over slippery rocks. Kublai didn't turn, content to stare out into the warm vastness, soaking in the sense of space and silence. He was weary after days and nights of hard riding, but feverish anticipation had him in its grip and his hands trembled. Arik-Boke was somewhere out there, beyond his sight. Kublai had made his plans and prepared his men, but it came down to waiting. If Arik-Boke rode out of Karakorum, they would be ready. If he stayed in the city, they would crush him like a flea trapped in a seam of cloth.

After so long together, it was odd not to have his most senior men around him. Bayar was still in the Russian north, Uriang-Khadai was out in the far hills, having returned from his mission to Hulegu. He missed them both, but neither more than Yao Shu. The old monk had grown too frail to ride with the tumans.

Yao Shu had set off for his monastery at last. Time and age stole away even the greatest of flames, Kublai thought. He sent a silent prayer that he might see his friend again.

For the first time in years, Kublai was alone with his warriors. Against him, Arik-Boke would have Mongke's tumans, sworn to his service. Kublai grimaced at the thought. Strength would not bring his brother to heel, not on its own.

It had been a risk to contact Hulegu. His older brother might have heard what Uriang-Khadai had to say and set out immediately to defend Arik-Boke's khanate. Uriang-Khadai had relayed Hulegu's words to him, but Kublai knew better than to trust them. If Hulegu moved to support Arik-Boke, it would add another year and another dead brother to the cost of the war. Kublai had no illusions left. In the silence, as his tumans stretched and rested and ate around him, he prayed his older brother would continue to show a little sense and stay well clear.

Kublai raised his head when he heard the jingling sound of bells, carrying far in the mountain stillness. No yam rider this time, but the small herd he had sent out with a couple of his scouts. On foot, he hoped they would have been able to get close to Karakorum unchallenged. He had not expected them back for another month and had made his camp in the hills, far from his brother's city. He tried to guess what their early return could mean and then gave up. He looked down the steep slope of grassy rocks below his position and saw the small figures of men driving goats and sheep before them. It would be a while yet before he heard whatever they had to say.

Kublai turned to see his son leaning precariously over the rocks to take a mouthful of water.

'Careful,' he said. 'It's slippery there.'

Zhenjin looked scornful at the idea of falling. He sucked at the stream of water, getting far more down his tunic than in his throat. Kublai smiled at him, but when he resumed his sentinel's stare, Zhenjin stayed where he was, easing back until he could lean against the rocks in something like comfort.

'I heard the men talking about what you're going to do,' Zhenjin said.

Kublai didn't look at him. 'I'm sure you know not to carry tales to me,' he replied.

The young man shifted his seat, pulling one leg up under him so that he could rest his elbows on the raised knee.

'They're not complaining,' he said. 'They were just talking, that's all.'

Kublai summoned patience. It was not as if he had anything to do until his spies reported.

'What did they say, then?' he asked.

Zhenjin grinned at him. 'They said you will be an emperor when this is done.'

'If I live, that is . . . true,' Kublai replied. 'I will be khan of the nation, but emperor of China.'

'Does that mean I will be an emperor after you?' the young man asked.

Kublai looked at him then, his mouth twitching to laugh.

'Is that what you want? To rule the world?'

'I think . . . I think I would like that, yes,' Zhenjin said, with a thoughtful expression.

'Then I will do my best to make it happen, my son. You are blood of my blood, bone of my bone. I will name a dynasty and you will carry the name.'

'Is that why we are going to fight, then? To be emperors?'

Kublai chuckled. 'There are worse things to fight for.' He looked over his shoulder at the bondsmen who rested in the mountain crags, the vast majority of his men invisible in the valleys and rifts behind.

'I think I would be a better khan than Arik-Boke, Zhenjin.

That is a reason as well. But a father works for his sons and daughters. He spends his strength and his youth to raise them up, to give them everything he can. When you have children of your own, you will understand.'

Zhenjin considered the idea with great seriousness.

'I will spare cities when I am emperor. I will be loved and not feared.'

Kublai nodded.

'Or both, my son, if you are lucky.'

'I would like to change the world, as you have done,' Zhenjin said.

Kublai smiled, but there was an edge of sadness to it.

'I used to discuss such things with my mother, Zhenjin. She was a woman of rare ability.' His eyes became distant with memory for a moment. 'You know, I said something like that to her once. She told me that *anyone* can change the world. But no one can change it for ever. In a hundred years, no one you know will be alive. What will it matter then if we fought or just spent our days sleeping in the sun?'

Zhenjin blinked at him, unable to understand his father's strange mood.

'If it doesn't matter, then why are we going to fight your brother?' he asked.

'Perhaps I haven't said it well. I mean it doesn't matter if we change the world. The world moves on and new lives come and go. Genghis himself said he would be forgotten and, believe me, he left a long shadow. It does matter how we live, Zhenjin! It matters that we use what we are given, for just our brief time in the sun.' He smiled to see his son struggling with the idea. 'It's all you can say, when the end comes: "I did not waste my time." I think that matters. I think it may be all that matters.'

'I understand,' Zhenjin said.

Kublai reached out and rubbed his head roughly.

'No you don't. But you will perhaps, in a few years.' He looked out over the crags to where his herdsmen were making their slow progress. 'Enjoy the peaceful moments, Zhenjin. When the fighting starts, this will be a pleasant memory.'

'Can you beat them?' Zhenjin asked, looking into his father's eyes.

Kublai realised his son was afraid and he made himself relax.

'I think so, yes. Nothing is certain.'

'They have more tumans than us,' Zhenjin went on, prodding him for a reaction.

Kublai shrugged. 'We are *always* outnumbered. I don't think I'd know what to do if I came across an army smaller than mine.' He saw the forced lightness wasn't reassuring his son and his tone became serious. 'I am not the first man to try to think how to counter the advantages of a Mongol tuman in battle. However, I am the first one of *us* to try. I know our tactics better than any man alive. I think I can find a few new tricks. My brother's warriors have spent the last few years growing soft around the capital city. *My* tumans are used to fighting every day, every step. And they are used to *winning*. We'll eat them alive.'

His son grinned at his bravado and Kublai chuckled with him.

'Practise your patterns now, Zhenjin. We won't be going anywhere for a while.'

His son made a show of groaning, but under his father's eye, he found a flat space in the rocks and began the flowing series of movements and stances he had learned from Kublai. Yao Shu had taught the sequences years before, each with its own name and history.

Kublai watched with a critical eye, remembering how Yao Shu had never been satisfied. There was no such thing as

476

perfection in a pattern, but it was always the aim to make every kick and block and turn as close to it as possible.

'Turn your head before you move,' Kublai said. Zhenjin hesitated.

'What?' Zhenjin replied without moving his head.

'You have to imagine opponents coming at you from more than one direction. It is not a dance, remember. The aim is to break a bone with *every* blow or block. Imagine them all around you and respond.'

Kublai grunted approval as his son turned his head sharply, then swept an imaginary kick away from him in a great circular block. As Kublai looked on, his son plunged a knife-hand into an invisible throat, his fingers outstretched and rigid.

'Hold there and consider your rear leg,' Kublai called to him. He watched as Zhenjin adjusted his stance, dropping lower before moving on. Kublai looked fondly at his son. It would be a fine thing to give him an empire.

Arik-Boke could smell his own sweat as he rode, the bitter scent of a healthy animal. He had not allowed himself to grow weak in his time as khan. His squat body had never been graceful, but it was strong. He prided himself on being able to exhaust younger men in any contest. From a young age, he had learned a great truth, that endurance was as much will as anything physical. He grunted to himself as he rode, his breath snuffling from his ruined nose. He had the will, the ability to ignore pain and discomfort, to push himself beyond the limits of weaker men. The righteous anger he had felt on hearing of Kublai's betrayal had not left him for a waking moment since that day. The aches and complaints of the flesh were nothing to him while his brother rode the plains in challenge.

His tumans took their mood from his, riding with grim

determination as they quartered the land in search of any sign of the traitor. Arik-Boke hardly knew the men with him, but that was not important as long as they obeyed their khan. His senior officers were spread out over an immense line, each commanding their own force of forty thousand. Any two would surely equal whatever army Kublai could bring to the field, Arik-Boke was certain. When all five came together like fingers curling into a fist, he would crush his brother's arrogance.

It gave Arik-Boke some pleasure to plan his vengeance as he rode. There had been too many men in the nation who thought they could rule. Even the sons of Genghis had warred amongst themselves. Guyuk Khan had been killed on a hunt, though Arik-Boke suspected Mongke had arranged it. Such things were already history, but he could make Kublai's death a hot blade sealing a wound. He could make it a tale to spread fear wherever his enemies met and plotted. It would be right to make an example of Kublai. They would say the khan had torn his own brother down and they would feel fear. Arik-Boke nodded to himself, savouring the sensations. Kublai had a wife and children. They would follow his brother into death when the rebellion had been destroyed.

He sat straighter in the saddle when he saw his scouts racing in from the west. The tumans who rode with the khan were the central block of five, while his orlok Alandar commanded the right wing as they moved south. Arik-Boke felt heat rise in him as he began to breathe faster. Alandar knew the orders. He would not have sent the scouts in unless he had sighted the enemy at last.

The galloping men raced across the front rank of the tumans, cutting in at an angle to where Arik-Boke's banners flew. Thousands watched them as they reached the khan and swung their mounts between the lines. His bondsmen used their horses to block the scouts from coming too close, a

478

sign of the new fear that had come to the nation since the death of Mongke.

Arik-Boke didn't need to wait for them to be searched and passed on through to him. The closest scout was just a couple of horses away and he shouted a question.

The scout nodded. 'They have been sighted, my lord khan. Forty miles, or close to it.'

It was all he needed and he waved the scout off, sending him running back to his master. His own scouts had been waiting for the word. As soon as they heard, they kicked their mounts into a lunging canter. In relays, the news would bring all the tumans in, a hammer of the most dangerous fighting forces ever assembled. Arik-Boke grinned to himself as he angled his horse to the west and dug in his heels. The blocks would turn in place behind him, becoming a spear to thrust into his brother's hopes.

He glanced up at the sun, calculating the time it would take him to make contact. The rush of enthusiasm damped down as suddenly as it had arisen. The scout had ridden forty miles already, which meant Kublai's forces had been free to act for half a day. By the time Arik-Boke's tumans reached him, it would be dusk or night.

Arik-Boke began to sweat again, wondering what orders he should give to attack a force he could not yet see, a force that would certainly have moved by the time he arrived in the area. He clamped down on his doubts. The plan was a good one and if he didn't bring his brother to battle until the following day, it would not matter in the end.

Kublai stared at a single point in the distant hills, waiting for confirmation. There. Once more he saw the flash of yellow, appearing and disappearing in an instant. He let out a slow breath. It was happening, at last. The bones had been thrown and he would have to see how they fell.

'Answer with a red flag,' he called to his scout. Miles away, the man who had signalled would be watching for a response. Kublai kept looking out at the blurred point as his man spread a red cloth as tall as himself and waved it before letting it fall.

'Wait . . . wait . . . now, yellow,' Kublai ordered. He felt some of his tension ease now that his plans were actually going into effect. Signal flags were nothing new over long distances, relayed from valley to valley by men on the peaks. Even so, Kublai had refined the practice, using a system of five colours that could be combined to send a surprising amount of information. The distant watcher would have seen the flags and passed on the message, covering miles far faster than a horse could ride.

'Good,' Kublai said. The scout looked up, but Kublai was talking to himself. 'Now we'll see whether my brother's men have the stomach to fight for a weak khan.'

CHAPTER FORTY

Alandar muttered to himself in irritation as his scouts came racing in, clearly expecting him to gallop off immediately in response to the news they brought. Instead, he had to balance his orders with the best tactical decisions on the ground. It was not a pleasant position and he was not enjoying the morning. Karakorum was over two hundred miles behind him and he had lost the taste for sleeping under the stars and waking stiff and frozen. His block of tumans had ridden at good speed, covering the land and staying in touch with Arik-Boke, but Alandar could not shake the feeling of unease that plagued him. Everything he knew of Kublai said the man was not a fool, but Arik-Boke was convinced he could be run down like a deer in a circle hunt. Alandar's own men expected him to roar battle orders at the first sign of contact, and as the scouts reported, he could feel their eyes on him, questioning. He stared straight ahead as he rode.

His four generals were close by and he whistled to bring the most senior man to him. Ferikh was a solid officer, with white hair and twenty years of experience under three khans. He trotted through the ranks at the summons, his expression serious.

'You have new orders, orlok?' he asked as he came up.

'Not yet. It feels like a trap, Ferikh.'

The general turned automatically to stare at where Kublai's tumans had been sighted, racing along a pass between two valleys. The contact had been brief, but just long enough to send Alandar's scouts pounding back with news. In relays, the news would be stretching out to the blocks in the long sweeping line.

'You do not have to respond, orlok,' Ferikh said. Alandar winced slightly to see the disappointment on the older man's face. 'The khan can decide when he has brought up the middle tumans.'

'Which will not happen until dark,' Alandar said.

Ferikh shrugged. 'Another day will not make a difference.'

'You think it's a trap?' Alandar asked.

'Perhaps. A brief sighting of a small group, no more than six or seven thousand. They might want us to go charging in after them and then stage an ambush. It's what I would do.'

Alandar rose as tall as he could manage in his saddle, looking at the hills all around them.

'If it's an ambush, they will have a large force somewhere near, ready to spring out as soon as we move.'

He was in a difficult position and Ferikh appreciated his dilemma. The men expected their officers to show courage and quick thinking. They had heard the news and they waited for the order to ride hard and fast, but Alandar had not spoken. If he fell for some ploy, he would risk the tumans with him and Arik-Boke's anger. Yet if he came across the tail of Kublai's army and failed to take the chance, he would look like a fool or a coward. He was caught between impossible choices and so did nothing, letting time make his decision for him.

In the distance, on his left side, his attention snagged on a blur in the air. Alandar turned round to stare and his expression changed slowly as he realised what he was looking at.

'Tell me I'm right that I can see dust beyond those hills, Ferikh.'

The general squinted. His long sight was not as sharp as it had once been, but he made a tube with his hands and focused down it, an old scout's trick.

'Has to be a large force to send up a cloud like that,' he said. 'Judging by where we saw the first ones, they'd be in about the right position to hit our flank.'

Alandar breathed out in relief. He would have a victory to report to the khan after all.

'Then I think we'll see some fighting today. Send five thousand between the hills after the ones we saw first. Let them think they've fooled us. The main tumans can cut through . . . there.' He pointed to a break in the green hills that would allow him to swing round and attack the army making the dust rise. 'Go slowly, general. If it's Kublai's main force, we'll stay out of range, ready to disengage. It will be enough to hold them in place until the khan reaches us.'

Alandar looked east, behind him, where the rest of Arik-Boke's army would be riding in support. 'We should have four more tumans coming up soon, then the khan's own tumans. The last will be here sometime after noon tomorrow. I'll give new orders as they arrive.'

Ferikh sensed the relief in the orlok at being able to make a decision. He bowed his head briefly, already enjoying the thought of confounding those who had tried to fool the khan's own army.

Five minghaans pushed forward towards the first valley and then Alandar gave the order for his main tumans to swing round and dash for the break in the hills. They surged into a gallop and the expressions of the warriors were cheerful with anticipation. They had all seen the faint trace of dust by then and they were already imagining the false khan's confusion as they appeared from a different direction, falling like wolves onto his flank.

Alandar was in the first line that entered the cleft, his tumans thundering behind him. He thought he had seen through whatever ruse Kublai was intending, but he was still aware that Kublai's entire force outnumbered his. Even so, he could not shake the sense of satisfaction that he could spring a trap on those who sought to fool him. He had not risen to command the khan's armies by making mistakes. For a moment, he thought of Mongke's orlok, Seriankh. He had been removed from authority for losing his master and fought somewhere in the ranks. Alandar still thought the man was lucky to have kept his life.

Alandar passed into the shadowed ground, with steepening slopes rising on either side. Somewhere ahead and to the right would be a force of warriors riding to surprise his tumans. He leaned forward in the saddle, his hand dropping to the long sword that slapped against his mount's flank. The land began to open out and in the sunlight he could see a green valley before him. In the distance, he thought he could hear sounds of battle as his minghaans met and clashed with the false group he had been meant to attack. Bows bent on either side of him as his warriors prepared a crushing volley of shafts. For a time they would ride without reins, using only their knees to guide the ponies at full gallop. Alandar could feel the moment when all four hooves left the ground as a rhythm beneath him. He would not use a bow that day, though he had one strapped to his saddle. He felt the excitement of the men around him, the quick breaths of air that seemed suddenly cold as the hills fell away and his front rank plunged out into the sun. His tumans feared nothing on earth and he led them.

It felt glorious as he craned forward for the first glimpse of the enemy.

Surprise and disappointment flashed through Alandar's tumans as they rounded the foot of the hill and were able to look down the valley stretching to the east. They shouted and pointed to each other as they rode further in, so that thousands of throats made a growling wail that fell away.

There were horses in the valley, thousands of them. It did not take a soldier of Alandar's experience to see they were not mounted by Mongol warriors. He gaped at the sight of Arab boys whooping and kicking at a milling mass of animals. Each one seemed to have some wide branch tied to its tail, so that it dragged on the dusty ground.

Alandar felt his stomach tighten in fear. If these were the distraction, where were Kublai's tumans? Almost without thought, he slowed his pace and the tumans matched him, coming down to an easy canter and then a trot. They were nervous at the sight of the trap, knowing they had been drawn in, but not yet seeing the danger.

Alandar jerked round in the saddle as he heard yells and warning horns sound behind. His tumans were still in the cleft between hills, stretched out. Something was happening half a mile behind him and he cursed aloud, yanking the reins savagely to halt. He could hear the sound of bows thrumming at the entrance to the valley, echoing back like the buzzing of bees.

For a moment, he could not think. The valley was too narrow to turn his tumans. The enemy was hitting them and he could not bring his force to bear. He raised his arm and ordered his men forward. If he could bring them all out of the valley, they would be able to manoeuvre once again. The lines surged forward with him, ignoring the boys on their horses as they

485

whooped and jeered. His lines stretched out and Alandar saw movement on his left. He almost cried out in frustration as he realised the position. With a dozen of his personal guard, he pulled his horse out of rank. Behind the knot of men, his tumans kept going, clearing the valley behind as his heart sank.

Mongol warriors were riding at full speed out of the hills there, straight for his flank. Alandar could only roar a warning and even then his men were exposed, under attack from the rear and the side at the same time. He showed his teeth in a grimace, then drew his sword. The enemy had worked him into the spot they wanted, but the games were over and it was time to fight. His generals bellowed orders and the first volleys soared out to meet the flanking force, blurring through the air. It was his one advantage over a flying column, that he could bring more bows to bear on their front rank.

They were already widening their line to fifty as the first arrows reached them. Alandar watched in shock as the enemy ranks raised cumbersome shields and seemed to snatch the arrows from the air. He had never seen Mongol warriors carry such heavy things into battle. They used the bow and the bow required two hands at all times. His generals were already turning men to face them, the orders running quickly down to the minghaan commanders and the leaders of each hundred in the tumans. His men were shifting from a running flank to a wide front, but it was one of the hardest possible manoeuvres and involved halting thousands in good order. Even so, it was beginning to happen.

Alandar felt hope swell in his chest, but then the enemy threw down their shields and raised bows. Shafts hummed back across the shrinking space between the racing armies. Alandar saw his ranks could not form up in time and he winced as the enemy archers poured volleys into the milling lines. He saw a dark stripe across his vision as something clipped his shoulder and went spinning away, rocking him back in the saddle. Another shaft thumped into his horse, sinking to the feathers in its throat so that the animal began to cough and spray blood from its nostrils.

Alandar panicked, dismounting with a stumble as the horse went down. His men had to clear the valley and they could do it only by riding hard and fast away from those who attacked. At the same time, he had to make a strong stationary line to answer the flanking attack. The orders clashed in his mind and he could not see a way through. The sun was warm on his face and arrows whirred past him without making him flinch. His guards were looking to him, but as he mounted a fresh horse from instinct, he sat with a blank expression, frozen. For a time, his tumans fought on their own.

His generals registered the lack of orders for a brief time, then filled the gap, working together. Those below them in the chain of command barely had time to grow worried before new orders came down the line and they were moving again. Jaguns of a hundred formed up in solid blocks, seeking only to hold back the flank attack until their main force was able to swing out of the valley.

It might have been enough to save the battle, but the tumans they faced were the veterans of the Sung territory. When the fighting was fluid, they moved in overlapping lines, so that they always brought the maximum force against the weakest points. When the fighting came down to swords and lances, they gave no ground, so that Alandar's tumans were smashed back.

Those in the valley ran clear at last and Alandar shook his head in disbelief as he saw the force that pressed them from behind. He had assumed it was no larger than the few thousand he had seen in the taunting glimpse that morning. Instead, the hills vomited warriors under Kublai's banners, such a flood of them that he realised he should have worked to keep them between the hills where they could do less damage. He was outnumbered by at least two to one and the Arab boys riding to make a dust trail watched open-mouthed as his tumans were crushed, hemmed in and hammered.

Alandar could see only chaos, too many groups racing back and forth. From his first move, he knew he had been dancing to Kublai's plans and the knowledge burned him. Arrows darted in all directions and men were falling everywhere. He could hardly tell them apart in the press, though the enemy tumans seemed to know their own. His guards had to fend off a yelling warrior barrelling past, using their swords to turn the man's lance away from Alandar. As the man went on, Alandar found himself thinking clearly, though he felt his guts twist in anguish. There was no help for it; he would have to call the retreat.

His own horn had been lost with his fallen horse and he had to yell to one of his officers. The man looked ill as he understood, but he blew a sequence of falling notes, again and again. The response seemed to be lost in the roiling mass of fighting men, except to call attention to that part of the battle-field. More arrows lifted into the air, seeming to move slowly, then dropping with a whirr all around them. One struck the horn-blowing officer high in the chest, puncturing the scaled armour. Alandar shouted in anger as the man slumped, wheeling his horse over and yanking the horn away.

He was panting heavily, but he raised the horn and repeated the signal. Slowly, he was answered by men too hard-pressed to disengage easily. They pulled back over the bodies of friends, raising swords and lances horizontal to hold the enemy off.

The gaps they made were suddenly filled with whining shafts. Hundreds more warriors were sent tumbling, choking on wooden lengths through their chests or throats. A few ranks made it to Alandar and formed around him, panting and glassy-eyed. They held position long enough for their numbers to swell to a thousand, then pulled back, joined by free riders as they went until some three thousand were moving across the field of the dead.

Of his generals, Alandar could see only Ferikh with him, though he had around twenty minghaan officers. They had all been in the fighting and they were battered and showing wounds and cuts. He saw the enemy tumans spot their moving group, men pointing across the valley floor. He felt the blood drain from his face as thousands of fierce eyes turned to see the orlok retreat.

His small force were still picking up stragglers as they struggled through to him, but by then the enemy were forming ranks, ready for another charge. Alandar looked across the battlefield. The losses appalled him to the point of illness: thousands of dead, broken bows, kicking horses and screaming men with wounds that poured blood onto the ground. One of the enemy rode to the front rank and said something to those near him. They roared a challenge, the noise making Alandar jerk in the saddle.

Barely five thousand battered men rode with him. He had thought to combine them with the rest of his tumans, but the fighting seemed to have stopped across the valley. With eight hundred paces between the armies, his men drew to a halt, exhausted and fearful as they looked to him for orders. Against him, the valley had filled with tumans, standing their ground in eerie silence as they all turned to watch. Alandar swallowed nervously and without a command, his remnant drew to a halt. He could hear the laboured breath of them, men muttering in disbelief. They had been outfought and outmanoeuvred. The sun was still up and he could hardly take in how fast it had happened.

'Behind us, the khan approaches with enough men to destroy these,' he said, raising his voice to carry to as many as he could reach. 'We have lost only the first skirmish. Take heart that you fought with courage.'

As he spoke the last word, the enemy leader roared an order and the enemy surged forward.

'Go!' Alandar shouted. 'If I fall, seek out the khan!' He turned his horse and dug in his heels, kicking the animal into its best speed. The Arab boys scattered before his men, jeering and shouting as they ran.

As soon as Alandar had ridden clear of the valley, Kublai called a halt. Uriang-Khadai came riding up to him in short order and they nodded to each other.

'Arik-Boke won't keep that formation now he's found us,' Kublai said. He did not congratulate the older man, knowing Uriang-Khadai would take it as an insult. Beyond a certain level of skill and authority, the orlok needed no praise to tell him what he already knew.

'I have often wanted to show Alandar the errors in his thinking,' Uriang-Khadai said. 'He does not react well under pressure, I have always said. This was a good first lesson. Will you turn for Karakorum now?'

Kublai hesitated. His army was still relatively fresh, the victory keeping their spirits high as they dismounted and checked their mounts and weapons. He had told his orlok he would try for a quick attack on the head of Arik-Boke's sweep line just as it became a column and turned towards them. After that, the plan had been to ride hard for the capital and seek out the families they had left behind.

Uriang-Khadai saw his indecision and brought his pony alongside, so that they would not be easily overheard.

'You want to go on,' he said, a statement more than a question.

Kublai nodded warily. His own wife and daughter were safe in Xanadu, thousands of miles to the east. It was not a small thing to ask his men to keep fighting with the fate of their families hanging over them.

'There is just a short time before my brother brings his tumans back into a single army. We could roll them up before us, orlok. If there were no women and children around Karakorum, would that not be your advice? To hit them again and quickly? If I head north now, I will be throwing away the opportunity to win. It may be the only chance we get.'

Uriang-Khadai listened with the cold face, giving nothing away as Kublai spoke.

'You are the khan,' he said quietly. 'If you order it, we will go on.'

'I need more than that at this moment, Uriang-Khadai. We've never fought an enemy with the lives of women and children in his grasp. Will the men follow me?'

The older man did not answer for what seemed like an age. At last, he dipped his head.

'Of course they will. They know as well as you that plans change. It may be the best choice to go on and fight again here, while we have the advantage.'

'But you want to head north, even so.'

The orlok was visibly uncomfortable. He had sworn an oath to obey, but the thought of his wife and children in the hands of Arik-Boke's guards was a constant drain on him.

'I will . . . follow orders, my lord khan,' he said formally.

Kublai looked away first. He had known many moments where hindsight showed him a choice, a chance to turn his life one way or the other. It was rare to feel such a moment as it happened. He closed his eyes, letting the breeze pass over him.

He felt death in the north, but the smell of blood was strong in the air and he did not know whether it was a true omen or not. When he turned east to face his brother's distant armies, he felt the same cold shiver. Death lay in all directions, he was suddenly certain of it. He shook his head, as if to clear cobwebs from his thoughts. Genghis would not have wasted a moment. His men knew death, lived with it every day. They slaughtered animals with their hands and knew when a child began to cough that it could mean finding them cold and still. He would not fear such a constant companion. He could not let it influence him. He was khan at that moment and he made his choice.

'My orders are to go on, orlok. Grab what arrows we can and chase Alandar into the tumans coming up. We hit the next battle group with everything we have.'

Uriang-Khadai turned his horse without another word, shouting orders to the waiting tumans. They looked confused, but they mounted quickly and formed up, ignoring the wounded and dying all around them. The sun was setting, but there were hours of grey summer light to come. Time enough to fight again before dark.

CHAPTER FORTY-ONE

Kublai gave thanks for his brother's poor decisions as he sighted four tumans riding hard against him. The great general Tsubodai had once employed the same system, five fingers stretching across the land in search of enemies. It was a powerful formation against slow-moving foot soldiers. Against the tumans he commanded, it had a weakness. His brother had formed a separated column a hundred miles long to search the land. Kublai and Uriang-Khadai had hit the end of the sweep and as the column turned to face him, he could work his way down it, bringing almost twelve tumans against each battle group as they reached him. Arik-Boke could still halt and let his tumans join up, but until he did, his warriors were vulnerable to simple numbers and overwhelming strength.

Overall, Kublai and Uriang-Khadai were seriously outnumbered, even after slaughtering Alandar's men. That disadvantage would dwindle as they cut through the snake piece by piece. In his head, Kublai went over his plans for the thousandth time, looking for anything to improve the odds yet again. He did not have to check Uriang-Khadai was in position. The orlok was more experienced than anyone Arik-Boke could field and his tumans showed it in the way they flowed over the land, moving well together.

The second block of his brother's tumans was too far away for Kublai to hear their horns, but over the vast plain of green grass, he could see them begin to shift and move in battle formations, reacting to his presence. He frowned as the wind whipped by him, checking the position of the sun. The soft grey twilight lasted for hours at that time of year, but it might not be enough. He hated the idea of having to pull out before the battle was done, but he could not be caught in one place. Every manoeuvre was intended to reduce his brother's ability to move, while enhancing his own. He could not be caught in the dark, with armies closing on his position.

Against stolid Sung soldiers, he would have kept his final orders to the last moment, too late for the enemy to react to them. As it was, the Mongol tumans he faced could shift and reply just as quickly. Even so, he had the numbers. With Uriang-Khadai keeping order, he sent his men forward in a column, like two stags rushing at each other. At a mile, he felt the first urge to give the final order, his heart beginning to hammer at him. Arik-Boke's tumans were moving fluidly, darting back and forth as they came on. He did not know who led them, or whether Alandar had reached the apparent safety of their ranks. Kublai hoped he had, so that he could send the man running twice in one day.

At half a mile, they were sixty heartbeats apart. Kublai gave his order at the same moment he saw the enemy tumans swing out to envelop his column head. He grinned into the wind as Uriang-Khadai and his generals matched the formation. Both hammer-heads widened, but Kublai had more tumans and he could imagine how they must appear from the enemy's point of view, spreading like wings at his back, further and further as his forces were revealed.

It seemed an instant before the arrows flew on both sides.

The wide lines could bring many bows to bear and the shafts soared out by the tens of thousands, one every six heartbeats from men who had trained to it all their lives. For the first time, Kublai felt what it was like to meet such a barrage in anger and he had to struggle not to flinch from the whirring air. The volleys spat like a war drum beating, crossing each other in the air. He could hear the thumps of them hitting flesh and metal, the grunts and cries of men on both sides and ahead of him. His own place in the fourth rank was not spared as shafts arced overhead and fell among them. Yet his wider lines could answer with thousands more shafts and the air was blacker on his side as they fired inwards, hardly troubling to aim against so many.

The first volleys broke holes in the galloping front ranks; the second and third tore men and horses away, so that those behind went piling into them. On both sides, the storm of arrows punched through armour. The heavy shields Kublai had picked up in Samarkand were long behind, left to rust on the valley where they had beaten Orlok Alandar. It had been a tactic worth trying, but the true strength of his tumans lay with the archers, the smashing power of bows of horn and birch, drawn back with a bone thumb ring and loosed at the moment when all hooves left the ground. The fourth volley was brutal, the air so thick with arrows that it felt hard to breathe. Thousands were hit on both sides and horses crunched to the ground, turning over at full speed so that their riders crashed down hard enough to kill.

Kublai's tumans kept their formation better than those they faced. They had spent years in battle against the Sung, against forests of crossbows and enemy pikes. The lines bunched in places where the arrow storm had been thickest, but the rest forced their way through with hardly a drop in speed. In the last moments before impact, they followed the routines drummed into them: bows were jammed onto saddle hooks and thousands of swords were drawn as they reined in slightly, allowing the ranks behind to surge ahead.

Through Kublai's front ranks came his lancers, each one lowering great lengths of birch as they went. It took enormous strength of arm and shoulder to hold the lances steady at full stretch. They brought them down in the final heartbeat, aiming the point ahead and leaning in, bracing for the impact. With half a ton of horse, rider and armour behind it, the lances slammed through the fish-scale chest-plates worn by the tumans. Kublai's riders wore no straps to keep hold of the long lances. As they bit, his men let them go, rather than break a collarbone or an arm trying to hold on. The air filled with spinning splinters as ten thousand lances struck and many shattered or broke at the hilt. The enemy rank went down, coughing blood or knocked still and white as they bled inside.

The crash of thousands of warriors meeting each other at full speed became a low thunder of hooves and roaring voices. The two fronts tangled together as they struggled with swords, hacking at each other with insane violence. Kublai's wide line spread rapidly around to the flanks as Uriang-Khadai continued to give calm orders. His tumans there had kept their bows and they sent another dozen volleys from each side, battering the men loyal to Arik-Boke.

They were answered with arrows every bit as powerful as their own, as warriors on the flanks loosed shaft after shaft back at them. The two sides were close in by then, drawing and loosing with grim stoicism, ignoring the deaths around them as they fought on. At the front, Kublai's tumans were pressing forward, killing and moving, crushing the head of the snake. The flanks began to crumple back, the aim of Arik-Boke's archers spoiled as those at the head were forced to give ground. Uriang-Khadai rode up and down his ranks barely two hundred yards from the main lines. As the hammer-head compressed, his men kept up their fire. The rain of arrows in return began to dwindle, but they loosed until their quivers were all empty, having sent more than a million shafts into the crush.

Mongol tumans did not retreat, did not surrender, but Kublai's forces were overwhelming them. His veteran warriors pressed forward at every slight give, forcing them to move back a step and then another, then a dozen more as two ranks collapsed. They could not move to the sides, where Uriang-Khadai watched with cold eyes. The tumans he commanded on the right drew swords with a sibilant rasp that sent a shudder through the flanks. They had the space to kick their mounts into a gallop. Uriang-Khadai yelled an order and his tumans snapped shut on the flanks, swords coming down in short, chopping blows.

The head of the column collapsed and those in the flanks felt the shift, panic swelling all around them. They tried to turn their horses, yanking savagely on reins as they were buffeted by unhorsed men and loose mounts on all sides. The edges of the flanks were hammered back as Uriang-Khadai's tumans tore into them and those in the very centre turned their backs on the battle and whipped their mounts desperately. Even then, with the decision made to retreat, they could not get clear. There was no room to move and the press of those behind kept them in place, yelling in fear or pain. The killing went on, with the flanks so compressed men could hardly move at all. Kublai's tumans cared nothing for those who tried to surrender. There was no possibility of mercy. It was too early yet to stop the killing and the carnage was terrible. Men raising their hands were cut down where they stood. Screaming horses had new wounds gashed in their flesh by racing warriors.

Kublai had not entered the fighting beyond the first charge. With a group of his bondsmen, he waited to one side, watching closely and giving orders to shore up the heaving lines. It was like watching a wave surge up around a rock, but the rock crumbled and fell into sand as he looked on. He caught a glimpse of his brother's orlok, fighting and roaring orders in the centre, already struggling to get away. Alandar would remember this day, Kublai thought with satisfaction, if he lived through it.

Kublai looked up as Uriang-Khadai sent a horn note across the battlefield. In the fading grey light, he could see fresh tumans coming. It would be the centre formation of Arik-Boke's sweep line and Kublai guessed his brother would be in the squares riding hard at him. The sun had set while the fighting went on. If it had been noon, he knew the moment was right to go on. His men had broken the tumans in the second battle group and lone riders were already streaming away, heading for the safety of their khan as he entered the field.

Uriang-Khadai sounded the horn again and Kublai muttered to himself. He was not blind, or deaf. Plans and stratagems hurtled through his mind and he sat still, trans-fixed by the opportunity. His men were weary, he reminded himself. Their arrows were gone and their lances were broken. It would be madness to send them in again, in the dark. Yet he could end it all in a day and the thought ate at him. He clenched his fists on his reins, making his gauntlets creak. The horn sounded for the third time, snapping him out of his reverie.

'I hear you!' he shouted angrily. Kublai gestured to his

waiting bondsmen. 'Send the signal to disengage. We've done enough today.'

He continued to stare out into the distance as the falling note droned out across his tumans. In the dim light, they had been expecting it and they pulled back quickly, forming ranks and resting on the wooden pommels of their saddles as they rode clear, calling and laughing to one another. The dead lay among the dying and Kublai could hear one man scream with astonishing volume, somewhere in the twitching piles they passed. He had to have broken legs to be left with breath to make such a noise. Kublai didn't see the warrior who dismounted and stalked over to the wounded man, but the sound was choked off mid-cry. He thought suddenly of Zhenjin, worrying for him. It was always a difficult line to walk for a khan and a father. The men understood he would be worried about his fourteen-year-old son among them, but he could give no sign of his fear, nor leave Zhenjin out of harm's way. Uriang-Khadai usually placed Zhenjin to the rear of any formation without making a point of it. Kublai looked across the field for his son, but he could not see him. He clenched his jaw, sending a silent prayer to the sky father that he was all right. Uriang-Khadai would know. The man missed nothing.

Thousands of Arik-Boke's forces had escaped the hammer-blow he had dealt them. They kept going as his men formed up and began to trot north. Kublai looked back over his shoulder, over the dead men and horses, to where his brother still rode in a cloud of dry dust. Already, Arik-Boke's distant tumans were merging with the gloom as darkness overtook them. Kublai tilted his head in a gesture of mocking respect. Orlok Alandar had won free in the final moments and Kublai only wished he could hear the man explain to his brother how he had lost so many men in just a day.

* * *

Arik-Boke raged as he leaned forward in the saddle and yelled 'Chuh!' to his mount, kicking it savagely in the loins to keep his speed. Sweat was dribbling into his eyes and he blinked against the sting of salt, peering into the distance. The light was almost gone and the tumans ahead shifted and blurred like writhing shadows. He could hear only the galloping horses around him, so that the battle ahead seemed almost dreamlike, robbed of the clash of swords and the screams of men.

The general of one of his tumans was angling his mount to catch up to the khan, the animal's head lunging up and down with effort. Arik-Boke ignored him, his focus only on those ahead. He knew he had lost contact with the tumans behind, that his long formation had been attacked at one end. He knew very well that the force with him might not be enough to send his brother running, that he should wait and re-form. He had only four tumans in close formation, but another eight were behind. Together, they would be enough, no matter what Kublai had managed to do. Arik-Boke spat into the wind as his brother's name flitted through his thoughts. His saliva felt like soup in his mouth and heat breathed out of every pore as he rode on, harder and further than he had galloped for years. It had to be Uriang-Khadai who had organised the attack. Arik-Boke knew he should have allowed for his brother turning over command to a more experienced officer. He cursed long and loud, making his closest men look away rather than witness his rage. He should have done a thousand things differently. Kublai was a weak scholar and Arik-Boke thought he would have made chaos of good tumans. Yet they had struck at exactly the right point, at the right moment. They had beaten Orlok Alandar and he could still hardly believe it. The right wing of his sweep should have been the strongest point, but they had rolled it up. Now darkness was coming and they would escape his vengeance.

The plain was long and flat, but the battle was still a tiny, surging throng of dust as darkness came. In the last moments before they were lost to sight, Arik-Boke was sure he saw tumans streaming away to the north. He clenched his jaw, the heat of his body feeling like fuel for the anger within. Karakorum had few defenders, with his entire army in the field. He felt sick at the thought that his brother could take the capital in a quick strike. He had ignored Alandar's feeble worries, convinced back then that his brother would never get in range of the capital. It should have meant nothing, but Arik-Boke wanted to roar his frustration. Whoever held Karakorum had a claim to rule. It mattered in the eyes of the princes and the small khanates.

His general had reached him, riding alongside and shouting questions into the wind. At first, Arik-Boke ignored the man, but then the darkness was on them and he was forced to rein in and slow to a canter, then a trot. Their horses snorted and breathed hard and the searing energy drained out of Arik-Boke, leaving a coldness deeper than he had ever felt before. Not till that moment had he seriously considered Kublai might beat him in battle. His mind filled with images of facing the scholar within the length of a sword. It was satisfying but empty, and he shook his head to clear it of foolishness. He rode on, into the night.

All around him, warriors coming the other way were streaming past, keeping their faces down in shame before those they knew. They were joining his tumans at the back in tens and hundreds, coming out of the blackness ahead. Arik-Boke saw one of them wheel his horse, turning to match the trotting line as he tried to come across it. The man was within a horse-length of him and calling out before Arik-Boke knew it was

Alandar. The khan's knuckles were white on the reins as his orlok reached him, bringing a stench of fresh sweat and blood that hung on him like a cloak.

'My lord khan,' Alandar said.

He did not need to shout over the noise of the horses any longer. They were barely trotting by then, the black grass flowing under their hooves unseen. Arik-Boke almost called for torches, but there were still hundreds coming away from the battle and he did not know if they were all his own men. It would not do to light himself up in the line.

'Orlok, I revoke your rank. You will not lead again in my armies.' Arik-Boke tried to keep his voice calm, but the rage threatened to spill out of him. He wanted to see the man's face, but the darkness was complete.

'Your will, my lord,' Alandar said, his voice unutterably weary.

'Will you report then? Must I drag it out of you word by word?' Arik-Boke's voice grew louder as he spoke, until he was almost shouting. He sensed Alandar flinch from him.

'I'm sorry, my lord. They set a trap to draw off my warriors, with a second position to make me think I had spotted the ruse.' Alandar had worked it out by then, though he was still dazed after such a day and so tired he could barely speak at all. He could not be seen to praise the enemy, but there was a grudging respect in his voice as he went on. 'They ambushed my forces once we had followed them into a valley. I saw some twelve tumans in all, under Kublai and Uriang-Khadai.'

'Were my orders not to wait until the main army came up to you, if you saw the enemy?' Arik-Boke asked. 'Did I not consider exactly what has happened today?'

'I'm sorry, my lord. I thought I saw through their planning and could strike a blow for you. I saw the chance to break them and I took it. I was wrong, my lord khan.'

'You were *wrong*,' Arik-Boke echoed. It was too much to have the man yammering his apologies at him. He turned to the general on his other side.

'Oirakh, take this man's weapons and bind him. I will deal with him when there is daylight to see.' He ignored the sounds of struggle as warriors closed on Alandar. Had he truly expected to live? The man was a fool.

As the crescent moon showed itself, casting a thin light, his tumans came to the edges of the battlefield Kublai had fled at the last. Some of the fallen men and horses were still alive, calling piteously for help to those who passed them. Arik-Boke picked his way carefully, slowing to a walk. The dead lay thick on the ground as he went on and he could hear wounded men sobbing with pain. The rage in him became a hard ball in his chest and stomach so that he could hardly straighten his back. Kublai's orlok had done this thing.

At the centre of the dead, Arik-Boke dismounted and called for lamps. The smell was appalling, and despite the darkness, flies were everywhere already, buzzing into the faces of his men so that they had to wave them away every few moments. Arik-Boke breathed deeply, closing his eyes as the lamps were lit around him and placed onto poles. They cast a golden glow, revealing staring eyes and cold flesh on all sides. Arik-Boke shuddered slightly as he turned on the spot, taking it in. His lips thinned in disgust and anger blinded him. His brother was responsible for all of it.

'Bring Alandar to me,' he said. He had not bothered to look in any particular direction, but the order was carried out quickly even so. Alandar was dragged in and thrown face down at Arik-Boke's feet.

'Were they heading north at the end?' Arik-Boke asked.

The man who had been his orlok struggled to his knees and nodded, keeping his head bowed as low as possible.

503

'I think so, my lord.'

'It will be Karakorum, then,' Arik-Boke muttered. 'I can catch him yet.' He knew why Kublai wanted that city. Tens of thousands of women and children had formed their own slums on the plains around Karakorum, waiting for their men to return. Arik-Boke drew a long knife from a sheath strapped to his thigh. The torn flesh of his men lay all around him and there had to be reckoning, a price to pay for all of it. He knew then what he had to do.

Alandar had heard the knife come free and looked up in fear.

'My lord khan, I . . .' His voice choked off as Arik-Boke took him by the hair and cut his throat with powerful strokes, sawing into the flesh.

'That is enough from you,' Arik-Boke said into his ear. 'Be silent now.'

Alandar jerked and struggled, the sharp smell of urine filling the air and steaming. Arik-Boke shoved him aside.

'Scouts! To me!' he roared into the night.

Two of the closest came in fast, leaping from their horses. They glanced at Alandar's cooling body, then quickly away.

'You have ridden hard today,' Arik-Boke said. 'But you will not rest tonight.'

The two scouts were both young men, not yet eighteen years of age. They nodded without speaking, awed at being in the presence of the khan.

'Take fresh horses and go to Karakorum. Use the yam stations for remounts.' He yanked a ring from his finger and tossed it to one of the young men. 'You will have to pass my brother's armies, so ride hard and fast. I want you to reach the city before him. Find the captain of my palace guard and tell him I said it was time. Do you understand? Those words, exactly. Repeat your orders.'

The two scouts chanted his words back at him and he nodded, satisfied. There was a price to pay for all things. By the time Kublai reached the city, he would learn the cost of his rebellion. Arik-Boke smiled at the thought. Perhaps Kublai's men would mutiny when they realised what he had cost them. Arik-Boke might return to his city to find his brother already dead at their hands.

CHAPTER FORTY-TWO

The night was cold and still as Kublai rode towards Karakorum. He and his men shared twists of black meat as they went, passing skins of sour milk or clear airag to ease parched throats. There was no time to stop and acknowledge the victories of the day, not with Arik-Boke's tumans so close behind. Kublai had seen his son for just a brief moment as Zhenjin rode past him on some errand for his minghaan officer. No doubt the man had suggested he ride close to the khan as he went. It was the sort of subtle gesture his men arranged and Kublai knew they were proud to have his son riding with them, with all the trust that implied. Kublai pitied the enemy who tried to take on that particular minghaan. They would slaughter anyone who came close to the khan's heir.

Though his thoughts were sluggish, Kublai worked through plans as he rode. He had to get clear before dawn, but his men had fought or ridden all day and were drooping with tiredness. Without rest, he would be robbing them of their strength, ruining his army just as he needed them at their sharpest and best. He had already given orders to ride in pairs, with one man napping as the other took the reins, but they needed to dismount and sleep at least for a few hours.

Uriang-Khadai was perhaps the oldest man under his command, but in the weak moonlight, he looked fresh and stern as always. Kublai grinned wearily at him, trying to resist the lolling motion of his head that led to a sudden start as he found himself asleep. It was one advantage of the high-pommelled saddle, that it held a sleeping man better than some designs, but he still felt he could fall if sleep took him. He yawned hugely every few moments.

'Do we know the losses yet?' he asked, more to keep himself awake than because he truly wanted to know.

'I can't be certain until there's light,' Uriang-Khadai replied. 'I think around two tumans, or a little more.'

'In one *day*?' Kublai demanded, the words bursting out of him.

Uriang-Khadai did not look away. 'We killed more. They have the same bows, the same skills. The toll was always going to be high.'

Kublai grimaced, raising his gaze to the stars. The numbers were appalling, as great as all his losses against the Sung. Many of them would be alive still, cold and lonely among the dead as they waited for Arik-Boke's warriors to find them and plunge a knife into their flesh. He shuddered at the thought of such a final vigil. After years with them in the Sung territories, each one was a loss. Arik-Boke had no concept of the sort of loyalty that had grown up with his tumans over the years. He brushed the thought away, knowing he would only become enraged afresh at his foolish brother. The depth of his anger could still surprise him, but it felt like an indulgence to give it rein.

'Four days to Karakorum,' he said aloud. 'And my brother's men will be behind us all the way.'

Uriang-Khadai did not reply and Kublai realised he had not asked the man a question. It made him smile that the older man could be so tight-lipped after everything they had endured together.

'I have one more bone to throw, orlok. Once we reach

507

Karakorum, we can turn to defend the city and our people. I will make Arik-Boke the enemy in the eyes of the nation. And when the battle is at its height, Bayar will hit him.' In the continuing silence, Kublai sighed. 'What do you think of that?'

'I think you have ten tumans or less to your brother's twelve and more,' Uriang-Khadai said at last. 'I think we are running low on arrows and lances. I cannot plan around a reserve force that has had to ride two thousand miles or more.'

'You came back from Hulegu. Bayar will get here,' Kublai said.

'And I will be pleased to see him, but we must prepare for the worst. We need weapons.'

Kublai grunted. He should have known better than to expect encouraging words. The Chagatai khanate had provided many of the supplies for his campaign. Lord Alghu had sent the Arab boys to raise the false trail of dust that played such a part in their first battle, and the food and drink they still had came from his cities. Yet Uriang-Khadai was right, arrows and lances were their most important stock and the last of them would go in one charge.

'If you can make arrows and lances appear in the next few days, I would thank you on bended knee, orlok. Until then, there's no point discussing it.'

Uriang-Khadai remained silent for a long time, thinking.

'There are stocks in Karakorum, enough to fill every quiver we have,' he said at last.

Kublai held back from mocking the idea. The older man knew the chances as well as he did.

'You think we could get them?' he asked.

'No, but Arik-Boke Khan could.'

Kublai winced at the words, but he nodded. 'The city knows nothing of the battles out here, not yet. I could send men in his name with orders to bring new shafts and lances out on carts. That's good, I think. That could work.'

'With your permission, I'll send out a few scouts with the order, ones I trust to play a part.'

'You have it,' Kublai replied. He gave silent thanks for the man at his side. In the darkness, it was somehow easier to talk to him than usual. Neither man could see the other well and Kublai considered sharing the secret he had learned years before, in the archives of Karakorum. His weariness made him slur his words, but on impulse, he decided to speak.

'I found a record of your father, once,' he said. The silence seemed to swell around them until he wondered if Uriang-Khadai had even heard him. 'Are you still awake?'

'I am. I know who he was. It is not something I am used to . . .' Uriang-Khadai's voice trailed off.

Kublai tried to cudgel his thoughts into order, to find the right words. He had known for years that Uriang-Khadai was Tsubodai's son, but the knowledge had never found a moment to present itself. Hearing that his orlok already knew was oddly deflating.

'I liked him, you know. He was an extraordinary man.'

'I . . . have heard many tales of him, my lord. He did not know me.'

'He lived his last years as a simple herdsman, did you hear that?'

'I did.' Uriang-Khadai thought for a time and Kublai kept silent. 'You grew up with Genghis as your grandfather, my lord. I suppose you know about a man's long shadow.'

'They seem like giants,' Kublai muttered. 'I know the feeling very well.' It was an insight into Uriang-Khadai that he had not expected. The man had risen through the ranks without anyone's name to help him. For the first time, Kublai felt he understood something of what drove the man.

509

'He would be proud of you, I think,' Kublai said.

Uriang-Khadai chuckled in the darkness.

'And Genghis would be proud of you, my lord. Now let us leave shadows to the night. We must find a river for the horses and I will fall out of the saddle if I don't rest soon.'

Kublai laughed, yawning again at the very idea of sleep.

'Your will, orlok. We will make our fathers and grandfathers proud, you and I.'

'Or join them,' Uriang-Khadai replied.

'Yes, or join them, one or the other.' Kublai paused for a moment, rubbing grit from his eyes. 'Arik-Boke will not stop now, not with us heading for the capital. He will push his men to complete exhaustion behind us.'

'You wanted him to be desperate, with everything he has focused on the city. If Bayar does not come . . .'

'He will come, orlok.'

The three days that followed were some of the strangest Kublai had ever known. He had been right about Arik-Boke pushing the tumans to their limits. On the second day, the armies passed four yam stations and knew they had covered a hundred miles between dawn and dusk. Scouts milled at the edges of each force, sometimes coming to blows, or drifting into range of arrows so that they were plucked from their mounts and sent sprawling to a great cheer from the nearest warriors. At sunset on the third day, the two armies were barely ten miles apart and neither could close or widen that gap. Kublai had lost count of the changes of mount as he and Uriang-Khadai did their best to keep their animals fresh, but there was never enough time to graze and they had to leave hundreds of horses when their wind broke or they went lame. All the time, he felt his brother's breath on his neck and he could only crane into the distance, looking for Karakorum.

Sunset was hardest on the men. Kublai could not call a halt until he was absolutely certain his brother was done for the day. With the armies in such close range, he dared not rest where Arik-Boke could spring a sudden attack. His own scouts relayed the positions back to him in chains, over and over, until finally they brought the welcome news that their pursuers had stopped. Even then, Kublai insisted on going on, forcing each precious mile in sweat and stamina. His men slept like the dead under the stars and had to be kicked awake by the changing guards through the night. Men cried out in troubled sleep, worn down by the constant threat of being pursued. It sat badly with natural hunters to be hunted, while those behind grew in confidence like a wolf pack, knowing they would run them down eventually.

Kublai had welcome news from his scouts long before the tumans under his command, but he did not pass it on, knowing they would enjoy the sight of carts laden with weapons coming from Karakorum. They were guided in to his spartan camp as the sun died over the mountains on the third day, greeted with whoops and shouting from his men. One climbed each cart and began throwing full quivers and lances to outstretched hands, laughing at the thought that the city had given them such a gift in error. The men driving the carts were left untouched and they knew better than to protest as they were shouldered aside and sent back to the city. Karakorum lay barely forty miles away and Kublai knew he would reach it by noon the following day. He wished he had thought to ask for fresh skins of airag to go with the arrows and lances, but it was enough to see the glee on his men's faces for what they had won with trickery.

Kublai felt a great tension ease in him as he settled down

for sleep that night, taking a moment to thump the grass beneath him when a lump dug into his hip. His men would fight with Karakorum in sight. They would battle an enemy just as weary as they were and they would give a good account of themselves, he was certain. Even so, he feared for them all.

Twelve men fighting ten was a rough match. The two extra tumans his brother could still field were a different proposition. Twenty thousand men would be able to pour shafts into his flanks, or hammer his men in charges while they were locked in battle. Against the Sung, he would have laughed at the numbers. Facing his own people, he struggled with despair. He had done everything he could and he thought again of the last bone he had to throw when Karakorum came into view. Somewhere out beyond the hills, Bayar had to be closing on the city. His three tumans would surely be enough to turn the battle.

He was still thinking it through when sleep took him in a black wave. Kublai knew nothing else until his son was shaking him by the shoulder and pressing a package of cold meat and hard bread into his hand. It was not yet dawn, but the scouts were blowing horns to signal that Arik-Boke's camp was getting ready to move.

Kublai sat up, cutting off a yawn as he realised it was the last day. No matter what happened, he would see an end before the rising sun fell behind the mountains. It was a strange thought, after so long.

His sleepiness vanished and he stumbled to his feet, taking a bite and wincing as it caught on a loose tooth. Karakorum had tooth-pullers, he recalled, wincing. His bladder was full and he put the bread in his mouth as he pulled back his deel robe and urinated on the ground, grunting in satisfaction.

'Stay safe today,' he said to Zhenjin, who merely grinned.

The young man had grown thin in the days of fighting or

512

riding, his skin darker than Kublai remembered. He too was chewing on the thick bread, hard as stone and about as appetising. The thick mutton grease was a gritty paste in his mouth and Kublai almost choked as Zhenjin handed him a small skin of water and he gulped from it.

'I mean it. If the battle goes badly, do not come for me. Ride away. I would rather see you run and live than stay and die. Is that understood?'

Zhenjin gave him his best look of sulky scorn, but he nodded. Scout horns sounded again and his rough camp jerked into faster motion as men mounted and checked their weapons for the last time. Arik-Boke's tumans were moving.

'Quickly now. Get back to your jagun,' Kublai said gruffly.

To his surprise, Zhenjin embraced him, a brief, fierce grip before he was sprinting back to his horse.

They rode hard through the long morning, covering miles at a smooth canter or trot while the scouts kept their eyes on Arik-Boke's forces and reported back constantly. Forty miles would have been nothing to fresh horses and men, but after days in the saddle, they were all stiff and weary. In his mind's eye, Kublai imagined them bleeding broken horses by the mile, turning the animals loose as they limped or collapsed. The sturdy little ponies were bred to endure and they went on, just as the men who rode them went on, ignoring the aches in their backs and legs.

It was a surreal moment for Kublai when he began to recognise the hills around Karakorum. The grey-green slopes shouted to his memories. He had grown up in the city and he knew the lands around it as well as anywhere in the world. His breath caught in surprise at the power of it, when he knew they had come home. In all his planning and manoeuvres, he hadn't taken into account the strength of that small thing. He was *home*. The city his uncle had built lay but a few miles further on and it was time to turn and face his brother, to test the men he had taught and learned from over thousands of miles of Sung lands. He felt tears prickle his eyes and laughed at himself.

Karakorum had originally been built with a boundary about the height of a man. That had changed when the small city was threatened and the walls had been strengthened and raised to include watchtowers and solid gates. Kublai no longer knew how many people it held, or how many more clustered round it in the tent slums. He had walked among them more than once when he was young and the memories were both vivid and sad. His people did not do well in one place. Though they came to Karakorum for work and wealth, they had no sewers and the gers there clustered so thickly in the sun that the stench of urine and excrement could make a strong man gag. As nomads, every camp was fresh and green, but when they were trapped in poverty, they made a slum where no woman and few men dared to go out after dark.

He could see the white walls in the distance when he gave the order to halt at last. He had avoided any thoughts of the future while his brother Arik-Boke was in the field against him. It seemed too much like dangerous pride to make plans for the years to come when he could so easily be killed. Yet as he stared into the haze behind him, he thought of the wide lands in the Chin territory around Xanadu. He could find them a place there. He could allow them to stretch out and live like men instead of animals, crushed into too small a space, too small a city. His people grew sick when they could not move, and not just with the diseases that swept through the city every summer. As the sun beat down, he shuddered at the thought of some pestilence raging through Karakorum as it baked in its own filth. If he lived, he could do better, he was certain.

Uriang-Khadai was like a wasp that afternoon, riding everywhere and snapping out commands so that the tumans formed in good order. Kublai's banners were raised far away from where he sat his horse, surrounded by bondsmen. With a wry smile, he looked across the field at the fluttering walls of yellow silk, decorated with a dragon twining on the cloth as if it were alive. The arrows would fall thickest on those men, volunteers all. They were the only ones still carrying heavy shields he had kept back, with their horses' chests armoured in fish-scale panels. Kublai himself would ride far from them in the fourth rank, invisible as he gave his orders.

Even with the losses, nine tumans and some six minghaans stood to face Arik-Boke's army. Most of them had fought together for years, against far greater numbers. Each officer had met and drunk himself senseless with his colleagues a thousand times. They knew the men around them and they were as ready as they would ever be. The khan's city lay at their backs and they had to win it for him. The khan himself fought in the ranks. There would be an ending on that day.

Arik-Boke still had ten miles to make up when Kublai had called the halt. It was time enough to empty bladders and take gulps of water from skins being passed down the ranks, then thrown down when they were empty. A hundred thousand bows were checked for cracks, with strings tested and discarded if they stretched or were too worn. The men rubbed grease on their sword blades to let them slip out of the scabbards easily and many of them dismounted to check their saddle cinches and reins for weak points that could snap under load. There was little laughter among them and only a few called to their friends. They had been hardened in the long ride to the city and they were ready.

Kublai kept his back sword-straight as he saw the first outriders of Arik-Boke's tumans. They appeared far away like black flies, shifting back and forth in the heat haze. Behind the scouts came the tumans in great, dark blocks of horsemen, riding beneath a cloud of orange dust that reached above them in spiralling fingers.

He tested his sword grip again, dropping the weapon in and out of the scabbard so that it clinked. The sick feeling that made a knot in his stomach was a familiar sensation and he raised anger to sear through it. The body was afraid, but he would not let weak flesh rule him.

The sight of his brother's army made his heart beat faster and fury surge in his blood, summoned by his will and stronger than the fear. Sweat broke out on his forehead while he sat like a statue watching them come. He could smell the horses around him, combined with the gamey stench of men who had not washed in months. *His* men, bound to him by oath and experience. Many of them would die that day and the debt would be Arik-Boke's. Kublai reminded himself that he knew his brother, no matter how he had changed in the years apart. The false position with the banners had come from that knowledge.

Arik-Boke would not just want to win the battle. The losses of his orlok had humiliated him. If Kublai still knew him at all, he would be half blind in wounded pride and rage, aiming his archers at that point. The bannermen would soak up the shafts. It was not a pleasant thought as memories of their youth flashed into his mind, but Kublai would use anything, any weakness. In silence, he sent a prayer of apology to his mother and father, hoping they could not see the battle he would fight that day.

Kublai looked right and left along the ranks of silent men. He wore no sign of his authority and his bondsmen were watching him with expressions of quiet pride. They were ready. He sent another prayer to the spirits of his ancestors that Bayar would come.

He saw Uriang-Khadai raise a hand and Kublai matched the gesture. It was time. He looked ahead to the vast army coming at them as his orlok gave the order. Horns began to sound across the ranks, a single, droning note that made Kublai's hands tremble before he gripped the reins hard. A hundred thousand warriors dug in their heels and began to trot forward to meet the enemy, his younger brother.

CHAPTER FORTY-THREE

Arik-Boke craned forward in his saddle, peering through the dust to where his brother waited for him. The scouts had reported Kublai's position long before, but he still waited for his own eyes to confirm it. Though the walls of Karakorum were painted white, he could see only a hint of paleness behind the darker lines of Kublai's tumans, like a reflection off metal. He nodded to himself, clenching his fist on his sword hilt.

His twelve generals were riding on either side of him, already looking back to their tumans and wanting his permission to ride with their men. Arik-Boke kept silent. His orlok had failed him and he had not appointed another, just to see him fail in turn. He was khan and he would command the battle. He could sense the unease of the senior men, as if the fools thought he would keep them in line with him right up to the first shafts in the air.

His tumans had ridden fifty miles that day without stopping. They were weary, but the sight of the enemy standing to face them would cast that weariness away. Arik-Boke did not feel it himself. Anger and excitement coursed through him as the range closed to two miles, less. He could see the formations of Kublai by then, still standing as if they had grown roots waiting for him. He struggled with colossal rage at the thought of them barring the way to his own city, standing in the khan's rightful path. His brother would answer for his arrogance, he promised himself.

His tumans matched his speed, though they were not idle. Spare horses were brought up from the rear in their thousands, pulled alongside, so that his warriors could jump across without slowing down. The ones they had ridden all morning fell back quickly without heels and whips to keep them going. Arik-Boke was close enough to see the bright yellow flags of his brother's position, standing tall on spears like bristling spines. At such a distance, he could not make out the symbol on them, but he had his first sight of the false khan's position. He could imagine Kublai looking out and a shudder went through him as if their gazes had locked over the empty plain.

'There is your target,' he called to his generals. 'I will give a province to the man who brings me his head. Which one of you will be a khan after today?'

He saw the stunned expressions as they understood and he was satisfied. They would drive their men ruthlessly for such a reward, falling on Kublai like a mountain dropping from the blue sky. It was a good thought.

He sent them back to their tumans and felt the change in just a short time as they began to roar orders. The speed grew and all the tumans matched the racing lines, each one subtly trying to manoeuvre to be in the best position to hit that small group of banner flags.

Arik-Boke grinned into the breeze. The armies were less than a mile apart and he had set bloody meat before the wolves. He had more men and they fought for the great khan of the nation. To ride to such a battle was the closest thing to joy he had ever known.

The scout was exhausted, drooping in the saddle as his horse reached the final yam station in the heart of Karakorum. It had not been an easy run to get around Kublai's tumans. He'd had to swing wide, beyond the scout lines, and then ride on through the darkness whenever he found a path or a road. He hadn't slept for three days, hadn't been able to with enemy scouts checking every trail and path. He'd spent some of the previous night with a dagger cutting into his bicep, using the pain to keep him awake as he peered out from a thicket and waited for a group of warriors to move on. He scratched at the bandage as he guided his exhausted mount down the city road to the yam station. His mind was playing tricks on him, making him hear whispers and see strange colours he could not name whenever he forced his eyes open. He had no idea what had happened to his companion. Perhaps he hadn't had luck with him and had taken an arrow as he rode.

The scout was eighteen years old and he had once thought of his strength as limitless, until the ride showed him the truth. Everything hurt and his mind felt like a solid lump in his skull, stupid and slow to react. Perhaps that was why he felt so little triumph as he almost fell from the saddle into the waiting arms of the yam riders. They did not laugh at the state and stench of him, the saddle still damp under his legs from the times he had urinated without stopping. With an army taking position outside the city, they were visibly worried. One of them took a wet cloth from a bucket and rubbed it over the scout's face roughly, waking him up a little as well as clearing the caked dust and filth.

'No message bag,' one of them said, with a twist to his mouth. None of them expected good news from the sort of message that could not be written down. He slapped the scout lightly on the face.

'Wake up, lad. You're here, you've arrived. Who were you sent to speak to?'

The scout brought his hands up irritably at the rough treatment, pushing them away as he stood on his own.

'From the khan. Captain of the Guards,' he croaked at them. One of the men handed over a skin of clean water and he gulped gratefully, spitting onto the floor to clear his gummed mouth. His words did a reasonable job of waking them all up to their usual efficiency.

'You walk him in, Lev,' the yam master said. 'I'll deal with the horse.'

The animal was blown, ruined, and in much the same state as its rider. The master took the reins with a grim expression to lead it out into the yard. He didn't want blood on the floor inside.

'I'll be expecting a few choice cuts for tonight,' one of the others called after him.

The yam master ignored the comment and the scout was led stumbling away with a man's hand on his shoulder.

The yam rider knew better than anyone not to question the scout and they walked in silence through the streets towards the khan's palace. It could be seen from a long way off, with its gold-capped tower. The scout looked up at it gratefully, hobbling along with each step sending sharp pains up his legs.

The palace gates were manned by Day Guards in polished armour. They nodded to the yam rider and looked askance at his filthy companion.

'Khan's orders. Captain of the Guard, urgent,' the yam rider said, enjoying the chance to make them move quickly for once. One of the Guards whistled and another one inside went running off at full sprint, his boots clattering on the stone corridors so that they could hear his progress for some time.

'Any news of that army?' the Guard asked.

The scout shrugged, his voice still rough.

'They were turning to face the khan, last I saw. It'll be over today.'

The Guard looked as if he wanted to ask more, but they

521

could all hear the running steps returning, with another along-side. The captain had not bothered about his dignity, not with a message from the khan and a hostile army outside Karakorum. He arrived at a flat sprint, skidding to a stop and putting an arm out to the gatepost to steady himself.

'Do you need to tell me in private?' he asked, panting.

'I wasn't told that. The khan told me to say "It's time".'

To the scout's surprise, the captain paled and took a deep, slow breath as he settled himself.

'Nothing else?'

'That's it, sir. "It's time."'

The captain nodded and walked away without another word, leaving four men staring after him.

'That doesn't sound good for someone,' one of the yam men muttered.

Kublai snapped his gaze back and forth, between the tumans riding towards him and his own. Both sides moved fluidly, shifting and overlapping as they came together, searching out weaknesses in the other and forcing them to react. To an outsider, it might have looked as if two great armies swept mindlessly towards each other, but the truth was a constant, darting struggle. Arik-Boke's generals would shore up one wing and Kublai or Uriang-Khadai would react to it. They would bring a new tuman swinging over to bolster another position, drawing the enemy back into line rather than risk a massed attack on a weak part of their formations. It happened at a canter and then a gallop, with each officer seeking the slightest advantage as they came within bow range.

At three hundred paces, the first shafts were sent flying up from both sides. The maximum range and the closing speeds meant they would hit overhead in the ranks further back. Kublai saw them soaring thickly to where his bannermen rode and he roared a final order to the closest general. They had only moments to react, but they drifted left, shoring up his own ranks and weakening the false position.

It was too late for Arik-Boke to react again. Kublai and Uriang-Khadai had been reading his formations, seeing the build of strength on his left wing. It was well hidden, with thousands of men screening the main shift, but Arik-Boke had taken the bait. He would hit the false position, where he believed Kublai to be waiting for him.

Kublai barely noticed the volleys thrumming out from both sides, one every six heartbeats, launching terrible death and destruction. He had eyes only for the enemy movements. They were throwing their strength into one side to reach where they thought he was, skewing their formations to bring the maximum numbers against that point of his lines and smash through.

In the last heartbeats, arrows buzzed between the armies by the tens of thousand, crossing each other in the air. Horses and men went down hard and Kublai had to wrench his mount out of the way of one fallen rider, then kick in to make a half-stumbling leap over another. He found himself in the second rank as the lances came down on both sides. He drew his sword.

On his right, Arik-Boke's tumans had brought lances to bear early, soaking up the arrow storm as they tried to punch right through to the yellow flags. Kublai could read his brother's rage in their formations and he shouted without words, a roar of sound that was swallowed in the screams and crashes all around him.

A lance came at him, aimed squarely at his chest. At first it seemed to be slow, then his mind adjusted and it struck at him like a darting bird, drawn in at the speed of two horses galloping head-on. He turned the tip of it with a grunt, forcing it wide so the lancer went past him on his right. Kublai slashed across the man's face as he went and felt a single spot of blood touch his cheek.

His own lance warriors took advantage of the weaker lines against them. Arik-Boke had committed his main strength to one wing, so that his tumans formed almost a spear on the land in the last moments. Kublai showed his teeth in the wind. He could not save the men who carried his banners, but he could hit the suddenly vulnerable flank they had helped to expose.

In just a few heartbeats, the two armies had slid past each other like dancers. It was a level of manoeuvre and formation only possible by the elite horsemen of the nation and yet Arik-Boke had made a mistake. As his tumans crashed deeper and deeper, throwing down lances as they broke, their flank was exposed to Kublai's main strength. Uriang-Khadai bellowed new orders at the exact moment Kublai did, sending fresh volleys of arrows into the streaming mass as they passed, punching hundreds of men from their mounts.

It took time to turn his tumans and every moment was agony as more and more of the flank poured past him. Kublai reined in savagely, using his strength to drag the animal into a tight turn. It stumbled again on a body, but came upright, snorting in fear. He pointed his sword at the tumans of his brother and his men dug in their heels, roaring 'Chuh!' to their mounts in a great burst of sound.

They struck at barely more than a canter in the space they'd had to leap forward, but Arik-Boke's tumans were focused forward and the swordsmen cut deep into them, hacking and slashing with the huge strength of men trained to the bow.

Kublai went with them, through the first rank galloping past him, then further as the lines crumpled. His minghaans kept his attacking line wide so that no single point could get ahead of the rest and find itself flanked in turn. With men dying on all sides, his officers kept calm and gave out a stream of orders. The khan's command had dropped to them and they were veterans, stolid and serious about their work.

Arik-Boke's flank collapsed as Kublai's tumans cut it to pieces. His men had bitten a huge bowl into the enemy, and despite the efforts of the minghaan officers, they were in danger of going too far into the crush. Before Kublai could give new orders, Uriang-Khadai had committed two more tumans, widening the attack and battering the flank with arrows and then a lance charge. They had the time to get up to speed and they tore into them at full gallop, lances down so that men and horses were broken and sent tumbling.

Kublai saw his yellow banners fall out of the corner of his eye. A great roar went up from Arik-Boke's tumans at the sight and they began to fight back with renewed ferocity. The single-minded drive that had ruined their formations for a single objective was gone. He felt the difference in moments as they pulled back from his men and began to re-form. He cursed. The arrows were still flying and he knew he would be the target if he gave the order.

Two of Arik-Boke's tumans had swung out from the battle to reach a good position. As Kublai watched, they drove back in, sending arrows before them, then shoving the bows into the saddle hooks and drawing swords. They believed Kublai was already dead and it gave them heart to keep fighting. He grimaced to himself, then nodded, turning to his bondsmen.

'Raise them up,' he shouted. 'Let them see how we fooled them.'

They grinned wildly as they unrolled great yellow streamers, sliding metal rings over the tips of banner-poles with practised efficiency. With a nod to each other, six of them raised the poles at the same time, sending Kublai's banners fluttering in the wind.

His tumans raised their swords and bows as they saw it, roaring at the top of their lungs. The crash of sound seemed to send Arik-Boke's tumans reeling back, but the reality was that Kublai's men surged forward. Nothing pleased the Mongols more than a good trick on the field of battle. Not only was Kublai alive, but Arik-Boke had wasted the lives of many thousands to tear down a false position. For a short time, Kublai's warriors laughed as they bent their bows and struck with swords, then the momentary giddiness dissolved and they were back to the grim-faced killing men of the tumans.

Over thousands of heads, Kublai could see his brother's banners, half a mile distant. He had ignored the position, with no desire to see his brother dead. He wanted him alive if possible, though if the sky father took him with a shaft or a blow, he would not regret the loss. His own bondsmen pressed close around him as those of Arik-Boke's archers in range sent looping shots high, hoping for a lucky strike. Kublai set his jaw as the air above him filled with whining shafts. He wished for a shield then, but he had not been able to carry one and maintain the deception. One of his bannermen was plucked away with a grunt and another man caught the falling banner as it was jolted out of his hand. Kublai made a growling sound as he saw he would have to pull back. The charge against the exposed flank had carried his rank deep into the enemy and he was exposed to the counter-attack that would surely come now his brother realised his true position.

For a frozen instant of time, Kublai searched the horizon for some sign of Bayar's tumans. His men had fought well and his officers had shown themselves as an elite. Perhaps four of his brother's tumans had been slaughtered for the loss of half that number, but the battle was far from over and Kublai was in desperate danger.

Even as he formed the thought, Uriang-Khadai brought

tumans across him, forcing the enemy back and allowing him time to get clear.

Kublai shouted to his men to find him a position out of the front ranks and they began to drift through the warriors. They cheered him as he went, still delighted at the deception that had allowed them to humiliate Arik-Boke. Men he knew from years among the Sung raised their swords in salute as he passed them, then pressed on with their tumans.

The battlefield had spread almost a mile from the original site, as the tumans shifted and struck, pulled back and charged again. As Arik-Boke's men pressed on in rage, Uriang-Khadai pulled four tumans out, leaving a sudden space. The enemy warriors rushed in after them, lost in the need to cut down the jeering horsemen, still hooting and calling to them as they went.

Uriang-Khadai made them run into fresh volleys of arrows from a halted line, emptying quivers by the ten thousand shafts. The broken lines they faced were torn apart, building lines of the dead. Their own archers replied without the massed force of a volley and were quickly cut from their saddles. Uriang-Khadai raised and dropped his arm to signal the shots, then rotated the front ranks to allow those who still had shafts to race forward. In the heart of the battle, the perfection of the manoeuvre broke the centre of Arik-Boke's forces. Those who survived it pulled back from their mad rush and formed up around their khan, ready to be sent in again.

Kublai had moved back three hundred paces, frustrating the enemy archers who sought him out. From that position, he saw Uriang-Khadai take over and heard the beat of volleys snap once more. He turned his head to see a huge block of fresh warriors detach from his brother's position and come swinging out. They rode around the wavering centre and Kublai swallowed hard when he saw Uriang-Khadai could be hit from the

527

flank and rear in turn. He looked around for the forces available to him, sending runners to his generals as fast as he could speak and shove them away.

Once again, he looked for Bayar on the horizon. Ever since his return from the Sung, he had dreaded the thought of a battle so closely fought that the armies of the nation destroyed themselves. He had already lost count of the dead, and if it went on, the empire of Genghis would be defenceless, with wolves all around them. He *needed* the men his warriors were killing. He needed them all. He looked for Bayar and sat frozen, his right hand clenching tight on the sword hilt. Tumans had appeared in the distance, dark lines of racing horsemen.

Kublai felt his initial surge of excitement fade as he saw the number of them. Too many. He breathed harder, feeling fear sink its teeth into him once again. Too many! He had sent only three tumans to Russia with Bayar. The army galloping towards him was far larger.

Kublai closed his eyes and bowed his head, breathing so hard and fast he felt his blood heat soar and his face grow flushed with every beat of his heart. He could surrender, or he could fight to the last man, the worst of all decisions. He wiped blood from his cheek in a spasm of anger, but Arik-Boke's men were shouting and the formations were moving again, as if to counter a new threat. Kublai's head jerked up, his breath held in his throat.

Not a reserve, then! Arik-Boke was already shifting his banners around, moving them away under a shield of tumans. Kublai felt dizzy and ill as his pounding pulse dwindled in his ears. He had known the agony of defeat, accepted it. He was not certain what he would have done, even then, but as the men around him shouted and cheered, he bawled with them, waving his sword to the tumans coming in at full speed.

'Lay down your swords!' Kublai shouted to the enemy.

His generals took up the cry, then his minghaan officers, then the men who ran each jagun of a hundred. In moments, thousands of voices were yelling the order at Arik-Boke's men and all the time, six tumans were galloping closer, fresh and deadly with full quivers and unbroken lances. Kublai repeated his order and his tumans repeated it like a chant. Uriang-Khadai pulled them back further, opening a new space between the armies. No one raced to close the gap and the tumans of Arik-Boke sat their mounts in stunned silence, watching sixty thousand men riding hard at them.

Kublai didn't see the first of Arik-Boke's men to throw his sword to the ground, followed by the empty quiver from his back. The officer was a senior minghaan and his thousand copied the gesture. Many of them dismounted and stood by their horses, their chests heaving. It spread through Arik-Boke's tumans, one after the other, beginning with those furthest away from their khan. By the time Kublai could read the banners of Bayar and Batu Khan with him, only a single tuman with Arik-Boke remained armed and ready, surrounded by their own men calling on them to surrender.

Arik-Boke's last tuman waited in grim silence as Uriang-Khadai gathered his tumans in silent ranks and Bayar and Batu Khan came into range with bows ready.

Under that threat, with a fresh army against them, the last tuman threw down their swords and walked away from the small knot of bannermen with Arik-Boke. He roared at their backs in furious anger, but they ignored him.

Kublai rode with the feeling that he had never been in more danger that day. He did not have to order his generals to form up around him. A single arrow could take his life and then Arik-Boke might yet rally his tumans again. He did not doubt his brother would fight to the end and leave the nation weak and wounded. He nudged his horse forward across the battlefield, not looking left or right as his men shouldered aside warriors they had been trying to kill just before.

It seemed to take an age before he found Arik-Boke. His brother looked older, Kublai saw, his ruined nose bright red with emotion. He still carried a drawn sword in his hand and Kublai murmured a command to those at his back. They bent their bows with an audible creak, a dozen shafts focused on one man who stared balefully at Kublai.

'Surrender, brother,' Kublai called to him. 'It's finished now.'

There was a bright gleam in Arik-Boke's eyes as he glared round at his men. His face was well made for the contempt he showed them and he leaned over to hawk and spit on the ground. For an instant, Kublai thought he would kick his horse forward at him and die, but his brother shook his head as if he could hear the thought. Slowly, he opened his hand and let the wolf's-head sword fall onto the grass.

CHAPTER FORTY-FOUR

Kublai stood alone in the throne room of the palace in Karakorum, looking out of the open window over the roofs of the city below. He hadn't noticed the grime and odour he carried with him before entering the palace. The clean rooms with the polished stone floors made him feel oddly out of place, like an ape in a garden. He smiled at the thought, imagining how he must look. The armour he wore was a far cry from the scholar's robe he had worn for much of his youth. Palms that had once been ink-stained were ridged with sword callus. He held up his right hand with a wry expression, seeing the pale scars on the skin. The grime that had worked its way into every seam and crevice of his fingernails was a mixture of blood, earth and oil.

He had not seen the city of his youth for many years and from the first steps through the gate, he had been struck by both the familiarity and the differences. The short ride through the streets to reach the palace had been a surreal experience. In his years away, he had entered many Sung cities, too many to count or remember. Karakorum had once seemed large and open to him, a place of wide streets and strong houses. To the man who came home, it was somehow small and shabby. None of the people within the walls had ever seen the delicate gardens and streams of a Sung city, or the vast hunting parks that were being shaped in Xanadu. Even the palace library where he had spent countless hours had shrunk in his absence, once golden treasures failing to live up to his memories. Walking alone through the palace corridors, he had visited many of the places of his youth. In the room where he had once slept, he found the spot where he had carved his name in oak. Standing there, he had lost himself in reverie for a time, tracing the primitive lettering.

Even the palace gardens were different, with shaded rows of trees grown huge. They changed the views and altered the sense of the garden, spreading patterns of shadows so that nothing looked the same. He had sat for a time at the bench and pergola built after Ogedai's death. There had been peace there, as the pale blossoms of a cherry tree stirred in the wind around him. The war was over. He had realised it truly as he sat there in the silence. All he had to do was rule.

The knowledge should have filled him with joy, but he could not shake the feeling of disappointment that weighed on him, as if all his years at war had won him only echoes of memories. He tried to dismiss the sensation as nostalgia, but the reality hung in the thick summer air, already sweet with the smouldering herbs that were said to ward off disease.

With an effort, he turned away from the window looking out over the streets below. If Karakorum was flawed, it was still the first city of his people, the boundary marker that Ogedai Khan had built to take them from nomadic tribes to a settled nation. It had been a grand dream, but he would do better in Xanadu. He would do better as emperor of China, with all the wealth of those vast lands at his disposal. Kublai realised he would have to appoint a governor for Karakorum, someone he could trust to make the city bright and clean again. Uriang-Khadai sprang to his mind and he considered the idea carefully, finally nodding to himself.

The place Kublai thought of as home had become a city of strangers. His place was in Xanadu, a bridge between the lands of the Chin and the Mongol homeland, exactly as he had planned it. From there, he would send out the tumans to dominate the Sung for all time. He clenched his fist as he stood in the silence. They had almost fallen to a Mongol general. They *would* fall to the great khan.

He heard footsteps approaching the polished copper doors that closed off the room from the rest of the palace. Kublai gathered his will once again, ignoring the weariness that made his legs and arms feel leaden. He had ridden and fought all day. He stank of horses and blood and the summer sun was setting at last, but there was still one thing he had to do before he could bathe, eat and sleep.

There were no servants there to answer the fist thumping on the outer door. No doubt they had all vanished as the conqueror came into the city, expecting slaughter and destruction. As if he would harm a single one of his people, the nation of his birth. He crossed the room swiftly and heaved open the copper doors. He was not aware of how his right hand dropped to his sword hilt, an action that had become part of him.

Uriang-Khadai and Bayar stood there, with his brother between them. Their expressions were grim and Kublai did not speak, gesturing for them to enter. Arik-Boke was forced to shuffle forward, his feet tied so he could take only the smallest of steps. He almost fell and General Bayar gripped him by the shoulder to keep him upright.

'Wait outside,' Kublai said softly to the two men.

They bowed briefly without protest, sheathing their swords as they went. Uriang-Khadai pulled the doors shut and Kublai watched the gap close on the orlok's cold eyes.

He was alone with his brother, for the first time in many years. Arik-Boke stood with his arms behind his back, straight

533

and strong as he looked around the room. The only sound was the hissing wheeze from the old scar across his nose. Kublai looked for some sign of the boy he had known, but the face had coarsened, grown heavy and hard, as Arik-Boke's eyes glittered under the inspection.

It was difficult not to think of the last time they had met in that place, with Mongke full of life and plans and the world before them. Much had changed since then and Kublai's heart broke to think of it.

'So tell me, brother,' he said, 'now that the war is over, were you in the right, or was I?'

Arik-Boke turned his head slowly, his face growing mottled as he flushed in slow anger.

'I was in the right . . .' he said, his voice grating, 'but now you are.'

Kublai shook his head. To his brother, there was no morality beyond the right of strength. Somehow the words and everything they revealed infuriated him. He had to struggle to find calm once again. He saw some gleam of triumph still in Arik-Boke's eyes.

'You gave an order, brother,' Kublai said. 'To butcher the women and children of my men in the camps around the city.'

Arik-Boke shrugged. 'There is a price for all things,' he said. 'Should I have allowed you to destroy my tumans without an answer? I am the khan of the nation, Kublai. If you take my place, you will know hard decisions in turn.'

'I do not think it was a hard decision for you,' Kublai said quietly. 'Do you still think it was carried out? Do you believe the captain of the Guard would murder defenceless women while their children hung around their legs?'

Arik-Boke's contemptuous expression faded as he understood. His shoulders dipped slightly and some of the spite and anger seeped out of him, making him look worn and tired.

'I trusted the wrong man, it seems.'

'No, brother. You *were* the wrong man. Even so, it is hard for me to see you like this. I wish it could have gone another way.'

'You are *not* the khan!' Arik-Boke snapped. 'Call yourself whatever you want, but you and I know the truth of it. You have your victory, Kublai. Now tell me what you intend and don't waste my time lecturing me. From you, *scholar*, I have nothing to learn. Just remember that our mother held this city and our father gave his life for the nation. They are watching you as you put on your false expression of regret. No one else knows you the way I do, so don't preach to me. You would have done the same in my place.'

'You're wrong, brother, but it doesn't matter now,' Kublai replied. He walked to the copper doors and thumped on them with his fist. 'I have an empire to rule, one that has grown weak under your hand. I will not fail in strength or will. Take solace in that, Arik-Boke, if you care about the nation at all. I will be a good master for our people.'

'And bring me out each month to parade me in my defeat?' Arik-Boke said, his face flushing once again. 'Or shall I be exiled for you to show the peasants your famous mercy? I know you, brother. I looked up to you once, but no longer. You are a weak man and for all your fine talk, for all your scholarship, you will fail in everything you do.'

In the face of his brother's spite, Kublai closed his eyes for a moment, making the decision with a wrench that felt like ripping the scab from a wound. Family was a strange thing and even as he felt Arik-Boke's hatred battering at him, he still remembered the young boy who had swum in a waterfall and looked at him in simple adoration. They had laughed together a thousand times, grown drunk and shared precious memories of their parents. Kublai felt his throat grow thick with grief.

Uriang-Khadai and Bayar entered the room once more.

'Take him outside, general,' Kublai said. 'Orlok, stay for a moment.'

Bayar took his brother into the corridor, the shuffling steps somehow pitiful.

Kublai faced Uriang-Khadai and took a deep, slow breath before he spoke.

'If he hadn't ordered the death of the families, I could spare him,' Kublai said.

Uriang-Khadai nodded, his eyes dark pools. His own wife and children had been in the city, at his home.

'The tumans expect me to have him killed, orlok. They are waiting for the word.'

'But it is your decision, my lord. In the end, it is your choice.'

Kublai looked away from the older man. There would be no comfort from him, no attempt to make it easier. Uriang-Khadai had never offered him the weak way and he respected him for it, as much as it hurt. Kublai nodded.

'Yes. Not public, Uriang-Khadai. Not for my brother. Put aside your anger if you honour me and make his death quick and clean, as much as it can be.' His voice grew rough as he spoke the last words.

'And the body, my lord?'

'He was khan, orlok. Give him a funeral pyre to light up the sky. Let the nation mourn his passing if they will. None of that matters. He is my brother, Uriang-Khadai. Just . . . make it quick.'

The summer sun was warm on the back of his neck as Kublai sat in the gardens of the palace, his son Zhenjin beside him. In the distance, a black plume of smoke rose into the sky, but Kublai had not wanted to stand and watch his brother's funeral.

Instead, he rested with closed eyes, taking simple pleasure in his son's company.

'I will be going on to Xanadu in a few days,' Kublai said. 'You'll see your mother again there.'

'I'm glad I had the chance to see this city first,' Zhenjin replied. 'It is so full of history.'

Kublai smiled. 'It isn't history to me, boy. It's my family and I miss them all. I rode with Genghis when I was younger than you, barely able to stay on a saddle.'

'What was he like?' Zhenjin asked.

Kublai opened his eyes to find his son watching him.

'He was a man who loved his children and his people, Zhenjin. He took the Chin foot off the throat of the nation and made us look up from the struggles of tribes. He changed the world.'

Zhenjin looked down, playing with a cherry twig in his hands, bending it this way and that.

'I would like to change the world,' he said.

Kublai smiled, with just an edge of sadness in his eyes.

'You will, my son, you will. But no one can change it for ever.'

HISTORICAL NOTE

There are few surviving details of Guyuk's khanate. It is true that he brought an army to attack Batu in his own lands, after Batu failed to give his oath at a quiriltai, or gathering. We know that Batu was warned by Sorhatani and then Guyuk died in a manner unknown, with the armies in sight of each other. People do just die at times, obviously, but as with the death of Genghis' son Jochi, some endings are a little too fortuitous to believe the official record. I should add that there is no evidence that Guyuk was homosexual. I needed to explain how he fell out with Batu on the return from Russia – a detail missing from the historical record. As he was khan for only two years and died conveniently early, I was thinking of him as a similar character to England's Edward II, who *was* homosexual. The development came naturally. Guyuk achieved nothing of note.

Guyuk's death cleared the way for Mongke to become khan, beginning a conflict within the Mongol nation as the forces of modernisation, as represented by Chin influence, struggled against traditional Mongol culture and outlook. Mongke was supported by Batu, who owed Sorhatani his life.

Mongke was about thirty-six when he became khan, strong and fit, with good years ahead of him. It is true that he began his reign with a gathering at Avraga, then a slaughter of the opposition as he cleared house, including Guyuk's wife, Oghul Khaimish. She was accused of sorcery.

Mongke began his khanate with a push outwards, re-establishing the Mongol war machine in all directions. He ruled from 1251 to 1259, eight years of expansion and slaughter. His brother Hulegu went west to crush the Islamic world, while at Mongke's order, Kublai was sent east and south into Sung China. Their mother Sorhatani died in 1252, more than seventy years old. In her life, she had ruled Mongolia in her own right and seen her eldest son become khan. A Nestorian Christian herself, she had her sons taught Buddhism and established mosques and madrasa schools in Islamic regions. For the breadth of her imagination and reach, she was simply the most extraordinary woman of her era. It is a pleasure of historical fiction that I sometimes come across people who deserve books all to themselves – Julius Caesar's uncle Marius was one. Sorhatani is another. I have almost certainly not done justice to her.

If it had not actually happened, a fictional account of Kublai's attack on Sung lands would be ludicrous. He had no experience in battle and had lived a mostly scholarly life. At that time, just one city in Sung territory held more people than the *entire* Mongol nation. It was, to put it lightly, an immense task, even for a grandson of Genghis. As a side note, home-made sheep-skin rafts of the sort I have described were used by Kublai and are still used today to cross rivers in China.

Mongke did give Kublai experienced generals. For plot reasons in previous books, I wrote Tsubodai as childless. In fact, Uriang-Khadai was Tsubodai's son and a renowned general in his own right. Mongke gave Kublai the best for his first campaign, as well as a minor first objective that he could accomplish with ease. There again, Genghis showed the way. As Genghis had attacked the Xi Xia kingdom first, to establish a back door into Chin territory, Mongke saw the Yunnan region with its single city of Ta-li as the way in to the Sung. Kublai's army would have been outnumbered, but that would not have been too worrying. They were always outnumbered. It is interesting to note that the popular idea of a Mongol horde overwhelming smaller armies is almost completely false.

Mongke offered Kublai a choice of two vast estates in China. In the history, Kublai had time to ask Yao Shu for advice and the old man recommended Ching-chao in the north as it had rich soil. In time, Kublai would establish thousands of farms there that produced a vast fortune and led to trouble with his brother over his income. It was on those lands that he began his 'Upper Capital', known as Shang-du, or in the more common English form, Xanadu. It may not have had a 'pleasure dome', as in the poem by Samuel Coleridge, but it did have an immense deer park within its walls, where Kublai could hunt.

The Assassin fortress in Alamut came under attack by Hulegu's forces around 1256. The head of the Muslim sect that held the fortress of Alamut was, in fact, Ala Ad-Din. I avoided his true name because of the similarity to 'Aladdin' and because I'd used one too similar in a previous book. Here I have used Suleiman. The Ismaili Shia Muslim Assassins were extremely powerful in the region at this time, with at least four major fortresses, though Alamut was the strongest, an impregnable eyrie in the mountains south of the Caspian Sea. Interestingly, the storyline around Hasan and the leader comes from the record of the Mongols written by Ata al-Mulk Juvaini, a Persian writer and historian who accompanied Hulegu both to Alamut and Baghdad, later becoming governor of that defeated city. We do not know it was Hasan who murdered his master, but he seems the most likely candidate. Hasan had been tortured over years for amusement, even to the point of being abused with his wife in the bedchamber. It is one of those interesting events in history that the leader of the Assassins was killed at exactly the wrong moment, making Hulegu's task simple. The Assassins were compelled to surrender and their new leader, Rukn-al-Din, was kicked to death on Hulegu's orders – a great honour from the Mongol point of view as it did not shed blood and therefore recognised his status as leader of the sect.

The fall of Baghdad to Hulegu is one of the most shocking slaughters ever to occur in the line of Genghis. Hulegu did insist on disarming the city, then went on to butcher at least 800,000 of the million population. The Tigris is said to have run red with the blood of scholars. The caliph was allowed to choose 100 of his 700 harem women to save, then Hulegu had him killed and the women were added to Hulegu's gers.

I have tried to contrast Hulegu with Kublai, as they had such differing styles. In many ways, Hulegu struggled to be like Mongke and Genghis, while Kublai became as Chinese as the most tradition-bound Chin lord – and greater. Baghdad was ransacked and looted, as Hulegu seems to have had a greed for gold that Genghis would never have understood. In comparison, it is true that Kublai spared cities if they surrendered, making it a central part of his style. He forbade his men indiscriminate killing of the Chin and Sung, on pain of their own execution if they disobeyed him. His character must be set against the traditional ruthlessness of his culture to understand what an unusual man he was. He was certainly influenced in that by Yao Shu, a man still revered in China for his Buddhist principles and the lives he saved.

Mongke still felt the need to join the Sung attack on a different front in the end. One source puts the size of the army he brought into Sung lands as sixty tumans – a true horde of 600,000 men, though a smaller figure is much more likely. Enemies of the khans always had trouble estimating Mongol army sizes because of the vast herd of remounts they kept with them. We do not know if Kublai had stalled, or whether Mongke had always agreed with his brother that a two-pronged attack would be necessary to unite the Chinese empires.

The manner of Mongke's death en route to Sung China is disputed. It was either an arrow wound that became infected, or dysentery, or cholera: such a wide range of possibilities that it allowed me to work with the idea that Hulegu's attack on the Assassins could well have earned their final vengeance. Kublai knew he had to pull back when the news reached him of the death of Mongke. It was an established tradition, and even Tsubodai's conquest of western Europe had been abandoned on the death of Ogedai. The Sung generals would have heard almost as soon as Kublai himself and their relief can only be imagined. Yet Kublai refused to leave China. He had already begun to divorce himself from the politics of home. China was his khanate, his empire, even then.

Mongke's army had no such reluctance and immediately abandoned their progress south in Sung lands. When Hulegu heard the news, he too returned from the Middle East, loyal to the end. He left only some twenty thousand men under General Kitbuqa (who did indeed insist on holding Christian Mass in conquered mosques). Without the other tumans in support, they were destroyed by resurgent Muslim forces, using, of all tactics, the feigned retreat so beloved by Mongol armies. However, Hulegu had won his own khanate, which eventually became modern-day Iran. Only Kublai ignored the call.

At home in Karakorum, Arik-Boke made a decision that would affect all the generations of his family to come. He had ruled the capital in Mongke's absence and was already established as the khan of the homeland. With the return of Mongke's army, he convinced himself there was no better candidate and declared himself great khan. The youngest son of Sorhatani and Tolui had come to rule.

In the same year, 1260, his brother Kublai declared himself khan while standing on foreign soil. Kublai could not have known that he was sowing the seeds of a civil war between brothers that would bring the empire of Genghis to its knees.

I have altered the order of Sung emperors rather than omit scenes with the boy emperor, Huaizong, who ruled slightly later in the period. Emperor Lizong had reigned for some forty years when he finally died childless in 1264. He was succeeded by his nephew, Emperor Duzong, a man of immense appetites. He lasted only ten years until 1274 and was succeeded by his eight-year-old younger brother, who in turn would survive only four years and see Kublai's triumph over his house.

On the subject of numbers: fourteen is extremely unlucky in Chinese culture, as the sound is similar to the words for 'want to die' in both Cantonese and Mandarin. Nine, as the greatest single integer, is one of the luckiest numbers and is associated with the emperor.

By this time, there were simply too many princes to include them all. Lord Alghu was son to Baidur, grandson to Chagatai, great-grandson to Genghis. He ruled the Chagatai khanate and initially supported Arik-Boke in the civil war before turning against him. It is true that he was the first of his line to convert to Islam, a fairly sound tactical move given the people he ruled in the khanate around Samarkand and Bukhara, in modern-day Uzbekistan. A century after these events, Samarkand would become the capital of the conqueror Tamerlane.

The answer Arik-Boke gave to his brother, 'I was in the right and now you are,' is part of the historical record and fascinating for what it reveals of the man. Like Guyuk Khan before him, Arik-Boke's death remains one of those oddly convenient occurrences in history. He was in the prime of his life, healthy and strong, yet shortly after losing to Kublai, he dies. It is not difficult to suspect foul play.

When I began this series, I intended to write all of Kublai Khan's life. The most famous events – meeting Marco Polo, both attacks on Japan – seemed like vital parts of the story. Yet it is a truth of historical fiction that all the characters are long dead; all the lives and stories have ended, and usually not well. Very few lives finish in glory and I have already written the deaths of Julius Caesar and Genghis Khan. For once, I thought I might finish a series with a character still alive and with all his dreams and hopes still to come. *I* might know that Kublai's wife and son died before him, leaving him a broken man given to drinking and eating far too much, but at this point in his life, *he* does not – and that is how I wanted to leave him.

There will always be loose ends with such a decision. Kublai defeated the Sung at last and established the Yuan dynasty of a united China, a name still used for the currency today. His descendants ruled for almost a hundred years before fading into history, though the bloodline of Genghis ruled other khanates for far longer.

This story began with a single, starving family, hunted and alone on the plains of Mongolia – and ends with Kublai Khan ruling an empire larger than that of Alexander the Great or Julius Caesar. Over just three generations, that is simply the greatest rags-to-riches tale in human history.

Conn Iggulden
London, 2011

GLOSSARY OF TERMS

Airag/Black airag
Clear alcohol, distilled from mare's milk.

Arban
Small, raiding group, usually ten men.

Bondsmen
Warriors sworn to personal service, guards to a khan.

Chuh!
Phonetic representation of the Mongol horse command for speed.

Deel
Lightly padded full-length robe with wide sleeves, tied at the waist.

Earth Mother
Earth spirit, partner to the Sky Father.

Gers
Circular homes of felt and wicker lattice, sometimes mistakenly called yurts.

Guest rights
The offer of temporary protection or truce while in a man's home.

Gur-khan/Great Khan
Khan of khans, leader of the nation.

Jagun
Military unit of a hundred men.

Khan
Tribal leader. No 'k' sound in Mongolian, so pronounced: 'Haan'.

Minghaan
Military unit of a thousand.

Nokhoi Khor!
Pronounced: 'Ner-hoy, Hor.' Literally: 'Hold the Dog!' – a greeting when approaching strangers.

Orlok
Overall commander of a Mongol army.

Quiriltai
A gathering of princes for the purpose of electing a new khan.

Shaman
Medicine man in a tribe, both a healer and one who communes with spirits.

Sky Father

Sometimes called Tëngri. Mongol deity, partner to the Earth Mother.

Tuman

Unit of ten thousand.

Yam stations

Stops for fast scouts to change horses, twenty-five miles apart.

INDEX OF CHARACTERS

Ala-ud-Din Mohammed
Shah of Khwarezm. Died exhausted on an island in the
Caspian Sea.

Alkhun
Senior officer of the khan's guards in Karakorum.

Arik-Boke
Youngest son of Tolui and Sorhatani.

Arslan
Master swordsmith who was once armourer to the Naiman
tribe. Father to Jelme. Died of disease in Samarkand.

Baabgai
The bear. A Chin recruit who becomes a successful wrestler.

Baidur
Son of Chagatai. Rules his father's khanate around modern
day Afghanistan.

Barchuk
Khan of the Uighurs.

Basan
Wolf tribe. Bondsman of Yesugei in *Wolf of the Plains*.

Batu
Son to Jochi and grandson to Genghis Khan. Leads a tuman with Tsubodai and becomes a lord with vast lands in Russia.

Bayar
General to Kublai.

Bekter
Oldest son of Yesugei and Hoelun. Murdered by his brothers.

Bela IV
King of Hungary at the time Tsubodai's tumans attacked.

Borte
Olkhun'ut tribe. Daughter to Sholoi and Shria. Becomes wife to Temujin/Genghis and has four sons: Jochi, Chagatai, Ogedai and Tolui.

Chagatai
Old storyteller in Wolf tribe.

Chagatai
Same name as storyteller. Second son of Genghis and Borte. Father to Baidur.

Chakahai
Daughter to Rai Chiang of the Xi Xia. A princess given as tribute. Second wife to Genghis.

Chen Yi
Criminal gang leader in Chin city of Baotou.

Chulgetei
General of a tuman under Tsubodai.

Conrad Von Thuringen
Grand Master of the Teutonic Knights.

Eeluk
Bondsman to Yesugei Khan. Becomes khan of the Wolves on Yesugei's death.

Enq
Olkhun'ut tribe. Father to Koke. Brother to Hoelun. Uncle to Temujin/Genghis and his siblings.

Genghis Khan (see also Temujin)
First khan of the Mongol nation. Husband to Borte. Father to Jochi, Chagatai, Ogedai and Tolui. Dies in *Bones of the Hills*.

Guyuk
Son of Ogedai Khan and Torogene.

Hasan
Brutalised servant in assassin fortress of Alamut.

Ho Sa
Officer of the Xi Xia. Becomes envoy and officer under Genghis. Dies in *Bones of the Hills*.

Hoelun
Wife of Yesugei. Mother to Bekter, Temujin, Kachiun, Khasar, Temuge and Temulun.

Hulegu
Third son of Sorhatani and Tolui. Grandson of Genghis Khan.

Ilugei
General of a tuman under Tsubodai.

Inalchuk
Governor of the city of Otrar. Dies when Genghis pours molten silver into his mouth.

Jebe (originally Zurgadai)
Chosen successor to Arslan. Becomes one of Genghis' most trusted and able generals. Leader of 'Bearskin' tuman. Friend to Jochi, Genghis' son.

Jelaudin
Son and heir to Shah Ala-ud-Din Mohammed.

Jelme
Son of Arslan. Later becomes one of Genghis' most trusted generals.

Jochi

First son of Genghis and Borte. Some doubt over paternity. Becomes general to 'Iron Wolf' tuman. Only general ever to rebel against Genghis. Killed in *Bones of the Hills*.

Josef Landau

Master of the Livonian Brothers, an order of European knights.

Kachiun

Fourth son of Yesugei and Hoelun. Becomes a general under Genghis.

Khalifa Al-Nayan

Leader of elite Arab cavalry for Shah Mohammed.

Khasar

Third son of Yesugei and Hoelun. Becomes a general under Genghis.

Kokchu

Shaman to the Naiman Khan and later to Genghis. Killed in *Bones of the Hills*.

Koke

Olkhun'ut tribe. Nephew of Hoelun. Cousin to Temujin and his siblings.

Köten

Leader of the Cumans, a refugee people who fled into Hungary and converted to Christianity.

Kublai
Second son of Sorhatani and Tolui. Grandson of Genghis Khan.

Lian
Master mason and engineer from Baotou, who makes siege machines for Genghis.

Mohrol
Shaman to Ogedai Khan.

Mongke
Oldest son of Tolui and Sorhatani.

Ogedai
Third son of Genghis and Borte. Husband to Torogene, father to Guyuk.

Oghul Khaimish
Wife to Guyuk Khan. Killed in purges by Mongke Khan.

Old Man of the Mountains
Traditional title for the leader of the Assassin sect. Father to Suleiman, who inherits his position.

Rai Chiang
Ruler of autonomous Xi Xia kingdom in northern China.

Rukn-al-Din
Son of Suleiman. Briefly inherits Alamut.

Samuka
Second in command to Ho Sa in his tuman. Dies in *Bones of*

the Hills.

Sansar
Khan of the Olkhun'ut tribe. Killed by Genghis in *Wolf of the Plains*.

Sholoi
Olkhun'ut tribe. Father of Borte. Husband to Shria.

Shria
Olkhun'ut tribe. Mother to Borte. Wife of Sholoi.

Sorhatani
Wife to Tolui, the youngest son of Genghis. Mother to: Mongke, Kublai, Hulegu and Arik-Boke. At one point, she was ruler of the ancestral homeland and co-ruler of the capital city. Three of her four sons become khan.

Temuge
Youngest son of Yesugei and Hoelun, brother to Genghis. Shaman and administrator.

Temujin (also Genghis)
The First Great Khan, or Gur-khan. Second son of Yesugei and Hoelun.

Temulun
Only daughter of Yesugei and Hoelun. Marries Palchuk. Murdered by Kokchu in *Bones of the Hills*.

Togrul
Khan of the Kerait tribe. Dies in *Wolf of the Plains*.

Tolui
Wolf tribe bondsman.

Tolui
Same name. The fourth son of Genghis and Borte. Husband of Sorhatani and father to Mongke, Kublai, Hulegu and Arik-Boke.

Torogene
Wife of Ogedai, mother to Guyuk. Rules Mongol nation as regent.

Tsubodai
Originally Uriankhai tribe. Becomes Genghis' greatest general and orlok – leader of his armies.

Uriang-Khadai
Orlok to Kublai.

Wei
Emperor of the Chin. Father to Xuan, Son of Heaven.

Wen Chao
Ambassador of the Chin court, sent into Mongol lands.

Xuan, Son of Heaven
Emperor of the Chin after the death of his father, Emperor Wei.

Yao Shu
Buddhist monk brought back from China by Khasar and Temuge. Becomes chancellor to the khans.

Yaroslav
Grand Duke in Moscow at the time of Tsubodai's attack.

Yesugei
Khan of the Wolves. Husband to Hoelun. Father to Temujin, Kachiun, Khasar, Temuge and Temulun.

Yuan
Master swordsman and guard to Wen Chao, a Chin diplomat in Mongol lands.

Zhi Zhong
General of Chin emperor Wei's armies. Becomes regent to Xuan after murdering his master.